"Say it. Say, 'I love you,' and make me believe it. Maybe then I'll let you stay."

"I love you."

It came without a moment's hesitation. So easily, so prettily and oh, so believably that Brice was left winded and pale.

"I...love you," Autumn repeated and realized in that instant that she did indeed love Brice Donovan.

His arms came around her then. His fingers twisted into the coiling copper-colored mass so suddenly she cried aloud in surprise. "Pretty little liar," Donovan hissed. "You'll regret having lied to me."

"I'm not!" she wanted to say, but the words wouldn't come. He kissed her then with raw abandon...

Other Avon Books by
Katherine Sutcliffe

DREAM FEVER
A FIRE IN THE HEART
RENEGADE LOVE
SHADOW PLAY

WINDSTORM

KATHERINE SUTCLIFFE

AVON BOOKS ◆ NEW YORK

I Dedicate WINDSTORM
To Neil, my husband, who makes *my* toes tingle.

To Bryan, Lauren and Rachel, who make me proud every day of my life.

To Peggy and James Cochran: Mom and Dad, who don't really understand my obsession but are there for me, anyway.

A Special Thanks
To Julia Bettinger, Phoebe Stell, Rosalyn Alsobrook and Shelley Darmon for all the letters and long-distance phone calls that, uncannily, seem to come when I need them most. I could not have survived this without you, ladies!

To Amanda Jay (Laura Kinsale), who eagerly shared her expertise when she really didn't have to.

To Ruth Cohen, my agent. Anyone who can listen to a crying, babbling writer half out of her mind with worry, then say, "Forget it, Kathy, you can say anything to me," deserves devotion. Thank you, Ruth.

And A Very Special Thanks
To Carin Cohen, my editor, who took the chance and gave me a chance, not once, but twice. I did this one for you.

WINDSTORM is an original publication of Avon Books. This work has never before appeared in book form. This work is a novel. Any similarity to actual persons or events is purely coincidental.

AVON BOOKS
A division of
The Hearst Corporation
1350 Avenue of the Americas
New York, New York 10019

Copyright © 1987 by Katherine Sutcliffe
Published by arrangement with the author
Library of Congress Catalog Card Number: 86-92050
ISBN: 0-380-75264-6

First Avon Books Printing: June 1987

AVON TRADEMARK REG. U.S. PAT. OFF. AND IN OTHER COUNTRIES, MARCA REGISTRADA, HECHO EN CANADA.

Printed in Canada.

UNV   10   9   8   7   6   5   4   3   2

Chapter 1

CHARLESTON, SOUTH CAROLINA

Fear. Autumn Sinclair could sense it in this steamy, earthen-floored cabin as she could in church—in the heat of summer—when the preacher railed about God and damnation and shook his fist in the air, proclaiming that every sweating, trembling soul in the room would perish in hell for his sins. Autumn would stare out the window, as she was doing now, focus her mind on the hazy shafts of light streaming through the glass and think of happier things than dying. But she couldn't think—not now—not when the approaching storm had sucked the air from the dilapidated quarters, when her nostrils burned with lye and her throat throbbed with the need to cry aloud. A scream rent the air, consuming and final, and for a brief moment Autumn wished for that red-faced preacher and his Bible-beating petition for lost souls.

Millie Tims was going to need him.

"Do something," Autumn pleaded, swiping a tightly clenched fist across her damp cheek. She turned toward the bed, a helpless face among the half dozen who wept and prayed over the obviously doomed black woman. Millie labored, knowing—accepting—the outcome. It didn't matter, as long as they could save the baby.

The midwife's eyes widened with distress. "Ain't nothin' I can do, Miss Autumn!"

"Miss Autumn, come away from here this minute."

Autumn lifted her eyes to the anguished black face of Millie Tims's brother. "Come away," he coaxed her.

"But it's my duty to help. I *want* to help. Please, I—"

"Ain't fittin'. Mr. Mitchell didn't mean for you to see this. Come away, now."

His calloused hands closed about Autumn's shoulders,

1

but another shriek turned her knees to water and she crumpled to the floor.

Millie's shoulders lifted. Her white teeth bared, she pushed and pushed, her bony fingers popping as she clutched the dirty sheets beneath her. Her husband, a mute shadow in the dimly lit corner, jumped to his feet as the midwife fell to her knees, accepting the infant feet first. The new mother dropped back on the bed. The spectators waited.

Slap! Slap!

Nothing.

They watched, listening for the first strangled cough and gasp of air.

When the baby wailed, pleasure brightened the spectators' faces—all but Autumn's. She looked sadly on Millie's still features.

"Millie's dead."

All heads turned toward Autumn. They hadn't noticed.

Autumn struggled to her feet, then turned accusing eyes onto Millie's husband. Where was the anger, or pain, or even the shame over having caused another human being such agony? There was only pride as he looked upon his son.

Calmly she walked out the door. "Go home!" she snapped to the curious bystanders. The men, women and the children, who were still too young to understand their lot in life, turned away, scattering through the row of cabins, their faces somber.

But by supper their friend would be a vague memory, a name who had once laughed and loved and existed only to die for the sake of . . . what? Millie Tims was gone.

What a waste.

Autumn, hands shoved into her breeches pockets, watched as a young woman swayed her hips coquettishly to a man who smiled and stepped up behind her. Fool! Millie Tims lay cold on her birthing bed—deathbed—because she had once thought a man more important than her life. Was a man worth that sacrifice? Autumn's own mother had thought so, had thought her husband deserved a place in the everlasting, so she gave him children. Not one but three—the more the better. The third one killed her, and Claude Sinclair had remarried within the year. That wife had died in childbirth as well. Autumn could still remember their

crucifying pain, punishment for being beautiful, desirable
. . . for being born a woman.

Autumn ran for her horse and mounted—up and over a
fence, the stallion's stride putting death behind her. She
had to escape the grim scene. She was cursed: born a
woman, a beautiful woman, but she wouldn't accept her
mother's fate! Not ever . . . ever!

Clouds threatened, roiling fingers of darkness and light
that wove through the mantle of pine trees at the Atlantic's
edge. Topping the bluff above Bachus Bay, the horse
reared, and before the heaving animal could stop completely, Autumn jumped to the ground. Her body trembling
and eyes shut tight, she tried to force the senseless loss
from her mind. Millie Tims had been Autumn's age: twenty.
The black girl had had every right to live!

A man stepped from the woods. "Autumn."

The rich, deep voice jolted Autumn from her thoughts.
Though she had only met the man three days before, she
knew instantly who he was. Roy Donovan. Just that morning she had turned down his marriage proposal. No "happily ever after" for her!

Donovan stepped up the path, his boots muddy, his
linen shirt damp and clinging to his skin. "I hoped you
would be here," he said.

Autumn stared out at the white-capped waves, thinking
of Millie.

Roy frowned. "What's wrong?"

"I . . . just watched a woman die, Mr. Donovan." Her
voice painfully tight, Autumn focused on the attentive man
and stated flatly, "I wasn't certain I would see you again."

"I rarely take no for an answer. Not when I want
something badly enough."

"And you want me."

"Is that so hard to believe?"

"I told you: I loathe being gussied up and paraded
before men like my brother's thoroughbreds. I intend to be
a partner to my husband, should I decide to marry, not
merely an ornament for his arm."

"Frailty in women might be appealing to some. I find it
tedious. You, my dear Miss Sinclair, are hardly that."

Autumn's mouth curved in a smile. "My wearing breeches doesn't bother you?"

"They would serve you better on the Île de Cayemite than a cumbersome skirt."

Autumn turned toward the water, thankful to find a topic to divert her mind from the past horrible hours. She was running again. She knew that, but as in those years long ago, after her mother had died in childbirth, she couldn't stop herself. All that mattered now was to escape the same fate. "Tell me again about Hunnington Hall." Convince me! she inwardly pleaded.

"The largest of two estates on Cayemite."

"In the Caribbean."

"Yes. My father bought it from a Frenchman over thirty years ago."

"You were born there?"

"The younger of two sons."

"And your parents are dead?" When he nodded, she asked, "Why was the estate left to you and not to your older brother?"

A sudden flush heated Roy's features. Staring out at the angry water, he spoke tersely. "My brother . . . is a wayward sort, prone to gambling and womanizing." He turned Autumn to face him, his long fingers digging into her shoulders. "Life on Cayemite is not one of leisure. There is little time for needlepoint and tea parties. There are few women other than the servants, and the woman I marry must content herself with my company and the building of an empire. It will take a special young lady, one who is capable of dealing with any unforeseen problems that might arise in my absence. *You* are that woman."

Autumn frowned. "But I don't—"

"Love me?" He pulled her closer. "That may come in time."

The drumming of hoofbeats caused them to turn. They watched as Jethro, her brother's black stable boy, cantered up to them.

"Miss Autumn, I been lookin' ever'where for you. Mr. Sinclair got more smoke coming outa his ears than my Aunt Lollie's seasonin' house!"

"Why is my brother angry this time?" She wiggled from Roy's hands.

"Why!" Jethro gaped in disbelief. "Miss Autumn, have you forgot the party Mr. Sinclair's wife be givin' for you tonight?"

Party. Autumn closed her eyes.

"I thought so!" Jethro exclaimed.

Forgetting Roy completely, Autumn hurried toward her horse. "Have guests begun to arrive?" she called over her shoulder to Jethro.

"Yes, ma'am. The Allens be here. So be the Carlisles, and . . ." He hesitated.

Autumn froze. "And?"

Jethro lowered his eyes. "Mr. Chandler and Miss Anita."

Gregory Chandler. That traitor! He was her dear friend, who had made a pact in blood with her that he would never marry and leave her. Well, he was leaving her, all right. Yesterday he had announced that he was marrying Anita Cunningham. Anita Cunningham, with her pale blond ringlets and upturned nose—everything he had sworn he loathed in a woman!

Autumn mounted her horse. Without speaking to Roy again, she rode back toward her brother's house.

"She's done it again, Mary."

"Calm down, Mitchell. The guests will hear you."

Arms akimbo, Mitchell Sinclair stared at the ceiling and asked, "Where did I go wrong? Before my father died, I swore I would raise Autumn as I would my own daughter. I gave her everything: clothes, education, yet she thumbs her nose at polite society, rebels against propriety and spites me every chance she gets."

Mary smiled at her husband. "Autumn is . . . different, dear."

"Different! Oh, she's different, all right. What other woman of her age—of *any* age, for that matter—would ride about the countryside dressed in breeches? She swings from trees, Mary!"

"I'm certain Autumn hasn't climbed trees in some years—"

"Not two months ago she was found swimming naked—"

"Lower your voice, dear."

"In the creek." He dropped into a chair.

Mary smiled sympathetically as her husband buried his head in his hands. "Autumn is a very special young woman, Mitchell. She's strong, independent—"

"Good God, you're actually defending her!" Mitchell jumped to his feet. "If I didn't know better, I'd swear that was envy on your face."

"Please, darling. Don't be too quick to criticize your sister until you learn the reasons for her tardiness."

"Well, she'd better have a damned good excuse for being late for her own birthday party."

"I'm certain she will." With a rustle of powder-blue silk, Mary left the room.

Palmyra's grand ballroom glistened beneath a thousand dancing candle flames. Soft music of violins and the sweet fragrance of gardenias mingled with the humidity of the impending storm. Along the far wall, young women and their escorts gathered about tables laden with sparkling punches and tempting canapes. Autumn's friends spoke softly, banteringly, occasionally casting curious glances toward the blue-gowned hostess greeting the arriving guests.

"I'll wager Autumn is up to one of her shenanigans again," William DeRosa said. "I wouldn't be surprised if she slid down the banister and plopped right at Mitchell's feet."

Anita Cunningham frowned and clicked her tongue. "Hush! You're such a bore, William."

"I wager your little announcement yesterday did much to unsettle the birthday girl," DeRosa commented to Gregory Chandler. "I always suspected that Autumn was in love with you."

"Nonsense," Gregory countered. "We are like brother and sister."

William laughed. "Like brother and brother, you mean. If she weren't so busy trying to be one of us, she might have landed herself a husband long ago. She's certainly pretty enough. But it is hard to conjure romantic images of a woman who wears breeches."

"Marriage and children are out of the question for

Autumn." Biting his tongue and silently rebuking himself for allowing his frustration to show, Gregory attempted a reassuring smile for his fiancée. His eyes shifted again toward the door. Mary Sinclair had disappeared from the room.

Autumn, shivering from the damp, stood at the foot of the stairs outside Mitchell's library door. "Where is my brother?" she asked her sister-in-law.

"Upstairs, attempting to recover from his state of apoplexy. Oh, Autumn, how could you forget the party?"

"I'm sorry. I was upset over Millie and"—she lowered her eyes—"I forgot."

Understanding erased the lines of irritation from the older woman's face. Autumn embodied the dreams, the secret yearnings, that occasionally unsettled Mary's contentment. Mitchell's sister was proud and defiant. Yes, Mary admitted to herself, perhaps she *was* slightly envious . . . but proudly so.

Lovingly, she touched the girl's flushed cheek. "Hurry upstairs and get ready. Lollie has your bath prepared and your dress laid out. I'll do something to pacify Mitchell."

"What will you do?"

Mary appeared thoughtful, then admitted, "Lie, I suppose. I don't know what else to do."

Taking the stairs two at a time, Autumn reached her room on the second floor. Lollie was waiting, her foot tapping and her face puckered in disapproval.

"You shoulda been home hours ago!" the Negress reproached her.

"I'm sorry."

"Sorry, you say. You been off poutin' over Gregory Chandler is all."

"I don't pout, Lollie." Autumn caught the tail of her shirt and pulled it over her head. Lollie snatched it from her hand. "Millie Tims died today," she said more softly.

"I know."

"It only proves my point—"

"We all know how you feel 'bout marriage and babies. And don't nobody know it any better than yore brother."

With her hands planted on her slender hips, Autumn

demanded, "Does he intend to parade his eligible friends before me during this soiree? If so, I refuse to attend."

Lollie scoffed and, pointing one knobby-knuckled finger in Autumn's face, responded, "Someday some man gonna sashay into your life and sit you right back on that breeches-clad behind of yores. I only hope I'm still alive to see it."

"Hell will freeze over first," Autumn said with such vehemence that Lollie pursed her lips. "I don't intend to fritter my life away in agony or perpetual tedium."

Lollie harrumphed and shook her head.

"Of course, if there was a man who offered marriage *totally* for love's sake, and *not* strictly to beget him a long line of namesakes, I might consider the holy state of matrimony." After a moment's thought, Autumn added, "Of course, he would simply have to be the most hand-some man on the face of the earth."

Dropping her breeches to the floor, Autumn stepped into the tub and sank to her shoulders in steaming water. She knew Lollie was staring. At the sound of the woman furiously clucking her tongue, Autumn lifted her face a fraction and frowned.

"You been spendin' time in the sun again without yore hat. Look at them freckles 'cross that nose. They is multi-plyin' like Mr. Mitchell's pet rabbits."

"Gregory Chandler says they add character to my face."

"Character! Lord, you just about 'charactered' pore Mr. Mitchell to death. And look at this hair." She lifted a fist of russet curls from Autumn's nape. "We shoulda been workin' on this mess hours ago. Ain't nothin' we kin do about it now."

"Certainly there is. Just twist it into one of those little knots on top of my head like Anita Cunningham wears."

"Anita Cunningham ain't got dis much hair. Ain't nobody got dis much hair but you."

Hair was the least of Lollie's worries. Mitchell Sinclair was not going to be pleased with his sister, regardless, so better to dwell on getting the girl clean and dressed. As soon as Autumn stepped from the tub, Lollie began rub-bing her charge briskly with thirsty linens until she tingled and glowed. Then she dashed Autumn's apricot skin with enough eau de cologne to make her sneeze, forced her into silk hosiery, layers of petticoats and a lacy chemise, then over it all pulled a figure-flattering creation that enhanced her generous bosom as well as her tiny waist.

Autumn hurried down the stairs. The distant music beckoned her to join her dancing friends, but the quiet timbre of Gregory Chandler's voice drew her toward the library. To her horror, as she approached the open door she recognized Mitchell's answering voice.

Gregory Chandler, his face expressionless, was staring at his host in apparent shock. "I'm sorry, Mr. Sinclair, but marriage to Autumn is out of the question. As you know, sir, I have already spoken for Anita—"

"But I believed you to be very fond of my sister."

"So I am, sir . . . in a brotherly fashion."

Mitchell hesitated, then said, "I am a very wealthy man, Greg. I could see you—"

"How dare you!" Autumn hurried into the room as Gregory and her brother whirled to face her. "Excuse us," she said to Gregory. "I've a few words to say to Mitchell in private."

Chandler, his face a mask, bowed stiffly and left the room.

"How could you humiliate me in such a way, Mitchell?" Autumn demanded. "Should I decide to marry, I can find my own husband!"

"I've seen no evidence of that." He moved to the open window. "You're too damned busy sticking your nose in the running of my plantation. Half the male population of Charleston is beginning to talk about my spinster sister who fancies herself more of a man than a woman."

"I'm hardly a spinster."

"For God's sake, Autumn, you swagger about the countryside wearing breeches, riding astride and telling jokes that would color a sailor's face. It's not proper, I tell you."

"Where is it written—"

"Stop it!" Slamming his fist against the wall, Mitchell shouted, "Dammit, Autumn, I don't want to hear again that if God had intended women to breed like rabbits, he would have given them long ears and cotton tails. It was funny when you were a child, but, by God, you're twenty years old, and it's time you settled down and fulfilled your obligation as a woman."

"Like Mama? Like Millie Tims?"

"Where would *you* be today had Mother chosen not to take that chance?"

Her chin came up. The defiance sparkling in her eyes dimmed slightly with tears.

"It's time you were married," Mitchell went on. "If I have to arrange matters myself, I will."

Gathering her skirts, she turned abruptly and left the room.

Applause greeted Autumn as she entered the ballroom. The group of friends surrounded their guest of honor and whisked her toward the dance floor. She smiled and laughed, but Mitchell's threat left Autumn shaken. She had done her best through the years to live up to his expectations of what she should be. For months she had floated about with a book on her head. For hours she had mulled over Mary's books on etiquette and plucked apart embroidery floss until her eyes crossed. But her true nature had inevitably won out. Autumn Dae Sinclair didn't care in the least that *Mode Illustrée* predicted crinoline underskirts would soon be the rage. They would do her little good on her jaunts about Mitchell's plantation. And she was far more interested in the ploughing of fields for next year's cotton than in the pickling of pigs' feet, or candle and soap making.

"Are you going to dance with me, Autumn?"

Autumn focused on Gregory Chandler's smiling face. "Are you certain it's proper? What about your fiancée?"

"Anita doesn't mind."

"Then I suppose I have little choice." She accepted Gregory's arm.

They glided a moment to the music, but when she could stand the tension no longer, she beseeched him, "Forgive Mitchell. He truly means well."

"The incident is forgotten, Autumn." Worriedly then, he added, "You're still angry with me?"

"We promised each other we would never marry."

"One of us grew up."

Autumn stopped. Gregory's eyes were troubled, his face flushed. She'd seen that look many times: when she'd forced her horse over a hurdle he had refused to take; when she'd accepted Bryan Holmes's dare to swim the entire width of Bachus Bay, a distance of over a mile.

Concern, anger, and . . . something else. "But we vowed—"

"Such vows are for children," he interrupted. "I'm a man with needs, Autumn. I want a wife who will hold me when I'm tired—"

"You want a mother."

"I want children! I want someone to come home to at the end of the day, whom I can talk to about something besides dirt and crops and last year's profits. I want to sit in front of a fire while my wife reads me Shakespeare and Rousseau. I want to be amused by unamusing gossip, dammit!"

Looking away, she forced a smile across her lips.

He continued in a tighter voice. "You've been my closest friend. My confidant. I've shared more of my life and my secrets with you than with anyone else. I wouldn't like that to end."

"But now you'll have a wife to share those things with," she said in a tremulous voice.

"Would I say good-bye to a friend just because I marry? You'll always be welcome in our home." His arm about her waist, he propelled her toward the petite blond girl across the dance floor.

"Autumn, how lovely you look!" Anita offered sweetly. Her smile faltered slightly as she looked up into her fiancé's rigid face, then again to Autumn.

"Thank you," Autumn said looking toward the pale blond knot of hair atop Anita's head.

A sudden clap of thunder shook the house. Wind pommeled the French doors, sending them back against the wall, spraying the floor with glass and rain. The room seemed to career crazily as all three chandeliers swung back and forth, and as another blast of wind whipped through the windows, every flickering candle was snuffed out.

Women screamed and grabbed their escorts, while attendants hurried to secure storm shutters and doors. "Don't panic!" someone called. "Stay where you are!"

"Autumn?" The voice was husky in the darkness. Autumn whirled and stared up into the man's shadowed face. He smelled of rain; he smelled of tobacco and rum. His sudden mysterious appearance caused Autumn's heart to race in her breast. "Come with me," he whispered. Sweeping her into his arms, he carried her out through the French doors, onto the veranda.

"Roy Donovan!" she exclaimed when released. "What are you doing here?"

"I want your answer. I want it now."

"What answer?"

"Marry me."

Thunder shook the wall at her back. "But I don't know you!"

"Will you stand by while your brother bribes another man for your hand?" Roy laughed at her astonished gasp. "I've a way of listening outside open windows."

Lightning outlined the sharp planes of Roy Donovan's face. He was a handsome man, with a wild, spontaneous nature to match her own. "But I don't know you!" Autumn repeated, trying to convince herself as well as Roy. She was shaking now, as much from nervous anticipation as from the wind and rain.

"You say you want to be a partner to a husband, not merely an ornament for his arm! You say you want to own the finest plantation on the face of this earth! You can have that!"

Autumn turned her rain-drenched face up to Roy's and cried, "On Cayemite?"

"Yes! Twenty thousand acres of the finest sugarcane ever grown and a fifty-room mansion overlooking the most beautiful stretch of turquoise sea in this entire world. Yours, Autumn Sinclair, if you will marry me!"

Autumn closed her eyes. She had dreamed of such freedom. Roy wanted a companion, a partner. He demanded nothing more of her than that. But Mitchell would see her married—and pregnant. Castigation would be forthcoming had she not birthed him a nephew within the year.

Dear God.

"Well?" Roy asked again.

Autumn held her breath, then finally stammered, "Y-yes."

He shouted a laugh to the turbulent sky before saying, "I'll contact you when the arrangements have been made." He kissed her, then was gone.

* * *

The stench of whiskey was as prevalent in the room as the blue-gray cloud of smoke hovering against the ceiling. The men seated about the table waited expectantly as Roy's fingers fluttered over his coins.

"Play or fold, Donovan. We ain't got all day."

His mouth dry, Roy Donovan threw a fistful of money onto the table. "I'll raise you five hundred."

Hugh Tyler, with his barrel chest and tree-trunk legs, clamped a hand onto his employer's shoulder. Bending to his ear, he said quietly, "We need to talk, Mr. Donovan."

"Later."

"Not later," he insisted. "Now, sir, or these men'll be pickin' yer bones before the game is finished."

Donovan's eyes shifted among the watchful gamblers. Laying his cards on the table, Roy joined his overseer, and both moved into the shadows.

"What the devil are y' doin'?" the Irishman demanded. "You've just gambled away what little profits we made on last year's crops. We'll be doin' good t' buy passage back t' Cayemite at this rate."

Donovan glanced toward the squint-eyed man who had goaded him into raising the stakes higher than he could afford. "He's bluffing," he said offhandedly to Tyler.

"And if he's not? You've already run up enough markers in this city. Any more and yer liable t' lose Hunnington completely."

"I'll get the money."

"Aye, you'll get yer money, all right. By marryin' Autumn Sinclair. It ain't right, maît."

"You just worry about making those arrangements," Roy muttered.

"I've made yer bloody arrangements!" Lowering his voice, the Irishman continued, "It weren't easy findin' a clergyman who would accept a bribe, but I did it. You've an appointment at ten in the mornin' t' be wed to Miss Sinclair."

A satisfied smile curled Donovan's mouth.

Hugh Tyler frowned. "Don't be lookin' too pleased. You'll have Mitchell Sinclair t' deal with."

"I'll handle Sinclair."

"I don't like what yer doin'. It ain't right, yer usin' the lass in such a way."

"Autumn is doing her share of using. She's using me to get away from that tyrannical brother. I'm doing her a favor, Tyler. In turn, she'll ask Mitchell for enough money to meet Hunnington's debts."

"And if she refuses?"

"And lose her chance to be a partner on a plantation instead of a brood mare for some paunchy, balding old man? She doesn't want a bunch of runny-nose brats hanging off her legs any more than I do. She won't refuse." After a moment's consideration Roy added, "I'm really quite fond of Autumn. I wager she'll keep me occupied nicely—"

"For a while. You'll get tired of her as quickly as you have the others. We both know there's only one woman who's gonna hold yer interest, and that's 'cause she was spawned by the devils . . . just like yerself."

Roy's head snapped around. His face went white and his body shook before he said, "Get word to Autumn that she is to meet me at ten in the morning."

Morning found Hugh Tyler cursing beneath his breath. Damn Patrick Donovan for taking pity on an *engagé* those twenty years ago. Better to serve out his sentence in prison than to be pawn to Roy Donovan's antics. Had he known the young hellraiser would waste his father's fortune on gambling and whiskey, he would have bid adieu to Cayemite years ago.

"So you lost all of last year's profits, sparse as they were." Sadly, Hugh shook his head and looked down on the semiconscious man. "Mother Mary, yer a mess," the Irishman continued. "It'll be *my* butt yer brother kicks for lettin' you get back into this state." Kicking the empty liquor bottles aside, Hugh reached for his employer, hoisting him to the edge of the bed. "You'll be gettin' dressed now," he said breathlessly. "You've the clergy t' meet. Have you forgotten, Mr. Donovan, yer t' be married today."

Roy laughed drunkenly. "So I am. To Autumn . . ."

"Sinclair. Mitchell Sinclair's baby sister. The man who's going t' bail you out of yer financial problems."

Donovan's eyes flickered open. "Those men—"

"I swore to 'em you'd have their money by noon. That'll give you enough time t' marry Autumn and see her brother." Grabbing one of Roy's two suits, he threw it on the bed. "Get yer pickled carcass dressed while I see t' our carriage." Turning away, he whispered, "God help our souls for wronging a woman."

Autumn read the brief message again before looking toward the church in the distance. She had ridden an hour to reach this fork in the road. There would be no turning back.

The clergyman looked up as she rode to the church door. He appeared worried, but not nearly so worried as the man fumbling nervously with Roy Donovan's cravat.

"Sorry I'm late." Autumn stepped hesitantly into the dimly lit interior.

After smoothing Roy's cravat into place, Hugh helped him from the pew. "Look who's here, boss. Yer fiancée."

His face gray and his mouth compressed in a sickly white line, Donovan stumbled forward.

"Are you ill?" Autumn asked.

"Just a mite," Tyler responded for him. "He overimbibed somewhat last evenin'. You know, celebratin' and all. Ain't that right, Donovan?"

Roy nodded. "I'm . . . glad you've come." Extending one trembling hand, he smiled.

Reluctantly Autumn lifted her fingers to his.

The touch of her hand brought Donovan back to his senses. He pulled her closer. "Little one, I thought you would never come."

"There was much to consider."

"What is there to consider? Cayemite needs you."

Autumn peered up into Roy's somber face. "Why the hurry, Donovan? Were you to approach my brother with respect to courting me, I'm certain you would meet with little resistance."

"There's no time, Autumn. I've been away from Cayemite too long as it is. Besides, my ship leaves this afternoon."

"This afternoon! I had no idea . . ."

Donovan closed his eyes. "I've no time for games, Autumn. You marry me this moment, or we'll forget the entire arrangement. What will it be?"

He was right. The past four days had given Autumn ample time to change her mind. And she might have done so had Mitchell not made good on his threat to present her to several prospective husbands. Again, she inwardly cursed her womanly lot. Had she been born a man these grievances would be laughable.

The ceremony was over quickly. Autumn closed her eyes as her husband pressed a perfunctory kiss onto her mouth. He then turned away to settle with the official. Of medium height, with strong shoulders and narrow waist, his hair neither blond, or brown, but a pleasant mixture of the two, Roy Donovan was a handsome man. His eyes were hazel, with lashes and brows slightly lighter than his hair. His skin was somewhat pale.

Autumn's eyes drifted curiously over his clothes. Although the cinnamon-brown jacket had been expertly cut to fit his shoulders, there was noticeable aging to its seams. The fawn-colored breeches were thin in places, and the heels of his knee-high boots were worn nearly to the soles.

Hugh Tyler walked away from the uncomfortable scene. For all the girl's bravado, there was vulnerability in the way she was staring at his employer. Damn, but he hadn't cared for this entire scheme. Stopping in the doorway, he didn't notice the approaching riders until they had rounded the farthest bend in the road. He cursed under his breath and turned on his heel.

Autumn leapt aside as the burly Irishman thundered down the aisle. He grabbed Donovan's arm, leaving both her and the clergyman perplexed at his urgency. "Missus Donovan," he said, "yer husband begs yer forgiveness for his abrupt departure. Go home and await his word."

"But—"

The rear door slammed. Autumn Sinclair Donovan sank onto the pew.

Chapter 2

"We all have certain responsibilities, Autumn. You, as a woman—a well-bred young woman—and my sister, whom I have attempted to raise as I would have my own daughter, have a responsibility to mankind and to me." Mitchell Sinclair paused in his pacing. "Are you listening to me, Autumn?"

"Yes, Mitchell." Autumn waited until her brother had continued his pacing before looking again toward the letter on her dresser.

"I have burned your breeches, and should you somehow get another pair, I will burn them as well. Do we understand each other?"

She glanced surreptitiously toward the wardrobe, thinking of the several pairs of breeches she had hidden there, but dutifully she said, "Yes, Mitchell."

"Good. You will begin our understanding by donning one of the dresses in your wardrobe. You'll be acting as hostess tonight."

"We're having guests?" Her small face tipped up, a quirk of irritation twisting one corner of her pressed lips.

"Jay Michaels."

"Again."

"Yes. We've business matters to discuss."

Suppressing a sigh, Autumn nodded. Mitchell left the room.

Jay Michaels again—just another in a long line of prospective husbands her brother had researched and found to be an excellent match for an "obstinate and slightly unmanageable little rowdy."

Still, Michaels was the only one who had returned after the first confrontation with her sharp tongue and even sharper wit. "Put a baby in her belly," she'd heard him

17

say to Mitchell, "and she'll mellow soon enough." Mitchell had looked toward the door, where she stood with her hands planted on her hips and foot tapping on the floor. His look of chagrin had reminded her of a child caught with his hand in a cookie jar.

But Michaels was becoming much too persistent. So was her brother. Something would have to be done . . . and soon. Striding toward her bureau, Autumn reasoned there was no time like the present.

Snatching up the letter, Autumn stared with burning eyes at her husband's scrawled words. How dare Roy Donovan profess his remorse over leaving her at the altar, his longing to bring her to Cayemite, then his need for money—in the same paragraph!

So, it was money that Roy Donovan had wanted from her. Nothing more. How conveniently he'd forgotten about her until his creditors started banging on his door. She closed her eyes, reliving the moment those four months earlier when several men burst into the church, hoping to force Roy into meeting his gambling debts. She'd realized then that Roy's tales of wealth and prosperity were lies. She should have admitted the truth to her brother then, but she just couldn't bring herself to do it. There had, after all, remained the hope that Roy would show up and claim her. Until now . . .

Moving toward her wardrobe, Autumn rummaged through her clothes. She shoved the canary-yellow satin aside, deciding on the nutmeg muslin Mary had given to her on her nineteenth birthday.

Autumn met Mary in the hall. Trying desperately to keep the nervous tremor from her voice, she asked in an odd, high-pitched voice, "Will I pass inspection?"

Fondly, Mary pushed an errant strand of hair over Autumn's shoulder. "You're beautiful, my dear. I'm certain your brother will be quite pleased."

Not for long, she thought.

"What do you think of Jay Michaels?" Mary asked.

"He's old."

Mary's eyes widened. "Forty-three is not old!"

Reflecting on the man's squat physique, Autumn managed only half seriously, "He looks like a toad."

"Oh!" Mary giggled and admitted, "Yes he does, a trifle."

Autumn peered thoughtfully at the ceiling, then wrinkling her nose, stated matter-of-factly, "I shan't marry him, you know."

"Oh, I never thought you would," Mary responded. She turned, as did Autumn, and both started down the hall. "I told Mitchell you knew exactly what he was doing. I'm just surprised that you've tolerated his meddling this long."

"I've humored him." Autumn, with a fond smile, looked sideways at her companion. "Mitchell finds such great pleasure in meddling in my affairs."

"He means well," Mary pointed out in the loving tone that made Autumn's heart ache with the thought of the pain she would cause them.

Pausing at the foot of the stairs, Autumn searched her sister-in-law's face. "I pray that Mitchell will forgive me," Autumn said softly. She prayed, too, that the woman who had been mother, sister and friend to her these many years could find it in her heart to understand her motives.

Leaving Mary at the door, Autumn squared her shoulders and entered the room where her brother and Michaels were waiting.

A delicious feast of rice, braised chicken and sliced ham filled Mary's finest china platters, spread over the linen-and lace-covered table. Autumn, however, had little appetite. She sat stiffly, avoiding any attempts to be drawn into conversation with Michaels and her brother. She dreaded the forthcoming confrontation more with each passing minute.

Michaels drew his linen napkin across his mouth before stating, "It seems, Miss Sinclair, that you have no taste for ham."

Unblinking, Autumn's eyes shifted over the man's beefy jowls, double chin and ruddy cheeks. His bold eyes had rarely left her bosom during the evening.

Mitchell cleared his throat. "Autumn, as you know, Mr. Michaels has been a widower for some time now."

"Two years," Michaels interrupted, "without female companionship."

Mitchell took a long drink of wine.

When Autumn still offered no response, Michaels fidgeted impatiently in his chair. "My deceased wife, God rest her soul, never provided me with children. You can understand how lonely Rivertree is."

Her father's face flashed through Autumn's mind. Claude Sinclair had been Michaels's age when he'd taken his second wife—a girl of just seventeen years. "What you are implying," Autumn responded with a stab at her chicken, "is that you would prefer a wife who is young enough to bear you a passel of children."

"Well, I—"

"Am *I* such a woman?" She looked down her tiny freckled nose, and with a lift of one brow, prompted, "Well?"

"I—"

"Are you attempting to propose to me, Mr. Michaels?" Autumn leaned slightly across her plate, holding the fork like a weapon in her shaking hand.

"Yes, I—" Michaels hesitated before repeating, "Yes, I guess I am."

Autumn dropped back in her chair. "Impossible."

"Autumn, you are being horribly rude to your guest," Mitchell said.

"*Your* guest," she emphasized. Looking back at Michaels, she continued, "It is nothing personal, Mr. Michaels, but, you see, there are circumstances which will not allow a marriage between us."

"And what might they be!" her brother roared, coming out of his chair.

Closing her eyes, Autumn took a deep breath. "I am already married."

Silence.

Autumn peeked from beneath her lashes at her brother. Mitchell stood at the head of the table, staring into his plate, his hands gripping the edges of the table.

"Married," he said. Finally he raised his head. Only then did she respond.

"Yes, Mitchell. I have been married some four months."

After an uncomfortable moment, Mary released a nervous laugh. "Oh, Autumn, stop teasing Mr. Michaels.

WINDSTORM   21

And look at your poor brother. You have practically caused him to swoon."

"I'm not teasing, Mary. I . . . I married Roy Donovan last March."

"Well!" Jay Michaels struggled to his feet. "Sinclair, I wish you luck with this young . . . young . . . *lady*. Good evening to you all!"

Mary came out of her chair, her face pinched with worry.

"Who the hell is Roy Donovan?" Mitchell's voice shook the table.

"My husband," Autumn told him.

Mary hastily suggested, "Why don't we retire to the library? I'm certain once we've all had time to calm down—"

"You've made me a laughingstock before this entire county!" Mitchell thundered.

Autumn was shaking. She had hoped and prayed these many long weeks that Roy would materialize on her doorstep and break the news of their marriage to her brother. But all her dreams had gone up in smoke with the arrival of Roy's letter. If she was to have the freedom he once promised awaited her on that distant island, it would cost her dearly.

Fool! For the first time in her life she had gambled on a man . . . and lost!

She covered her face with her hands. Disappointment, disillusionment, hammered inside her head as painfully as Mitchell's anger against her ear. No more! Her chair tumbled backward as she jumped to her feet. "Stop it! Roy has not deserted me! Once his affairs are in order, he is going to return here and take me home to Hunnington Hall!"

"And just where the hell is this Hunnington Hall?"

"The Île de Cayemite . . . in the Caribbean."

"Good God!"

Autumn threw herself at Mitchell, the tears she had suppressed the past horrible months spilling down her cheeks in a torrent. "He swore he would come back for me, and he will!"

Mitchell caught Autumn in his arms. Never since their

mother had died had he witnessed his sister weeping like this. Chastened, he looked helplessly toward his wife. "Take Autumn upstairs. Perhaps she could use one of your powders to calm her down."

Burying her face in Mitchell's coat, Autumn said chokingly, "I don't need a powder to calm me down!"

"Hush," he soothed her. "Autumn, I'm sorry, so dreadfully sorry that I've brought you to this."

"He promised me!"

"Yes, I'm certain he did." He looked beseechingly toward Mary, then surrendered Autumn as his wife extended her arms.

"Donovan? Sure I've heard the name. What do you want to know?"

"Who is he?" Mitchell Sinclair stepped back as the stevedore tipped a hogshead onto its side and rolled it across the dock.

"Depends. There's two of 'em."

"Roy Donovan."

The man mopped his brow with a red-and-white kerchief, then barked an order to several draymen. "Roy Donovan. Don't see him around much anymore. Heard his place fell on hard times a while back. Can't say as I'm surprised. He has a bad habit of gambling away his profits."

"From?"

"Cane. Got most of an island where he grows the stuff."

"Cayemite."

"Something like that."

Mitchell turned away. There was only one thing to do.

The Île de Cayemite jutted from the turquoise water like a polished jewel on the horizon. Against a sapphire sky rose purple tree-clad mountains lush with vegetation and crowned by billowing white clouds. Even from a distance, fingers of white sand beaches could be seen stretching toward the sun.

Within minutes the tiny port of Bovier came into view. The sparse docks were empty but for several weathered skiffs bobbing and bumping against the rotting pilings.

The street of thatched huts looked deserted. From all appearances, the town might have been closed completely. Still, a bubble of excitement surrounded Autumn's heart. Towering palm trees and deserted beaches were fantasies belonging to books and the yarns of sea captains. But the vision before her was real. Roy Donovan had not lied about Cayemite's beauty!

Mitchell spoke with the captain as his wife and sister prepared to depart. "We will be joining you on your return voyage, Captain."

"All of you?"

"That remains to be seen." Lowering his voice, Mitchell asked, "You're certain there is more to the island than this poor excuse for a town?"

"I'm familiar with the Donovans, Mr. Sinclair. Hunnington Hall is some five miles out of Bovier."

No other passengers debarked. As the wind filled the *America*'s sails and sped her out to open sea, the sound of the captain's voice faded, replaced by the flapping of palm fronds and the shifting of sand through the trees.

"I don't like it, Mary." Sand crunched beneath Mitchell's boots as he approached the nearest shack. "Where the devil is everyone?"

"We're not expected," Autumn reminded him.

A dog barked. Somewhere drums were beating a rhythmic tattoo.

"Moin dit, monsieur!"

The three spun.

"Bonjour!" the approaching man called.

"Thanks be to God. Hello!" Mitchell responded.

"Welcome to Cayemite. How may I help you?"

"We have come to see Donovan."

The stranger stepped back, looking suspicious. With a frown he shook his head. "No one can see."

"But I am his wife," Autumn said.

"Tonnerre!" he exclaimed. *"Nan point taureau?* No bull?"

She lifted her chin. "Certainly not."

Opening his jacket with an air of importance, Mitchell withdrew his purse. "We would like to hire a carriage to take us to Hunnington House."

"Ca va reglé." His eyes on the coins in Mitchell's palm, the man whistled. From nowhere men, women and children appeared on the street.

It was too soon to feel a sense of relief, Autumn warned herself, yet as the donkey cart was produced from behind the nearest shelter, she couldn't help sharing a quiet giggle with her sister-in-law. Knowing that Mitchell's sense of propriety did not include being hoisted about in the rear of a rather filthy tumbril, their only hope was that their trip would be as expeditious as possible.

They traveled through vegetation so thick that at times the occupants of the bouncing vehicle were convinced that the driver had left the rutted pathway and become lost in the jungle. Autumn leaned her head back against the side of the cart and stared overhead at the canopy of green. A paradise of fruit trees, lagoons and waterfalls surrounded them. Birds squawked and primped their feathers. Brightly colored flowers filled the air with their heady-sweet fragrance.

As the cart left the rain forest behind, the Sinclairs stared in disbelief at the countryside around them. As far as they could see, the earth undulated with fields of waving cane.

"Donovan habitation!" the driver announced.

The Greathouse was perched on the top of a hill, its steeply pitched shingled roof outlined against the sky. From a distance the gray stone walls of the three-story structure appeared sound enough, but as the cart drew closer to the house, its crumbling facade became more clearly visible. Mitchell and Mary exchanged glances. Autumn, however, was blind to everything but the mansion's weathered magnificence.

"It's . . . it's beautiful!" Autumn bounded up the broad stone steps. Arms open wide, her face turned up to the sun, she exclaimed, "Have you ever seen anything so wonderful!"

"The damned house is falling down," Mitchell grumbled.

Scaling the steps, she stopped outside the arched portico and looked back on a garden of hibiscus, bougainvillea and towering mahogany trees. Autumn longed to cry with exhilaration and relief.

"I am Autumn Sinclair . . . Donovan," Autumn announced to the somber-faced woman who answered the door. "Roy Donovan's wife," she added with a little less enthusiasm.

The servant's black eyes shifted among the three strangers' faces. No response.

"Is . . . is Monsieur Donovan here?"

"No." The woman began to shut the door.

Mitchell jumped forward, bracing his shoulder against the door. "See here, young lady, I have not traveled hundreds of miles to have this damned door slammed in my face. I demand to see Donovan this moment."

The servant shook her head. "No can do. Go now. Go!"

"The devil, we will. I said—"

"Moin dit, assé-a!" came the thundering command. The attendant jumped aside, allowing the door to swing open. In the long hallway stood a woman of such immense size that Mitchell and Mary stepped back in surprise, leaving Autumn standing stubbornly inside the door. "Who be you?" the black demanded.

Undeterred by the woman's size and booming voice, Autumn squared her shoulders and stepped forward. "I am Donovan's wife."

"Tonnerre!" she said. "Donovan's woman." With hands planted on her hips, she offered, "Donovan's woman, you are welcome. I am Celie."

Autumn drew a long breath and stepped into the house. "Is Monsieur Donovan about?"

"No."

"Has he . . . mentioned me?" Celie's kerchiefed head bobbed up and down. Relieved, Autumn asked, "Will Monsieur Donovan be returning soon?"

"Maybe."

They followed Celie from the foyer, entering the first room to their right. Furnishings were draped in sheets. Decay lingered in the air, musty and damp, along with a hint of smoke. Celie pulled away the settee's covering, scattering dust that hung in the hazy shafts of light spilling through the half-closed jalousies. She left the room.

An hour later Mitchell was still pacing about the cluttered quarters. "The place is falling apart." He glowered at his sister. "It's not fit to live in."

"I don't agree." Leaving her chair, Autumn strode about the room. "Rugs will hide the marred floors until we can have them refinished."

"Good God, you don't believe I'm going to allow you to stay here!"

Her head snapped around. "I think you have little say-so in the matter."

"Balderdash! By the time I get my hands on Roy Donovan, there will be little left to call husband."

"Is that why you have come here, to do him some harm?"

"I could hardly break his lily-livered neck from Charleston."

"But I like it here, Mitchell. I *want* to stay."

"For God's sake, Autumn, what is there to like? The heat is insufferable. The help is rude, those damned drums won't shut up and the roof is certain to fall in any minute. No. Your staying here is out of the question."

"But—"

"You have my final word on the matter."

Angrier than Mary or Mitchell had ever seen her, Autumn whirled to face her brother. "It is up to Donovan whether I stay or go!"

"I dare say he will tell you to go, as obviously he did not want you here in the first place."

"Mitchell!" Mary sprang to her feet.

Shoulders back and eyes glittering with amber fire, Autumn announced bravely, "Until my husband arrives to dictate differently, you are in *my* home, as *my* guest and you will keep your opinions to yourself."

"Damnation."

Autumn jerked open the door. Celie was there. "We are to be shown to our quarters now," Autumn directed.

Autumn lay on her husband's bed, watching one corner of the gauzy mosquito *baire* flutter each time the wind whipped through the open window. It reminded her of a butterfly, the kind she had chased as a child before her

arrival at maturity had made it improper to engage in such
childish pursuits.

She hoped there were butterflies on Cayemite.

Fanned by a breeze, the candle flame next to her bedside leaped and danced, casting shadows that undulated
with the rhythm of the drums. The drums, with their
ceaseless call . . . She didn't hear them any longer, though
she knew they were there and as persistent as ever. The
drums didn't concern her—her husband's absence did.

Unable to stand the waiting any longer, she slid to the
floor. She had refused the use of Donovan's room at first,
acquiescing only after being informed that only one other
was available. Upon arriving on the second level of the
house, she understood why. Her senses had not deceived
her when she thought she'd smelled smoke. Many of the
rooms had recently burned.

Two hours after midnight Autumn realized her reunion
with Roy would have to wait another day. Perhaps it was
just as well. Autumn wasn't looking forward to the confrontation between Mitchell and her husband. She had
sworn to her brother that Donovan would return to her
after he had settled his urgent business matters on Cayemite.
And though she suspected that Roy had married her only
for her brother's money, she hadn't informed Mitchell of
her suspicions. She didn't want to believe that her husband's only reason for marrying her had been so material.
She was certain she had felt affection in his kiss.

Moving around his quarters, she found the need to know
her husband far more compelling than going to sleep. His
room was grand, the ceilings high, the furniture without
the delicate French and English lines that were so popular
in Carolina. Leather and mahogany conjured images of
security, strength and presence.

Ignoring a disquieting feeling, Autumn opened the wardrobe. A pleasant scent of musky cologne filled her nostrils.
Ignoring the fluttering of her heart, she ran her fingers
over the row of coats: dark blue broadcloth, forest-green,
cinnamon-brown and white. There was a black velvet
jacket with a satin waistcoat and matching trousers, as well
as work breeches of fawn-colored nankeen and buckskin.
The clothing was exquisitely cut, expensive and in very

good condition. Had her earlier perception of Roy Donovan's state of affairs been wrong?

She closed the wardrobe door with a quiet creak. The tips of her fingers lingered, tracing over the scrolled woodwork, searching out the reason why she was drawn to something so inanimate as a piece of wood. Then her fingers found the carving. Down. Around and up. *D*—Donovan, of course. Donovan.

She jerked her hand away.

The open window enticed her. Moonlight poured through the jalousie and illuminated a patch of floor. She stepped into the light and turned her face to the sky. The wind gently molded her gown to her curves, and she felt a surge of freedom. With the wind on her face and promise stretching boundlessly across the horizon, her future was here. Autumn Sinclair Donovan had come home at last!

A movement caught her eye. Watching the shadows, she realized that the lamp behind her would offer any voyeur a display of her silhouetted curves, she bolted across the room and extinguished the flame. Retracing her steps, she stared toward the line of trees beyond the stone fence. The grounds seemed darker somehow, the shadows deeper, the drums louder.

At the tree line, an orange light arced, hovered, then pulsed on a man's upturned face. Autumn caught her breath as his indistinguishable features glowed for an instant in the fire's light, then disappeared.

Backing away from the window, she returned to the bed and pulled the counterpane to her nose. She was acting like a child, Autumn told herself. On a plantation this size, men were always about. Squeezing her eyes closed, she attempted to sleep.

Autumn floated in and out of dreams, tossing in her bed until the dampened sheets clung to her feverish skin. She dreamed of shadows with eyes, shadows that gyrated with the drums. Then she was suffocating, the acrid smell of smoke assailing her nostrils until she sat upright in bed. No. Even that was a dream, because the man in the shadows had moved up to her room. He was watching her, moving toward the bed . . .

"Madame, s'il vous plaît!"

Her heart racing, Autumn opened her eyes. A woman's face, the color of coffee-and-cream and crowned with thick dark hair, was peering into hers.

"I am Jeanette," the stranger said softly. "You were dreaming, *oui?*"

"Yes." Thank God.

"I have brought you breakfast." Gracefully, Jeanette reached for the silver service at Autumn's bedside. "The drums will take some getting used to. They are used during the day to relieve the strain of the combite—the men and women working in the fields. At night they are used for entertainment and celebration. It is the way of my people."

Autumn looked up. "Your people?"

"We are descendents of the ones who inhabited these islands before your Columbus sailed here."

"You're Indian?"

"My mother was." Jeanette poured the coffee. "The drums, do they bother you? If so, we can have them silenced."

"No," she lied. With trembling hands she accepted the cup of steaming black coffee. "Is my brother about?"

Jeanette nodded. "He and his wife are now speaking with Donovan."

"Donovan!" China clattered as Autumn rolled from the bed. "My husband is home?"

"Husband! Donovan is your mate?"

Autumn ran for the dress Jeanette had placed across the back of a chair. "I married Roy last spring," she responded over her shoulder.

"Roy?"

Glancing at the lacy undergarments, Autumn threw the dress aside and ran to her trunk. She searched through the meticulously folded clothing and pulled out her breeches.

Mary Sinclair perched on the edge of her chair, neither moving nor blinking as she looked first at her husband and then at the man silhouetted before the open window. Never, in her wildest imagination, had she ever dreamed that Autumn's husband was so handsome.

"By God, Donovan, if I were a dueling man, I would

call you out. You have taken advantage of a simple girl who was gullible enough to believe your lies.''

"And they were?"

Mitchell leaned on the desk. "That you found her irresistible, for one. Of course I can understand now why you found the need to lie." When there was no response, he roared, "You want my money!"

"Do I?"

"Certainly. You lost your profits by gambling, and you thought by marrying Autumn you could again face your creditors. Very well, Donovan. Name your price. What will my sister's freedom cost me?"

Donovan's chair creaked, and, lifting his weight from the seat, he braced both hands against the desk top and leaned to within inches of Mitchell's face. Smiling unpleasantly, he said, "Since the moment you barreled through my door, you have not ceased to malign your sister or myself. Tell me, Sinclair, why I should not call *you* out."

It was at that moment that the door burst open. Mary jumped from her chair. Mitchell spun about. Her unbound hair spilling in auburn waves to her waist, her face animated and her eyes flashing golden-brown, Autumn's sudden appearance was as startling as the first blast of a cool autumn breeze on a suffocating summer day.

"I overslept," she panted. Halfway through the doorway she stopped. "I'm sorry, I—" Mary saw a look of consternation cross her face.

Before Autumn could finish, Donovan was around his desk. In three pantherlike strides he reached her, wrapped one hard arm around her waist and pulled her weightless body against his. He stared down into her brown eyes.

"Autumn."

She blinked rapidly.

"God, darling, I've missed you." A slow grin tilted one side of his mouth as he demanded boldly, "Haven't you a kiss for your *husband*, Madame Donovan?"

Before Autumn could respond, his mouth found hers with overwhelming intensity. Mary's eyes widened at the scene. For a moment she thought the man would consume her sister-in-law completely. His eyes were absorbing Autumn's every detail, his fingers tracing each delicate feature, from her moist, parted lips to the shell of her dainty ear. "Mitchell, perhaps we should offer Autumn and Mr. Donovan their privacy," she said softly.

Before Autumn's brother could recover from his shock, Donovan turned to face him. "Your wife is a sensitive woman, Monsieur Sinclair. I will speak with Autumn alone."

Mitchell looked toward his sister and the tall man whose arm was wrapped protectively about her waist. Drawing his shoulders back, he agreed. "But only for a moment," he added. "'You have a great deal of explaining to do, Mr. Donovan."

Autumn opened her mouth to object, but as Donovan's deep-set, gray-green eyes shifted down to hers, all ability to speak seemed to desert her.

Mitchell escorted Mary to the door. She looked from Autumn to Donovan and again to Autumn. She then left the room.

Donovan moved with controlled grace toward the door. He closed it, then, turning slowly, faced the spellbound girl. Amusement deepened the curves about his mouth as he smiled and said:

"Madame Donovan . . . I presume."

Chapter 3

His eyes reminded her of the sea. Not the turquoise blue of the magnificent Caribbean, but the churning, muddy-green waters of Bachus Bay back home—murky, deep, calm on the surface but dangerously turbulent beneath. The under-tow could suck a swimmer into its depths in an instant if he wasn't careful. Those gray-green eyes peering at her now were doing just that—and she was drowning.

Slowly he crossed the room, allowing her to study him from the top of his black-brown hair to the tips of his glossy knee-high boots. Her eyes passed over his fawn-colored breeches, indecently snug, hesitated over his slender hips, then jumped over broad shoulders clad in linen and leather back to his eyes. Cautious eyes. Damning eyes. She struggled to breathe.

Easing onto the desk, he crossed his arms and waited.

Autumn was speechless.

"Haven't you something to say?" he asked. "According to my brother's letter, you're quite the conversationalist."

"Brother?"

"Your husband," he said. "You *do* remember your husband?"

"But . . ." Autumn closed her eyes to clear her mind of its confusion. Then again meeting his cold gaze, she stated firmly, "Roy Donovan is my husband. *You* are not Roy Donovan."

"Tell me, *chérie,* would you know my brother if you saw him again?"

The question was cool, the words brittle. Autumn sensed his earlier affable manner had been a veneer for an under-lying hostility. "I would know him. Now tell me where he is and why you have taken it upon yourself to act as buffer between him and Mitchell?"

32

Donovan's eyes narrowed into two pinpoints of green light. "Did you love Roy?" He extended one hand, brushing her cheek with his thumb and causing her to move away.

"Where is he?" She was trembling. "And why this farce with my brother?"

He studied her face. "Does it matter?"

"Meaning?"

"I think any man would do for you."

Her jaw dropped.

"You only want to escape your brother's domination."

Autumn wanted to run from his eyes. They were as green and sharp as broken glass and as condemning as his words. She backed away. His presence was sapping her strength, and she had the horrifying premonition that if he made one move toward her, she would scream. "Where is Roy?" she demanded.

"Dead."

She reeled as if someone had hit her. She couldn't breathe or move or speak, and she would have fallen had he not grabbed her. She sank into a chair. A tinkling of crystal penetrated her shock, then a glass was forced into her hands.

Brice Donovan stared at the dazed woman before him. Autumn. She looked it, by God, with those golden-brown eyes and that fall of russet hair. He damned himself for his unthinking response to her. But his equilibrium had been shot to hell the moment Autumn Sinclair Donovan entered the room. His brother's letter had hinted that she was beautiful, and his dawn visit to her room had confirmed it. But during the time from dawn to the moment Mitchell Sinclair burst into the library, he had convinced himself that his sister-in-law was a money-hungry little termagant who cared for nothing more than bettering her station in life.

But her exploding through that door, hair and face and eyes like autumn fire, had been his undoing.

"Dead." Autumn gulped her drink. "Roy is dead. I don't understand. How? When?"

"Two months ago. There was an accident. . . ." Her eyes were on his—rich, limpid pools of golden-brown a

man could drown in. Brice found himself recalling the way
her lashes had fluttered against her cheeks as he kissed
her, the taste of her mouth . . . He cleared his throat. "He
was drinking and smoking in bed. He must have passed
out."

"God, he burned to death!" Autumn covered her face
with her hands. "Poor man," she stated shakily. "How
very horrible."

Brice moved away. He had anticipated a burst of hyste-
ria. Then he could have accused her of hypocrisy. He had
expected her to weep on his chest, to tilt her delicate face
up to his and beg for understanding, perhaps help. Then he
would have had an excuse for foiling her brother's attempt
to gain her freedom. But there she sat, pale and stunned,
not trying in the least to hide her feelings. She was upset
that Roy was dead, but not destroyed, and it occurred to
Brice that her underlying strength might have offered Roy
a calm port in Cayemite's tumultuous storm. What, Brice
wondered, might it offer him?

"Donovan! Donovan! *S'il vous plaît*, Donovan!"

Brice and Autumn looked toward the door.

A slender boy with curly black hair bounded into the
room. His great green eyes were dancing with excitement;
his mouth was open—poised for a bloodcurdling scream.
Behind him came Jeanette.

"Non!" she called. Jeanette was stopped in her tracks
as her son threw himself into Brice's arms. She looked
guiltily toward Autumn. "I am sorry, Maîtresse Donovan.
Forgive my Pierre. He is only a child and—"

"I've told you repeatedly," Brice interrupted. "You
and Pierre are free to move about the house as you please."
He focused then on the child. "But you must tell me what
all the excitement is about."

A curl fell onto the child's smooth brow as he tipped his
head toward Autumn. *"Azeto."*

Jeanette gasped. *"Non!"*

Autumn looked up and found Donovan staring down at
her, his eyes reflecting amusement. There was something
disturbingly similar about the man and child, both peering
at her through thick black lashes and their mouths twisted
in the same irregular smile. *"Azeto?"* she asked.

"Witch."

Her face froze.

Brice looked again at the child. "Does Maîtresse Donovan look like a witch?"

Pierre thought a moment. "*Non*. She is very pretty."

Autumn's face turned warm, then hot as Donovan's green eyes shifted again onto her features. "*Oui*," he responded softly, "she is very pretty. Now run tell the others what you have found."

The child scampered from the room. Curtsying, Jeanette followed.

Autumn sat back in her chair. "I have been called a great number of things, but never a witch."

The morning sun spilling through the window caused an aurora of color to reflect from Autumn's hair, all reds and golds, like fire. Those tilted amber eyes were bewitchingly beautiful. Pulling from his trance, Brice offered, "He is only a child, *chérie*. You must not take it to heart."

Moving to her feet, Autumn approached the open window. Before her stretched a colorful vista of sun-splashed gardens, and beyond that, through the tips of trees, was a world of churning, white-tipped blue. Had it been only last evening that she had tossed in bed dreaming of running barefoot up and down those shores? Damn the self-pity that swelled inside her mind and heart. Roy Donovan was dead; so were her dreams.

"Why did you lie to my brother?" she asked dispassionately.

"I was given little opportunity to do otherwise."

"That's a sorry excuse." She turned. "You could have clarified your identity the moment I walked into the room."

Donovan shrugged, unwilling to admit to himself that his need for Autumn's companionship might surpass even his brother's. "Perhaps I felt it in your best interest to break the news of Roy's death privately."

"You're very kind."

He cocked one brow.

"But now we must consider the consequences. My brother believes you to be my husband."

"So he does."

He withdrew a thin black cigar from his vest pocket,

then slipped it between his lips. Orange light intensified
the dark hollow between his prominent cheekbones and
chiseled jaw as he lit the cheroot and inhaled. Autumn
stiffened in recognition. It was he. *He* had been watching
her from the gardens last midnight!

A knock sounded, and Hugh Tyler stepped into the
room.

Autumn recognized the man instantly. The Irishman's
eyes widened as she strode confidently across the room
and stopped before him, her hands planted firmly on her
hips and her head thrown back as she looked up into his
startled face.

"Tonnerre! Mistress Donovan, ye're a sight for sore
eyes, and that's a fact. Welcome t' Cayemite.''

"Charlatan!"

"I take it the two of you have met," Donovan said.

Ignoring him, Autumn demanded, "Have you slept these
past months, Mr. Tyler? I assure you, I haven't. How
many other gullible young women have you swindled
since leaving me in Charleston?"

Rolling his broad-brimmed hat in his hands, Hugh had
the decency to duck his head and look perfectly guilty.
"Ye're the only one, ma'am."

"How very comforting."

Clearing his throat, the man stepped gingerly around the
furious young woman to face Brice Donovan. "I don't
mean t' be intrudin', maît, but there's trouble in the
combite."

"What's the problem?" Donovan crushed out his cigar.

"Boar."

Brice jerked open the desk drawer, grabbed a ring of
keys, and, proceeding to an adjacent door, unlocked it. It
swung open to reveal a cabinet of weapons.

Autumn's eyes widened as Donovan withdrew a cross-
bow and arrows. Stepping aside as he swung a quiver over
his shoulder, she frowned and demanded, "Haven't you
forgotten something?"

His eyes flickered over her upturned face. "Hardly,'' he
responded after some thought. "But there will be little
work done on this habitation unless the boar is found and
destroyed."

"May I come?"

"No."

"What am I to tell my brother?"

Donovan paused at the door. His hand resting on its mahogany frame, he stared out into the foyer of the grandiose home before saying, "That's up to you, Mrs. Donovan." With that he and the Irishman left the room.

It was a long ride to the far side of the island, but it gave Brice time to think. He knew the main reason Roy had married Autumn Sinclair was that he'd needed money. Mitchell Sinclair had recognized that fact soon after arriving on the island. The house was in disrepair, most of the cane was unfit to be harvested, and that meant there would be no profits to carry them over the next year.

Breaking through the copse of trees, Brice reined in his horse. The field of faintly trenched earth, overtaken with weeds, stretched before him. On the stump of a tree at the field's edge hung the skull of a horse, beneath it a wooden cross and the shriveled casings of desiccated limes.

Within the desolate clearing the men knotted in little groups. As Donovan and Tyler approached, the workers broke and ran to Brice's side. "Maît Donovan, Maît Donovan; *baka!*" they exclaimed.

Sliding from his horse, Brice plowed through the men to the solitary figure who stood a head taller than the others. "Who the devil started this *baka* madness?" he demanded of the towering, well-built simidor who was overseer of this particular combite.

Jonas frowned and pointed to the distant hill. "Maîtresse Rose tell them all: Beware the *baka*. She seen him with her own eyes."

Tyler placed a hand on his employer's shoulder. "I warned ya, Donovan, that the woman was doin' her best t' keep these people out of the fields. She knows the only way short of murder is t' scare them with their own beliefs. What better way than to spread the rumor that one of her workers defied his god and was changed into a *baka* that took the form of a boar."

Brice's head whipped around. His straight black hair, tousled from his ride and a sudden gust of wind, fell into his eyes. "And you've allowed her to continue with this ridiculous ploy?"

"What was I t' do? I'm fightin' beliefs that go back five hundred years, and when ye've got a woman who's intent on controlling every soul on this island in any way she can . . ."

Hugh was right, Donovan realized. He moved toward his horse. "Tyler, see these people back to the house. I suspect we'll see little enough work from them for the rest of the day."

"Are y' comin'?" Hugh's sun-browned face was creased with worry as he peered up at his employer.

"I've a *boar* to kill," Brice said. Taking up the reins, he headed toward the trees.

The boar's tracks were easily visible at first, but as Brice ventured further into the dense forest, they disappeared completely. He moved his horse into a clearing. A direct sun baked the trees, and within their shelter of tangled and twisted limbs the air smelled dead and stale, almost impossible to breathe. Sweat trickled down the back of Brice's neck as he listened to the quiet, disarming in its intensity. These forests were never quiet. Unless . . .

Brice slipped from the gelding and shifted his eyes about the bushes. To his left there was a quivering of leaves, behind him, a trembling of reeds. His nostrils flared as he perceived the stench of boar. Then—

"Christ!"

It appeared from nowhere. Its hump fanning gray bristles, it charged at Brice with its ugly head down and its menacing tusks poised for attack. Too late to draw his bow, he jumped for the horse. The animal screamed and shied, and for a terrible moment man and mount battled for a foothold against the rampaging boar.

Ears back, the horse bolted into the trees. Brice danced momentarily on the end of the boar's nose, and with a quick toss of its shaggy head the *baka* sank its yellow tusk into his thigh. Brice hit the ground with a thud, scattering arrows through the air. The bow snapped beneath his weight. The animal was on him again before he could recover, flicking its deadly bristles across his arms, grunting, squealing and coughing its sour, hot breath into his face.

He heard someone screaming—ah, shame—it was himself. He flailed with his arms, striking the animal on its snout. He kicked its matted underbelly and heaved it aside. But efforts to reclaim his legs were useless. Brice fell onto his back, closing his eyes. He felt little pain. The laceration in his thigh burned, but the nicks about his arms were nothing more than an annoying sting. It was as if the damnable beast had been intent only on scaring him to death.

Silence. The world was a bowl of green. Here and there shafts of sunlight broke through the leafy canopy. Had Brice's father been here at that moment, he would have cursed his oldest son for sweating and trembling and praying for the strength to overcome his fear. Yet even as Brice lay on his back, fingers coiled into the palms of his hands, he knew the terror that left his mouth dry and his hands sweating had nothing to do with a *baka*.

"Donovan."

Brice rolled.

At the edge of the clearing stood a man, ebony in color and magnificent in his naked stature. "*Baka!*" he hissed, then disappeared through the trees.

Donovan stared disbelieving at the yawning green void where the man had stood, and outwardly struggled with reason. It was *only* a man, he told himself over and over.

Cursing, Brice struggled to his feet. There could be only one person behind this tactic. By damn, he would not tolerate it any longer!

Barrett Hall was half the size of Hunnington House, but twice as opulent. Before Donovan could rein his frothing animal to a halt, three manservants hurried from the house, one to heed the prancing horse, one to help Brice from his perch and one to escort him to the stately front doors.

He ignored them all, shoving the last Negro aside as he burst into the house. Standing within the marble-floored foyer and staring up the curling flight of stairs, he thundered, "Goddamn you, Annee Rose!"

"You are bleeding on the floor, my darling Donovan."

He pivoted on his heel. Standing within the doors to the adjoining room, the statuesque figure could have been cast of porcelain. Straight, blue-black hair hung to her silk-draped hips.

Annee Rose smiled. "But you're so angry."

"You're damn right I'm angry. Why the hell are you trying to scare my workers to death?"

Her violet eyes drifted across his thighs. "What has that to do with your injury?" She floated toward him.

Brice backed up. "Stay away from me. I'm here on business."

"And so very angry." Her long, white fingers plucked at the silk scarf around her waist, exposing most of one breast and thigh. She slid to her knees at Donovan's feet. "You seem to be in desperate need of my *traitement*, love," she purred. "Let me heal you, Donovan."

He was sweating, and he cursed. "Don't touch me, Annee." The dry command came out like a croak, causing Brice to wince inwardly. No woman had ever made him cringe like Annee.

"Donovan, Donovan, you must learn to relax." She pressed her mouth against his wound.

The blood left his face.

She licked her lips, then wrapped the crimson scarf about his thigh, tying it gently to stem the flow. Her fingers fluttered lightly over the swelling between his legs.

"Stop it," he snapped. He roughly caught her wrist and yanked her slender body so close to his he could feel her warm breath through the coarse material of his breeches. "I'm here to warn you, madam, that should you continue with this little ploy, I will see you and your cohorts run completely off this island. My father and brother may have been gullible enough to fall for your ridiculous antics, but I assure you, I am not."

Her head fell back, spilling raven hair onto the floor. Her free hand cupped and molded him until his entire body was like stone. He cursed her, threw every vile name he had ever heard into her face.

She only laughed.

Donovan thrust his hands into her hair, closed his eyes

and cursed the day thirteen years ago when he'd taken Annee Rose's virginity.

The crab scuttled sideways, its mantle of shell looking strangely cumbersome for its tiny body. It shimmied, then disappeared into the sand at the water's edge. Autumn fell to her knees as she watched intently for any sign of its resurfacing. Water broke across her thighs, and with a sharp gasp and delighted giggle, she jumped and ran, the water racing her to the nearest boulder. She outdistanced the wave by a mere second and stood laughing and holding her sides as the water splashed at her toes.

God, how was she to leave this?

Sobering, she sat down on the rock, curling her legs beneath her. She had made such grand plans since arriving the day before. Thoughts of how she could rebuild Hunnington Hall to its former magnificence had occupied her every thought those long hours between midnight and dawn. Perfumed breezes from the nearby forest would replace the stench of smoke and neglect, once the rooms were opened. Draperies could be cleaned, rugs beaten. Wax would bring back the luster of those breathtaking mahogany floors.

Damn Roy Donovan for tempting her with visions of paradise. Damn him for dying.

Autumn looked glumly over the water, wondering how to explain to Mitchell that the man posing as Roy Donovan was actually his brother. Just say it, she told herself, but the simplicity of the idea brought her no peace of mind. She didn't want to admit the truth, for with such an admission her future would be irrevocably buried.

Squaring her shoulders, Autumn returned to the house. She had successfully avoided Mitchell throughout the morning, pleading headache, nausea, then finally refusing altogether to answer the door when he knocked. But there was no avoiding the inevitable. She had arrived on the Île de Cayemite and found neither husband nor home. There was no reason for her to remain.

She knocked on the library door. No response. Entering the imposing room, she stood for a moment on the fringed edge of the Oriental carpet. The room had survived the neglect into which the rest of the house had fallen. Its gleaming paneled walls smelled of wax. The furniture appeared to have been frequently dusted.

Autumn's fingers drifted over the unmarred desk top before she sank into the cushioned leather chair behind it. The table suited Donovan . . . the stranger Donovan, not her husband. She somehow imagined Roy's becoming lost behind this massive mahogany frame. But Roy's brother complimented its strength and darkness. Autumn shook away the image of his rising from this very chair. A great sleek cat, lithe of limb and graceful.

Perhaps if they discussed her problem as two adults would, something could be arranged . . . She would leave him a note, make certain she had a chance to speak with him again before he saw Mitchell.

Autumn noted the quill and ink on the corner of the desk. She needed paper, and eyed the drawer at her waist. It yielded to her exploring hand with little effort.

The papers lying askew on top of the open vellum pouch appeared to have been shoved hurriedly into the drawer. She might have ignored them completely had Roy's scrawled signature not attracted her eye. Casting a cautious glance toward the door, she tugged the unsheathed pages into the light.

Autumn skimmed the penned words with a disinterested eye at first, then more slowly, pronouncing each syllable aloud. She went cold, then hot. She shook from disbelief, then anger, and finally excitement. It had to be a trick! But no . . . She reread Roy's will.

"I leave one-half of Hunnington Hall and all its properties to my brother: Brice Donovan. The other is to be left to my wife: Autumn Sinclair Donovan, of Charleston, South Carolina."

Half of Hunnington Hall was hers?

Autumn struggled to her feet.

Brice Donovan had shown no inclination at all of ever telling her. The man was a thief!

But why should she be surprised? Roy Donovan had jilted her at the altar, had bartered his name in hopes of gaining a pot of gold to ease his impecunious state. Why should his brother be any different?

The clatter of hooves on the cobblestone drive announced Donovan's arrival. Autumn steeled herself for the confrontation. What she was *not* prepared for was the drastic change in the man's demeanor.

Vest ripped and shirt hanging in tatters, Brice stormed through the door, his dark face a study of anger and frustration. He limped slightly, but he'd shoved aside his thoughts of pain for more immediate problems. They did not, however, include Autumn Sinclair Donovan. He'd totally forgotten about her.

Standing before the open window, her hair an explosion of copper-red, she appeared little more than a silhouette at first. But as his eyes became adjusted to the darker room, he paused, darted a look again toward the window, then froze.

"What the devil are you doing?" he snapped.

Slowly Autumn advanced, her eyes flickering curiously over his bedraggled state. She was holding a sheaf of papers. "Haven't you something to tell me?"

"Who gave you the right—"

"I have every right," she interrupted. "Every right, since half of this plantation belongs to me."

"Aha." His mouth twisting into a grim smile, Brice moved stiffly toward the crystal decanters of whiskey across the room. He poured himself a drink before facing Autumn again. "Truth, at last. You came here hoping for a windfall. Now you have it."

"You're a cheat, Brice Donovan." Autumn shook the papers between them, then let her arm fall to her side. "It seems deceit runs as thick as blood through the Donovan veins."

"And you know us so well."

His innuendo brought fire to her cheeks. "As well as Roy knew me. He knew what I wanted, knew what I had to offer, while I could only chance that he was being honest with me."

Brice raised his glass. "Well, " he said, "it seems, Madam Sinclair, you have fared far better than my dear dead brother."

"Donovan," she reminded him in a cold voice.

He winced with pain. Autumn frowned, but he stopped her incipient question by drawling, "Donovan." He tipped his glass to his lips and drank deeply. The liquor went directly to his head and the world was instantly reeling. When he spoke again, his voice was deeper, sluggish and tired. "If you want only to be rid of your brother, then that can be arranged. I'll buy your half of Hunnington and you're free to settle wherever you please." Her eyes were round. There was a flicker of distress in their brandy-brown depths. "You've no business on this damned island," he mumbled, then looked away. When he moved toward the nearest chair, he stumbled.

She was against him in a moment, grabbing his arm and bracing his weight against her shoulders. Such small shoulders—just how much burden could they support? Her face tipped up to his, her skin like apricot satin. In her amber eyes he saw reflected himself—the face of a condemned man whose own soul had been lost twelve years ago. If anyone was in need of a redeemer, then surely it was he.

She blinked and the image was gone, the amber sheen eclipsed by black as her eyes widened. "How did this happen?" Her voice was unsteady.

"Doesn't matter." Dropping into the chair, he dismissed her with a flip of his hand. "Cayemite doesn't need you, Madam Donovan. There are enough souls in this stinking harbor for it to feed on."

"If you loathe it so, why do you remain?"

His head dropped back against the chair. "I was born here," came his gravelly voice. "The first sound I heard was those drums. When other children were occupied with playmates, I was content with praying to my loa. It's in my blood. No matter where or how far I run, when I close my eyes at night, the drums are still there."; His voice lower, he finished, "Run while you can, love, while your dreams are easy and your mind your own."

Her face thoughtful, Autumn slid onto the desk. "I need Cayemite, Mr. Donovan."

"No you don't."

"I want it."

"You're a fool."

"Was your father a fool?"

Brice looked away. "Keep my father out of this."

"This was his dream," Autumn pointed out. "Once Hunnington must have prospered."

"At the cost of everything he loved."

"Meaning?"

Angrily, Brice shoved both hands through his damp black hair and cursed to himself. Autumn Donovan was lancing old wounds, though she didn't know it. "Hunnington prospered, but not without sacrifice. Patrick Donovan gave up everything he loved for the money and prestige of being maît of Hunnington Hall. Now tell me, Lady Donovan, just where the hell it got him."

She didn't flinch. "If money was all I wanted, I would accept your offer."

"The frigging cane is rotten!" he thundered, causing her to shy and jump to her feet.

She backed away as he came out of his chair. "New crops can be planted."

"The house is falling in."

"With effort it can be restored."

"The workers won't accept you."

"It may take a firm hand—"

Donovan's roar of laughter echoed about the room. He moved clumsily toward the girl planted stubbornly in the middle of the floor. She didn't budge, but lifted her chin in defiance. "Ah, you are a contrary little minx, aren't you?" he drawled more quietly. He caught her jaw in his fingers. "I can see why Roy was so fascinated by you. When he wrote me he had married a rapscallion with copper hair and brandy-brown eyes who sashayed about the country-side wearing men's breeches, I believed he had again imbibed too much whiskey. Would you believe, my fiery little sweet, that my brother was really very smitten with you?"

"You're hurting me," Autumn forced between her teeth, but she didn't whimper.

His face closer, he smiled. "You haven't experienced pain until you fester on this island, my love."

"Let me be the judge of that."

He dropped his hands, turned and with head down leaned against the desk for support.

Autumn stared, waited, jumping as the tall case clock in the foyer chimed the hour.

Brice spun about and planted his long legs apart. "What do you want?" The query held a faint note of surrender.

"Two months." Autumn carefully tested her footing to make certain her wobbly legs would support her weight. It was those eyes again, staring at her through his unruly dark locks. "If—if in those two months I am unable to carry on my duties as mistress of this house, I will forfeit it all to you."

He took several moments to consider her request. "Very well," he said. "Two months. But during that time should I feel it in your best interest to leave this island, you will do so."

Autumn's face brightened. She offered her hand.

"A gentleman's agreement?" His mouth smiled. His eyes didn't.

"Would you prefer it in writing?" she asked less steadily.

"I don't think so."

Gently his hand closed around hers, and the heat from his palm shot up her arm like a lightning bolt. Her immobilizing fear mingled with an odd sensation, a complete, heart-stopping rush of blood to her head. She hid her confusion by laughing. "Is there something more?" she asked.

"Never seal a bargain without first reading the fine print. There are clauses to consider."

"Meaning?"

"Your brother, for one."

She tugged on her hand.

"I'll wager he won't be pleased with the prospect of his baby sister abiding on this rock with a man who is *not* her husband." Donovan's brows met as he considered. His face seemed leaner now, and darker. The smile had compressed into a thin white line. Then he continued, "I might be convinced to play out this little farce for the price of—"

"What?" Her question was hollow.

"What is your freedom worth, *ma chérie?*"

A look of fury crossed Autumn's face, but she managed steadily, "So it is blackmail the Donovans practice as well. You expect me to sell myself—"

"You did once."

"Devil!"

He laughed, a low sound laced with pain and disarmingly haunting. "Sweetheart," he drawled, "you haven't begun to know hell."

Chapter 4

A shuffling of paper disturbed the lazy silence. Mitchell Sinclair pulled the leaf-shaped candle holder closer to the open ledger, then peered more intensely at the scrawled entries.

"Interesting," he said.

Autumn's head bent over the column of numbers. "Profits. Substantial, by the looks of them." She couldn't hide her smile.

Mitchell lifted his eyes to hers. "It's a bit soon to be so pleased. These entries could be falsified easily enough."

"Why would I want to?" Donovan stepped from the shadows. He had remained quiet up until now, using the darkness to conceal his interest in the girl. "If I wanted your money, it would hardly pay me to falsify those figures."

Mary entered the room carrying a tray of tea and cakes. She smiled brightly, if somewhat nervously, toward Donovan. "I thought you gentlemen might be ready for a break."

"And so we are," Mitchell responded, leaving his chair.

Autumn remained, studying the ledger. Donovan moved up behind her. "Are you pleased?" he asked softly.

Her head came up.

"What I don't understand," Mitchell ventured, "is why the estate appears ruined, when there's money aplenty for renovation."

Brice smiled and accepted Mary's offered tea. "I can hardly deny Hunnington's former indebtedness. Suffice it to say, I've attempted to rectify earlier misjudgments."

"How?"

Cup halfway to his lips, Brice shrugged. "Lucky ventures."

"Gambling."

"Investments."

"With your history, Mr. Donovan, you must understand my questioning your reliability. Should Hunnington lapse into its former insolvency—"

"It won't. Roy Donovan's days of gambling are over. Buried, so to speak." He tipped the cup to his lips, wishing for something stronger.

Skirts swishing, Mary rounded the desk and hugged Autumn happily. "How wonderful, dear. Perhaps before I leave we can discuss some much needed renovations for the house." A pleasant smile on her face, she tilted her head meaningfully toward Brice. "Now that you've a wife, I'm certain you'll be anxious to restore the Hall to its former condition."

Autumn frowned, her eyes still wandering over the ledger. "It will take a great deal of money."

"Darling, your husband can afford it, according to these figures. You should have little to worry over."

Brice walked away.

Excitedly, Mary continued, "Oh, Autumn, you can travel to Montego Bay with us when we leave. We have a two-day layover. We could spend the entire time shopping!"

"Do you think so?" she asked.

Mary looked again at Donovan. "Roy? It *is* Roy? . . ."

She knew. Mary Sinclair could stand there smiling and laughing like merry little bells, Brice mused, but she knew he wasn't Roy Donovan.

At a nod of his dark head, Mary beamed. "Wonderful!"

China clattered slightly as Brice placed his cup and saucer on the desk. "Now," he said, "it's been a long day—and an even longer four months."

Autumn fixed her eyes on the book and didn't move.

Mary exchanged looks with her husband.

Brice moved around the desk. His hands on Autumn's tense little shoulders, he stated quietly, "I'll join you shortly, my love," then physically lifted her from the chair.

Face white, she moved woodenly toward the door, Donovan's insistent nudges poking her sharply in the back the entire way. She didn't bother to turn, but disappeared from the room.

The ceiling creaked. Brice slouched in his chair, watching the chandelier quiver each time Autumn paced again across the floor of his bedroom overhead. "Stew awhile," he said toward the round-bellied little cherub whose arms held the melted blob of wax above its head.

He drank steadily. When the glass slid from his numb fingertips, he lifted the decanter to his mouth and prayed the potent sweet liquor would finish him completely. It didn't, but sluggishly inched through his inebriated mind and pounded against the back of his eyes. Memories battled with a new surge of hope, the warm flame of promise that had engulfed his heart the moment he set eyes on Autumn Sinclair . . . Donovan.

His brother's wife—his dead brother's wife.

She wanted no part of Brice.

Hunnington Hall was her reason for living. As he had escaped Cayemite those years ago, she had fled Charleston in search of a dream. Call it what one liked, hell could be as enticingly beautiful as heaven.

"Donovan."

The soft voice was familiar. Brice smiled as Jeanette moved soundlessly across the room.

"The boy's asleep?" His speech was slurred as he tried to sit up.

"*Oui.*" She dropped to the floor beside him. "It will storm soon. He'll be frightened."

"I'll be here if he needs me."

Her soft mouth curving in a smile, she said, "I'm glad you're home."

"I'm glad you're glad."

Jeanette laughed. "It was an empty place without you."

"I should have taken you with me. Perhaps then—"

"Don't." She smoothed her fingers over his troubled brow.

The ceiling creaked. Both looked up. Brice's smile was suddenly white in the semidarkness of Hunnington's smallest drawing room. Then he laughed quietly.

"Will you make her go?" Jeanette asked.

"I can't do that."

"You *won't* do that. Why?"

"Do you know," he said, avoiding her question, "that, as a child, I would pretend that those damn cherubs were my guardian angels?"

She looked toward the chandelier.

Thunder rumbled. The crystal prisms on the overhead fixture tinkled with the vibration. As a sudden burst of light pulsed inside the room, Brice looked down into Jeanette's frightened face.

"Leave here," she implored him. "It's you Annee wants. For my sake and Pierre's, leave before it is too late."

"I can't." It was dry, the response, resigned and tired. "I can't run again."

Burying her face in his lap, Jeanette wept, soft, whimpering sobs that tore at his heart. "Don't cry," he pleaded, and stroked her hair. "Ah, damn. I hate it when you cry."

Mary fluttered about the room, a nervous little bird, unable to light for more than a moment in any particular spot. With the parcel tucked behind her back and hidden within the folds of her red velvet dressing gown, she looked like a little elf, except for the concern on her slightly flushed face. "Oh dear," she finally said with a sigh.

Autumn turned from the window, her face wet.

Mary stopped her prancing and scowled. "Come away from that window, dear, you'll get the sniffles."

It wasn't rain dampening Autumn's face. She blotted her cheeks with the cuff of her sleeve. "Is something wrong?" she asked her flustered in-law.

"Well," Mary began, her laughter ringing nervously. She withdrew the package and, offering it in her upturned palms, smiled apologetically. "I bought this for you when we stopped at Havana."

Autumn crossed the room. "What is it?" Mary didn't respond, and Autumn accepted the gift with a smile and trembling fingers. She turned for the bed, froze as her eyes acknowledged the sheets Celie had earlier turned down, then swiveled on one heel and dropped into a nearby chair.

Mary continued, pacing, "I hope you like it. I found it when you were bartering with that dreadful little man over those leather riding boots. The shop on . . . oh, let me see . . ."

"I remember." Autumn nudged the ribbon, as if checking to see if it would spring at her hand and bite.

"Yes. Well." Mary took a deep breath. "I thought the color . . . of course Mitchell doesn't know. He was too busy buying those smelly old cigars and—" Her hands clasping beneath her quivering chin, Mary blushed, and in a sudden rush of apologies beseeched her husband's sister, "Please forgive me. It's horribly brazen, isn't it? And on your wedding night, too. I should have purchased something more . . . more . . . well, I wasn't really certain if . . . I mean, you made no mention of having . . . oh, dear."

A cloud of gold silk, the negligee poured from Autumn's fingers and spilled across her lap. She stared at the diaphanous bodice, what there was of it, and briefly considered throwing herself out the window.

"Oh, but it is beautiful, isn't it!" Mary exclaimed.

Autumn forced her eyes from the shimmering gown and stared at her sister-in-law. Mary's eyes were glassy with emotion, her lower lip pinched so tightly between her teeth Autumn thought at any moment the dear woman would draw blood.

Mary tenuously ran her fingertips over the lace edging of the skirt. "I thought the color would suit you, and the form reminded me of something Diana might wear." She pointed to the single shoulder strap. "You've the height to carry it quite nicely, I think."

Autumn smiled fondly. "It's beautiful, Mary. I must thank Mitchell—"

"No!" Catching herself, Mary released a tight laugh. "You know your brother, dear. He might not . . ."

"Approve?"

Mary nodded. "Not that there is anything at all wrong with it. Why, I would dearly love . . . well . . ." She dismissed the confession with a wistful sigh. Autumn ducked her head, and Mary smiled. "It's not so bad, Autumn. Mr.

Donovan is a very handsome man. And he seems quite fond of you.''

Autumn jumped to her feet, spilling tissue paper onto the floor. She paced toward the window, silk trailing from her fingertips.

''Why, I've never seen such a look of pleasure on a man's face as I witnessed on his when you burst through that door. And at dinner—oh, my, but he couldn't keep his eyes off of you.''

''I didn't notice.''

''You're understandably nervous, dear.'' Mary joined Autumn and both stared into the rain-drenched darkness. ''I've always been a fair judge of character. Mr. Donovan, though a bit imposing, seems a decent sort.''

''He's a cheat.''

''Yes. Well. We all have our little quirks, I suppose.'' Her voice firmer, Mary continued thoughtfully, ''Not many men would be so willing to accept a woman as his partner. And to be given a free hand in the restoration of Hunnington is more than generous. I think, at times, that I would sacrifice anything to be treated as equally as Mr. Donovan has treated you since your arrival.''

Slowly Autumn turned and, unblinking, looked down into the smaller woman's wistful face. ''Anything?'' she repeated.

''Anything.'' Mary nodded.

Her fingers plucking at the gossamer material, Autumn released her breath.

A smile tugged at the corners of Mary's mouth, and with a careless giggle, she approached her sister-in-law one last time. ''Will you try it on, the gown? So I'm certain it fits you.''

''Of course.''

The last thing Autumn longed to do was to step behind that screen and undress. And to don the transparent wrapper with its gossamer lace bodice was almost unthinkable. Flannel was more to her liking—a formless sack with a thousand buttons. She would prefer to itch to death in wool than subject herself to Brice Donovan's blackmail!

The floor creaked as Mary busied herself snuffing some of the candles and adjusting the jalousies. The wind had shifted, and the rain that had earlier masked Autumn's tears now made a puddle on the dull mahogany floor.

"I suppose," came Mary's light voice, "that you are aware of the, um, well, the responsibilities . . . that's really not the appropriate word, I suppose—"

"It's all right, Mary." Autumn stared at the tapestried screen ornamented with naked nymphs and dropped her breeches to the floor. "I know where babies come from."

There was a clatter of something being dropped, then Mary's nonplussed, "Oh, my. Good."

The negligee was a whisper, a thistledown softness against her skin, lacking the security of her flannel, long-sleeved gown. Good heavens—she was naked!

Autumn stepped from behind the panel and Mary stopped. Her blue eyes widened momentarily, then she smiled tremulously. "Don't cry," Autumn told her.

"Oh, I shan't. Really. It's just . . ." Mary blinked rapidly and looked away. "You've grown up."

Autumn turned. Slowly Autumn turned, giving Mary every advantage to view the filmy creation. Facing her sister-in-law again, she froze. Mary's face was radiant. Beyond her, however, a dark silhouette filled the doorway.

Her dressing gown belling around her knees, Mary whirled. "Mr. Donovan!" She backed protectively toward Autumn before catching herself.

He said nothing.

Autumn stared at the back of Mary's head, biting her lower lip and wondering just how far a drop her window was from the ground.

"You will excuse us?" Donovan finally said.

Mary hesitated, started to turn, but checked her movement. Instead, she moved reluctantly toward the shadow in jerky little steps, stopping near the door as he refused to move. Finally, he shifted.

"Good night," he said softly, repeating "Good night," as she dissolved into the dark hallway.

Brice and Autumn watched each other in silence. She wanted to hide. She knew those eyes by now, knew their unblinking perusal was swallowing her every minute detail.

"Very nice," he stated smoothly, causing her to jump. He stepped into the room, and she bolted toward the

bed, grabbing her dressing gown and clutching it to her
bosom like a blanket. "Stay away from me," she said,
and backed away. "You—how dare you come in this
room without knocking."

"It is my room."

He stood in a pool of yellow light, holding an opened
bottle of champagne and a glass. A satyr with the smile of
Adonis. Autumn tried to look at the floor, but her gaze
stopped at his open shirtfront and wouldn't budge.

"Is something wrong?" he asked her.

Her eyes sprang to his face, and she flushed to see him
smiling. "Do you always saunter about half-clothed?" she
asked, thinking if her heart pounded any faster she would
pass out completely.

"Do you always wear breeches?" he responded with the
lift of one raven brow. Then, acknowledging both of her
bare shoulders, he teased, "Obviously not."

Autumn gasped, turned, and wiggled fiercely into her
dressing gown. When she turned back, she was surprised
to find Brice resting quite comfortably on the horsehair
sofa against the wall. One long leg was stretched out
before him, the other curled slightly toward the settee. He
was running one hand up and down the bottle in a light,
caressing motion that somehow made her dizzy.

"Sit down," he ordered suddenly. His head came up,
sleepy-eyed and lazily smiling, and she thought that she
might scream. He repeated the command and Autumn
obeyed, sitting beside him on the settee, though such
compliance was most unusual for her.

Brice watched her closely. She looked like a young
lioness, with that mane of copper hair and those cat's eyes
of amber. Her tiny nose was sprinkled with freckles. Her
mouth wore a very slight pout, and at one corner of her
rosy lips was a single freckle. How very stalwart she tried
to appear, with that defiant little chin thrust just so and her
body poised for a ready escape. "Relax," he said.

She didn't blink.

He reached for the glass he had earlier placed on the end
table and filled it with champagne. He offered it to her.
Lifting his bottle, he touched it to the rim of her goblet.
"To lasting partnerships, Autumn Donovan."

Brice watched as she drank the champagne. Her dark lashes fluttered slightly as the liquid slid down her throat. Her cheeks glowed becomingly. "More?" he asked. She nodded and drank again. Soon she was leaning relaxed against the back of the settee. Her face had lost that mask of indignation. In its place was confusion and worry, and just a little anticipation.

Autumn lifted her empty glass. "More, please."

"I don't think so."

Her eyes widened frantically. "Are you going to ravish me now?"

Brice took the glass, carefully avoiding her fingers. "Do I look like the kind of man who would take advantage of a drunk woman?"

"Yes," she responded after some thought, "you do."

His green eyes narrowed as he smiled. "Then perhaps we should get on with business." He meant only to discuss their circumstances, but Autumn didn't take it that way.

Her shoulders snapped back at the suggestion. She looked first toward the door, then the window, to the bed and finally at Brice. Her fingers dug into the sofa as she waited. He watched as she nervously moistened her dry lips, and Brice's amusement evaporated like a mist. "You seem to find my company less companionable than my brother's. Perhaps if I were a bit drunker, or more forceful in my intentions . . ." Smiling coldly, he prodded, "Or perhaps we've known each other too long. Perhaps you prefer to strike bargains in business and in bed with *total* strangers."

The response was instinctive. Autumn slapped her open hand against his cheek. Before he could recover, she jumped up from the sofa and stood planted with her back to the window, her breasts heaving beneath the multitudinous folds of her dressing gown, her face white with fury. "Don't come near me." She sucked in an unsteady breath, then, backing to the window, announced bravely, "I'll jump."

"Promise?" He left the sofa.

Autumn retreated again. Where was her strength, the resolve that had hardened in her when Mary had announced that *she* would sacrifice anything for the freedom this man offered? He was before her now. With his long legs thrust apart he looked like a sleek cat, cunning and beautiful, wild. He was causing her heart to race, but she would be damned and dead on the cobblestones below that window before she would admit that those feelings were caused by anything other than anger.

Lightning flashed over the water. Suddenly his arms were around her, lifting her, spinning her around, but when her head fell back in anticipation of the kiss that would certainly follow, she was plunked without ceremony onto her feet and deserted.

Brice closed the jalousie completely before facing Autumn again. "Stay the hell away from these windows when it storms," he ordered. They stared at each other for a long moment; then, attempting to ignore her, Brice turned and strode as casually as possible toward the bed.

"What are you doing?" Autumn asked. The champagne caused her to sway unsteadily.

"Going to bed."

"There?" She grabbed the bedpost for support and pointed with a wavering hand toward the plump white pillows.

Donovan dropped onto the bed. His thigh was suddenly throbbing, and the ache in his head was little better. "Come to bed," he said tiredly.

Silence.

He looked back over his shoulder. "Come to bed," he repeated. "I won't touch you."

"A likely story."

One boot hit the floor, then another. Brice lay back on his pillow, left arm crooked over his face, blocking the light from his eyes. "Christ," he groaned. "Come to bed."

"I've been thinking," she said in a small voice.

"Saints preserve us."

"Perhaps this isn't a very good idea, Mr. Donovan."

"I won't touch you," he stressed more forcefully. "As long as you stay on *your* side of the bed and keep your hands to yourself, you're safe enough . . . tonight."

Autumn stared unblinkingly at the man's outstretched

form. He dwarfed the bed, and the sight of his shaggy black hair spilling onto the crisp white pillowcase did funny little things to her stomach. His shirt was open, flaunting a well-muscled chest with fine black hair. His stomach was flat. The wide belt around his waist rode indecently low around his hips . . . and those breeches—how he managed to move without popping their seams was beyond her imagination. The unconscionable roué was an insult to a delicate woman's sensibilities!

Her eyes widened as she realized he was watching her now, from the crook of his elbow. "Do you sleep standing up?" he asked her.

"Are you always so sarcastic?" Autumn lifted one brow and leaned a little harder against the post.

Donovan groaned again and rolled to his side, offering his back. "If you don't get into bed now and put out that light, I'm going to take off all my clothes. That's how I usually sleep. In that case, I can no longer guarantee my behavior and only hope, for your sake, that your brother is a sound sleeper."

Autumn skittered across the floor and hit the bed in two seconds. She glared at his back. "Promise."

"I promise. Good night, Autumn."

Her name had a ring to it, sounding magically musical from his lips. She would have to remind him tomorrow that when out of her brother's company he was to address her as *Missus* Donovan.

The room appeared cavernous in the dark. Autumn clutched her dressing gown about her bosom and considered sneaking from the bed and donning her flannel night-gown. Silly girl. Already, the discomfort of wearing the heavy robe to bed was causing her to sweat. She could feel the perspiration trickling down her ribs and between her legs. She stretched, recoiling as her bare toe touched his leg. It was impossible to move without touching Donovan. He was everywhere!

Autumn sat up. Where was the breeze that, with the *baire,* had entertained her so the night before? She turned and stared toward the restless dark form at her side. It was unimaginable that she should be resting beside a perfect stranger, watching him sleep and wishing for a candle so she could better study his face. Brice Donovan had a nice face, it somewhat grim. And she imagined that he would have a nice smile, should he smile sincerely instead of smirking in that fiendish way. Autumn suddenly regretted having slapped him. He hadn't even retaliated. Just jerked her away from the window when he'd thought her in danger from lightning.

She left the bed and paced. What was she to do about her situation? Roy Donovan she could have dealt with, but Brice Donovan was a different matter altogether. With one glance from those sharp green eyes he could cut her to the bone. Without uttering a word he could rend her speechless. Autumn yanked up the champagne bottle, and without thinking, tipped it to her lips. "Cheat," she said then, and hiccuped. "Think you can just saunter around this house with your shirt unbuttoned and your breeches so tight you can hardly move, and I'll just puddle at your feet like Jeanette must have done."

She padded across the floor and stared down at the sleeping figure. "Do you hear me?" she barely whispered, jumping back slightly as he mumbled in his sleep. Autumn drank deeply from the bottle, then tiptoed closer to the bed. Tilting her head, she bent lower and stared down into his left ear. "How dare you kiss me that way in front of my brother," she mouthed silently. "How dare you kiss me at all. No one has *ever* kissed me like that. Why, your mouth was open. That's disgus'ing, Misser Donovan, and if you ever do it again I shall . . ." She lightly touched the black hair above his ear. "I'm sorry I slapped you," she said more loudly.

Brice groaned and rolled to his back.

Autumn began pacing again, tipping the bottle one last time to her mouth. "Roy warned me about you," she continued. "Said you are a womanizer 'n' a gambler. Well, Misser Donovan, I believe it. You are a scoundrel to think I would le' you kiss me like that again." Stopping, she pointed at him and said, "You just try to kiss me like that again."

Brice opened his eyes, drifting on a sea of confusion. The dreams were back again, frightening, haunting him with voices from the past. And, as always, there was Annee, her smile beckoning as she called: "Donovan."

"No." His head rolled back and forth on the pillow. "Donovan, Donovan."

"Leave me alone, Annee; God, leave me in peace."

"My darling, Donovan."

Brice struggled to breathe. To his horror he felt himself slipping, sliding into the black hole of no return. And there awaited Annee, her beautiful face a mask of death, a porcelain temptation that had induced stronger men than he to thrash in eternal damnation. Still, he battled her allure like a drowning man battles that first burst of water flooding his lungs. But she was reaching, pointing taloned fingers in his face and accusing: "It's your fault. All I ever wanted was you."

His father's and brother's faces appeared behind her, hollow-eyed, and their hands thrust toward him, beckoning Brice to join them. "Ah, God," he groaned, "don't. Don't." Crossing his arms over his face, he wept. "Enough, enough," he cried, until Annee was close enough to touch.

He sprang then, capturing the delicate wrists in his grasp and twisting until, with a cry of surprise, she fell beside him. Her hair was like silk in his fingers, her skin like satin against his hand. He pressed his mouth against the throbbing pulse in her throat and growled, "Is this how you want it, Annee?" Soft whimpers escaped her, sounding hauntingly like a child's. But then she could be like a child—soft and sweet—until she had him where she wanted him, which was between her legs. Then he couldn't turn back. She wouldn't let him, regardless.

"Stop," she pleaded.

"New games, Annee?" He kissed her with all the tenderness and forcefulness he could muster. He would kiss her, then kill her, be done with her forever. But, oh, Christ, her mouth . . . like wine. He hadn't noticed before.

With his tongue he traced her lips, like rosebuds and cherries. They quivered, parting beneath his. The inside of her mouth was hot and smooth, and her tongue was deliciously sensual against his, timid, at first, then bolder until their mouths fused together so completely he wondered if they would ever separate again. That thought was startling. Annee was getting better at her games.

She turned her head away, her soft gasp for air sounding harsh in his ear. "Please," she cried softly. "You promised."

She was trembling, and he smiled. She'd always made him tremble, made him quake and blunder like a virgin— like the time they'd fallen together in the northernmost cane field and he'd fumbled clumsily for five minutes before he'd managed all his buttons. All the while he'd been looking back over his shoulder, afraid his father would ride up on his big black horse and thrash him for "fooling" with a respectable white girl. But then, Patrick Donovan didn't know Annee Rose. That came later.

But that day, with the sun baking down on his naked back and buttocks, with stones cutting into his knees, he'd taken Annee's virginity with all the ferocity of a buck in rutting season. She hadn't minded the pain, reveled in it, as a matter of fact. They'd enjoyed it so damned much they did again. And again.

A sudden flash of light brightened the room, and in that instant, Donovan froze.

"You promised," Autumn repeated, and he closed his eyes.

"Yes. Yes, I did. Sorry." But he didn't move.

Autumn shoved at his chest. Her cheeks were burning and she was suffocating with anger. "If you're so lonely for your mistress, Mr. Donovan, I cannot fathom why you are here."

He lay his head on her shoulder. "Mistress?"

"Does Jeanette know about Annee? However do you manage them both?"

"Jeanette?"

His hair was tickling her nose. His head was heavy, and Autumn was infuriated by the fact that she liked it there, on her shoulder, nestled warmly in the hollow of her throat. "Have you a son with Annee as well? Perhaps a daughter." She wiggled fiercely.

"A son?"

"Pierre."

He laughed then. "The lady is jealous already."

"Jealous!" she squeaked. The man was the most conceited, bad-tempered rakehell she'd ever had the misfortune of meeting. "Oaf," she blustered breathlessly, "get . . . off."

"I think," he whispered, "that I may like it here."

They stared at each other, nose to nose, listening to the constant dripping of rain as it plopped on the veranda outside the window. Autumn's world was spinning, the champagne and the kiss having set her senses reeling. "I told you not to do that again," she said, not nearly so angry now.

"Do what again?" he asked.

"Kiss me like that."

"Like what?"

"With your mouth open." He shifted, pressing his hips intimately between her legs and causing a sudden ache to grow uncomfortably between her thighs. "It's rude." She stared at the offending mouth.

"What's rude?"

"Your tongue."

"I can think of ruder things to do with it." He grinned and peered down at her through narrowed eyes.

Wind rattled the jalousies as Brice continued to stare, feeling the tide of desire rising in his loins, a slow, throbbing fire that burned hotter each time she moved beneath him. It seemed natural to rotate his hips against the mound of femininity at the juncture of her legs. "Do you like that?" he asked huskily.

"No." Her breath fluttered against his mouth like wind from a butterfly's wing.

"I do." He brushed her temple with his mouth. "Would you like me to show you what I can do with my tongue?"

"No!"

He caught her face with his hand. "Open your mouth." Autumn twisted away. He dipped his tongue into her ear, laughing quietly as he heard her gasp. "Isn't this fun?" he asked.

Autumn's head snapped around. Staring up into his taunting face, she cried, "This is all a game to you, isn't it, Mr. Donovan? Like a cat toying with a bird—"

"Rat," he corrected.

"Before he eats it!" Donovan buried his face in the curve of Autumn's neck, and to her horror, she realized he was purring. "Oh, don't. Please!" Her fingers twisted into his shirt. It seemed every nerve ending throughout her body was vibrating, and the short bursts of hot breath against her ear were growing more discomforting by the moment. *"Please!"* she tried once more. "You promised!"

Very slowly his head came up. Damp spikes of hair clung to his brow, and the drumming of his heart against hers seemed to punctuate the momentary silence. "So I did," he finally said. "But would a womanizer and gambler give a damn about a promise he made under the influence of champagne? I think not, pet. That's left up to honorable men like my brother; the kind who lie to their wives, beat their mistresses and reject their bastard children."

Autumn felt the sudden tension in Donovan's body. She stared up into his still, shadowed face and held her breath. A bead of sweat rolled from his brow, onto her cheek. He caught it with his tongue and swept it away. That wet velvet touch was a spark to the building heat in her breast, and before she knew what she was doing, she caught the back of his head and pulled it down to her arched throat.

His response was overwhelming. His groan of pent passion shaking the very foundation where they lay, he pressed painfully between her legs, the folds of her robe and the silk of her bunched gown the only barriers between the hard swelling within his clothing. She could lie to herself all night, but she couldn't deny that Brice Donovan had awakened something within her with his kiss. And that frightened her. It caused her to quiver as he feathered kisses along her jaw. It caused her to quake and tremble as he ran one hand along the outside of her thigh. These responses went against her every belief; they defied her own resolutions.

The shocking realization that she could desire a man in that way appalled her. She had to stop it—now. Before those overwhelming sensations could grow even more out of control.

"Aren't Annee and Jeanette enough for you?" she forced herself to ask, hating herself even as she spoke. "Or is having your dead brother's wife somehow gratifying to you?''

He froze. ''Bitch,'' she thought he said, and Autumn closed her eyes. Surely she had imagined the pain in his voice as he rolled away, the same as she'd imagined the vulnerability of a man almost weeping in his dreams as she stood over him in the dark. The very same as she had imagined his saying ''I need you,'' just before she'd made her caustic remark about his having his dead brother's wife.

''I'm sorry,'' she wanted to say, but didn't. Instead she lay painfully stiff as he rolled away. She felt dreadfully empty. And, more important, in that instant she felt lonelier than she had ever felt in her life.

Chapter 5

No man had ever caused Autumn Sinclair to weaken in her resolve, though many had tried. It had become a game around Charleston. Who would melt the ice lady first? Gregory Chandler had jokingly confessed that even he had wagered a little bet on the outcome, thinking Autumn would dismiss the jesting with the same indifference as she always had. And outwardly she did. Inwardly, however, she had hurt. She wasn't opposed to loving a man. Truthfully, she longed to love a man. She was human, after all. But loving a man brought complications, responsibilities that she couldn't allow herself to accept. Love brought marriage, and marriage, pregnancy . . . pregnancy, death. What man could love a woman who was *afraid* of having children?

Autumn sat ramrod stiff by the window. She had no reason to feel this way: confused, angry and afraid to face Brice Donovan. It was only the circumstances, Autumn told herself, and the circumstances were only temporary. When her brother returned to Charleston, she would move into the other room, and need never set eyes on Brice Donovan again after bedtime. He could come and go as he pleased. No need to skulk from the room under cover of darkness. He would be quite free to visit his mistress whenever he wanted.

Both of them.

Dawn had come and gone with splashes of gold and primrose pink staining the sky and sea, and she hadn't even noticed. Her eyes were riveted on the road, watching for the return of her . . . partner. After all, how was she to explain to her brother that her *husband* had been called away on urgent business before dawn?

Jolted from her musings by the light tapping on her door, Autumn turned in her chair. "Yes?"

"May I come in?" It was Mitchell.

"Certainly," she responded.

The door creaked slightly, just as it had at half past two this morning. She'd been awakened by that, not by the stealthy way Donovan had sneaked from the bed and put on his boots. She had, of course, pretended sleep, even as he slipped out the door, closing it softly behind him.

"Good morning," Mitchell greeted her.

She tried to smile.

Shoulders erect, Mitchell stepped gingerly into the room. "Are you all right?" he asked uneasily.

Her cheeks turned hot as she watched him look from her to the bed and back again. "Fine," she responded, wishing he'd leave before she cried.

"Where's your husband?"

"My husband? Oh. Yes. Roy. He's . . ." She thought a minute. "Out."

"He'd mentioned showing us around the plantation."

"He'll be back momentarily. There was some problem, I think. Mr. Tyler called him out early."

"I see." Sliding his hands into his pockets, Mitchell stared at his boot tips. "Mr. Donovan certainly keeps irregular hours."

Autumn turned back toward the window and shivered.

Celie entered the dining room, her beefy hands laden with silver and china bowls on a silver tray. She set the tray on a sideboard and stood back, overseeing a slender boy who rushed to dish out fresh fruit and pour the coffee.

Mitchell cleared his throat before looking toward the enormous woman. "Will we be granted the pleasure of Mr. Donovan's company this morning?"

"Don't rightly know," Celie responded. "Maît Donovan don't usually take his breakfast here."

"What does that mean?"

"Mitchell, please." Mary glanced concernedly toward Autumn, then toward her husband.

His face beet-red now, Mitchell wadded up the white linen napkin in his lap and flung it on the table. "Am I to simply sit here twiddling my thumbs while that blackguard makes a fool of my sister?" He glared at Mary. "I knew the man couldn't be trusted."

"You don't know that," Autumn stated quietly.

"Then you might tell me what he was about at two-thirty this morning."

"Perhaps he couldn't sleep," Mary joined in.

Autumn met her brother's glare, her eyes flashing in disbelief. "Did you spend your evening with an ear pressed against the wall?"

"Of course not." He sat back in his chair.

"Then you might inform me why *you* were about at two-thirty this morning."

"I have a right, Autumn, to be concerned over your welfare."

Autumn blushed with shame. Mitchell had been both brother and father to her since Claude Sinclair died ten years ago. He'd given her a home, love, everything she'd ever wanted, and she'd rewarded him with a deception that would eventually break his heart. But she wasn't a child any longer. He just wouldn't see that.

"Good morning."

The greeting hung in the air. Autumn choked down the thick black coffee before looking toward the casually dressed man in the doorway. He wasn't alone.

"Say good morning to our guests," Brice directed Pierre.

Pierre was peering at Autumn over Donovan's shoulder, his arms wrapped snugly about Brice's neck and his gray-green eyes dancing with mischief. The child giggled and hid his face.

"Well, I'll be . . ." His chair legs thumped against the floor as Mitchell scrambled to his feet. Stiff-necked and unblinking he said to Donovan, "How dare you, sir, flaunt that . . . that . . . *child* before my sister."

A flash of something dangerous darkened Brice's face. Gently, he lowered Pierre to the floor. "I'll see your mother later," he told the boy. Pierre scampered from the room. Slowly, more slowly than Autumn could ever recall seeing a man his size move, he slid into his chair before looking directly at Mitchell.

Donovan looked guilty, confused and angry all at once.

His jaw was tensed, and Autumn went from hot to cold as she watched his mouth compress into a tight white line. She remembered how that mouth had felt on hers last midnight and the morning before. She felt the sudden urgent need to protect him. He was, after all, innocent of any misdeeds toward her. Guilty only by association. Then she thought of the way he had so conveniently forgotten to inform her that Roy had left half of Hunnington to her, and she became angry all over again.

Still, she said quietly, "Thank you, Mitchell, but I assure you the child is no concern of mine. Or yours."

Mitchell appeared surprised. "You're certainly taking this all in stride. Your husband is keeping a mistress at his beck and call, not to mention a son—"

"Then I shan't have to worry over giving him one, will I?" Autumn stabbed her fruit, Mary asked for coffee and Donovan . . . Donovan just stared.

The sun was warm. It was all Autumn could do not to rest her head on that brawny shoulder at her side and doze. But she wouldn't. The arm resting along the back of her seat was disturbing enough. Occasionally Brice's hand would slip and rest on her shoulder, his fingers idling in little circles along her arm. She caught him smiling at her once, slanting that infectious grin her way when Mary and Mitchell were watching. She caught herself smiling back and wishing he would grin at her that way when Mary and Mitchell *weren't* watching.

The well-worn wagon tracks disappeared into a tumble of fallen cane. The driver pulled the buggy to a stop. "This is it," Donovan said. "All of it."

Mitchell shook his head. "A shame. A damned shame. You've a king's fortune in profits just rotting to perdition."

Brice cocked a glance toward Autumn. He was amazed at how easily she had played this little game of deception up until now, but thought she might possibly change her mind after viewing the circumstances in their entirety. The excitement sparkling in those constantly assessing eyes told him otherwise. "Still so eager to make a go of it?" he asked her, knowing before she opened her saucy little mouth what her answer would be.

"Certainly." She offered her back and swung down from the buggy with all the dexterity of an acrobat. He watched her walk confidently toward the cane, prim little shoulders pulled back so far he expected her elbows to clatter together any minute.

He pulled his eyes back to Mary and found her smiling. Then Mitchell left the buggy, leaving Brice and Mary alone. The minutes clicked by while he waited for her to make some comment about his walking out on Autumn at two-thirty that morning. He wondered, remotely, what his excuse could possibly be.

"My," she suddenly said.

Brice waited.

"It's certainly beautiful here, Mr. Donovan."

"Yes, ma'am."

"I suspect Autumn will be very happy on Cayemite."

His eyes went immediately to the girl in the distance. She was knee-high in brambles. "Careful," he called, then leaning forward, braced his elbows on his knees. When Autumn looked his way he warned, "Snakes." Up went her chin and back went her shoulders as she waded even farther into the rotting mess.

"She *is* a bit headstrong," Mary volunteered.

Brice studied the muddied tip of his boot before nodding.

"I always suspected it would take a very special man to mellow her."

Job, perhaps. "No doubt, Missus Sinclair."

"Please, call me Mary."

With tiny, white-gloved hands Mary twirled her blue India muslin parasol against her shoulder. She was all ruffles and lace, pink-cheeked and proper. He wondered why a woman of such apparent propriety would accept the situation between him and her sister-in-law.

"I must admire her, though," she went on. "She has the courage to follow through on her convictions."

His head came up as he smiled. "There is a fine line between courage and muleheadedness. I suspect the young lady has a little of one and a lot of the other."

Mary laughed aloud, causing both Autumn and Mitchell to look curiously toward the buggy. "Oh, my." Mary

70   **Katherine Sutcliffe**

allowed one last giggle through her cotton-tipped fingers. "Oh, I do like you, Mr. Donovan."

"You," he crooned in a voice rich enough to make her blush, "don't know me, Missus Sinclair."

"But I do, sir. I do. I pride myself on being a good judge of character."

Brice fished inside his shirt pocket, withdrawing a thin black cheroot. He rolled it between his thumb and forefinger before saying, "But I'm a gambler, Missus Sinclair."

"Certainly not in cards, sir."

"I have a different mistress for every day of the week."

This made her frown. "Perhaps," she said, "but love has been known to turn more than one profligate around."

Donovan sat back. "Love has nothing to do with this."

"Doesn't it?"

For once he was speechless.

Mary smiled again. "I think it does." She looked toward Autumn. "Oh, yes. I think it does."

"You don't know the first thing about sugarcane, Autumn." Mitchell followed his sister, taking much greater care than she as he dodged one bramble after another, regarding with great distaste the rank smell of putrid cane that hung in the air.

"I know enough to realize this crop should have been harvested months ago." She tried hard to keep the disappointment from her voice. More lightly, she ventured, "Really, Mitchell, I suspect one crop is much like another. We'll simply clear the field and begin again."

"And how do you propose *we* do that?"

Autumn stopped. She hadn't noticed Donovan's approach, but there he stood, a head taller than the cane, his hands on his hips and his boot-clad legs braced apart. He was testing her—and taunting her. She wasn't certain which agitated her more, the test or the taunt.

She looked around, down the zigzagging row of yellowish stalks, and slapped the grit from her hands. "We . . . burn it."

He frowned and cocked his head, cupping one hand around the back of his right ear. "Pardon?"

Autumn blushed, threw a cautious glance toward Mitch-

ell, who seemed intent on other business, and said louder.
"We burn it, Mr. Donovan."

"Au contraire, mon amie." He clucked several times
before smiling. "If we burned this much cane, the clouds
would be dripping molasses." He caught one rotted stalk
with his foot and pushed it to the ground. It snapped under
his boot heel. "We cut it back, to just above the ground,
and hope it continues to grow. Do you know"—he shielded
his eyes against the sun—"just how long, and how many
workers, it would take to clear this land?" Before she
could answer, he finished, "Months, if not years."

Go ahead and smirk, she thought, and was glad she'd
slapped his face the night before. Autumn pirouetted on
the toe of her boot and continued ambling as casually as
possible down the eroded furrows of earth. His footfall
thudded behind her, but she didn't turn.

"Go home," he said quietly. "You don't know the first
thing about sugarcane. Tell them all I'm a son of a bitch
and I lied through my teeth. I'll buy your half of the estate
and—"

"No."

"For God's sake, Autumn—"

"Missus Donovan to you, sir."

"Won't your brother think that's a bit odd?"

"No stranger than your slithering out of my bed into
someone else's." She turned then, stepping back to better
see up into his swarthy face. Autumn hadn't realized how
close he was standing. "Just where exactly did you go,
Mr. Donovan? To see this . . . Annee?"

"What I do is no business of yours." His face was like
stone now, and as black as the clouds collecting over their
heads.

"Indeed? And how am I to explain your deranged
behavior to my brother? Remember, sir, who you are
supposed to be."

"As long as you remember who I am not, which is your
husband, thank goodness. I'm not certain I like the idea of
finding a woman in my breeches. *Wearing* my breeches,"
he amended hastily. "Do you ever wear anything besides
those tacky leggings?" he goaded.

Insufferable cad, she thought.

"Is that why you married my brother, because no one in Charleston would have you?" That's mean, Donovan, he thought.

"Oh! How dare—oh! I'll have you know that men were lined up from Charleston to Columbia, just hoping for my hand in marriage."

"Then why the hell didn't you marry one of them!"

A raindrop fell. Then another and another—great clear teardrops that plopped on their shoulders and heads and dripped off their noses. They didn't notice.

"Why!" she exploded. "Because they're just like you, all spineless and mindless and believing a woman is good for nothing but preserving and sewing and birthing babies every nine months until she withers up, or dies." Sticking her face closer to his, she hissed, "Well, I shan't. Do you hear me? I'll stay on this island and cut every stalk of cane myself before I go back and subject myself to that!"

Her face was wet. So was her hair. The blousing linen shirt she wore to hide her femininity now clung revealingly to two of the most perfectly shaped breasts Brice had ever seen. But it was those eyes that riveted his attention, golden-brown and flashing and overflowing, making him ashamed for ridiculing her breeches.

"I'm sorry," he said, feeling soaked and foolish. "Don't cry."

"I'm not crying. It's the rain, I . . ." She swiped at her face.

"You're crying, dammit."

"Very well, Mr. Donovan, I'm crying. Are you satisfied now?"

"That's a stupid question."

"So I'm stupid as well as unattractive."

"I never said you were unattractive." His eyes dropped to her breasts. She crossed her arms to cover herself, and her face turned a marvelous fuchsia color that almost made him smile.

Neither had remembered Mitchell, but as Autumn stared up into Donovan's tumultuous face, her brother's image appeared through a break in the cane, coat dripping and brown hair hanging in spikes over his brow. He was quite pale. She wondered how much of their conversation he'd overheard.

His mouth opened and closed, but he said nothing.

"Is something wrong?" Autumn asked him.

"Ah." Mitchell pulled a sodden handkerchief from his vest pocket and attempted to wipe his brow. "Ah," he repeated.

"Well?" Donovan barked, causing Autumn to frown and push him aside as she approached her brother.

Mitchell half turned, pointed feebly toward the cane and mumbled something that sounded oddly like, "Adudbuddy."

"Adudbuddy?"

"A . . . dead . . . body."

"Oh." She stopped in her tracks.

Donovan pushed past her in a flash, moving up beside her brother. The remote thought hit her that Brice seemed perfectly suited to these surroundings, while her brother, poor, pale Mitchell . . .

"Are you certain?" Donovan stared down into the smaller man's ashen face.

"Certainly. It was, ah." He again pointed toward the cane.

"There?"

Mitchell nodded. "Everywhere, I think."

"Show me."

Autumn's brother appeared to shrink. "Must I? It's really very . . . messy."

"Autumn," Donovan said, "get back to the buggy." His face was a mixture of concern and anger. Grabbing Mitchell's arm, they disappeared into the jungle of cane.

The downpour had stopped as suddenly as it started. Autumn stood in the clearing, staring at the row of cane and smelling earth and rain and the starch evaporating from her damp shirt. The intense noon sun, its rays reflecting from standing puddles of water and limp cane, scorched her skin and clothes and her bare head, making it pound.

A dead body. There must be some mistake.

By the time she reached the wagon, her boots were caked with mud and her breeches were spattered. Mary perched on the edge of her seat, parasol hiding the upper portion of her face, and her skirts clinging to her knees.

She lifted her hand as Autumn approached and pointed toward the driver.

"The gentleman seems . . . upset, dear."

Autumn stared at her sister-in-law, wondering if she should mention the horrible discovery before Mitchell returned, then deciding against it, looked toward the driver.

"Is something wrong?" she asked.

His eyes wide, he gestured toward the field and chattered something unintelligible.

"I don't understand you."

Taking up the lines, the man began turning the buggy. "No stay here, no ma'am. This no place for Tullius."

"Put down those lines," Autumn demanded.

Tullius was standing now, his shoulders hunched and his knees bent as he snapped the whip over the animal's back. The big horse stumbled in the wagon tracks. Mary rolled in the seat as her parasol somersaulted off the side of the buggy and into the mud. Autumn jumped for the harness, but the horse wouldn't stop. *"Asse-a!"* she yelled to both animal and driver. "Enough!"

The whip cracked, but when she might have jumped away, her sleeve hung upon the harness, and to her horror, she felt herself lifted from the ground as the terrified animal rose upon his back legs, dancing and twisting as the frightened driver attempted to rectify his mistake. The animal lunged and bolted. Autumn was running now, knowing that should she trip and fall beneath the racing animal she was doomed, yet it was all she could do to keep up with the horse's quickening pace; her boots were like weights, dragging her down with each step she struggled to take.

Stepping from the cane into the middle of the track, Donovan was a brief flash of white-and-black as he planted himself, legs astride, before the runaway buggy. Just as the animal bore down upon him, he shifted, threw his weight on the animal's neck, dragging the horse nearly to its knees. The material encasing Autumn's arm finally gave. She hit the ground, instinctively rolling from the animal's path, and for an instant the world was a sea of confusion, of mud and murky water and brambles that tore at her skin and made her want to cry. But she wouldn't cry. She wouldn't!

"Autumn!"

Tenderly Donovan rolled her over. She wanted to slap his face, as she anticipated the mocking arrogance that would laugh at her miserable state and proclaim "I told you so!" Instead, the concern she found there was disarming. It made her want to bury her face against his chest and relieve the burden in her bosom.

"Are you all right?" he asked her gently.

She thought, He's going to kiss me. But he didn't, and an odd and infuriating disappointment rekindled her agitation and set her face on fire, a fire hotter than that caused by the thornbushes, and far more painful.

Brice shook her slightly. "Are you all right?" he repeated.

"I'm alive," she snapped. "Disappointed?"

His smileless face turned wooden. Without responding, he lifted himself from his knee, towering, towering until the sky was blotted by his wind-tousled hair, his broad shoulders and eyes as roiling and green as a storm-tossed sea. He was staring at her as if she were some funny little bug he might squash beneath his boot.

They both, at that moment, became aware of Tullius. Clambering down from the buggy and knocking aside a huffing Mitchell attempting to reach his wife, the driver threw himself at Brice's feet.

"Grace, Maît Donovan, Tullius no bad!"

Autumn struggled to her knees. "Don't hurt him," she pleaded.

"The hell you say!" Donovan thundered. "He might have killed you both!"

"He's only frightened!"

He was over her then, setting her on her feet as one would a child. Brice shoved her toward the buggy. She stumbled toward a pale-faced Mitchell. "Tell her!" Donovan gritted his teeth and advanced toward the cowering Sinclairs. "Tell her, Sinclair, what Tullius is frightened of."

Mitchell croaked something, then clearing his throat, tried again. "A man has been murdered."

Autumn sucked in her breath.

Brice's fingers curled into her shirt, lifting her until they were nose to nose and his tobacco-sweet breath was hot against her mouth. "Would you care to see for yourself, Maîtresse Donovan?"

"I . . . I don't believe you," she said weakly.

"Well, then"—he began dragging her back toward the cane—"let me show you, love, just exactly what living on this rock has in store for you."

No, no. She didn't want to see!

"Donovan, let her go," came Mitchell's wavering command. Then, in a stronger voice, he added, "By God, sir, I said release my sister!"

The hand on his shoulder was surprisingly insistent. Donovan hesitated, turned, but before he could react, Mitchell had planted a fist across his jaw with enough force to send him careening to the ground.

"Oh, my!" Mary cried.

Autumn's jaw dropped as her brother planted himself over Brice and proclaimed, "Damnation, but I've wanted to do that since the moment I learned you'd taken advantage of my sister. Get up, Donovan, and face me like a man."

Brice closed his eyes. A weight hit him then. He thought, at first, that it was that demented Sinclair, railing about making him pay for sins he hadn't committed and how he should have killed him on sight. Then he opened his eyes.

"Stop it," Autumn commanded her brother. "If you lift a hand against him, I will never speak to you again." She looked down from her protective perch atop Brice's chest and asked concernedly, "Are you all right?"

No, he thought.

Closer now, so close he could count the freckles across her nose, she frowned and lightly touched his jaw. She was all warm and soft, just where she should be, and, oh . . . "So beautiful," he whispered.

"What?" The corner of her mouth twitched as Autumn tried to decide whether she should laugh or scold him again for his outrageous behavior.

"You're beautiful," he repeated, and her cheeks caught fire. Wrapping his arms around her shoulders, he pulled her against his chest, nestled his face in her hair and thought, Don't leave me. Ever, ever.

Chapter 6

Crossroads. Twelve years ago Brice might have climbed from this wagon, fallen to his knees and prayed to Legba, spirit of all loas, to allow him passage through these crossroads. But that was behind him. He wasn't the same boy who had grown up praying to his loa and following on the heels of the island doctor, learning how to cure with herbs and *farine Guinée*. "You are destined to be a great doctor," Henri had proudly proclaimed. But Brice hadn't wanted to be a doctor. And he hadn't wanted to spend his entire life isolated on this island, a hundred miles from civilization.

With the sun hot on his bare shoulders, Donovan balanced on the tumbril seat and stared out across the sea. Gulls soared, dipped and dived toward a patchwork of blue-and-green crystal-clear water. It could be so peaceful here, with the wind in his face and the stinging bite of salt on his lips. At times he could understand his father's obsession with Cayemite. To a man eager to make a quick fortune, these islands appeared to offer every opportunity: fertile land, constant temperatures and easy access to the shipping lines. But what it had offered to Patrick Donovan and to every soul who had thought to rule over these islands, even before Columbus had discovered them shrouded in mist over three hundred years ago, was ruin, heartbreak and death. The legend of five hundred years had continued. And that was what frightened Brice most. His father was dead. His brother was dead. By inheriting Hunnington, Brice was given a certain supremacy over it all. His workers called him maît—master. Those who lived on Trempe Mountain knew him as chief. They had condemned him, as ruler of this cursed paradise, to certain madness.

* * *

The shack sat perched on stilts, just above the Marilius Marsh, lopsided and fragile looking, no better or worse than it had twelve years before. Brice's eyes swept the terrain, noted the thatch-roof *humfort* and its *poteau-mitan*—the little house with its "meeting" post painted in brilliant splashes of red, blue and white. "Hello!" he called. The rich sound echoed somewhere down the marsh.

Brice swung from the wagon, paused for an instant, then dropped to his knees. Humor him, he thought, and smiled at the ground. *"Atibo-Legba, l'uvri baye pu mwe, agoe! Legba, l'uvri baye pu mwe. Pu mwe pase."*

"The barrier is open. You are welcome."

Brice concentrated on slapping the dirt from his knees and wondered where *hungan* Tousainnt was hiding this time. Come out, come out, wherever you are, he thought.

The hut was empty. Donovan stood at the half-door and noted the straw bed, a table laden with coconut bowls of boiled maize, bread soaked in oil, *afibas*—slices of small intestine lying congealed in their own fat in the bottom of an iron pan—unrefined sugar and *clairin:* all food for Zaka, loa of crops. He noted too, the tools of Touisannt's trade: a *paquett* full of healing herbs and powders.

The old dog lying inert beneath the hut roused itself, stretched and wobbled to its legs. Brice offered his hand. The animal sniffed, rolled its yellow-tinged eyes his way and lifted its limp tail in friendly greeting. It then dropped back into the shadows onto its side and groaned.

"He is as old as I," came the uneven voice.

"And how old are you?" Brice asked without turning, remembering the game.

"Old. Is that not enough?"

"The sea is old. You are a babe compared to the sea."

The old man humphed and said, "Come here."

Brice turned and knew the minute he saw him that Henri had been there all along, watching. The man might have been Legba, guardian of gates, protector of homes. Dressed in rags, a pipe jutting from between his teeth, and his feeble frame ransacked by time, he was no different than he had been thirty years ago.

"Come here," Henri repeated.

Brice did as he was told.

The dark, puckered face turned up to his. Button-black eyes squinted and thoughtfully assessed him. "I knew you would come," Tousainnt said past his pipe.

Right.

"Tell me, little boy, are you happy in . . ." He looked to Brice for help.

"Virginia," he helped him.

"Do you respect your loa in Virginia?"

Brice shoved his hands into his pockets and toed a pebble with his boot. He didn't respond.

"Have you forgotten what I taught you?" Henri demanded. "All that I taught you?"

Brice looked away.

"Why have you come here?" the old man asked, pouting. His twisted fingers worked deftly, pulverizing ash into fine, fine powder. His eyes, however, never left Brice's face.

"I have something for you."

"Bring it to me." Tamp, tamp, tamp went his stone in the bottom of the bowl.

"I can't." Brice took a deep breath. "It's in too many pieces."

Brice wasn't surprised that Henri reached for a crutch. Legba, after all, walked with such an apparatus. They ambled toward the wagon, but on reaching it, Brice fell back and waited.

Henri lifted the canvas. His teeth clamped tighter around the stem of his pipe.

"Do you know him?" Brice asked.

Henri shook his head.

"You're a liar, Henri."

Henri's eyes opened wider. Stumbling backward, he opened his arms to the heavens. "Have you heard?" came the high-pitched lament, and his body appeared to vibrate with tension. "He questions my honor, O Legba, maî-bitasyon, what shall I do? Eh?" He jutted his bony jaw toward Brice and peered at him from the corner of his twinkling eye. "Eh?" he repeated.

"I'm sorry." Brice sighed.

"Eh?"

Louder Brice said, "I apologize." Henri appeared pleased.

Brice followed the old man back to his chair. "Do you remember the times you came to me?" Henri asked. "I taught you all that I know."

"Yes," he replied, remembering.

"You turned your back on all I offered."

"I'm sorry," Brice repeated, wanting desperately to ignore those stirrings of guilt in his breast. Yet it was there, the guilt, festering. It had been for twelve years.

"You thought that if you returned the guilt would end. Has it?" Henri turned his grizzled face up, and Brice wanted to hit him.

"No."

"You came here to help your brother."

"He asked for my help."

"Did you? Help him?"

Hands clenched, Brice fought back his anger.

"Did you?"

"No!" he exploded.

"No. You were safe in . . ."

"Vir-Virgin—ah, damn."

"Ah, yes. Virginia. Far, far away."

Brice dropped to his knees. Palms pressed against his thighs, he stared at the ground and tried hard not to vomit. But the anger was building, as it always did. He might have controlled it, until . . .

"You broke your father's heart by leaving."

He was like a sparrow in Brice's hands. His fingers lapped about Henri's scrawny throat, he shoved the man to the ground, straddled him like a horse and swore in his face, "Damn you, damn you!" Henri's Adam's apple seesawed against his palms, and the fact that he was laughing infuriated Brice even more.

"Go on." Touisannt's gaping smile beamed up at him. "If hitting me will help you sleep better at night."

He wanted to; he wanted to obliterate all reminders of his responsibilities as Patrick Donovan's oldest son. But he couldn't. They were all around him—in every stalk of putrid cane, in every rundown shanty and rotting eave of Hunnington Hall.

"Just help me," Brice pleaded past his trembling hands.

"Tell me who killed my family and that poor bastard in the back of that wagon."

"I don't know."

He lifted Henri, sitting the old man up on buttocks that were barely more than skin and bone. Brice cupped the leathered face in his hands and beseeched him. "Why not? You know everything that happens on this stinking island, old man. Is it Annee? It is, isn't it?" He shook him. "Did Annee Rose kill my brother?"

"Does it matter?" Henri responded.

"I have to know. For my own—"

"Sanity?" He blinked his rheumy eyes and asked, "Are you afraid, little boy? Afraid your father and brother have passed their madness to you?" Brice turned cold as Henri said, "Madness begins with fear."

Touisannt's head snapped back and Donovan shook him again. "I'm not mad," Brice argued in a raw voice.

"So your father said . . . just before he killed himself."

Ah, God.

"So your brother said the day before he burned."

His fingers twisting in Henri's shirt, Donovan hissed, "She did it. I'm here to prove Annee Rose killed them both! And you're going to help me prove it, old man, or I'll submit your soul to Guede, I swear to God."

Henri's face was a mask of fear as he fixed his eyes on Brice's chin. "Too late," he said simply.

Brice looked then, over the old man's shoulder, beyond where the dog lay with its tongue drooping wetly from the side of its mouth, past the *poteau-mitan* to the trees beside the marsh.

Annee watched him.

And she was very angry.

Autumn studied Brice from behind the curtain. Donovan jumped from the tumbril, put on his shirt and waited as a servant hurried from the stables. Brice tossed him the lines. Horse, cart and boy moved slowly around the house, but Donovan stayed until Autumn wondered if he intended to sleep there the night. She noted that his legs appeared longer, his shoulders wider and his black hair blacker. But then, she hadn't compared his height before to the bougainvillea bush growing profusely next to the drive, or the color of his hair as it looked against an azure sky, light and dark . . . hell and heaven. She dropped the curtain.

The house was alive with chatter; from every room lively conversation could be heard. She liked it, this French Creole dialect. It was musical; the servants nearly sang when they spoke. She had picked up a few words already: *Asse-a*, meaning enough, *tonnerre*, meaning thunder and *azeto* . . . witch. She'd learned enough to know what the help called her—Donovan's witch. She liked that, too, though she couldn't imagine why.

Autumn dawdled in the drawing room doorway, staring toward the front entrance. A stray leaf, caught up in a whirlwind of cross breezes coming through the open windows, danced across the marble floor—this way, that way— then scuttled toward the door that slowly, slowly, was opening. She felt a childish urge to hide and a more adult need not to.

She noticed right off that his face was pale. She noticed, too, that Mitchell and Mary were arguing in the distance. They seemed to be doing that a lot lately. Celie had promised her something called *akee* for her evening meal, and she could smell it now, wafting between the scents of bougainvillea and roses. Smells invoked tastes . . . with her tongue she touched her lips, remembering Donovan's taste.

That's how he found her, pink-tipped tongue teasing the corner of her lips, her freshly washed hair cascading to her waist in loose curls. She'd changed her breeches and cleaned up her boots. She was lounging against the door-frame, arms crossed over her breasts—yes, she undeniably had breasts—and she was smiling, remotely, but smiling nevertheless. The Sinclairs' voices carried clearly.

"Mitchell, I must insist you stay out of this. Autumn is a married woman, and it is her decision whether or not she stays on this island."

"Enough, Mary. What kind of brother would I be if I didn't see after my sister's welfare?"

"But she loves him!"

"Balderdash!"

"It is written all over her face!"

"Poppycock!"

Do you? Donovan's eyes asked hers, and she looked away. In one fitful moment he was flooded by desperation.

Autumn shifted her stance; her nerves were jangled to their very core. She told herself it was because of her matchmaking sister-in-law's unwitting blunder, but why then did she try to avoid those eyes, the ones that obliterated her reason one moment, and the next . . .

"Autumn."

The sound was haunting. It settled about her shoulders and seeped into the very marrow of her bones. It rooted her to the floor, and though she tried, she couldn't tear herself from her spot and escape. She could only stare into his eyes, gaze at his open shirtfront and the lean hips that heralded his masculinity. He came toward her, not so confidently as before, wavered halfway there and stopped. His face was as bleached as the white muslin shirt that up until now had exaggerated the duskiness of his tanned skin. "Are you all right?" Autumn asked worriedly.

He didn't respond, only stared at her with eyes as glassy as a millpond.

"Donovan?" She frowned.

Mary and Mitchell's bickering punctuated the silence. Elsewhere, Celie was railing about stolen cookware and how she would hang the culprit when she caught him. There was hammering and laughing and the undulating song of the *simidor* as he beat his drum to the combite, along with the sudden overpowering scent of flowers that must have drifted through the window. All this was obliterated by the man wobbling so precariously before her.

He reached for her, and for the very first time she felt a wave of exhilaration as his fingers curled about her arm. It swept her like a blast of heat from Lollie's ovens, like a gust of winter wind as it whipped over the icy water of Bachus Bay, hot and cold, cold and hot. It made her heady, queasy and giddy all at once.

"Kiss me," he said. "Show him . . ." His voice trailed off, but she realized what he meant.

Autumn stared at his mouth, moistened now by his tongue. A lock of his hair had spilled to the top of one arched brow, and Autumn noticed, not for the first time, that it lacked the greasy dressing that other men, including her brother, used to keep their hair swept back from their faces. His hair had a soft, inviting look.

She felt herself drawn to Donovan, and she wondered if he had somehow hypnotized her with those bewildering, bewitching eyes. His eyes followed her, his lids lowering until his lashes were sooty wings against his cheeks. His lips moved again, silently saying: "Kiss me."

It suited a purpose, she rationalized.

One arm went around her waist, the other up her spine as he cradled the back of her head gently, his fingers entwined in the curls that tumbled over the back of his hand. "Help me," she thought he murmured, then his head tilted and his mouth found hers and all thought left her.

She had convinced herself until that moment, when his mouth molded to hers with a hunger that left her breathless, that his kiss had been no different than Roy's or any other of the half dozen eager young men who had attempted to woo and win her over the past years.

Oh, but it was different, so very different—painful and wonderful all at once. Cocooned in his arms, she felt the pounding of his heart against hers, the uneven rise and fall of his chest, the warm, intoxicating breath against her face. He kissed her endlessly, insistently, and her senses thrummed with a strange anticipation, a splintering of all rational thought. The sounds of the lazy afternoon now dulled into a low buzz, no more noticeable than a distant humming bee.

But in that instant she noticed that the fragrant scent of roses had not wafted through the open door. It was coming from Brice. It was hers: Annee's. He was kissing her while reeking of his mistress! Tearing her face from his, Autumn stumbled away.

"Autumn?" Brice searched her eyes.

Mary and Mitchell appeared at the top of the stairs, falling silent as they looked down on the tense scene, and Autumn knew more inexplicable anger than she had experienced in her lifetime. Smiling coldly, her gaze fixed on Brice's bewildered countenance, she asked as quietly as possible, "Was the perfume a gift from you, Mr. Donovan?"

His face paled further.

Whirling, she left the room.

Autumn hesitated at the top of the stairs. She should have sent Celie to fetch Donovan, but she needed these private minutes to collect her thoughts. Her brother was incensed, ranting about failed crops and murder. Autumn, Mitchell informed her, would be the death of him yet.

She didn't think to knock—a mistake, she realized, as she stepped into the room. He stood naked, with his back to her, in a great brass tub of soapy water. The sun spilling through the open jalousies reflected a rainbow of colors from the puddle of bubbles on the floor, the bubbles on the backs of his calves and . . .

She covered her mouth with her hand. She'd be struck blind if she looked upon a naked man, Lollie had once told her. But Lollie wasn't here.

He was scrubbing his arms with a stiff-bristled brush, from his hands to his shoulders, across his chest, down to his stomach—she averted her eyes—back to his hands. *Shush-shush*—the sound was painful. He turned his palm to the ceiling and scrubbed it as well. But her eyes weren't on his hands; they were on his back. She stared at the scratches across his back.

He must have sensed her there. He stopped his scrubbing and turned his head. "Close the door," he ordered her. When she took an uncertain step backward, he repeated, "Come in and close the door." He reached for a linen and wrapped it around his hips. She shut the door. "I need your help," Brice said in a strained voice.

"Let me get Celie—"

"No!" He didn't turn, but stepped from the tub and crossed the room. There, before the window, he braced his big hands on the window frame and lowered his head. "I want you to do it."

"One woman ministering to the injuries from another— does that give you some sort of satisfaction, Mr. Donovan?"

"Please," he murmured in a pain-laced voice, looking down at the floor.

"I'm sorry—"

He slammed his fist against the wall. "I'm not asking for your pity, madam, I'm asking for your help!"

She stormed across the floor. "Wonderful! You go tumbling with some other woman and come back to me to kiss your wounds."

His head jerked around. "I didn't realize you cared."

Her brown eyes narrowing, she purred, "I don't."

They glared at each other before Brice snapped, "Damn you, woman, you're enough to try a saint."

"A saint," Autumn crooned, "you're not."

The attempt to straighten up cut off his breath. His evident pain made Autumn consider their earlier meeting. How stalwartly he must have denied the discomfort as he held her and kissed her. "What do you want me to do?" she asked quietly, tugging her eyes across the massive sweep of his shoulder and back to his face. She studied, momentarily, the soft swirl of hair that covered most of his ear.

"Get the brush," he said.

"Surely you don't mean to use that on your back?"

"The brush," he repeated.

She did as she was told.

Brice resumed his former position. This time, however, his legs were splayed and his body had taken on a rigidness that was as palpable as the tension crackling between the two of them. "Do it, Missus Donovan." Scrub every last trace of the bitch from my back, he thought. This was his baptism. Autumn Sinclair Donovan would save him from Annee Rose, from her madness and his. He'd known that the first moment she'd come barreling into that room the day before.

She stared at his back and said, "You might tell her to trim her nails next time."

"There won't be a next time," he said, his gaze averted.

She didn't move. Finally Brice looked back over his shoulder.

"I don't care if you see her." She met his eyes.

"I know that."

"It's none of my business."

"That's for sure."

She lifted the brush. "I . . ." The admission trembled

on her lips. "I don't want to hurt you, Brice . . . Mr. Donovan," she corrected, confused over such a slip of the tongue. Higher went the brush. Still she hesitated. "She must be very beautiful," she stated, wanting him to deny it.

Donovan looked back out the window. "No more than you. She just knows how to use it to her best advantage." Autumn went stiff all over as he looked around again and, with a strained smile, teased, "I guess you're pretty adept at that yourself, come to think about it."

A warm feeling passed between them that suffused Autumn's face with color. "I suppose when people want something badly enough, they'll do everything in their power to get it," she commented sheepishly.

"You must have wanted Hunnington Hall pretty badly, then," he said. "Or could it be that you were in love with Roy?"

That was the second time he'd asked her if she had loved Roy. She didn't know how to answer. No, she hadn't loved Roy. That made her sound cold and calculating and unfeeling. He was, after all, a dead man. But an admittance of love was a lie. She had loved what the man could offer her: a chance to escape what most women hold ideal, a conventional marriage that would lead to childbirth. Could Brice Donovan understand that? She decided to say nothing.

Autumn stared at the angry welts across Donovan's back and wondered what had been the reason behind such flagrant cruelty. It conjured up disturbing pictures in her mind. She wasn't ignorant of how "it" was between a man and woman—she knew how babies were conceived—but the thought had always been formulated in a conquer-and-submit image, the woman disdainfully submitting to the odious act while the man vented his animal lusts in the most brutal ways possible. Once she had happened on a young couple who had stolen to the edge of her brother's cotton field . . . oh, but the poor girl's pain must have been horribly intense, the way she kept whimpering and groaning and writhing all over the ground. On that day Autumn had come to the conclusion that a woman would never voluntarily submit herself to that, unless, of course, she was desperate to have a baby.

"Well?" Brice prompted.

Autumn dropped the brush. "I think, Mr. Donovan, that you probably deserved it." She walked to the door, paused, then looked back over her shoulder. He hadn't moved, just stared out the window while the breeze riffled his dark hair with easy familiarity. For a heart-stopping moment she wished it were she with her fingers in his hair.

Amid the ruins of Patrick Donovan's obsession, Brice slouched in his chair, hating himself and the house that had snatched his mother's youth and life, his father's and brother's lives and his own. The weight of conscience hung like an albatross around his neck, dragging him down until his own achievements were little more than a penance for leaving the island in the first place. He could find no thrill in success; never once had he savored the thrill of accomplishment, though he had longed to do so and tried many times. When he'd received Roy's letter he had foolishly believed that the chance to make amends was at hand, that he could somehow make up for his selfish and cowardly escape from Cayemite twelve years earlier.

But he had arrived too late.

There was only one thing to do. He had to face it, accept it with all the courage he could muster.

Suicide was never easy. But he wasn't going alone. Annee was going with him.

Hugh Tyler stepped to the door. "There y'are. I might've knowed, cuddled up to that bottle like it was yer mother's breast. Damn if y' ain't more like yer pitiful brother every day."

Donovan sat back in his chair. "Try being a little more straightforward next time," he said, smiling crookedly.

"Y're a sot, Brice."

"Not yet, but I'm working on it."

Tyler shook his head. "Y'ain't got it in y', maît. Y' got too much up here." He tapped his temple with one finger. "Y' were always the bright one around here, so it just don't figure, yer actin' in such a way."

"If this is preaching, it must be Sunday."

The Irishman ambled across the drawing room floor. "I got no room to preach, considerin' my background."

"Aye."

"But I promised yer father I'd do my damnedest t' see his dream complete. Y're not makin' it any easier for me, Brice."

Donovan stared into Hugh's weather-ruddy face. His brows, bleached by years in the sun, framed eyes as blue as Cayemite's coves. Patrick Donovan had been dead nearly seven years, but Tyler was as faithful to Brice's father's memory as he had been to the man himself. "It's a bit late for you to be out, isn't it?" Brice asked, wanting to avoid any discussion about Patrick Donovan.

The big man ignored the query. "The *America* docks tomorrow. Is the lass leavin' on it or not?"

"As far as Montego Bay." Hugh shoved his hands in his pockets and met Brice's eyes. Donovan shrugged and stared again into his bottle of rum. "I tried. She won't sell out."

"Have y' tried explainin' to 'er?"

"Explaining what? That her life is in danger because there's a madwoman on the island who wants me and this plantation and will stop at nothing to get both? That these islands are cursed, and anyone who holds supreme power is eventually driven mad?" Brice laughed, then asked, "Would you believe it?"

Pursing his lips, Tyler turned toward the window, a bleak look on his face as he stared out across the moon-drenched waters of Ravel Bay. "I'm wonderin'," he said thoughtfully, "just how much of that yer believin' yerself." Brice was staring into his rum bottle as Hugh turned back toward the desk. "Donovan?"

"Sometimes . . ." Brice forced his eyes from the bottle. The nearby candle reflecting from the amber liquid had reminded him of brandy-brown eyes and the intoxicating sweetness of the freckle at the corner of Autumn Donovan's mouth. "Sometimes I believe it. When these people look at me with fear on their faces, or when I think of how my father turned from a gentle, loving man to one who was twisted enough to beat his wife and kids. And Roy—"

"Roy was never any good," Hugh interrupted quietly.

"When these people look at you, they're still rememberin' yer brother. He was a cruel bastard; y' know that. Give 'em time."

Brice laughed to himself. "Time," he went on, "I'm running out of time, my friend. The next body found butchered might be either one of us, or . . ." His head came up. Their eyes locked.

"Will y' be goin' to Montego with Autumn?" Tyler asked.

"She'll need money."

"Aye. It'll be good to see the old place restored to its former splendor."

"Let's not go that far." Brice took another drink. "I'm not sinking all I've got in the place."

Hugh was smiling now. "Half of what's in them coffers is hers."

"Half of nothing is nothing."

"That ain't the way she and that watchdog brother of hers has seen it, thanks to yer quick jimmyin' with them figures."

"So I'll talk to her, once Sinclair is gone." Propping his elbows on the desk, he made a steeple with his fingers and rested them against his chin. "She can't do much damage in two days."

Tyler's deep guffaw bounced off the walls of the austere room and struck Brice's ears. "Give a woman two days of unlimited spendin' of a man's money and he'll go t' his grave a pauper. Y' mark my words, Donovan, y'll feel this all the way t' Virginia. Y're gonna have t' sell a lot of them fine cigars t' make up for this little dalliance. Is she worth it?"

His green eyes shifting to Tyler's, Brice said, "Roy must have thought so."

"So y're doin' this for Roy and his widow?" Hugh shook his head. "Y're still tryin' to make up for leaving here twelve year ago. Y' did the right thing, Brice; when are y' gonna wake up and see that? It's no one's fault but Roy's that this place went t' wrack and ruin after yer father died. No one held the boy down and poured that damned stuff down 'is throat." He pointed one big, roughened finger toward the rum bottle centered between Brice's elbows.

"But the rum didn't kill him, Hugh. Did it?"

The question hung between them as audibly as the distant pounding surf.

"We don't know that," the Irishman finally responded.

"*I* know it." The bitter weariness edged again into his voice as Brice sat back in his chair. He stared at the ceiling. "I know who killed him and why—for the same reason she killed my father and the same reason she killed that poor dismembered bastard we found in the cane field this morning."

Angry, Tyler leaned over the desk and glared at Patrick Donovan's son. "So y'er just gonna lay yerself spread-eagle on Annee's doorstep and be her next victim, right, Donovan? Should we bury y' down at the crossroads with yer brother . . . that is, if there's anything left t' bury? Tell me now, lad, so I'll know what t' do with yer bones when the time comes."

When Brice didn't respond, Hugh grunted to himself and straightened up. "Take my advice; sell to Clarence Dillman and get out."

"Roy's made that just a wee bit hard to do."

"Dillman will buy yer half. He's been itchin' to get his hands on this land for years." Hooking his thumbs in the waistband of his breeches, Tyler looked askance at Brice and ventured, "Course I'll understand yer not wantin' t' sell if y've got designs on Autumn Donovan. Course if y' do, more's the pity. She came here for one reason: freedom. If y're longin' t' settle down and play house, y'er barkin' up the wrong skirts, ah—breeches. That lass is about as likely to whelp you a bunch of babies as Annee Rose is apt to sprout a halo and go to heaven. They've both got certain things in common, though, come t' think on it."

"Aye," Donovan agreed. He stared toward the luminescent little angels on the chandelier and grinned. "They're both beautiful."

"Aye. Y' know what the workers are callin' Autumn, don't y'?"

"Witch."

"Donovan's witch. Every time y're around 'er, yer eyes go all glassy, so y' look like y' drank one of Henri's potions."

"Haven't you something else to do?" Brice looked again at the grinning Irishman and thought of the girl as she had stood before him the night before, swathed in gold silk and hiding behind Mary's fluttering little form. At this very moment Autumn was, no doubt, bundled up in that ridiculous dressing gown and sweating a bucketful of water, waiting for him to make good on his "blackmail." Chuckling, Brice turned the bottle over his glass.

Casually, Tyler moved toward the door, remarking over his shoulder, "Never thought I'd see a Donovan have to get barley-brothed before facing a woman."

"Depends on what woman he plans on facing, I suppose." Brice then laughed into his upturned glass.

Hugh stopped, but he didn't turn. "I'm hopin' it's the one upstairs . . . Donovan?"

"Good night, Tyler."

"Don't see Annee, lad."

The rum depleted, Brice turned his glass over the bottle neck, his eyes to the bronze angel now weeping wax, and pillowed his cheek tiredly in his hand. "Good night, my friend."

The drums again.

Autumn lay back on the bed and watched the flutterings of the mosquito *baire* overhead. One, two throbbed the drums. One, two . . . They were different tonight. The undulating rhythm was disturbing, its pounding adding to the suffocating heat of the sweltering room. Where was Donovan? She left the bed.

Standing before the window, she looked out across the gardens to the darker chasm that was Ravel Bay. Earlier she had watched its diamond-topped waves sparkle beneath the moon, now lost behind clouds tumbling across the midnight horizon. One, two . . . the drums. Autumn closed her eyes. Her hips swayed.

She was floating, weightless, feeling every beat that pounded in time with the distant waves. She scarcely breathed, for the rhythm had settled in her stomach and suffused her body with a tide of its own. One, two. The heat—unbearable.

Like a pulse it surged through her body, his vision, mouth moving, eyes moving, hands moving, stirring. Hot and cold. Autumn shivered. One, two, the pulse, pounding, thrumming. In and out . . . the heat. Painful. Her head fell back. Was he with her now?

Annee. Donovan.

Oh, God. Was he touching Annee? Did his presence leave her aching, throbbing in the most private of places? She looked down the stone steps, to the edge of the garden. Donovan was there, his back to her, his head down. He was moving, too, with the drums—slowly, side to side. To and fro, his hips. One, two . . . the drums.

The heat, the unbearable heat, was sluicing up her legs, coiling there where her thighs met, and, oh—

Donovan. Elusive warlock.

He turned his face to the heavens and the clouds parted, bathing him in moonlight. The coil tightened. Her breath stopped. Donovan. The drums pulsed.

Beyond the stone wall, against the shimmering satin sand where the feathered waves indented the land with probing fingers, the horse appeared, ghostly white beneath the chasing moon, prancing and rearing in time to the haunting drumbeats.

"Donovan," came the feminine rider's voice.

"Donovan," Autumn repeated softly. "Don't go."

Don't go.

She moved away, her eyes never leaving the window. Lying back on the bed, she counted the flutterings of the mosquito *baire* overhead, feeling the drums. One, two. One, two.

Don't go.

Donovan.

Chapter 7

Excitement crackled throughout the city. Hawkers barked their prices to the stevedores who walked in droves up and down the bleached-gray docks. Gulls circled above the tall-masted ships, their keen eyes on the nets of fish being hoisted to the nearest vendors.

The lighter that had transported the passengers of the *America* to Montego's docks dipped and lurched against the ropes that bound it to the wharf. Near the end of the dock Mary and Mitchell were overseeing the baggage that would be transported to the nearest lodgings by horse-drawn dray. Autumn had little choice but to lag behind, waiting for her "husband," who seemed more concerned with his conversation with the *America*'s captain than with seeing to her interests.

Around her the array of dialect was dizzying: French, English, creole, Spanish, all mingling with excited barter-ing over fish, rum, tea and cotton. "Higher, higher, who'll see 'er higher!" chanted the auctioneer in the distance. His eloquent cajoling worked the eager vendors into a frenzy.

They had been warned, when arriving at Montego Bay, that the lodgings would be first come, first served. And as there appeared to be several ships already docked, Autumn sensed that if Donovan did not finish his dallying, they would find themselves bunked again on that poor excuse for a bed they had shared the night before . . . or attempted to share. At some time past midnight he had left the cabin, not returning until just before dawn.

"Donovan! Brice Donovan; by damn, I can't believe my eyes!"

Autumn and Brice turned their astounded gazes on the man approaching from the far end of the pier. Beyond him, Mary and Mitchell's attentions were centered on the dray, and much to Autumn's relief, they were too busy to have heard the newcomer's welcome.

The stranger was slender, long-legged and handsomely dressed. He had a youthful face, belying his balding pate, with a dazzling smile that produced dimples and side whiskers that swooped almost to his jaw. His coattails flounced around his thighs, adding to the joviality of his appearance. She liked him, Autumn decided.

Brice stepped past her, brushing her in his haste to greet his arriving friend. The men clasped hands, then, feeling such a greeting totally inadequate, embraced each other wholeheartedly.

The stranger, gripping Donovan's upper arms in his hands, stepped back and smiled warmly at his friend. "It's been years, Brice; what the devil are you doing in Montego Bay?"

"Business, mostly."

"How's life in the Southside?"

Brice laughed before admitting modestly, "Comfortable."

The stranger's bushy brown brows shot up. "Indeed? Then perhaps we can do business ourselves while you're here." His eyes then landed on Autumn. "Donovan, you ole dog, have you taken the plunge without letting us know?" He looked back and forth between Autumn and Brice.

Before Brice could respond, the stranger had sidestepped him and extended his hand. "Since my friend has so completely forgotten his manners, madam, let me introduce myself. The name's Laurence Nelson—Loz for short, and you are? . . . His blue eyes trailed down her trousered legs before returning, with a twinkle, back to her face.

"Autumn," she could barely respond without laughing. The man's good-naturedness was most contagious.

"Autumn! Jehoshaphat, but what an outrageously delightful name. Let me see." He searched the heavens above her head, his index finger tapping at one ruddy cheek in contemplation, then teased, "You were born on a crisp day in November—"

"March." She smiled again.

Loz frowned. "You don't say."

Autumn nodded. "My middle name is Dae."

"You don't say. Autumn Dae—outrageous!"

"Yes, it is, isn't it?"

Loz laughed a little harder, and shaking his head, again faced a slightly smirking Donovan. "Wherever did you find her, Brice?"

"You might say," he drawled, looking at her askance, "that she found me."

Autumn refused to acknowledge Donovan's innuendo, and focused instead on the couple approaching hurriedly from a distance. Mitchell stormed down the dock, his coattails flapping and his face set in rigid determination. Mary, skirts whipping about her ankles as she attempted to keep up with his longer stride, and bonnet bobbing precariously, appeared more than a little concerned.

A thousand thoughts flashed through Autumn's mind. Had Mitchell overheard Mr. Nelson's greeting to Donovan? Should her brother learn now of her deception, the consequences to her would be dire, as well as to Brice. Donovan would hardly take another assault lightly—his jaw was still sporting a bruise that looked pitifully like raw meat—and she had, on more than one occasion, witnessed him slowly manipulating his jaw back and forth as if testing it to make certain it was still operable.

"Autumn, will you be joining us or not?" a winded Mitchell asked. He refused to acknowledge Donovan.

Mary frowned while attempting to straighten her bonnet. "Mitchell, I'm certain Roy will see to her comforts. Please, darling, the dray is leaving with our baggage."

"Roy!" came Loz's surprised exclamation.

All eyes turned toward Nelson. He looked from one to the other, but it was Donovan's gray-green stare that brought him upright. Clasping his hands behind his back, Loz rocked on his heels and amended, "What I mean is . . . *Roy* will be staying with me. At my home. And his . . . and Autumn, as well, of course."

They waited a tense moment before Mitchell looked back at Autumn. "I want to talk to you."

"Your dray is leaving." Autumn pointed down the pier.

Mary tugged on Mitchell's coattail.

Brice pulled a cheroot from his coat pocket, nipped its

end and spat the tip into the water. "I'll contact you," he said to Autumn.

The egotistical goat is trying to get rid of me, she thought, before looking back at Mitchell. If she agreed to her brother's demand she would be bombarded every moment with the reasons why she should not remain with Donovan. And at this point, with the task of having to say good-bye to him and Mary inexorably approaching, she was afraid she *might* give in to his harassment and put Cayemite behind her forever. She couldn't take that chance.

Looping her arm through Donovan's, she replied as stoically as possible, "It would be terribly remiss of me not to remain with my husband, Mitchell."

Mitchell's face turned from red to purple. Autumn, however, hardly noticed. Brice's hand had closed over hers with the declaration, and she was somehow immeasurably glad.

The horse, a dappled gelding with arched neck and a high prancing gait, led the way out of town, past the cultivated fields of fresh earth and rippling emerald seas of ripening cane. Autumn didn't listen to the conversation between Donovan and Nelson. She was too busy taking in the spectacular view ribboning one side of the road. Endless sand stretched as far as she could see in either direction, but it was the vision of turquoise water that held her spellbound. The curvature of the earth was clearly definable from the beach, all blue and green and feathery-white in places. Upon that curve perched a single sail. It was a lonely sight, so isolated and remote, and it brought a lump to her throat.

The road twisted. Its head lowered, the horse strained a little harder as it began the ascent up the constantly changing path, and with more than a little disappointment Autumn said good-bye to that lonely voyager and the vista of blue-green tranquility. She stared now into trees not unlike those on Cayemite, towering, smooth-trunk trees with leaves that rattled with the wind.

Autumn had discovered that, while the morning held the briskness of dew and delightfully cooler temperatures, the evenings were special in another way. The waters changed color beneath the descending sun. Great splashes of primrose-pink, goldenrod-yellow and sapphire-blue swirled like a kaleidoscope on the horizon. Flowers blossomed into fragrant blooms as deliciously sweet as the rarest perfume. This was Autumn's favorite time. The sun made her sleepy and content. She wanted to stretch and yawn, turn her face to that great, melon-colored ball in the sky and drift blissfully to sleep. Not a good idea, she realized, as she looked up to find both Donovan and Nelson staring at her intently.

Loz was the first to break the silence. "I was just telling Brice; you couldn't have come at a more exciting time. My wife is due to deliver a baby any day now."

Was there any place on the face of this earth where women were not having babies? Autumn mused. She attempted to smile, aware that the color had left her face. She was cold suddenly, and that nagging fear gripped her stomach so painfully that she felt fully capable of passing out completely. Breathe deeply, she told herself. Insensitive, foolish little girl. "How very nice for you," she finally managed.

"It's our first, you know. After ten years of marriage, we'd almost given up hope. I'm sure as a woman you can appreciate my wife's excitement, so please forgive her if she seems just a trifle overwrought."

She looked up at Brice. He was grinning in that infuriating way that made her light-headed. "Perhaps we should have remained in the city," she suggested.

"Miss me already?" His smile broadened.

"I beg your pardon?"

"At least here we'll have separate rooms."

"I hadn't noticed we'd shared one, Mr. Donovan." She returned his smile, aware that her allusion to his leaving to see Annee every night had met its mark. Yet there was no anger reflected in those green eyes that, when turned upon her, swam with her own reflection. They were clear and startlingly sharp. There was a twinkle of amusement in their depths.

Lowering his head, he whispered into her ear, "When you're ready to see out our bargain, my pet, just let me know. I think it would take very little on your part to entice me into staying the complete night in your bed."

Autumn shot a glance toward Nelson, who was going to great lengths to pretend interest in the most uninteresting scenery they had encountered since leaving the city. "Do you think you could squeeze me in between Annee and Jeanette?" she responded in a voice so soft Brice had to lower his head further to hear her.

Donovan's burst of laughter sat Autumn flush back against the seat. "Certainly not," he replied loud enough for Nelson's driver to hear. "I was thinking of only the *two* of us, but if you care for company I would be more than happy to accommodate, my love."

Confused and embarrassed, Autumn stuttered, "Oh! I—no, I—I only meant . . ."

"Yes?"

He was bestowing on her one of those lazy, devastating smiles that made her toes tingle, and she wondered with great consternation if Annee and Jeanette responded in such a way when he looked at them. Her eyes narrowing, she spat, "It will be a cold day on Cayemite before we *ever* see out that bargain, Mr. Donovan!"

Sitting back in his seat, Brice shrugged one shoulder noncommittally and ventured in a dulcet voice, "Don't look now, sweetheart, but I believe that's snow clouds in the distance." He pointed toward the horizon, and Cayemite Island.

Shelley Nelson was as vivacious as her husband. Her honey-blond hair, swept away from her face, was twisted into a coil around the back of her head. She had pixielike features, rosebud lips and cheeks of naturally high coloring. She sat on the edge of her chair, her legs spread and her elbows propped on her knees, so her stomach lazed comfortably between her thighs. Her eyes were bright with excitement as Autumn finished her explanation of *how* she came to be Brice Donovan's partner.

"Imagine," she bubbled, smiling. "Your own plantation."

"Not exactly," Autumn reemphasized. "Donovan *does* own half."

"Which half?"

"Well, I . . ." Frowning, Autumn shook her head. "I don't know."

Shelley threw a cautious glance toward the door, making certain neither her husband nor Brice had returned to the parlor. "What do you know about sugarcane?" she asked her.

"Nothing," Autumn responded truthfully.

"Oh!" Shelley sat straighter. "Well, then, the first thing to consider is just where to begin." She lowered her voice. "Hunnington is a dry-weather estate, from my recollection, and—"

"There you are!" Loz stood in the door, concernedly glaring at his wife. "You're supposed to be resting," he admonished her.

"Oh, fiddlesticks. We were only discussing the weather." Shelley sat back primly and smoothed her hands over her stomach.

His hands behind his back, Loz ambled into the room. "So I heard. If I didn't know better, my dear wife, I might believe you were about to give Missus Donovan an abbreviated course in crop raising." Autumn smiled as he looked her way. "Brice is counting on your failing," he said to her. "He hates Hunnington almost as much as your husband did."

"Then he should leave Cayemite and go back to wherever he came from," Autumn countered.

Nelson laughed before admitting, "He would like nothing more, I think."

It was in that moment that Donovan entered the room. Autumn looked away. There was a porcelain bird in a glass-enclosed cabinet; she centered her eyes there, thinking she would be safe from the unsettling breathlessness his presence provoked. Alas, it was not to be, for his image was multiplied a hundred times by those etched-glass panes. A hundred Donovans dressed in black broadcloth and staring down at her!

"Have you rested?" he asked her in a surprisingly gentle voice. The room grew uncomfortably warm.

Loz cleared his throat. "I believe our meal is ready."

He offered his arm to Shelley. "My dear, if you'll allow me . . ."

Brice offered his hand. Autumn stared at it, then at his arm, at the cravat tucked neatly into his white shirt collar and finally at his mouth, beginning to curl lazily at one end. How easy it would be to slip into those gray-green eyes and drown. She didn't want to look, but she did.

Autumn lost her breath. Had he noticed? Those eyes didn't change, nor the sardonic twist to his lips. But she changed—not outwardly, of course, but there, in her stomach, where a thousand butterflies fluttered for escape. She stood before him, dressed in cotton breeches and a muslin shirt, and he made her feel like that porcelain bird in yonder cabinet, all fragile and tiny, encased in glass that might shatter if he touched her the wrong way. Catching her hand, he lifted her from the chair. Her urge to bolt was distressingly strong, and as if he sensed it, he stepped before her, barring her escape.

Don't touch me, she mentally implored him.

Touch me, she implored him.

He offered his arm. "Autumn?"

He was smiling, and Autumn wondered if her brother was hiding behind some door Donovan knew about. It was a sincere smile, like the ones he bestowed on her when Mitchell and Mary were about, when they were pretending that they were in love. She looked around the room.

"Hungry?" he asked her.

"I . . ." His hair was combed so neatly. "No, I . . ." She recalled the soap bubbles on the backs of his thighs and swallowed hard. "Yes," she whispered.

Autumn wasn't aware she'd accepted his arm, or that they had left the roomy parlor, walked through the cross-shaped foyer with its gleaming breadnut floors and entered the dining room. White-coated attendants stood at each corner of the table, and suddenly it seemed all eyes were on them.

Oh, no.

She jerked her arm from his, left him standing at the door while she strode alone to her chair. And when he hurriedly moved to pull out her chair, she grabbed it from

his hand and did it herself. He hesitated behind her. He
was staring. She could feel it. She could feel those eyes.

She was attracted to Brice Donovan. What a startling
realization. Autumn stared at her naked toes and recalled
how he had smiled at her during dinner. By dessert he'd
actually had her blushing and giggling like . . . Anita
Cunningham! It was the wine, she mused. She hadn't
giggled since she'd turned fourteen.

Stopping at the far end of the portico, Autumn turned
her face into the night wind and tried to think of something
other than Brice Donovan. Impossible. The man was a
mystery. One moment he was scorning her for remaining
on the island, the next, he was wrapping his arms around
her and in his own way pleading with her to stay.

Loz Nelson stepped from the shadows. "So tell me,
Missus Donovan, what do you think of Jamaica?"

Startled, Autumn looked up. "It's beautiful," she
responded, feeling naked without her shoes.

If he noticed her toes, he didn't let on. "I can't imagine
living anywhere besides this island," Loz remarked casually. "Do you know that three-quarters of the landowners
throughout the islands live someplace else? England, mostly.
Imagine living in that cold, stale place when they could be
bathing in these beautiful waters and basking in sunshine."

They met beside the balustrade. "It's been a good year
for sugarcane," Loz continued. "Just enough rain, you
see. I suspect Cayemite could still see a small profit, if
harvest is begun as soon as you return. Of course, there
will be other crops to see to as well." He paused meaningfully, then looked down into Autumn's eyes. "There are
red beans on the mountains. They'll have to be picked.
Millet should be planted soon for the cattle and horses. If
one hurried, new fields of cane could be planted. As my
dear wife stated earlier, Hunnington is a dry-weather estate.
It could yield, oh, say, two and a half tons of cane an
acre. An astute planter would know that the best crops will
be planted in soil that is neither too heavy with clay nor
too sandy. If there's too much sand, the rain evaporates
too quickly and leaves the cane dry. Clay soil retains the

water in pools and will rot the crop." He lifted one brow.
"Do you understand what I'm saying, Missus Donovan?"

She nodded and wondered why he was telling her this.

"Now, take the Barrett plantation." There was a wine glass in his hand. He stared down at that. "Barrett is a planting estate, placed on higher ground. Most of it was once covered with forest; the ground is made up of dense black mold. Oh, it makes a brilliant first crop, but it also lends itself to rapid soil exhaustion. Maîtresse Rose has to replant every year." He looked again down at Autumn. "Annee would like nothing more than to get her hands on your estate."

"Among other things," she stated under her breath, but loud enough for Loz to hear.

He laughed softly, then said, "Yes, I won't pull any punches where Brice and Annee are concerned. She wants him. She's made no secret about that."

"Why are you telling me this?" Autumn asked.

"My wife thinks you should be warned." Loz took a deep breath and added, "So do I. You've managed to place Brice in an uncomfortable position. He doesn't want Hunnington, but—"

"He wants Annee." Autumn gritted her teeth and looked away.

"No," he surprised her with his reply. "He wants you."

Her head snapped up. "I—I beg your pardon?"

Nelson wiped his palm across his brow and swallowed hard. "Oh, he probably doesn't realize it himself. But I've known Brice since we were boys. He lived with us for two years after leaving Cayemite and, believe me, had he wanted some frivolous little skirt, he would have had his pick of the women on this island." He glanced at Autumn and smiled. "Don't you like him just a little?"

Autumn opened and closed her mouth. Two days ago she would have vehemently denied any fondness for the man, but now . . . now what was she feeling? She had thought only last night that perhaps, just perhaps, they might try harder to get along. They would be spending a great deal of time in each other's presence, after all.

"Yes," she surprised herself by admitting. "I do like Mr. Donovan."

Loz's face appeared to brighten. He lifted his glass between them. "Then I toast your partnership." He quaffed the red wine, then stepped back. "Now, if you'll excuse me, my wife is no doubt growing quite stiff with her ear pressed against that glass." He motioned toward the nearest darkened window and winked. In a moment, Autumn was alone.

Autumn stood alone outside the French doors to her room. With her hands in her pockets she stared out over the gardens. The road was a pearl-gray ribbon in the darkness. At one end of the portico, crouched in shadow, was a stone lion with one raised paw, its mouth open in what resembled a lazy yawn. There was a potted plant next to it, its flower now closed tight and tucked within itself. Autumn entered her room, thinking of that flower.

She knew immediately that she wasn't alone. Brice slouched in a chair, a halo of orange light wreathing his face as he smoked. "Why are you here?" she asked, never taking her hands from her pockets.

"I was lonely," came the response.

"Missing Annee?" She cocked her head and smiled.

"Come here." As he drew on his cigar, a burst of light settled like torches in his lazy eyes.

Autumn shook her head. She nibbled her lower lip and stared down at her toes.

"We need to talk," came his smooth voice, cutting through her resolve like a hot knife through butter. She wanted to run from those eyes, that voice and the very presence that caused her emotions to reel crazily. "We need to talk," he repeated. "Man to . . . whatever."

Autumn stiffened.

"Does that annoy you?" Brice taunted, then chuckled.

She took the chair facing Brice. Knee to knee, they stared at each other for a long moment. Slowly, and with all seriousness, he removed a cigar from his shirt pocket and offered it to her. With no apparent surprise, or hesitation, she took it from him.

He waited.

She fingered the cigar.

He grinned and offered to light it.

She wrinkled her nose and started laughing.

"That's nice," he said softly.

"What?" She stuck the cigar in her ear and he started laughing. "Isn't this the way it's done?" she teased him, and he laughed that much harder. Autumn fell against the back of her chair, arms wrapped around her ribs and bare feet suspended above the floor. This was so silly. There was really no reason at all to laugh. But there they were, each hee-hawing away in the darkness as if there were no tomorrow.

Then, suddenly, he wasn't laughing. With elbows propped on his knees, he was watching her laugh, and smiling. He'd never heard her laugh. It was such a feminine sound that it made his chest ache.

"Is something wrong?" She was aware, now, that Donovan was no longer laughing.

"Take the cigar out of your ear," he commanded quietly.

"Why?"

"I have no intention of kissing a woman with a cigar in her ear."

Slowly she removed the cigar.

"Come here," he repeated.

"No." Autumn ducked her head. Her breath was coming in sharp spurts. Her palms were sweating.

"Don't you *want* me to kiss you?"

Squeezing her eyes closed, she confessed, "Yes. I want you to kiss me."

"Then come here."

"No." Autumn opened her eyes. He was so close. So very close.

A flash of anger crossed his face. With his elbows digging a little deeper into his knees, he stressed, "If it's guilt you're feeling over Roy—"

"Roy has nothing to do with this!"

They stared into each other's faces, each watching the play of emotions that swept the other's features. "Then what is it?" he finally asked.

"You're a man, Brice Donovan; you couldn't possibly understand."

Brice sat back slightly, a look of dawning in his eyes.
"You're wanting me to seduce you," he said bluntly, and
Autumn's mouth dropped open in surprise. "Is that how
Roy did it? Did he say, 'I think I'm in love with you,
Autumn—' "

"No!"

"Or did he say, 'Every woman who came before you
was wiped from my mind the first moment I laid eyes on
you'?"

His words were like velvet, sending ripples of yearning
down her spine. Wringing her hands and sitting on the
edge of her chair, Autumn shook her head. "No," she
repeated, a frightening urgency in her voice. "He said
none of those things!"

"Well he sure as hell must have done something!"
Brice's voice vibrated with frustration.

They both came to their feet. Staring up into his obstinate face, Autumn hissed, "Keep your voice down, Mr.
Donovan. I don't wish for this entire house to think I'm
entertaining you in my room!"

"I'm certain no one in this entire house gives a damn,
Missus Donovan, except you. And I have to ask myself
why a woman who would go to the lengths that you did to
seduce a ne'er-do-well like my brother into marriage would
care what other people think."

"Oh! I did not seduce your brother!" Her fingers curled
into tight, white knots.

"Ha!" he laughed sharply. "It was your body or your
money. On second thought, it must have been your money.
What the hell kind of a fool could be seduced by a little
hoyden who's too afraid even to admit that she's a woman!"

His arms went around her then, putting the lie to his
own words. He lifted her from her feet. She beat at his
shoulders. She thrashed her head, avoiding his mouth.
Then all too suddenly she was staring up into his eyes, her
lips were parting, and he was kissing her fully, hungrily,
with as much tender passion as he could allow his starving
body.

Dancing on the tips of her toes, Autumn clutched weakly
at Donovan's shirt. Her world was tumbling in a thousand
sensations. He was molding her lips with his, pressing,

forcing her mouth open until his tongue could plunge and plunge in a rhythmic, suggestive fashion that seemed to reach all the way to her loins. She wanted desperately to breathe, but the arm around her back wouldn't allow it. She yearned to run, but the hand twisting into her hair made escape impossible.

"Ah, witch," he murmured when finally he released her. "You cast your spell the moment you barreled into my room, and now you torment me with your coy indecision: yes, no, yes, no. You make me swear not to touch you, then taunt me with the curve of that lovely throat. What am I to think, Autumn? How would you have me respond, if not like this?"

"Do not respond at all!" she cried.

"Madam, I am only human." His fingers digging into her arms, he set her from him and demanded, "What are you, Autumn? My brother wrote of an enchanting child—"

"Child?"

"Who wears men's breeches, and yet here you stand before me and flaunt your womanly beauty every time I turn around. Look, but don't touch, your eyes tell me."

"Then don't look!"

"How can I help it? You're there when I eat my breakfast, when I bathe and turn down the light for bed. You're there when I dream, with the smell of your hair as it spills over my pillow, and I am expected to act the gentleman and yield my shoulder as you mold your body against mine in your sleep. Ah, God." Thrusting his hands through his hair, Donovan turned from Autumn and in a shaking voice, confessed, "You've driven me from my own bed, indeed, my own house, and I'm at a loss as to what I should do. My common sense tells me to send you from the island for your own good, yet my need for you bids me to let you stay. And *why?* I ask myself. Why? When it is obvious you care no more for me than any of the other poor besotted fools back in Charleston you must have mesmerized with those bewitching eyes."

"You *need* me?" She blinked in surprise.

"Perhaps if I understood why you married Roy in the first place . . ." He paced toward the door, then stopped. Moonlight spilling across his shoulders, he turned again toward her and asked, "Have you some reason for fleeing Charleston, Autumn? Did something happen there that would forbid you from remaining? Another man, perhaps?"

"Another man?"

"That's it, isn't it?" His voice was suddenly tight and full of anger. "You've been hurt, and to make certain it won't happen again, you've been parading about in those disgusting breeches, hoping to avoid a similar relationship. Perhaps everyone was aware of the affair, and believing no one would accept a 'soiled dove,' you chose the only alternative: Escape Charleston with a stranger who was so desperate for money that your somewhat tarnished reputation didn't matter."

"I think, Mr. Donovan, that you have been smoking too many of those cigars. The smoke has gone to your brain."

"It's not smoke that's addled my mind, Autumn, nor is it better judgment. Very well. Keep your secret. But know this: There are more patient men than I. We have a verbal contract, you and I, and I just might decide to collect on our little bargain sometime in the future. Those damn breeches may prove a barrier to the rest of the world, but I assure, my love, they will be no barrier to me. You will find Cayemite a very small island if—when—I decide I want you. With that thought, Missus Donovan . . . good night."

Chapter 8

"You're aggravated, Donovan; what's it about?"

"She's driving me completely mad with her come-hither, hands-off routine."

Nelson's laughter was rich. "Ah, the good fellow has met his match. Forgive me, my friend, but I can recall when you actually gloried in turning the ladies' heads. You've left many a concerned mama soothing a daughter's broken heart."

"Never intentionally," Brice responded. "I have never vowed a love to which I was unwilling to commit."

"And have there been many?"

Donovan stared into his snifter without responding.

"Somehow I imagined your populating Virginia with a half dozen little Donovans by now."

"I vowed never to marry until I could offer my wife something more than a plot of tobacco and a one-room house."

"I would call two thousand acres a trifle more than a plot. And, forgive me, but I could have sworn you mentioned something about a house with twenty-two rooms. I think if you tried, you could squeeze in a wife and a child or two."

"Willow Bend is an isolated place. Most women would find it . . . tedious."

"Most, but there are always exceptions. Take Autumn, for instance."

"I would like nothing better." Pushing himself up from his chair, Brice rotated his head, attempting to relieve the tension at the back of his head. He stared at the ceiling and stated, "I've seen with my own eyes what that damnable isolation can do to a marriage."

"You cannot blame your parents' failed relationship totally on Cayemite's isolation."

"Aye, but I blame Cayemite. She's a bitch, Nelson; a whore who lured my father and the men who came before him with promises of something brighter. She takes and takes, and gives nothing in return."

"You must respect Patrick for trying," Loz reasoned. Leaving his chair, he joined Brice at the window.

"I know." His voice hoarse now, Donovan stared into his drink, watching the swirl of memories take shape before his tired eyes. "Patrick Donovan *was* a man to respect, in the beginning. But how can I continue to respect the memory of a man who was driven mad by greed?"

"You might try placing the blame on the Cayemite legend," Loz teased, wanting only to lighten his friend's mood. But the stormy, troubled eyes that looked back at him were hardly relieved.

"If I'm to believe that, then I'm to believe that *I* am next in line for madness," Brice whispered. "Do you know what it's like, questioning my own every motive, wondering every morning when I open my eyes if this might be the day I snap?"

"Then leave Cayemite," Nelson stressed.

"Ah, God, if only it were that simple." Brice's head dropped between his shoulders, heavy, pounding and fuzzy with brandy. "I worked five long years trying to forget Cayemite and my father. Then Roy's letters started: Patrick was ill—my leaving Hunnington had destroyed him. The crops were rotting—as if *I* had anything to do with the damned rain that wouldn't let the island alone. Every nail I drove into Willow Bend was a betrayal of Roy and Patrick."

Brice tipped the drink to his mouth, then looked his friend directly in the eye. "The day I sold my first crop, I received word of my father's death. He killed himself, so I'm told."

"I don't believe that," Loz said softly. "I saw Pat in Kingston just a few days before he died. He'd just negotiated a loan and was looking forward to rebuilding the old mill on Trempe Mountain. He spoke fondly of you, Brice, and asked if I'd heard from you recently. He sent his gratitude to my father for helping you when you left Cayemite. He was perfectly rational, not the kind of man who would kill himself.''

How he wanted to believe that. Donovan searched Loz's face, afraid to let the hope show in his eyes. ''If I thought he had forgiven me for leaving, perhaps I could sleep at night,'' he said looking into his empty glass.

''He forgave you, Brice.''

''But Roy—''

''Was mad.'' Donovan's head snapped around. ''Roy was mad,'' Loz repeated. ''Mad the day he was born. You can blame legends or curses or whatever you please, but he undermined everything you and your father ever did. He was sick, my friend, so place no reliability on anything he might have written in an incoherent moment.'' Stepping closer, Nelson pressed a comforting hand on Brice's shoulder and offered in a kind voice, ''Go to bed and sleep easy tonight. Forget ghosts and legends and curses that mean nothing. You are not going mad from anything but guilt and loneliness, and there are those of us who will help you through that.''

Shelley Nelson stepped to the door. ''Laurence?'' she called softly.

Brice watched as Nelson hurried to his wife's side. ''Are you all right, darling?'' he heard his friend ask.

''Certainly. I missed you is all.''

''I'm on my way up.'' Loz turned and smiled at Brice. ''Good night,'' he said.

Brice remained, staring after his friends who walked together to the foot of the stairs. With little effort Loz lifted his very pregnant wife in his arms and carried her up and out of sight, their quiet laughter underscoring the emptiness Brice felt in that moment. He was so tired of the emptiness.

He took the decanter of brandy, then mounted the stairs.

A dark-skinned maid greeted Brice as he stopped at the head of the stairs. She was beautiful, her skin reflecting like ebony in the candlelight. ''May I be of any assistance?'' she asked him, her teeth bright, her smile suggestive.

He touched her cheek, his fingers sliding below her ear

and around the nape of her neck. "Thank you," he said, "perhaps . . . another time." She left him and he continued down the hall, passing empty rooms and darkened corridors. Autumn's door was ajar. Brice hesitated, staring down at the sliver of yellow light from her room that angled across the toe of his boot. He could smell her, that slightly sweet hint of jasmine that drifted in her wake when she moved. With one finger he slightly nudged the door.

She stood at the end of the bed, her back to him. Her breeches lay in a heap at her feet. Her shirt dropped from her hand to the foot of the bed. Brice closed his eyes briefly, unable to believe the vision before him was real. Her apricot-colored skin seemed to glow in the tallow light, whiter over her buttocks, but firm. Her legs were slender and long. The loose-fitting linen shirts she wore had adequately hidden the delicate bone structure of her shoulders and the feminine curve of her back. Then she turned, and he almost dropped his brandy.

Shaking, Donovan stepped back from the door, hidden in the darkness of the hallway. He watched her hair slide like copper silk over her breasts, all but hiding their creamy perfection. They were generous breasts, but not too large. They would fill his hand. His eyes trailed downward, over the inward curve of her tiny waist, to the apex of her thighs. He was sweating now. His breeches were uncomfortably tight.

With his tongue he wet his lips and did his best to swallow the low groan of desire that crept up his throat. Autumn was more beautiful than he had allowed himself to believe. Dressed even in her baggy shirt and breeches, she was more woman than most he had met. But now . . .

Gripping the neck of the decanter in a stranglehold, Brice attempted to drag his eyes from that russet triangle. He felt like a kid again, peeking at the native women as they crowded about the Marilius Cove to bathe and swim. Damn Autumn Donovan for making him respond like a kid again.

Autumn opened a bottle of lotion, poured it into her tiny cupped palm and began rubbing it on her arms. Then, propping her foot on the end of the bed she massaged the cream into her thighs, up and down and around, her fingers occasionally brushing that baby fine nest of hair. Her hands moved up, over her stomach to her breasts, and she rubbed them as well until her skin gleamed like white alabaster in the light. A tight smile curved Donovan's mouth. Autumn Donovan could deny her femininity to the rest of the world, but behind closed doors she gloried in her own womanhood.

Her face was serene, her whiskey-colored eyes closed and her gold-tipped lashes a thick brush on her smooth cheeks. He stared at the freckle at the corner of her mouth, then at her lips, curled upward as if she were smiling at some secret thought, or memory. That somehow made him rigid with anger . . . or was it desire? Lust! he thought disgustedly, ashamed at standing in the dark like some perverted voyeur and staring slack-jawed at the vision before him. How his brother could think of Autumn as a child was beyond comprehension. There was nothing child-like in that form, or the sultry way her mouth parted and her tongue darted in and out, moistening her lips.

The thought of his brother with Autumn brought Brice upright. His face flushed. His jaw tensed and the fingers gripping the crystal decanter flexed so rigidly that a thinner glass would have shattered. He had never liked his brother overly much; had tolerated him more than anything, out of necessity. Loz had been right; Roy had undermined and manipulated everyone and everything since he was old enough to lie. Had he somehow manipulated Autumn, too?

Sure, he grunted to himself. Manipulated her right into his bed. And while he was in a besotted state of ecstasy, she convinced him to marry her. He stared at her breasts and swallowed hard. She could probably do a lot of convincing, even if Roy hadn't been drunk.

"Monsieur?"

Brice jumped as the maid he had earlier encountered came up beside him carrying a tray. She looked from him to the door, then back to Brice. She blinked innocently, but her smile was knowing.

"I've brought the young lady tea," she whispered. "Would you care to join her?"

His face burning, Brice stepped back, shaking his head and feeling slightly lower than a worm.

"Good night, monsieur." The girl giggled.

Spinning on his heel, Brice strode as casually as possible to his room.

The sun had barely crested when Autumn left the Great House with Laurence Nelson. She had breakfasted on warm banana porridge and akee. She had slept soundly in the four-poster bed and felt rested enough on this new day to meet whatever obstacles Brice Donovan or her brother might place in her path.

The pungent stench of stewing sugar brought Autumn to a stop just outside the boiling house doors. "You'll get used to it," Nelson assured her. Autumn wasn't so certain. Still, she knew if she was to rebuild Hunnington to its former worth, she must pay close attention to the workings of Nelson's estate. Loz had been kind enough to plead an excuse when Brice ventured into town, remaining at the house voluntarily to show Autumn just where she should begin her efforts when returning to Cayemite.

"First, you'll need the employees," he stated, raising his voice to be heard over the *busha*'s thundering order to "skim light!"

"We have employees," Autumn responded. She mopped her brow and wondered how anyone could work in the enclosed surroundings with four fires burning beneath *taches* of bubbling, spewing liquid.

Loz rolled his shirtsleeves up to his elbows and nodded. "You have Hugh Tyler and two dozen Indians who won't work unless given money. Patrick Donovan was a good man, with good intentions, but by freeing his slaves he gave them every right to leave the island if they so chose. Unfortunately most of them did."

Autumn stepped from the building and stared toward the three huge steel cylinders that were pressing the yellow juice from the cane. "But the Indians—"

"Like all free men, the Indians and remaining blacks won't work for nothing. They have families to feed and clothe, and with no maît to provide them with even the simplest of necessities, they demand the salary they feel they deserve."

"And Patrick couldn't pay them?"

"Wouldn't pay them fairly. So many of the bloody buggers took off to the hills. You'll meet them yet. They've survived very nicely up on Trempe Mountain."

They wandered farther down the well-plodded path, past barns and pens of cattle, goats and pigs. Everywhere men, women and children were scurrying to their chores. She was reminded of Palmyra, but even Palmyra had not teemed with such energy.

"You'll need to hire a bookkeeper," Loz went on. "I suspect Hugh has done a respectable enough job, but he has his limitations. You also need a mason, a carpenter, a blacksmith and a cooper, if you intend to reopen the mill. Those damned fermenting casks are always in need of repair."

They returned to the house. Loz was met at the door by a young girl toting a great silver tray, and on it, a tankard of rum punch, sweetened with cool coconut juice. He accepted the drink before asking the girl, "How is my wife?"

"Resting," she said in her clear, smooth voice.

"She's not ill?" Nelson's face paled noticeably.

"Overly tired, Massa Nelson; nothing more."

Loz frowned and said softly, "By Jove, Dani, I wish this ordeal was over. I'm not certain my nerves will stand this tedious waiting."

Dani's robust laughter filled the entrance hall. Tucking the tray beneath her arm, she smiled then at Autumn and teased, "He act like the only mahn whose wife have baby."

A sheepish smile on his face, Nelson turned back to Autumn and admitted, "She's my life; what can I say? without Shelley all of this would mean nothing."

Autumn thought of those words all the way into town. She was still thinking about them when she met Mary outside the hostelry. Her sister-in-law greeted Autumn with open arms. "Have you had a tolerable visit with Mr. Donovan?" Mary asked, planting a brief kiss on Autumn's cheek.

"I suppose tolerable is an appropriate word," Autumn answered with a half smile. Hooking arms, they strode leisurely down the broadwalk to the center of the small town. "Where is Mitchell?"

"Sleeping. He was coaxed into one of those horrible card affairs last evening and couldn't tear himself away until dawn. He's to meet us at luncheon, however, as is Mr. Donovan."

Her step faltering, Autumn looked sideways at Mary. "Oh?"

"Oh, yes. I saw him earlier. He was on his way to the bank, I believe; something about extending credit and robbing Peter to pay Paul." Mary laughed gaily and confessed, "I fear I barely listened. The man is attractive enough to make even me giddy in the mind. He was as cantankerous as a bear, though. He slammed the door of the establishment so loudly I heard it all the way down here."

The bank. Autumn stared down at the paper in her hand, a letter of introduction to Mr. Amos Edwards, executor of credit, from Laurence Nelson. Frowning, she crumpled it up and flung it among the boxes of garbage that lay strewn along the streets. She had never been one to accept charity from others. She had no intention of starting now.

The Bank of Jamaica was small compared to those in Charleston. Autumn stood inside the establishment, regarding the three closed doors at the far end of the room. Finally a stoop-shouldered man with wire-rimmed spectacles looked out from behind his cage and asked, "May I help you ladies?"

It took a poke in the back from Mary before Autumn moved forward. "Is . . . is Mr. Amos Edwards in?"

He squinted slightly to see her clearly in the shadows. "Is he expecting you?"

"No." She shook her head.

At that moment a door opened. A tall man with gray hair stepped from the office, his eyes falling expectantly on Autumn and Mary. "A young lady to see you, sir," the man with the glasses announced.

"You don't say." Edwards's beaming smile put Autumn at ease. "And you are?"

"Donovan." Autumn stressed the name. "Autumn Donovan. Roy Donovan's wife."

A look of surprise and befuddlement flashed over the banker's features before he responded, "I see." Rearranging his expression slightly, Edwards approached, extending his hand. "My condolences, Mrs. Donovan, on the loss of your husband. I must admit . . . I wasn't aware that Roy had married."

At Edwards's reference to Roy's death, Autumn glanced at Mary. She had suspected her sister-in-law was aware that Brice was not her husband, but she hadn't been certain. Mary smiled knowingly before looking back at the stranger. Autumn released her breath.

"Please, Mrs. Donovan, come into my office." He escorted Autumn and Mary into the comfortable room. It smelled of beeswax and leather. The window behind his desk looked out over the bay. Autumn sank into one of the matching high-backed chairs before his desk and tried to draw some courage from the view out that window. "How can I help you?" Edwards prompted, sitting down behind his desk.

Autumn stared at his square hands, at his well-manicured nails, at his fingers now folded casually together, and wished she hadn't discarded Nelson's letter. "I . . . I need money, Mr. Edwards."

Those fingers opened, then closed a little more tightly together. "I see," the banker said.

"I intend to restore Hunnington Hall," Autumn added bravely.

Edwards's brows bounced up and down, first in surprise, then concern, before he responded in a flat voice, "Then you're here about a loan, Mrs. Donovan." His eyes, for the first time, appeared to acknowledge her breeches.

"Yes." Autumn squeezed her knees tightly together, thinking the room had grown uncomfortably warm.

"That would take a rather sizable loan. Have you some sort of collateral?" he asked her.

"Collateral?"

"Something of equal value—"

"Oh, certainly," she interrupted, smiling. "Hunnington Hall."

Edwards sat back in his chair rather suddenly. "Hunnington . . . My dear lady, you wish to risk the chance of losing Hunnington Hall on such a venture?"

"I shan't lose Hunnington Hall. I fully intend to restore the estate to a profitable plantation."

"Do you realize what size loan we are discussing, Mrs. Donovan?"

"A rather sizeable one, I imagine."

Leaning forward, the man asked, "Have you full title to Hunnington Hall?"

Autumn swallowed hard. "It is owned by the Donovans free and clear, I believe."

"Donovans?"

"I own half of the estate, Mr. Edwards. Brice Donovan owns the other half."

"And does he know you are here?"

"No." Autumn stared out the window.

"I'm sorry, Mrs. Donovan, but in such a case I can do nothing without approval from both parties. If you were to default, Mr. Donovan would lose his half of the estate as well. It simply cannot be done without his permission." Again sitting back in his chair, Edwards smiled so condescendingly Autumn felt like spitting. "I really think you should reconsider this idea of mortgaging Hunnington Hall. Perhaps we could arrange a much smaller loan, something to help you purchase a few trinkets for the house—"

"I wish to buy steel rollers and *taches,* Mr. Edwards, not trinkets for the house. I would like money to pay our employees fairly until the cane is cut, milled and sold."

Edwards sat a little straighter.

"Hunnington is a dry-weather estate and should yield approximately two and a half tons of cane per acre. From my recent inspection of the property I would estimate that there are one hundred acres of cane that could be harvested, had I the manpower to do it. But to hire them and pay them wages, I must have money."

"This is *most* unusual, Mrs. Donovan."

Autumn left her chair. Her slender shoulders squared,

she looked down into the man's dazed face and asked, "Are you refusing me the loan, Mr. Edwards?"

"I'm sorry. I cannot mortgage Hunnington Hall without Mr. Donovan's permission. Perhaps we might assign something smaller, were you to have a cosigner on the loan—"

"A cosigner?"

"Someone who would be willing to fulfill your monetary obligation should you be unable to meet your financial responsibility."

"But, I don't know—"

"Oh!" Both Autumn and Edwards looked toward Mary and her little gloved hand fluttering for attention. "I'll be more than happy to sign such a loan," Mary exclaimed, her cheeks flaming with excitement.

Edwards lifted one brow. "You, madam?"

"Oh, certainly: I'm her sister-in-law, you see." She looked at Autumn.

"I see. And you, madam, are financially able to shoulder the loan in case it is forfeited to you?"

"Of course. My husband owns one of the largest and most productive cotton plantations in Charleston. That's in South Carolina, you know."

Edwards smiled the same smile he had earlier bestowed on Autumn. "That's most generous of you, dear lady, but your husband will have to sign the note."

"But that's impossible!"

"I'll sign the note," came a resonant voice from behind them. Autumn whipped her head around and Mary jumped from her chair. Both looked up into Brice's smiling face. "Ladies," he greeted them.

Her eyes narrowing in anger, Autumn demanded, "Is your eavesdropping at open doors a habit, Mr. Donovan, or simply rude behavior?"

His smile widened. "I wasn't eavesdropping, Missus Donovan. I simply walked out of Mr. Thompson's office and overheard you." Tipping his head toward Mary, he said pleasantly, "You're looking lovely today, madam."

"Oh, my, thank you." Mary blushed and ducked her head.

Autumn blushed, too, as Brice's green eyes cut back to her. "Have you some business here?" she asked him.

"I did. I've done with it now."

"Then good-bye, sir." He didn't move, causing Autumn's face to color further. "Is there something more?" she demanded. Her toes were tingling again, fanning the anger she was feeling over his obvious intent to humiliate her in front of Mary and Amos Edwards.

Brice leaned casually against the doorjamb. He was perusing her with so lazy and insolent an eye she felt like crossing her arms over her breasts. "I like your . . . boots," he finally said.

Clearing his throat, Edwards left his chair. "Mr. Donovan, we were just discussing you."

"Indeed."

"Mrs. Donovan has seen me about a loan."

"I heard."

"There was some discussion about mortgaging Hunnington—"

"No." His eyes softening somewhat, he looked at Autumn directly and shook his head. "I will not allow you to mortgage Hunnington." Up went her chin, and for a moment he wanted to grab those delicate shoulders and shake the stubborn pride from her face. "I will cosign a loan for you, however," he added, anticipating the backlash that would immediately follow.

"I don't need your assistance, Mr. Donovan! Nor do I *want* it!"

"Aha. Then I suppose you'll be asking for your brother's help?"

Frustration and helplessness showed in her face. Visibly shaking, Autumn gripped the back of her chair and considered the ways she would gladly murder Brice Donovan, given the opportunity.

Richard Thompson stepped from his office then. Barreling into the room, he announced brightly, "Oh, good job, Donovan; I'm glad you're still here, old man. You've met Amos, I see. Good! Amos, Mr. Donovan has just reopened Hunnington's line of credit. We are to extend to him and his partner all monetary considerations they might need in restoring Hunnington Hall." He came to an abrupt halt as his eyes found Autumn.

"My partner," Brice murmured in a voice dripping with amusement.

Ignoring Thompson, Autumn stared at Brice. He was standing upright, shoulders filling the doorway, legs braced apart while he slapped his leather riding gloves against his hard thigh. "I don't know what to say," she finally managed, aware of her voice fluctuating maddeningly between excitement and disbelief.

"You might try 'Thank you.' "

Relief melted the obstinancy from Autumn's face. She would never have gone to Brice Donovan to plead for his help, truly believing he would turn her down. But he was not only offering her his acquired resources but was willing to cosign a loan so she might have her own, as well. "Thank you," Autumn said, and smiled.

Donovan watched those rose-red lips turn up in the same sultry way they had the evening before, and the memory of those few secret moments caused the blood to simmer in his veins. Aware that this was no place to let such ardor show, he turned abruptly from the door and flung back over his shoulder, "Your debts are mounting up, my love. You might begin to consider just *when* you intend to pay me back."

Autumn and Mary followed Donovan from the bank, Autumn doing her best to ignore Mary's inquisitive glances, and Mary doing her best to keep up with Autumn's longer stride. "Oh, do slow down," Mary finally beseeched her. "I fear I'm going to expire in this intolerable heat."

Autumn watched Donovan's retreat up the street, noting the women who coyly smiled and flirted as he passed. "What did you say?" she asked, turning back to her friend.

"It's dreadfully hot, don't you think?"

"I hadn't noticed."

Primly blotting her upper lip with a handkerchief, Mary sighed and looked after Donovan. "No, I suppose you hadn't, dear."

On tiptoe Autumn peered over several shoulders, taking great interest in the young lady who appeared to have caught Brice's eye. "Oh, for heaven's sake," she muttered under her breath. "The ninny has dropped her kerchief."

"What?"

"What a thoroughly feminine thing to do, dropping a hankie at his feet."

Mary laughed and waved hers under Autumn's chin. "Would you care to borrow mine, dear?"

"Certainly not." Autumn glared down at Mary before both turned up the street.

Wyndham's was packed with the luncheon crowd. Donovan had found his way to Mitchell's table, as had Loz Nelson. Autumn desperately hoped Nelson would avoid asking her about his letter of recommendation, then, realizing he was aware of her situation with Mitchell, decided she had little to fear. All three rose from their chairs as she and Mary approached.

Mitchell jumped immediately to attend his wife. "You look ravishing as always, my dear. Have you had a pleasurable morning?"

Donovan moved around the table, reaching for Autumn's chair. She took it before him, however, leaving him empty-handed, as she had the night before. Sensing his irritation, she threw her head back slightly and needled sweetly, "Sorry, old man, but I thought you might be too fatigued from gathering hankies from the street to bother with me."

"Au contraire," he responded with a startling smile. "I rarely find beautiful women fatiguing, but I must admit to a certain boredom with breeches-clad poseurs who cannot decide *what* they are."

A sleepy-eyed waiter ambled to the table.

"By Jove, it's warm," Nelson remarked. Pulling at his shirt collar, he proclaimed, "I think I should like a rum punch."

"Make that two," Donovan said, taking his chair.

"Three!" Mitchell added.

"Four!" Autumn announced, and all heads swiveled her way. Setting her chin, she stared back with determination.

Mitchell went pale, then, as Mary declared, "That will be five, sir. Five rum punches to quench our thirst!"

They began their meal with turtle soup. Mutton pie and yams followed. Mary, to everyone's concern, had grown quite giddy from her punch and rambled good-naturedly about everything from sewing to the deteriorating state of the economy. The room buzzed with lively conversation, the tinkling of crystal mingling with the denser, heavier thud of pewter tankards against the tables. A burst of laughter every now and again seemed to coax the ongoing conversations to a higher pitch.

The gay chatter diminished so gradually that no one in Autumn's party noticed, until finally the only voice heard throughout the strangely quiet room was Mary's tipsy babbling. As all about the table became aware of the silence, they glanced at one another expectantly, then looked around the room. All eyes were transfixed on the door.

Autumn knew the moment she put eyes on the woman who she must be, though she had never seen her face except in her imagination. But she had known the moment Brice Donovan called out her name in his sleep that she would be more beautiful than anyone she had ever met. She was, Autumn thought, with a shaky sense of desperation, the most beautiful woman she had ever seen.

Slowly the woman crossed the room. Her perfect hips, outlined beneath clinging emerald silk, swiveled gracefully from side to side. Her plunging décolletage was far too daring to be acceptable, yet there was not one man or woman in the establishment who did not look upon Annee Rose with anything but awe. She slowly passed tables with slack-jawed men who clambered to their feet and bowed, as if paying homage to royalty. Yet she never turned her startlingly brilliant violet eyes to theirs.

Onward she came, past gaping waiters who appeared to have forgotten the trays of food balanced upon their palms. Her red lips parted in silent laughter as one ogling man's wife, with a huff, flounced from her chair and, with nose in the air, left Wyndham's in a flurry of taffeta skirts. Onward she came, her eyes never straying, the swish of silk and the light tap of her parasol upon the floor the only sound in the room. Onward . . . straight toward Donovan.

He hadn't moved. Even as Nelson and Mitchell left their chairs, he stared down into his rum punch, face set, the tips of his fingers white to the cuticle as he gripped the

pewter rim of his tankard. His brow was moist. The smile
tugging at one corner of his mouth was hardly pleasant, a
grim curl that hinted at silent fury. Autumn wasn't certain
which disturbed her more: Annee or the effect she was
having on Brice.

Still, Autumn watched him. She couldn't do otherwise.
Her face was burning—for Donovan's discomfort, for her
own comprehension of why he would leave her own bed
for Annee's. Annee Rose was the *other woman*, at least in
the eyes of her brother. Yet she realized with a jolt that
Annee Rose was the other woman in her own eyes as well.

Then, with great effort, Brice forced his eyes from
inside the walls of that pewter tankard and looked at
Autumn. Not at Annee, but at *her*. They were pleading,
those opaque pools of green, so full of question and confusion, anger and desperation, that they seemed to say,
"Help me."

Autumn reached over and took his hand.

The swirl of silk and the rap of Annee's parasol stopped.
They continued to stare, Autumn at Brice and Brice at
Autumn, while around them the entire room was buzzing
with twitters of curiosity.

Donovan looked down at their hands, found some strength
there, and took a breath. Only then did he look up at
Annee.

Chapter 9

"Hello, Donovan."

He left his chair very slowly, forgetting the napkin on his lap that tumbled in a crisp heap to the toe of his boot. His knees were shaking, and he thought, as he swallowed nervously, that he would embarrass himself further by croaking his reply. So he didn't respond at all.

Annee slanted him a smile as she faced Donovan's staring companions. "Gentlemen," she greeted Mitchell and Loz. Then to Nelson she asked, "Is your wife better?"

He smoothed back his hair rather nervously before responding in a curious tone, "Better?"

"She was ill this morning. Tired, I think."

"But how . . ." He blinked, frowned and accepted her extended hand. "Charmed," was all he could manage.

She turned then to Mitchell. "Sinclair," she purred smoothly, a rich sound that flushed his cheeks with color. "You're just as handsome as I imagined."

"I am?"

"Certainly." Tipping her chin toward Donovan, she cooed, "Won't you introduce us, darling?"

Brice waited in wooden silence as Annee lifted her fingers virtually to Sinclair's mouth. Mitchell pressed his mouth against her gloved hand before Brice responded in a tight voice, "Annee Rose. Of the Barrett Plantation." He waited, watching as her eyes shifted to Mary, acknowledged her wide-eyed appraisal with a tolerant smile, then with apparent cordialness, looked down at Autumn.

"So," Annee said softly, "We meet at last."

Autumn said nothing.

"Why, she's charming, Donovan. Simply charming. And as pretty as you claimed. No wonder you became so smitten by her while in Charleston. I know we'll become fast friends. I thirst so for female companionship on Cayemite. It can be such a lonely place, as you'll soon discover, Autumn. May I call you Autumn?''

"Certainly," Autumn responded dryly.

"Wonderful. As soon as we return to Cayemite, we must get together. I've such marvelous tales to share with you, mostly about this scandalous husband of yours. We've known each other since we were children, you know. Why, Donovan has been my *closest* friend for years. Isn't that right, darling?'' She looked at Brice, and smiled.

Brice stepped from behind the table, ignoring the query. Looking down at Autumn, and appearing to forget the others, he allowed her a shadow of a smile and said, "My apologies, but I'm late for an appointment. I'll see you back at the Nelsons' this evening?''

Her face pale, she nodded briefly.

He looked at Annee. His outstretched arm motioning her toward the door, he invited with mocking gentility, "Allow me the honor of seeing you out . . . my love.''

A flash of pleasure and anticipation crossed her features, apparent to everyone around the table. "Yes!" she responded in a giddy voice that sounded oddly out of character for the woman who had mesmerized the room only moments before with her aloofness. Casting a short look down at Autumn, she offered, "Tomorrow we must get together, dear. I'll show you around Montego Bay; there's a delightful little shop that carries the latest fashion plates from Paris. Adieu!''

Brice walked calmly out the door with Annee on his arm, aware of the eyes that followed and the low hum of speculation that vibrated the crystal on the tables. Stepping from Wyndham's, he breathed deeply, allowing the salt air of the cloudless day to cleanse the thoughts of murder from his mind. He lifted his hand, recognizing Annee's chaise in the distance, and whistled at the nodding Negro who had grown drowsy in the afternoon sun.

In a moment the door of the elegant traveling chaise swung open. Brice had not yet acknowledged the woman on his arm. He didn't trust himself to speak to her. But as he caught the tender flesh above her elbow to lift her inside the chaise, the anger he was so desperately controlling became evident enough from his iron grip to bring a soft gasp of surprise and pain from Annee's mouth.

The swooping brim of her hat fluttered in the wind as her face swung around to his. "Get in," he said, looking into her startled eyes.

She did so, feeling her cheeks burning. She stared out the window to her right as the chaise sagged momentarily to one side as Brice climbed in. The door slammed. The hot air inside the confined space was unbreathable.

"Shall we have William lower the calash, darling?" she asked him.

"Don't call me darling. Not now."

"Later, then." Annee tipped a smile his way and sank back against her seat.

William swung the chaise around in the middle of the street. A dog nipped at the horse's hooves before the driver whacked the mutt's scrawny haunches with the tip of his whip. They passed the docks, the sounds of seamen and vendors drifting through the windows of the carriage, distracting Brice momentarily from his anger. But it was there, in his stomach, gnawing its way up through his chest and swelling in his throat.

They traveled the coastline with its snatches of sea grape and clumps of mangrove. It was tortuous riding inside the carriage, the road full of ruts and rocks jostling the riders within. The sun was high in the sky and beating fiercely down on the countryside, too hot, even, for the gulls that were so unnaturally absent. The air burned brilliantly with hard yellow light and bleached the usual sapphire sky colorless.

The chaise was like a furnace. Even so, Brice refused to remove his coat. He sat unmoving, like an oil portrait on canvas, with one crooked elbow propped on the sill of the window and the other outstretched, the palm of his hand resting on his thigh, gloves dangling limply in his hand.

The air radiated with Annee: the nudge of her arm against his as they hit yet another rut in the road, the smell of her perfume, as stifling as it was intoxicating. He thought that if he allowed himself to hang his head out the window he would be sick.

"You're brooding, Donovan." Annee's voice came so

suddenly and tonelessly, Brice flinched. He squeezed his fingers, choking his gloves. "Have I displeased you?" she asked.

He finally looked her way, down into the milk-white cleavage that quivered above the plunging décolletage. He felt his Adam's apple catch on his cravat as he tried to swallow.

"I thought you would be happy to see me," she went on. Leaning slightly against his tensed arm, she thrust out her full lower lip like a child and teased, "You've hurt my feelings."

"Have I?" he managed to ask, aware his voice sounded as though he'd just swallowed a cupful of dust.

"Certainly. You were such a naughty boy, leaving Cayemite that way, forgetting to mention that you were leaving. You can imagine what I thought."

"No." Brice looked back out the window. "What did you think, Annee?"

"That you had deserted me again. That you had run away with that horrible little breeches-clad urchin your brother had the bad judgment to marry." Her bejeweled fingers drifted down his arm to his thigh. "Are you pleased with the way I played your little game, pretending you were Roy for that cow-eyed brother of Autumn's?"

"Yes." He looked down at Annee's hand and thought of killing her now and being done with it.

"Don't I deserve just a small token of appreciation?" She slanted a glance up into his blank face. "After all, one slip of my tongue and Autumn Donovan would find herself hustled aboard that boat tomorrow and on her way back to Charleston."

Donovan smiled coldly. "Are you blackmailing me, Annee?" Her hand slipped beneath his coat to the tight, hot bulge at the apex of his thighs. He laughed flatly. "I do believe you are."

"You know what I want, Donovan."

Sweat trickled down Brice's temples and behind his ears. "Doesn't Autumn's presence on the island threaten you just a little?" he asked her, watching a bead of perspiration zigzag its way into the cleft between her breasts.

"I can take care of Autumn."

"As you did the others?"

Her chin came up. Her eyes narrowed. "I don't know what you mean."

He caught her wrist as Annee attempted to pull away. Aware that his fingers were crushing the sparrowlike bones at the heel of her hand he squeezed harder and demanded, "Don't play games with me, Annee. It's too damned hot and I'm too damned mad."

Her eyes flashed violet fire. "You're hurting me, Donovan."

"But I thought you enjoyed pain, love."

The excruciating ache slid like quicksilver up her arm and burned into her shoulder. Her breathing quickened. She responded by lifting her mouth to his.

And he did kiss her, brutally—the way she liked it, knowing even as he forced her mouth open with his, his teeth grazing her tongue and the sweat over his upper lip combining with hers, that this was exactly how she wanted it, how she'd planned it. Their tongues danced, as wet as their faces and palms and the secret, forbidden places within the folds of their clothes. They battled for the same air, and unable to share it, broke apart, gasping lungfuls of harsh salt air that dripped with their scent of arousal.

"How much *do* you want it?" he taunted her, pulling away.

Her eyes flew open. "Don't tease," she whined. Unbuttoning the bodice of her dress, she locked his hand to her naked breast. The roll of the chaise knocked him against her and she felt the tightness between her legs knot like a fist around her womb. She was sweating now, all over. She could feel it under her arms, beneath her spine where it lay buried in silk, and between her legs.

Pulling back his hand, Brice leaned out the window and said to William, "Stop here, please."

William stopped the chaise.

"What are you doing?" Annee attempted to sit upright.

"Leaving."

"I won't allow it." She clutched at his arm.

Raking her with insolent eyes, Brice grinned out of the

side of his mouth and said, "Do you intend to stop me, looking like that?"

"You'll walk back to town!"

"Exactly."

He flipped open the door and jumped out into the road. The sun was intense on his shoulders, but the air, at least, was breatheable. No sooner had he closed the door and turned his back to the chaise, than the door flew open again. Annee followed Brice into the sunlight. He didn't turn, but continued walking back toward town, tugging his coat sleeves back down over his wrists and dusting off his lapel as if leaving a woman standing bare breasted in the road was the most natural thing in the world.

"You'll pay!" she screeched behind him.

· He continued walking. The pounding of her feet against the earth, however, was enough warning for him to whirl in time to catch her upraised hands before she could sink her nails into the back of his neck. "No," he said so deadly quiet that her mouth dropped open. "You sank those damned claws once into my back when I wasn't expecting it. You won't do it again."

"It's her, isn't it?" she hissed. "You want *her* now and think you can discard me as if I meant nothing to you. Well, I'll see that little slut off Cayemite if it's the last thing I do, Donovan."

Suddenly his hand grabbed her cheeks, fingers digging so cruelly into her flesh that she couldn't help but whimper. "If you so much as look crossways at Autumn . . ." Brice swallowed his anger, knowing should he give Annee any more reason to hate Autumn, he'd be sealing her fate, as well as his. "I won't be manipulated," he threatened in a soft voice. "And I won't be watched. I came to Montego Bay on business that has nothing to do with you. You had no right to intrude."

She stared up at him with eyes damp and childlike. "I—I was frightened, Brice. Frightened you had left me again. You know I love you, only you. I've never loved another." She pressed her body against his, felt him tremble, and smiled. "You love me, too, Brice. I know it. No other woman could do for you what I could, if you would only—"

"Don't." He backed away, aware that the brief response of his body had been acknowledged by Annee. Before, in the chaise, he had been too angry to think of anything but making her pay for humiliating him in front of Autumn, for humiliating Autumn. But now, anger was struggling with the desire that had sucked stronger men than he under her spell. Added to that, the picture he had carried in his mind of Autumn as she was the night before . . . it was a dangerous mixture that was having a cataclysmic effect on his senses.

She stepped closer, ran her hands inside his coat, around his ribs. Her hips brushed his. "Come home with me, Donovan. I've sent word to have the house opened and dinner prepared. We'll have all night. Just the two of us. I'll make you forget about Hunnington Hall and Autumn Donovan. You'll forget there's another woman on the face of this earth. I swear."

Mitchell ran his hands through his hair before turning frantically from the window. "For heaven's sake, Mary, I was not ogling that woman!"

Mary wailed in response. Forearm over her eyes, she lay on her back on the bed and wept, "You practically made love to her with your eyes. I—I'm so humiliated!"

"Tell her!" he beseeched Autumn. "Tell her I did no such thing!"

Autumn stared at her nails and sighed.

His eyeballs popping, he choked, "You, too? Well, at least I did not leave the establishment with her as did Donovan!"

Mary wailed louder.

Autumn left her chair. "Keep Donovan out of this." She needed no reminders of Brice's desertion.

Mitchell spun on his heel and, lying across the bed, tried one last time to reason with his distraught wife. "It's that damnable punch, sweetheart. It's made you imagine the most despicable things."

"You couldn't take your eyes off her décolletage!"

"It—it was just so—"

"Beautiful?"

"Well . . . yes."

"Oh!"

Mitchell blinked in disbelief as Autumn started for the door. "You can't leave me now. Please, talk with your sister-in-law, Autumn, and remind her I am only human. When a woman that beautiful—"

Mary came off the bed. "Are you implying that *I* am not that beautiful?"

"Oh, for God's sake, Mary, be reasonable!"

"You never stared at *my* breasts like that!"

"You don't *have* breasts like that! What I mean is . . ."

Autumn opened the door. "What do you mean, Mitchell?"

"I mean"—he stared up into Mary's glazed eyes and sputtered—"you don't have breasts that . . . yours are not . . . oh, good grief."

Stepping from the room, Autumn quietly closed the door behind her.

The streets were busy. Autumn stood outside the hostelry and stared at the people moving hurriedly about the businesses. She spotted Nelson. Loz dodged around the ox-drawn wagons and milling bondsmen who were weaving through the throng with baskets of fruit on their shoulders. He shot her a dazzling smile as he stepped up beside her.

"Is Mary better?" he asked.

She shook her head and tried to smile.

"Oh, dear." Loz mopped his damp brow with a handkerchief while looking out across the bay. "That's a shame."

"I fear it was the punch."

"Combined with the heat."

"Yes," she said. "It was the heat."

They both knew it was Annee.

Tucking his kerchief into the inside pocket of his coat, Loz feigned a lighthearted tone and offered, "I have wonderful news."

"Oh?" She stared down the road and wondered if the news had anything to do with Donovan.

"I spoke with Mr. Weir. The rollers I ordered last spring to expand my mill should be arriving within the next few days. I can have them shipped directly over to Cayemite. I shouldn't mind reordering a new set and waiting a few months to begin my own expansion."

He caught her arm and both moved out of the hostelry door. They continued walking, not bothering to talk as they passed the construction of a new business; the din of hammering and sawing would only drown out their conversation.

"Thank you," she finally said, when the noise was behind them.

They walked toward the wharf, finding it a quieter place, and cooler. At the end of Bachman's Dock a fat Negro woman squatted, shoulders bared to the sun and skirt hiked to the tops of her heavy thighs. Around her were bowls of fruit, black with flies; on mahogany trays at her feet were mounds of sticky cakes made from sugar. A dog sniffed at one of the trays, then tucked its tail between its legs as she shooed it away.

As they stopped at the end of the dock, Loz stared out at the droghers, watching their small white sails hurry them into the bay. Finally he asked, "Would you like to talk about it?"

"It?" Autumn wished she were a better liar.

"Donovan and Annee."

"No. I don't think so."

"I warned you about her, you know. She'll stop at nothing to get him." He cocked a conspiratorial glance at Autumn and teased, "You must fight fire with fire, my charming child, if you wish to douse the inferno."

"I didn't come here to fight fires."

"No? Then why *did* you come to Cayemite?"

"To find my husband."

Loz laughed quietly, then added, "Don't skirt the issue. Were you running from a man, or to one?"

"Neither."

He looked around.

"I came to Cayemite because I was lured here. Roy offered what no other man had been willing to do. He promised I was under no obligation to conform to the normal obligations of marriage and would have the freedom to do whatever I wanted with Hunnington."

"Define normal."

"Children."

He stared. "I see. You don't want children. You don't like them?"

"Quite the contrary. I like children. I just don't care to . . . have any." The admission brought color to her face. She was thankful when the wind blew her hair across her cheek.

"Well." Loz's voice sounded slightly disappointed. "You certainly married the man for that. Roy loathed children and everything they stood for."

"I don't loathe children," she said quietly to herself, surprised at her own adamance.

Staring again out over the water, Nelson asked bluntly, "Is that the reason for the breeches and baggy shirts? You honestly believe that if you dress in that getup, men will find you so unappealing they wouldn't want to have children with you?"

Autumn glared up at him and demanded, "Why shouldn't women dress any way they desire, Mr. Nelson? By what right does someone dictate to us that we must dress in a particular way to be accepted?"

Facing her, his arms out to his sides and palms turned up, he answered, "For the same reason I'm standing out in this heat with this damnable coat on, Mrs. Donovan. It is an established convention."

"And you, Mr. Nelson, are sweating buckets, while I, on the other hand, am simply pleasantly warm and not soaked in my own perspiration." She twirled on her toe and stormed back down the dock.

Nelson remained, mopping his face with his sweat-dampened kerchief and staring out to sea.

The stench of fermenting rum hung about the city. Combined with the decay of garbage and offal that lined the streets, the smell was enough to turn Autumn's stomach. She thought of checking on Mary, then decided against it. She thought of shopping, but the small, dingy businesses lining the dusty streets didn't seem to offer much in the form of afternoon recreation. Still, she stopped outside one shop and stared for a long moment through the window at the bolts of brightly colored material within.

"Lady see something she like?" came the lilting voice behind her.

Autumn focused on the image reflected in the window. The woman's dark face broke out in a smile. Before Autumn could respond, the Negress gently took her arm, and led her into the store.

It was close inside; the only light in the room filtered through the streaked window in pale yellow shafts that highlighted floating particles of dust. The proprietress of the shop left Autumn's side and sauntered unhurriedly around the burdened tables of gray and blue osnaburg. She stopped behind a counter piled high with brightly colored plumes, picked up a blood-red flower, freshly picked, and offered it to Autumn.

"You see something you like?" she asked Autumn again.

Autumn moved her eyes around the store. In one corner, tucked between bolts of cheesecloth and velvet, were several rounds of cheese. A ham was suspended from the ceiling. Tins of tea and bottles of wine were nestled against the wall farther back. Gentlemen's boots were lined up on the floor. On a table close to the window were ladies' gloves and ribbons of every color imaginable. But it was the clay figure of a woman that caught her eye.

"What is this?" She carefully picked up the fragile piece, gently running her finger over the contours of the woman's nude curves.

"Zemi," the woman responded. "You like?"

"Zemi?"

"Indian spirit." She pointed to another, sitting further back. "That different zemi. Both good spirits and bring much good luck."

"They're very beautiful." Autumn smiled, wondering why she should be so moved by such a simple trinket.

The Negress's throaty laughter responded. "They much like you," she continued. "See?" Pointing to the flowing hair and wide eyes she said, "She bring you good magic. Mattie know, when I see you out front, what you would like. You need good magic in your life."

"Do I?" Autumn laughed, but didn't look up.

"There be shadow behind you," the woman said, and this time Autumn looked up. She looked behind her, misunderstanding the woman's remark. "Evil," the Negress explained.

A chill crept in, causing Autumn to shiver. She shifted her eyes about the room wondering from where the draft had suddenly appeared.

Leaning her immense girth over the table, the proprietress picked up the statue and held it in a shaft of light. "This one will keep you safe. That one," she pointed to the object in Autumn's hand, "will keep you happy. You take both."

Autumn shook her head. "I can't."

"But you must."

"I've no money with me."

"You bring money another time. Take both zemis. You must feed them each day and they will protect you from evil. Someday"—her face beamed Autumn a bright smile—"someday you will thank Mattie. You'll see."

Chapter 10

She saw the cloud of dust ahead of her before she saw the rider. Autumn stopped her horse and waited.

Billy Boyd, the Nelson's stable boy, emerged from the dust and reined his horse by Autumn. "It's Missus Shelley!" he proclaimed. "I'm searchin' fo' d'massa!"

"In town. Is Shelley all right?"

"D'baby is fair near t'comin', yes'm. You know where d'massa be?"

Her heart turning over, Autumn shook her head.

"Lawd, Lawd," he groaned. Digging the heels of his bare feet into the horse's flanks, he tore off down the road toward town, leaving Autumn to stare with dread back up the road before she continued toward the Nelson house.

The doors and windows were open, allowing every breeze to enter the house. No sooner had Autumn scrambled from her horse than Dani appeared on the front porch, waving one skinny arm and yelling, "Missus Shelley be calling for you all morning. Hurry!"

Autumn froze.

"Come on," Dani coaxed her.

Swinging the cotton bag slowly from her shoulder, Autumn stared down at the zemises and released her breath.

Shelley looked up as Autumn entered the room. "Oh, Autumn, you're back." Shelley's face was a brilliant red. Her honey-blond hair, wet and clinging to her brow, was now dishwater-brown. She lay on her back in the center of her bed, knees up and open and draped with a sheet. Smiling unsteadily she asked, "Will you stay awhile? Until my husband comes?"

Autumn stood in the door, unable to move.

"Have you had a pleasant day?" Shelley stared at the ceiling.

"I drank rum punch at Wyndham's." It was the only thing pleasant she could recall about her day.

"Really!" Rolling her head toward the door, Shelley laughed gaily, blinked the sweat from her eyes and teased, "We'll make an islander out of you yet. Did you see Brice?"

"I saw him. He's with Annee now."

"Oh." Shelley motioned Autumn in. "You must tell me all about it."

After assuring herself Shelley was experiencing no discomfort at the moment, Autumn cautiously approached the bed.

"Sit." Shelley pointed to the chair beside the bed. Autumn sat.

"What have you there?" She referred to the bag dangling from Autumn's fingers.

"Zemis."

"Really! Will you show me?"

"Are you certain you're up to it?"

"Certainly. Show me your zemis." Shelley's eyes grew wide with pleasure as Autumn extracted the first statue. "Why, Autumn, she looks like you."

"Does she?"

"And the other?" When Autumn held the figure high, Shelley laughed and asked, "Whatever are you doing with that?"

"The woman said it would keep me happy."

"I certainly think it would. It's a zemi of fertility."

Suddenly Shelley clutched her bedding and buried her head back into her pillow. Autumn leapt out of her chair. Shelley gasped for air, then begged, "Oh, do give me your hand, Autumn!"

Autumn stared blankly at the damp palm waving pitifully in the air. She took it, then sank back down into her chair.

"That's better. Oh, my. It is hot today, isn't it?" Curling her fingers around Autumn's, Shelley smiled weakly, and said, "It is good to have you here. It's not often I meet young women close to my own age. I know we'll become wonderful friends, you and I. I knew it the moment Loz brought you and Brice home. We'll visit. You will come here for a week and we shall come to Cayemite for a week. Perhaps two. Did you say you had spoken to Brice?''

"He's with Annee.''

"Oh, well. We'll simply have to do something about her, won't we?''

Autumn closed her eyes, awash with shame. She wanted nothing more than to run from this room, from this house, from this island—from the ordeal she must face with her friend.

"Is something wrong?'' came the soft query.

Looking at Shelley with imploring eyes Autumn asked, "Is the pain unbearable?''

"Is that what's bothering you?'' Shelley squeezed her friend's fingers. "Please don't worry. The pain is intolerable only for a moment. It's worth it in the end.''

Not if you're dead, she thought. Please don't die, she thought.

"We've waited so long for this baby. I dare say Loz will make a fool of himself over the child.'' Gripping Autumn's hand more tightly, she forced, "Have you seen my husband?''

"In town.'' Autumn squeezed back and leaned more closely to the bed. "He's selling me the rollers he bought last spring so I might begin harvesting soon.''

"I thought he might. He thinks a great deal of you. And Brice . . . oh . . . they are like brothers. Closer, even, than brothers, I think.'' She stared at the ceiling and panted. Sweat rolled down her temples. "Did—did you know Brice lived here for two years?''

"In Jamaica?'' She clutched Shelley's fingers with both hands.

"Here. In this house. When it belonged to Loz's father. Patrick, he . . . b-banished Brice from . . . oh, Autumn, help me!''

"I'm here!''

"Aren't I silly? Silly me!''

"You're not. The pain must be terrible.''

"Yes. Yes, it is. Bu-but it's worth it, isn't it?''

"Would you like some water?''

"Yes, I think so. When the pain ends. Forgive me for making you sit here. Would you like to leave?"

"No."

"Are you certain? I wouldn't blame you, you know. Leave if you like."

"No." She felt stronger for saying it.

Dani came in. She threw the sheet back from Shelley's knees. Autumn stared down at her friend's nude stomach and became light-headed. "Open wide, Missus Shelley, so I can tell what's happening." Autumn watched in disbelief as Dani gently probed with a greased hand inside her friend. "It's gonna be a while," Dani said.

Shelley smiled calmly at Autumn. "I'll have that water now."

Autumn quickly fetched the pitcher and glass that were placed near the window. Returning to the bed, she lifted Shelley's head slightly from her pillow and nudged the glass onto her mouth. Dani left the room and returned with a basin of cool water and a cloth. Autumn took it and bathed her friend's brow.

Shelley watched drowsily as Autumn wrung the cloth into the basin. "Did you love Roy?" she suddenly asked.

Their eyes met.

"No."

"Then you couldn't understand. Not really."

Autumn studied the cloth, folding and unfolding and folding it again.

"My going through this pain must seem so silly to you."

"I don't think that at all."

"Autumn Donovan, you're a terrible liar. You're wondering why a woman would endure this ordeal for a man. Aren't you?"

Autumn crossed her arms and stared out the window. "I think you probably had little choice in the matter." There. She had admitted it and felt better for it. Her head swung around as Shelley laughed.

"No one made me have this baby. As a matter of fact, Loz was more than concerned about putting me through this. But I had some say-so in the matter. There are precautions I might have taken. We aren't forced to have children if we don't want to."

Autumn stared down at Shelley. "Then, why?"

"Because I love him."

"Can you love a man and *not* want his baby?"

Shelley looked up through spiked lashes with surprise on her face. "I can't imagine that. Living with the ache forever . . . well . . ."

"Ache?"

"To have his child. I can't explain it. You'll know it when it happens. Like you know when you fall in love. The ache starts in your heart and melts into your stomach. It's in every breath you cannot find when he enters the room, in every jolt you get when he touches you with his eyes." Conspiratorially, she lowered her voice and admitted, "My breasts tingle when Loz enters the room."

Autumn felt her face color.

"Oh, my. Have I embarrassed you?"

"No. I was only . . ." Thinking about my toes, she thought.

They both looked around as Loz entered the room. His face was white as he fell to one knee beside the bed and grabbed Shelley's hand. He couldn't speak. Just pressed her palm against his mouth and closed his eyes.

Shelley smiled into Autumn's eyes before staring more seriously at her husband. "Have you had a pleasant day?" she asked him.

He shook his head and pressed her hand more firmly against his face.

"I was just telling Autumn: It's terribly hot, isn't it?"

Loz nodded.

Lifting her head slightly off the pillow she asked, "Would you like a punch, darling? No? A powder, perhaps?"

"I—" He cleared his throat and began again. "I wish I could go through this for you."

Autumn backed away.

"Silly boy," Shelley teased. "Would you deprive me of something I have yearned for since the moment I met you?"

"If it meant saving you from the pain. I cannot bear the thought of your going through it alone."

"But I'm not alone. Autumn is with me. And Dani. Isn't it wonderful that Brice is here as well?" Her head dropped back then; her hands clawed at his.

"Shelley!" he said. "Oh, help her, please!"

Autumn turned her back on the scene and stared out the window, her mind swimming with memories: her mother's face, her stepmother's and Millie Tims's. And there were the faces of Millie's husband and Autumn's father—one tired and haggard and uncaring, the other disappointed only briefly. There would be other women to have other babies, after all. This caring, this sharing, this love Autumn was witnessing was something new. And it shook her. It rocked the very foundation on which she had mapped out her life. Men wanted women for only one reason: children. And women were expected to comply, whether they wanted to or not.

And what about the pain each woman had so stoically faced? Shelley Nelson had sworn it was worth it. How could anything be worth the suffering she was now enduring? How could anything be worth the sacrifice of one's own life?

She turned, glared at Nelson's back and wondered if Shelley's breasts were tingling now.

"Oh, God."

Loz's lamentation made Autumn's brow pucker with concern. "I think you should go," she told him. He looked around, his mouth twisted to one side and his lower lip gripped between his teeth. "I think you should go," she repeated.

"Autumn's right." As the contraction eased, Shelley peered dazedly at her husband and smiled. "You'll only upset yourself, dear."

He blinked at Autumn. "You won't leave her?"

"No."

"Well." He squeezed Shelley's hands in his and released his breath. "I don't know."

Shelley licked her lips and Autumn knew by watching the sheet grow taut across her belly that her friend was contracting again.

Hesitantly, Loz moved to his feet. "Are you certain?" he asked his wife.

"Please." Her fingers gripped the bed sheet; sweat beaded her brow.

He stood rooted to the floor until Autumn, sensing Shelley's desperation, grabbed his arm and ushered him to the door. "It's for the best," she assured him.

"But I—"

"But nothing. You're a hindrance, Mr. Nelson."

"A hindrance!" His long legs seemed to tangle up with one another as she shoved him toward the door. "But she's my wife."

"You should've thought about that before you got her in this situation."

She slammed the door in his face as he yelled, "But that's why she's in this situation!"

Leaning against the door, Autumn looked back at Shelley and said, "Now!"

Her shoulders curling toward her breastbone and hips burrowing into the mattress, Shelley pushed until her face turned as red as the fire under her husband's *taches*. She fell back on the bed then and panted, looking to the ceiling. "Thank you," she managed to say after a moment. "I thought he would never leave." Getting no response, Shelley looked toward the door. "You don't look so good yourself, Autumn. Would you like to leave as well?"

"Yes."

"But you won't."

"No."

"Are you certain?"

"No."

Shelley closed her eyes and laughed. "I'm glad you're here," she said. "Awfully glad you've stayed."

Heel to toe, there were exactly thirty-five feet from one wall of the Nelson's bedroom to the other. Autumn had counted them no less than a dozen times in the last three hours. The contractions were coming more frequently now. It was less than two minutes since the last one. Shelley's water had broken with the last onslaught; now they would wait again.

Oh, but she was tired of waiting! Autumn paced again to the bed and pressed a cloth against Shelley's damp brow, thinking that if she sweated any more, she'd wither like a raisin. Her friend was dozing between each contraction; her lids fluttered as Autumn skimmed the hair back from Shelley's brow with her fingers.

"It's taking too long." Shelley's voice was dry.

Autumn didn't respond, just sat down heavily into the chair and leaned her elbows on her knees.

Shelley opened her eyes. "Am I going to die?"

"I'm going to die, Autumn." Those had been Autumn's mother's last words.

"No. I won't let you die."

She'd said those words *then*, too. It was hard to believe them now.

"If it comes down to me or the baby—"

"It won't."

"Take the baby."

"Why?"

"He deserves to live. I am half-finished with my life. While he . . . well, he can do it all over again. He can do all the things I dreamed of as a child. He can play all the games I long to play but am too old to play. He can dream of growing up while I . . . can only dream of growing old."

She took Shelley's hand. "Let's not speak of dying."

Shelley smiled weakly. "All right."

Yet the thought was there. As the pain washed over her friend again and the contraction contorted Shelley's face and hands and abdomen, the overwhelming urge to flee the room and horsewhip Laurence Nelson made Autumn giddy. How dare he sit within the sanctuary of well-being in some other part of the house, sipping on sherry—or was it brandy—smoking cigars and boasting that it had all been nothing, and that given the first opportunity, *they* would do it again.

If Shelley Nelson died, she would see to it that Laurence Nelson hung for murder!

The scream was a blast of anguish that sent Autumn scurrying from her chair to the window, then back to the bed, gulping air and attempting to alleviate the woman's pain with comforting words that sounded shallow even to her own ear. Dani was there as well, her face thin beneath high cheekbones and her mouth pursed like a dried berry in August. Her arms were locked tightly across her bosom.

"Do something," Autumn pleaded, and flashes of Millie Tims and Charlotte Sinclair and, yes, Mabel Sinclair, too, popped in and out of her mind, their faces frozen in the grimace that had accompanied them to the grave.

She ran for the door.

Dusk had settled in the corridors. Autumn took the stairs two at a time, dodging in and out of shadows until she reached the bottom. The library door was partially open. She hit it in full stride, sending it flying against the wall. As Nelson pulled his face from his hands she slapped him across the cheek. Once for her mother. Once for her stepmother. Again for Millie Tims.

Hands closed over her shoulders, and spun her around.

"Get your hands off me!" She struggled and beat against the chest and arms that were confining her.

"Hush," he coaxed her. "For God's sake, Autumn, get hold of yourself."

The voice jarred her halfway back to normalcy. "Y-you!" she sputtered up at Brice.

Loz grabbed her arm and twirled her back around. "My wife!" he cried, with frantic eyes and a bleeding lip. Where was Claude Sinclair's and Joe Tims's indifference? "How is my wife?"

"Pregnant!"

"Ah, God; still?"

"This is all your fault!" Autumn accused Loz.

"Autumn, stop it!" Brice shook her.

She turned and with all the power she could muster drove her fist into Donovan's chest. "There!" She gloated at his groan. "And there and there and there!" She did it again and again until he wrapped both his arms around hers and lifted her kicking and squirming from the floor.

Nelson fell back into his chair with a groan.

Brice hauled his spitfire out the door, through the foyer and into an alcove decorated with elaborate rococo moldings of puffing cherubs and tumbling clouds.

"Let me go!" she demanded.

"Like hell."

"Brute! You're all brutes, all animals preening over your damned urges and women be damned!"

"Lower your voice." Brice looked back over his shoulder. Then, pinning her more forcibly against the wall, he peered down into her tear-stained face and asked, "Has something happened?"

"Happened? Oh, my, how could I have forgotten? How could you possibly have known? You've been out with your mistress and up to your hips in silk. Well, let me enlighten you, Mr. Donovan. The dear lady up those stairs is having a baby and has been for these past many hours."

"I know that."

"Do you?"

"I know," he reassured her.

She noticed, for the first time, that his face was pale. His white shirt collar was open and soiled; his cravat was missing.

"You shouldn't have hit him," he said looking into her eyes. "He's suffering enough."

"*He!* And she is not? The woman up those stairs is not a brood mare, Mr. Donovan. Birth for her is not reclining in a field of clover and—"

"I never said it was."

She thumped her fist against his shoulder.

"That's damned annoying, Autumn. And it hurts."

"Good!" She hit him again. "I hope it hurts as badly as my mother and stepmother and Millie Tims hurt. I hope—I hope it kills you like it killed them!" She covered her eyes with her forearm. She didn't mean it—not a word of it. But it helped to say it, nevertheless.

Brice pried her arm away. He stared down into her child's face—wide eyes and freckled nose—and finally understood the reason for her anger and fear and why she had escaped to Cayemite. He understood her breeches.

"Shelley is not going to die," he assured her softly.

Autumn clutched his shirt in her fingers. "They didn't care. Don't you see? The men didn't care whether their wives died as long as they had children to carry on the line. Well *I* won't. Do you hear me?"

"All right. You don't want babies? *We* won't have babies."

She blinked. He smiled. She thought she'd misunderstood. He stopped smiling and wondered what in God's name had happened to his senses.

The wail came from the upper story. "Au-u-ut-u-umn!" and with a lunge, she shoved him aside and ran for the stairs. She beat Loz by two strides and, reaching the room, slammed the door again in his face.

Dani was on her knees between Shelley's legs. "It's coming!" Dani yelled without turning. "Push, Missus Shelley, you can't rest now!"

"I—I can't!"

"The hell you can't!" Autumn responded. In an instant she was on the bed behind Shelley's head, lifting her friend's shoulders from the pillow and sliding her knees beneath her shoulder blades so the woman was sitting partially upright. Shelley reached back and grabbed her hands.

"Push!" Autumn coaxed her.

Shelley's fingernails dug into Autumn's flesh. She pushed. So did Autumn.

"Breathe!" came the next command.

Shelley panted and sweated and tried a little harder. So did Autumn.

Their strength merged and grew and—"Push!"—Autumn wept.

They all pushed: the women and the men, who had materialized through the door. There was a moment of silence, then . . .

"It's a girl!" Dani announced excitedly.

Autumn collapsed back onto the bed.

Loz whirled, grabbed Brice around the waist and lifted him from the floor.

Shelley laughed looking up at the ceiling.

The baby wailed.

Autumn lay on her side in the four-poster bed and asked out loud to herself, "We?" No, no. *"You"* won't have babies." But "you" and "we" sounded absolutely nothing alike. She'd misunderstood, that's all. She'd been crying and he'd been angry. And with Shelley bawling upstairs everything had gotten so confused, she'd simply distorted his words.

Imagine Brice Donovan even considering marriage to her. Why, she was a nuisance. He'd implied that every day since her arrival on Cayemite. Why would a man like that be remotely interested in her? She wasn't overly pretty. Most men teased her about her freckles. Her eyes were a little too wide, and her stride was too long when she walked. And though she could read and write and cipher better than most young women, she wasn't the least bit interested in entertaining a man with babblings from Shakespeare or dashing off invitations to luncheons on the lawn.

She could imagine Donovan with a woman like . . . Annee. Yes, the woman was certainly beautiful enough. She complimented Donovan wonderfully, with her willowy height and fragile features. She could imagine their growing up together, as she and Gregory had, sharing secrets and playing make-believe husband and wife. The difference, Autumn mused, was she had slapped Gregory's hand away and reminded him that if there were to be babies *he* would have to bear them.

The thought of Annee having Brice's baby brought a knot the size of a doubled fist to her stomach.

Then she reminded herself that he was a cad. A cheat. A liar. He was arrogant to the point of boorishness. And he was Roy Donovan's brother, which said a lot. Besides, there was no way she would ever marry again. Why should she? She had everything she had ever wanted: a home to do with what she pleased and a life safe from the excruciating ordeal Shelley had just experienced.

Her stomach growled. Autumn realized she had not eaten since lunch, and thanks to Annee's untimely arrival she hadn't even finished that. She'd stared into her plate of mutton pie and yams until both had congealed into a unpalatable lump.

The memory of lunch brought the memory of Mary and Mitchell's tiff over Annee. And with the thought of Mary and Mitchell came the sinking realization that by this time tomorrow night they would be gone. Gone. Mitchell had been there all her life, so much older and wiser. Then there was Mary. Autumn could still recall the day Mitchell had brought Mary Bedell home to meet their father. Claude had snickered behind her back and called her plain. But Autumn had liked her. And when Claude died, Mary had been there for her always, sometimes a conspirator in her schemes, sometimes not. Mary loved with a loose rein. Oddly enough, it was the times she pulled in those reins that Autumn loved her most.

Distant laughter caused Autumn to roll to her back. She listened in the darkness. There was Shelley's feminine giggling, the hum of Loz's resonant response, and another voice. Leaving the bed, Autumn slipped on her dressing gown, fumbled in the dark with the satin ribbon beneath her chin then tiptoed out of her bedroom. She made her way down the corridor, its breadnut floors reflecting pools of yellow light from sconces placed every few feet on the walls.

Her feet slowed as she neared the master bedroom. She'd forgotten her slippers, she realized, staring down at her toes. Then she studied the arched niches in the wall, each with a Louis XV bust. Between each were plaster ovals of Joseph Vernet's marine scenes in gilded frames. She edged a little closer to the room, and peeked around the door frame.

Shelley looked up and smiled. "Autumn! Oh, do come in, please!"

There was a table laden with fruit and empty tankards that must have held punch earlier. A cloud of smoke that smelled like sweet tobacco hovered against the high ceiling. Candles glowed around the room—Autumn counted six of them with a glance. There might have been more, but as Donovan's gray-green eyes turned up to hers, she forgot about candles and punch and tobacco.

Brice held the baby in the crook of his arm. Sitting relaxed in his chair, with one long brown finger crooked and poised on the baby's chin, he stared at Autumn and smiled in that infuriating way that made her . . . toes tingle.

"Did we wake you?" Loz asked, rising from the chair by Shelley's bed.

"I couldn't sleep." Focusing on her feet, Autumn crossed the room, knowing Brice's eyes were watching. She won-

dered if she would make it as far as the chair before her
knees gave out completely. She perched on the edge of the
chair, thinking her tingling toes had absolutely nothing to
do with Brice Donovan.

"We were just talking about you, Autumn," came Nelson's voice over her right shoulder.

"That must be it, then; my ears were burning." Autumn
pointed to her right ear and smiled.

Shelley smiled back. "I was telling Loz that you really
should be with us to celebrate, considering you're Sara's
godmother."

The blood crawled up her chest and rushed to her ears.

Loz clapped his hands on Autumn's shoulders and teased,
"Darling, you really shouldn't spring that kind of thing on
Autumn. After all, she might not care to be Sara's
godmother."

"But she helped bring Sara into the world! I couldn't
have made it without her, I'm certain." Shelley reached
for Autumn's hand. "Will you, Autumn?"

She'd entered this room feeling like an outsider. Now
they were honoring her with such a request? She'd been
moping in her room, thinking that tomorrow she'd have no
one left in the world, while, all along, her goddaughter lay
snuggled in . . . Her eyes bounced reluctantly from Shelley
to Brice, then back to Shelley. "But if anything happened
to you—"

"Raising her would be your responsibility."

Recalling their conversation on the dock, Autumn looked
up at Loz. He squeezed her shoulder reassuringly. "I'd be
honored," she told him, beaming with pleasure that seemed
to radiate from her entire body.

"Wonderful!" Shelley clapped her hands. Exchanging
meaningful looks with her husband, she added, "And with
Brice as godfather, I can't think of two nicer people with
whom to share our daughter."

Their eyes met and sparred, Autumn's with Brice's and
his with hers. A tiny pink hand waved by a tiny pink arm
jutted under Brice's chin, and the thought hit her that *they*
would be sharing a daughter. And for one heart stopping
moment the child in his arms was theirs. It felt so wondrous, the tears sprang unbidden to Autumn's eyes before

she could remind herself that her emotionalism was not due to such a ridiculous fantasy, but to her family's leaving the next day.

And the ache in her breast had nothing to do with the fact that her heart had melted to her stomach.

Absolutely nothing!

Chapter 11

Donovan was standing at the bottom of the stairs dressed in a fawn-colored nankeen coat, a white shirt open at the throat, buckskin breeches and black knee boots. His feet were braced apart, and his hands were on his hips. Autumn watched his Adam's apple slide up and down as he looked over Dani's head and found her there, half in sunlight, half in shadow, at the top of the landing. He stared at her a full thirty seconds before he realized who she was.

"Is something wrong, Donovan?" Autumn smoothed her kid glove a little tighter onto her hand. She felt so . . . conspicuous!

Brice raised one black brow and stared a little harder.

Loz entered the foyer behind him, bounded up the stairs to Autumn's side and let loose a whistle that made the blood rush to her face. "By Jove, Missus Donovan, you do almost as much justice to that dress as my wife does. You look splendid!"

The compliment was not without its desired effect. Autumn ducked her head slightly and smiled.

"I've brought the chaise around." Loz smiled into her blushing ear before looking down at Brice. "By golly, old friend, I believe you're underdressed."

"So it seems," was all he said.

Excusing himself, Nelson continued down the hall to Shelley's room, his gay whistling saying more than words ever could.

Autumn stood planted at the top of the stairs.

Brice stood planted at the bottom.

Deciding that Donovan had no interest in the mug of rum punch on her tray, Dani disappeared through the nearest door. Autumn followed her with her eyes, wishing she could drink it.

152

She decided to ignore him. But, somehow, ignoring Brice Donovan while she was wearing breeches was much easier than ignoring him dressed as she was. Why could this armor of silk, crinoline and whalebone make her feel more vulnerable than her simple cotton frocks? She felt all fluttery and weak and breathless. Descending those stairs was one of the hardest feats she had ever attempted.

He watched her descend, her gloved hand on the gleaming banister. The skirt of her honey-gold dress reflected in the brass balusters at her side. Occasionally he would catch a glimpse of ivory petticoats beneath the frilled hem of her skirt, the graceful curve of her instep as her toes searched carefully for each step.

She paused halfway down, before the John Booker mirror on the wall, and he expected to see her affect a coy pose and pretend to tame some stray wisp of hair about her temple, perhaps pinch her cheeks to heighten their color. But she didn't even glance at her reflection.

But he looked. He caught a glimpse of the delicate skin behind her ear, of the baby-fine tendrils resting against the lily-white nape of her neck. Her pearl-studded tortoiseshell combs winked in the ray of sun spilling through a window at the top of the stairs, and Brice wanted nothing more than to release the array of curls from the top of her head and send them spilling to her waist, so he could bury his face in them.

She stopped on the second stair from the bottom and stared Donovan in the eye, wishing he would discontinue his cool appraisal and say something.

Finally, he said, "Nice dress."

"It's Shelley's."

"It's still nice."

"Thank you."

"You're welcome."

Without taking his green eyes from hers, he tugged his gloves from the waistband of his trousers and slapped them absently against his leg. "So."

"So." She stared at his mouth, and sure enough, it began to curl up at one end. Autumn felt like giggling. Nerves, she told herself.

"This is the big day, I guess."

She nodded. "You're going into town as well?"

He nodded. "As your *husband*, I should be with you when Mitchell leaves."

"Oh." She appeared surprised.

"Why else would I go into town?"

"Annee."

His face went blank. He had the good grace to blush. "No, I—I'm not seeing Annee."

Her heart flip-flopped. I don't mind, she lied to herself. "Now that Mitchell is leaving, well . . ."

"Well, what?" He was frowning.

"You're free to do whatever you please."

"Am I?"

"Certainly. I know how difficult these past days have been for you—"

"Do you?"

"Certainly." She swallowed and clutched her reticule with both hands. "Now that Mitchell's leaving, we can go our separate ways. We should rarely need to see each other, except at mealtime, of course, and to discuss business. I won't infringe on your personal life in any way." Staring at her toes, she offered, "I'll move my things from your bedroom just as soon as we return to Cayemite."

"That won't be necessary."

Her head snapped up. "Oh?"

"You can have the room."

Oh, no, he's moving in with Annee! she thought.

"I'll move into the other."

"Oh! Oh. Well . . ." Her fingers fluttering around her purse strings, Autumn shook her head. "No, that won't be necessary. I'll move out. Perhaps when renovations are complete, I'll move into another wing."

"Autumn."

Her mouth went dry. Blood pooled in her ears and rang like church bells on Easter Sunday.

"Look at me," he said.

She did.

The slap, slap, slap of leather against his thigh suddenly stopped. He gazed into her face with an intensity that caused his words to ooze like warm molasses through her veins. "About last night . . ."

"Last night?" She nervously checked the tiny earring on her right ear, knowing she hadn't lost it. "Yes?" Her eyes strayed reluctantly back to his.

"We were upset."

"Yes?"

Brice took a deep breath. "I just wanted you to know."

"Go on."

"The things we said, you said; I want you to know I understand your feelings."

"Oh." Her throat ached too badly for her to swallow. She reminded herself that it was only because her brother was leaving in a few hours.

Brice stared at her lips and wondered why he couldn't say what he wanted to say. But the words, *"Autumn, the blunder I made about our having children was a mistake and of all the women in the world I would marry, you would be the last,"* just wouldn't form in his mouth. Instead, he allowed his eyes to fall to the apricot column of her neck, to the fluttering of her pulse at her throat. All the reasons he had rehearsed the previous morning of why he couldn't marry her had disappeared with the jolt of seeing her atop those stairs. Autumn Sinclair Donovan was one of the most beautiful women he had ever known, and it had nothing to do with the dress, with her breeches or her *without* them.

They said nothing during their journey to town. Refusing to look at Donovan, Autumn stared out over the ribbon of sand beside the road. She counted the coconut trees, watched their fringed fronds wave in splashes of green touched with gold as they reflected the sun. Bamboo plumes stood in erect little clumps near the water's edge. Occasionally a patch of blue lignum vitae would catch her eye, a shocking contrast to the vibrant crimson and orange blossoms of the bougainvillea and hibiscus shrubs.

She wished Brice Donovan would find her as interesting as he found the countryside.

Brice stared out the other side of the chaise toward the purple-shaded ridge of mountains jutting from the center of the island, their steep peaks still obscured with morning mist. Toward those mountains, the gradual inclines of earth were framed in a giant checkerboard: great squares of green cane interspersed with the burnt-yellow splotches of grazed pastureland or sections of harvested fields.

He wished Autumn Donovan would find him as enthralling as she did that damned fish-infested ocean.

As they rounded the bend and Montego Bay came into view, with its few businesses backed by a sloping, crescent-shaped sweep of land, dread settled like lead in the bottom of Autumn's stomach. The image of independence, once glowing like gold in her daydreams, now seemed dull when Autumn considered saying good-bye to what little family she had left. And for the hundredth time she asked herself if this was *truly* what she wanted.

"Having second thoughts?" came Brice's voice.

Her eyes swept the terrain before reluctantly finding his. "Are my thoughts so predictable, Mr. Donovan?"

"It's a big step you're taking."

"I'm a big girl."

"And big girls don't need companionship. Right?"

She gave him a tight smile. "I don't see that companionship has anything to do with my remaining on Cayemite."

"You will, once you've lived on it long enough."

"It's not as though I'll be living on the island alone. There's you—"

"Not forever."

The buggy jarred in and out of a rut in the road.

"Annee seems to have done all right for herself," she went on, ignoring the constriction in her chest.

Again, Annee. Brice sat a little straighter and thought of confessing everything: The figures in Hunnington's ledgers were a ploy to deceive her brother, and that to reopen Hunnington's account at the bank and at the surrounding businesses, he had paid out of Willow Bend's coffers just short of thirty thousand pounds, depleting his tobacco profits for the past year completely. He wanted to confess that her life was in danger; Annee Rose was as deadly as she was beautiful, that she wanted Hunnington as much as she wanted Brice, and she would stop at nothing to have full control over both. He wanted to admit that the solitude, the loneliness and the craving for companionship had killed his mother and destroyed his father. And the ache

for a soft shoulder on a stormy night had been enough,
almost, to drive Brice into the arms of a madwoman. He
wanted to confess that Autumn Sinclair Donovan had been
his salvation from the loneliness and from Annee since the
moment she arrived on that godforsaken island.

But he didn't.

The driver stopped the chaise outside the hostelry. Brice
dismounted first, offered his hand to Autumn, which she
accepted after a moment's hesitation, then helped her to
the ground. His fingers lingered on hers a moment longer
than necessary before pulling away. Both sensed it. Both
looked away, to opposite ends of the street.

Twisting her purse string round and round her fingers,
Autumn gathered her courage before casting a glance back
at Brice. His body faced her, but his head was turned. He
was studying the bay with strict concentration. His hands
were on his hips again; his coat was open and caught
behind his wrists. The stance was authoritative. He was
accustomed to control, she realized.

"Will you come to Mitchell's room?" Autumn took a
short step backward as Brice's head turned sharply around
toward her.

"I have an appointment," he said.

"I see."

"I assumed you wanted to visit with your family alone
before they left."

"Since you're my husband—"

"But I'm not." He dropped his hands. "Am I?"

"No," she snapped. Her body grew hot. The whalebone corset seemed to dig more viciously into the tender
skin below her breasts. Shielding her eyes from the sun,
she looked back down the street, and grew even hotter.
"Here comes your appointment," she cooed sarcastically
to Donovan.

"Darling!"

Brice stiffened.

A vision in white, Annee Rose floated up the walk with
the grace of a wraith, her full skirts and slippers defying
the swirl of dust about her ankles, a silk-and-lace parasol
shading her delicate features from the sun. Her hair was
swept away from her face, caught slightly above and behind

her ears with white satin ribbons that were left to trail to
her shoulders. Her step slowed as she recognized Autumn.

Annee flashed the Donovans a bright smile, but it was
to Brice that she spoke. "You look wonderful, as always."
Rising onto her toes, she pressed a kiss onto his cheek.
Then to Autumn she said, "You look dreadfully uncomfortable, dear, positively miserable. Those clothes don't
suit you at all."

"Oh?" Autumn smiled sweetly—a little too sweetly.

"Certainly." She tipped her chin up at Brice and
appeared to forget Autumn completely. "I've missed you,"
she told him.

Annee's hands closed possessively around Brice's arm.
Autumn watched his dark head tilt over Annee's and she
was stunned at how beautiful they were together.

"What do you want?" he asked Annee so quietly
Autumn had to strain to pick up his words.

"My darling Donovan, was there ever any doubt in
your mind about what I want?"

"I have an appointment." He pried her fingers from his
coat sleeve, then dropped her wrist as if it had burned him.

Not at all flustered, Annee twirled the parasol on her
shoulders and probed, "With whom?"

"Clarence Dillman."

"Cla—why are you seeing Dillman?"

"None of your business."

Red-faced, Annee shot a glance at Autumn. "I'd like to
speak to Brice."

"By all means." Autumn didn't budge. But she did
smile.

"Alone," she stressed through her teeth.

"That may prove difficult in a street full of people."

Slamming the tip of her parasol onto the wood walk so
violently Autumn felt the vibration under her soles, Annee
glared up into Brice's amused face and hissed, "Stay away
from Dillman!"

"Stay out of my business, Annee."

"I won't allow it, I tell you!"

"I'm . . . not . . . your . . . property."

Annee's face turned gray. Her mouth turning down into

an ugly red gash, she snarled, "I've waited too long, Donovan. I won't lose you again."

His hands clenched into tight bronze fists, he warned, "Don't threaten me, lady."

"You'll regret the day you were ever born, I swear it."

He stared more intensely into her violet eyes and grinned mirthlessly. "Tell me something I don't already know."

"Bastard!"

"Tut-tut, Maîtresse Rose; you're not making a very good impression on Missus Donovan."

There was something in the way he drawled "Missus Donovan" that brought Autumn out of her shock over witnessing their rather vocal displeasure with each other. Annee appeared to have heard it, too, for her face paled further.

"Now"—Brice reached a hand slowly, deliberately, for Autumn's arm—"I'm taking Missus Donovan into this establishment. By the time I return, I want you in your buggy and out of town. Do we understand each other?"

"But—"

"We'll continue this discussion later."

She had little choice, it seemed. Summoning her bruised pride, Annee planted her parasol back on her shoulder and, without so much as a glance toward Autumn, marched toward the chaise parked further down the street. Brice, squeezing Autumn's arm above her elbow a little too tightly, ushered her to the front door of the hostelry.

"I'll see you later," he said. Then, turning, he headed in the opposite direction from Annee, leaving Autumn to wonder just who Clarence Dillman was.

The door opened so abruptly Autumn jumped in surprise. Mitchell stared at her for several seconds before realizing who she was. "Autumn!"

"Yes." Autumn clasped her hands at the small of her back.

"Have you been there long?"

"No." Another lie.

Mitchell stepped to one side as several burly men hoisted his and Mary's trunks from the room. "Come in," he told her, when they were gone.

Mary was perched on the bed. She turned her red-rimmed eyes up to Autumn as she entered the room. "You came," Mary squeaked. "And you look so, so . . ."

"Lovely," Mitchell finished.

"Thank you." Feigning pleasure in her attire, Autumn turned a full circle between them. "Shelley Nelson lent me the dress. I thought you might enjoy it."

"You needn't have gone to such bother," Mitchell told her. But he was pleased. Autumn could hear it in his voice.

"I thought it was the least I could do, considering . . . everything."

"Everything?"

"All the problems I've caused you."

The rattle of a carriage from the street below carried through the open window. Mary sniffed and buried her face in her hands.

Mitchell dropped his eyes to the floor. "I guess we'd better be off," was all he said.

They walked the short distance to the docks. Stiffly, silently, they jostled their way through the other travelers who were making their way to the *America*'s lighters. With each step Autumn's throat closed more tightly, and the band about her chest squeezed that much harder. Her eyes and nose were burning, and it had nothing to do with the stench of fish or offal, or even with the cloud of gray smoke from the nearby sugar works that huddled over the city on this otherwise cloudless day.

Donovan was there, at the end of the dock, standing behind the fat Negro woman and nibbling on a sugar cake. Autumn's heart raced a little faster. Odd how she had come to rely on his strength when hers faltered.

A sudden gust of wind whipped his hair and snapped his coattails against his thighs. Looking up, Brice dropped the sugar cake he was eating to the mongrel lying at the ledge of the dock. He shoved his hands into his pockets and waited for someone to speak.

It was Mary who spoke first. "Oh, Mr. Donovan, we're so glad you came. Aren't we, Mitchell?" She nudged her husband in the ribs.

"Yes," he said. Then more forcefully he continued,

"There are a few things I would like to say to you privately, Donovan."

Brice pursed his mouth in a way that said, "I thought as much."

Mitchell clapped a steely grip on Donovan's arm and pulled him from the others. They walked a short way down the dock, shoulder to shoulder, each watching his toes and thinking about the young women behind them.

Finally Mitchell's head came up. He stared squint-eyed toward the mouth of the bay. "I love her, you know." That's all he said.

"I know."

"And I'm damned hurt that she did this."

"That's understandable."

Mitchell stopped. The effort to smooth his ash-brown hair back from his forehead did little good. "I did my best. She was just so damned . . . stubborn. I felt if she found a decent sort of man, with enough patience, he might settle her down. It was her fear of having children, though." He shook his head. "It's just not natural, a woman *not* wanting to have babies."

Brice looked back down the dock at Autumn.

"I thought I could bend her. All right, dammit, manipulate her. Get her married, then she wouldn't have any choice but to have a baby. That would settle her down, for sure. I had no idea she would run off with some ne'er-do-well just to spite me."

Brice pursed his mouth again.

"All I ever wanted for Autumn was happiness. A nice, stable man who would love her, despite her shortcomings, who could provide a comfortable existence for her and teach her that marital responsibilities aren't so intolerable. Is that so much to ask?" He looked directly at Brice. "What do I get for a brother-in-law, I ask you? A philanderer. A gambler. A cheat and a liar. And for the life of me, I cannot understand why I am continuing to permit it."

"I'll take care of her," Brice said quietly.

"Yes, man, but you do not love her, and that breaks my heart."

The sun reflected from the sea in a burst of blinding

white. Brice turned away and stared at the wagonload of puncheons ready to be transported to the distant, high-riding schooner.

"Why *did* you marry her, Donovan?"

He thought of the letter. "I was lonely."

"But why Autumn?"

"She was . . . special." Roy's words. "I needed a companion who would keep me entertained out of bed as well as in. And she was willing."

"If you hurt her, I'll kill you."

"I won't."

They turned and walked back down the dock.

And Brice casually mentioned something about a successful brother he had in Richmond, Virginia, who wasn't a gambler or a cheat and very rarely lied. He suggested, just as casually, that Mitchell should look him up.

Mary dabbed at her tears one last time. "I'm such a crybaby when it comes to good-byes." She sniffed into her hankie.

"Everyone aboard!" called the first mate from the lighter.

Mitchell stepped up beside his wife. "It's time to board," he announced, sounding resolutely cheerful.

Autumn swallowed hard.

Mary pressed a hand across her mouth and made a croaking sound into her palm.

Autumn looked up at her brother, and all her false bravado fell away when she saw that Mitchell was crying.

She threw herself into his arms, tears of shame and regret falling hot onto her cheeks and soaking the front of his coat. "Oh, don't!" she pleaded. "Oh, please don't!"

"My God, I'll miss you."

"Don't, don't."

"I love you, little girl. Never forget that. I couldn't love you more if you were my own daughter."

She wept that much harder.

"I did my best. Always my best, because I loved you. I only wanted you to be happy."

Burying her face in his chest, she rocked back and forth.

In a lower, tear-filled tone he whispered, "I'm a fool for leaving you here, but . . . but he'll be good to you. He'll be good *for* you. I don't know why I know this, but,

by God, I know it. Just give him a chance, Autumn.'' He
pried her arms from about his chest, then held her at arm's
length. ''You've leaned on me long enough. It's time to
let go. You're a grown woman, a beautiful woman in
dresses or breeches, and I'm so damned proud of you; I
always have been.''

He was speaking to himself. Everyone knew that, and
understood.

''Everyone aboard!'' called the man from the lighter.

Mitchell tipped Autumn's face to his. ''Be happy.''

''I—I shall.'' She tried to smile. ''I can go barefoot
now and run on the beach. Remember how you hated my
running barefoot on the beach?''

''I was afraid you'd step on one of these damnable
jellyfish.''

''Really? You never told me that was the reason.
Remember how you hated my riding astride?''

''I was only worried that you would . . . well . . . hurt
yourself in some way.'' His face turned red.

''Oh. Oh, my, you never told me that, either.''

''I made a lot of mistakes.''

So did I, she wanted to tell him, but he turned away.

''Will you write?'' he asked over his shoulder.

She nodded, not trusting her voice to speak.

Mitchell boarded the lighter first, then Mary. Autumn,
arms crossed and locked across her stomach, watched
numbly as the barge moved away from the dock and grew
smaller as they neared the *America*. Occasionally she would
see Mary's little hankie flutter in the air, Mitchell's hand
raise hesitantly above his head, and all she could do was
think of all the good times they had shared together. The
bad times were completely forgotten.

''Oh, God,'' she asked aloud, ''what have I done?''

Brice had kept his distance during those final good-
byes. Now, as he moved quietly up behind her, he laid a
comforting hand on her shoulder. ''Autumn—''

''Don't!''

He jerked his hand away.

''I want to be alone, Mr. Donovan. Just leave me
alone!''

Complying, he moved down the dock, his hands in his

pockets and shaming himself for feeling grieved because Autumn was shutting him out of a very emotional moment in her life. It wasn't, after all, as if they really meant something to one another. They had been thrown together out of necessity. Now that Mitchell was gone they could— how had she said it?—oh, yes, go their separate ways. They needn't share their lives, their bedroom, or even their meals if they didn't care to. He could go back to the life he knew before Autumn Sinclair Donovan—before she burst into that library with her eyes flashing excitement and her auburn hair flying about her shoulders. He could eat alone, bathe alone, sleep alone. Talk business matters over with himself, and foremost, he could soon wash his hands of the estate and return to Virginia . . . to eat alone and sleep alone and . . .

There was a child selling flowers. He bought one and stood facing the turquoise water, twirling the delicate bloom back and forth beneath his nose, allowing its pungent-sweet scent to replace the rancid odor of decaying fish and the stench of stagnant water trapped beyond the pilings. He listened to the hurried footfalls of boots upon the wharf, but heard, instead, Autumn's laughter two nights before as they sat knee to knee in her bedroom—laughter over nothing more than a cigar stuck in her ear. And he wanted desperately to hear her laugh again.

He looked out at the *America* and was suddenly shaken by his mind's image of a lost young man who had given up everything, family and home, to chase a dream, thinking that beyond that blue-and-green rainbow of water were promises of freedom and happiness and riches beyond his imagination. He had stood on the deck of that departing ship, looking back at all he had lost, and felt more alone and afraid than he ever had on Cayemite. If there had been one soul to hold onto those next months, perhaps he wouldn't be the shell of a man he was today. He'd learned to cope with the emptiness, the loneliness, by shutting off his emotions and convincing himself that he didn't *need* anyone. He was now thirty years old, and the freedom and riches meant nothing because he was alone. He couldn't let that happen to Autumn.

Brice turned back down the dock, his eyes searching for

her curly russet hair and prudish high-collared dress that
made her look little more than a girl. He bumped and
nudged his way through the stevedores, around the bondsmen whose naked black torsos glistened with sweat. He
found the very spot on which he had left her. But Autumn
wasn't there.

His first instinct was to check the water, feeling foolish
even as he dropped onto his hands and knees and peered
under the dock. Autumn wasn't there. Brice jumped to his
feet, brushing grit from his hands and wondering if she
had somehow passed him on the dock and returned to their
chaise. He looked the other way, beyond the dock and past
the vendors.

The skirts of her dress clung to her knees. She ran down
the beach, her hands clutching her sodden dress as high as
possible as the waves surged about her legs. Her hair had
fallen from its combs.

Brice ran after her.

She ran until she could run no farther. She ran until the
ship weighed anchor and the mainsail bulged with the
same south wind that whipped her hair around her neck.
Autumn thought she saw Mary wave once, but she couldn't
be certain. She imagined Mitchell standing there in his
rigidly correct manner. But she couldn't see him. Oh, if
she could only see him.

"Good-bye!" she called. "I'll miss you. I love you.
Oh, I do so miss you. I lied, Mitchell. This man is not my
husband! I'm sorry. I'm so sorry, and if I could do it over,
I'd be so good. I'd marry Jay Michaels if it would make
you happy. I wouldn't wear breeches or ride astride. I'd
keep my nose out of your business and do nothing but
stitch and help Mary plan the menu."

"Autumn."

"Good-bye!" She waved at the ship.

"Autumn," he repeated, closer now.

"Oh, God, what have I done?" She turned, stumbling
as a wave broke across her legs. Donovan stood just
beyond the water's reach, his coat blown open by the wind
and his hair, wet with spray, clinging to his brow. "What
have I done?" she asked him.

He didn't respond.

"I suppose you think this is all very funny, don't you? Is that why you followed me, Donovan? To—to see me cr-cry?"

"No."

"Well, I *can* cry. See?" She opened her arms and started crying like a baby. "Don't look at me!"

"All right." But he looked, anyway.

"I'm scared. Is that what you want to hear?" Lifting her skirts and fighting the water's sucking current, she trudged onto the beach and stared down at her bare feet. "The rocks cut my feet." She wept.

He moved up beside her, into the wave and mud and kelp that clung to her ankles, and lifted her into his arms. "Hush," he soothed her.

"I'm such a fool," she choked, leaning into his shoulder.

"No, you're not."

"A fool. I've no one, don't you understand?"

"I understand," he whispered against her temple.

"How could you? How could you know what it's like to leave everyone and everything you love?"

"I know. I swear it."

He dropped to the sand and cradled her in his arms.

"He said he loved me. He never told me that before."

"He should have told you."

"J-just once would have been enough." She wiped her nose on his shirt.

Brice only smiled.

"Donovan?"

"Hmm?"

"What if I fail?"

"You won't."

"But what if?"

"I won't let you." He looked down her leg. "How are your feet?"

She shrugged.

The wind changed. It rushed from the north, and the vendors' chants were carried in the opposite direction. They listened to the water as it hissed and reached blue-green fingers onto the beach. They could hear the sand shift through the nearby trees.

Autumn took a shuddering breath and looked down at his hand. "What's that?" She touched his fingers. They slowly opened.

"A flower."

She giggled. "What's happened to it?"

"It's wrinkled, I think." Slowly he tucked the bruised petals behind her ear. "Welcome home," he said into her glistening eyes.

"Do you mean it?"

He nodded.

The *America*'s sails were tiny white specks on the sweeping horizon. He held her closer as they disappeared completely from sight. Her body was shaking, and he wondered how anyone so small could cry so hard and be so quiet about it.

"Yes, man, but you do not love her." Those words came to mind.

A lot you know, he should have said to Mitchell Sinclair. But he hadn't, so he said them now, softly and to himself.

"A lot you know."

Chapter 12

The days that followed found Autumn busy with plans for renovating Hunnington Hall. The activity kept her mind off Mitchell and Mary. Brice joined her on her jaunts into Montego. They visited Mattie and paid her for the zemis. While they were there, they bought cheese and wine and picnicked on a cliff overlooking the tiny, uninhabited Bogue Islands just to the west of Montego Bay. The conversation rarely strayed from business. Donovan appeared to listen intently, if somewhat disinterestedly, as Autumn discussed her fascination with the cane mills and her hopes of rebuilding Hunnington's to an even grander scale than Patrick Donovan had ever dreamed.

He reminded her that men had tried before, that Charles Bovier had settled on the island fifty years before, when the main island of Cayemite had been nothing but a rain forest and a tribe of Indians. With the help of slaves and Indians he had built the Greathouse in just under two years. It had taken another five years to clear enough land to begin planting. His first crop was ruined by drought, the second by rains. To raise enough money to continue his efforts, he sold a smaller section of land on the opposite side of the island to Everard Barrett, hoping the two might form a friendship as well as a partnership. It never happened. While Barrett's crops did well, Bovier's died of disease and insect infestation.

"Why did Barrett's thrive and Bovier's die?" Autumn asked him.

Brice turned his green eyes to the Bogue Islands and said, "He made a deal with the gods."

"Gods?"

"Cayemite has her own gods."

Fascinated, Autumn encouraged, "What was the deal?"

168

"His firstborn child."

"A sacrifice?"

"Her soul."

Brice went on to tell Autumn of Ester Barrett, Everard's wife, who, when learning of the pact made with the gods, aborted her own child. Rumor was that she went insane and killed herself: the island gods' vengeance for taking what supposedly belonged to them. He returned to England in hopes of finding another wife, but the idea of living in such a remote place didn't appeal to the young ladies, so he returned to the island alone.

Everard was a handsome man, and as fate would have it, he and Charles's wife became attracted to each other. Charles was too busy trying to save his deteriorating crops to realize what was going on. Everard's aspirations eventually outgrew Barrett Plantation; he wanted it all. He convinced Maureen Bovier that if Charles were out of the way, they could marry and join the two estates. Charles Bovier died peacefully in his sleep, slowly poisoned to death.

The gods appeared to Barrett then and reminded him of their pact. Maureen was in her forties, as was Everard by that time. She was beyond childbearing age. He refused to marry her, admitting his only interest had been in Bovier Hall. She, in turn, refused to sell the estate and left the island, returning to her native Ireland.

Everard, having fired his bookkeeper and overseer for indulging too frequently in his *clairin*, was the only white man left on the island. For companionship he began visiting the Indian village up on Trempe Mountain. There were enough young women there to satisfy his baser needs, and all had visions of moving into the Barrett habitation.

Barrett was delighted when one of his favorite young ladies informed him she was to have his child. The pact, it seemed, would be complete; perhaps his deteriorating crops would be saved in time, after all. He took the girl to the Greathouse, and though he wouldn't marry her, he treated her like a queen. He was taking no chances that he would somehow lose the child, as he had before. His daughter was born seven months later.

But the gods weren't pleased. The child's soul was

rebellious and defied them at every turn. They came to fear her; her power was stronger, and soon the gods of light began leaving the islands, relinquishing them, it was said, to the gods of darkness, the same gods who had controlled the islands in an earlier time, when the Cayemite islands were veiled in mist and mystery.

"Tell me about these gods." Autumn was enthralled with the fairy tale.

Donovan explained that once, before the Indians found their way to the islands, a great battle had raged between good and evil. The islands shook, the seas rocked and the mountains exploded in rivers of liquid fire. Defeated, the gods of light surrendered all power to darkness, and for thousands of years the islands lay obscured by fog. Then the Indians arrived, and they brought their own gods: their zemis. The spirits of darkness tolerated their presence mostly because they had become lazy and overly confident of their own strength.

But the Indian spirits, the zemis, were many in number, and they were as good as the gods of darkness were bad. Tiring of the injustices the dark ones perpetrated on their people, they rose up against the evil ones and banished them from the island. But legend has it that the dark spirits have been returning in human and animal form and are waiting to retake the island when their forces are large enough. The old ones say there will be so great a battle that the entire island will be destroyed.

Autumn laughed, then teased, "So tell me, sir storyteller, just how your father came to live on the island."

"Maureen Bovier, in her old age, was heavily in debt. My father bought Bovier Hall from her, changed the name to honor my mother—her maiden name was Hunt—and they moved to Cayemite."

"What happened to Everard Barrett?"

"Dead twenty years."

"What of the young woman who gave birth to his daughter?"

"Afraid of her daughter and believing she had released great evil on the island, she went to the mountain and threw herself from the top, thinking that if her soul joined the afterlife, there would be one more spirit to battle the dark ones' takeover.''

''And—and Barrett's daughter?''

''Annee Rose.''

Autumn thought of those words throughout her busy days, but she didn't speak of them. It was all legend and lore, after all, and deserved no more than a moment's consideration. Instead, she focused her attention on the expansion and renovations of Hunnington and its mills. With Brice she spent long hours on another plantation watching the cutting of cane. She observed the hacking at the roots and the shaving of the leaves. Together they watched the children running up and down the rows as they collected the crop and deposited it into the ox-drawn wagon that stood in the paths that divided field from field. Much to her displeasure, she witnessed the whipping of several slaves and was glad Hunnington practiced no such barbarism.

But because of Hunnington's enlightened policy came an additional problem: that of hiring enough workers to work Hunnington. She posted Help Wanted notices about the town. After two days with no response, she learned the notices had been removed. So she appealed for help through the newspapers: the *Bay News,* even the *Royal Gazette* in Kingston. She stood on the docks and handed out fliers to the seamen, with Brice at her side, his arms locked across his chest and his eyes daring the randy sailors to make one questionable move toward her.

It was after such an afternoon, when Autumn sat on the piazza with Shelley, watching her cradle Sara in her arms, that she noticed the cloud of dust on the horizon. Loz left his chair and stood at the edge of the porch, his pewter tankard sweating onto his fingers as he stared down the road. Brice joined him.

The Negroes emerged from the dust, their lanky frames balancing bandboxes, bundles and even heavy trunks on their shoulders. They came at a quick pace, more like a trot, their movements synchronized with the rhythmic tune they were singing. The trunk fleet, it seemed, had arrived.

''Good Lord.'' Loz groaned and turned to Shelley. ''It's your parents.''

Within the hour the first horse appeared, a handsome gray pacer with a shuffling gait. Shelley's father came first. A portly, dignified-looking man, he had removed his coat in the heat. He wore long trousers of Russian sheeting and a white kerchief under the front of his Panama hat. Next came her mother, as round as her husband, her long riding habit sweeping down below her shoes, a white-and-green hat perched jauntily on her gray head, under which was a white handkerchief that wrapped around her face and was pinned across her nose. Behind her was a very young girl, Shelley's sister, Autumn surmised. She was dressed almost identically to her mother.

Loz went immediately to help his mother-in-law dismount. Brice offered his help to Shelley's sister. Autumn noted the girl's delight as he lowered her to the ground.

There was little discussion over the baby, and Autumn was given the impression that the infant had very little to do with Shelley's parents' visit. She was also vaguely aware of her own irritation over their disinterest in their grandchild. Just what could be more important than Sara?

That thought sat her back in her chair.

After offering the baby a chuck under the chin, Edward Drake settled into one of the matching wicker chairs, his belly protruding over his lap and his hat hanging upon his knee, and expelled, "By God, Nelson, this is excellent cane growing weather!"

"That it is, sir."

With the mention of cane, Shelley stood from her chair, as did her mother and sister; they excused themselves and entered the house. Autumn remained, eager to listen to the men's discussion about their crops. She was taken aback when the men all turned to stare at her.

"Is something wrong?" She sat a little straighter in her chair.

Brice, who had seated himself beside her, leaned slightly toward her and whispered, "It is customary for women to excuse themselves when men discuss business."

She felt the blood creep up her neck and pool in her cheeks. "Is that so?"

"Yep." He had the gall to grin.

"What a foolish custom."

Brice's smile widened as he taunted, "It is a well-known fact that women have no minds for business."

"Oh?" Her face got hotter.

Sitting back in his chair, stretching his long legs out and crossing them at his ankles, he responded simply, "Yep."

A Negro boy appeared, carrying an ornate silver tray, whereupon a selection of cigars was neatly arranged. As each man chose his smoke, the boy produced a tiny pair of scissors and clipped the cigars' tips. "Fire!" Edward bellowed so loudly Autumn jumped. Another boy appeared from within the house, a wood sliver flaming at one end, and proceeded to light each man's cheroot. They all puffed away silently until a cloud of smoke collected over their heads.

Finally Brice looked again at Autumn. "Sorry, love, would you like a cigar? You must promise me, however, that you won't stick it in your ear." He smiled so shamelessly Autumn nearly slapped him.

Instead, she only smiled back. "I'll tell you exactly where I'm going to stick that cigar, Mr. Donovan."

Loz cleared his throat. "Edward, Missus Donovan is now part owner of Hunnington Hall on Cayemite."

"That so?" Edward looked neither right nor left, but stared straight ahead, rolling the cigar between his lips with fingers that were as short and fat as his cheroot.

"She plans on renovating."

He guffawed at that.

"Is there something funny?" Annoyed, Autumn frowned.

"Patrick Donovan failed at it. So did Charles Bovier. What, my dear, can you do that either of those men couldn't?"

This is your chance, Autumn, she told herself.

Completely dauntless and wearing a look of total confidence, she took a deep breath and attacked the subject with as much enthusiasm as she could muster, considering that every man and boy on that piazza was staring at her with his mouth agape. She talked nonstop for half an hour, completely ignoring Drake's occasional burst of laughter and the fact that Loz had walked to the far end of the veranda and stood staring out across the gardens. Oddly, however, it was Donovan's intense appraisal that kept her going. He was listening, actually listening, and more than that, he agreed with her on more than one occasion. Oh, not verbally, of course, but she had perceived that almost inconspicuous nod of his head when she mentioned the former owners' overplanting of cane, and the Indians' need for more productive land of their own. But it was the mention of using manure on the crops that stood all three men on their feet.

"Dung?" Edward asked chokingly.

Autumn wondered if his surprise had more to do with hearing a woman speak the word than it did with the actual idea. "And compost," she added. "It worked very well on my brother's crops."

"And tell me," Edward went on, "what makes you think it would benefit cane?"

"It is most obvious." She looked at Brice. "I cannot imagine why your father or Monsieur Bovier never realized. Those areas now growing the healthiest cane were once part of the rain forest, were they not?"

Brice looked at Nelson. They both looked at Drake.

"A rain forest is a prime example of fertile land. Vegetation falls to the ground and dies, rots and richens the earth. Why, there would be endless reserves of compost at our very fingertips."

Settling back in his chair, Edward puffed on his cigar while contemplating her words. Then he said, "That won't help your worker shortage."

Autumn dismissed the remark with a wave of her hand. "Sharecropping will eliminate that."

This time it was Brice who choked on his cigar. "Impossible!" he finally managed.

"Be reasonable, Brice."

Their eyes met. Her face turned pink with the realization that she had addressed him by his Christian name. This time, unlike the time before, she didn't correct her blunder. It had been no blunder.

She continued, her voice less steady and her breath a little short. She curled her toes inside her boots and swallowed hard. "By planting less, we'll need fewer workers," she finally responded.

"You still have to pay them," he argued.

"Buy you some bondsmen!" Drake was perched on his chair like a hoot owl with his feathers ruffled.

She didn't blink. "No. Slavery, sir, will someday be abolished. We must all be prepared for that. It is an abomination that won't be tolerated for much longer."

"She's right," Loz joined in. "Just last month in Saint Thomas parish, Chaloner Archdecker's slaves rebelled, burning half of Golden Grove. And look at what happened to Saint-Domingue in 1804."

"Go on," Brice urged her. "Tell me your idea on sharecropping."

She spoke only to him then. "I realize we can't afford to pay them all a proportionate salary, but we could offer them land as incentive to work. At the end of each year they would be awarded with a section, one or two acres per family, to a maximum of, say, one hundred acres. They would be expected to grow a certain percentage of cane, and to sell it to us upon harvest. We process it ourselves into rum or molasses or sugar and sell it at three times what we gave the Indians in the first place."

Edward puffed a little harder on his cheroot. Loz stared down the drive. And Brice stared at her.

She felt conspicuous again, as she had when she'd stood at the top of the stairs in Shelley's dress. Even then, she had been waiting for his reaction. Now she was waiting again, but this time the anticipation was greater. She wished he would say something. But there he sat, legs outstretched, elbows propped on the arms of the chair and fingers laced casually across his flat stomach. The cigar jutting up between his fingers was little more than a nub. She watched it smolder nearly to the fine black hairs on his knuckle before he absently flicked the ashes away.

He must realize what his silence is doing to me, she thought. He must know that by staring at her like that he could cause her heart to flip-flop in her stomach. Yet he continued to stare, so she simply stared back, picking the white paint from the wicker chair with her thumbnail. It peeled off in long flakes that scattered over her breeches and fluttered to the red-tiled floor of the piazza.

His eyes flicked down over her lap, watched the miniature snow of white paint sprinkle the floor around her feet.

He wondered if she had looked at Roy that way when they were discussing plans to marry. Her voice was all full of breathless expectation, excitement and nervousness. Her cheeks were ablaze and her eyes—ah, those eyes—they could look at him so guilelessly that he wanted to shake her. More than that. He wanted to sweep her up the stairs and into his room and show her exactly what was in store for her if she remained on Cayemite with him. He'd been more than patient, allowing Autumn her futile fantasies, but he had a few fantasies of his own that had nothing to do with that stinking cane.

Then he reminded himself that her expectation, excitement and nervousness had nothing to do with him. Cayemite was her sanctuary, her life, *her* fantasy. She wanted no part of his dreams.

"Well?" Autumn moistened her lips and waited.

Brice threw his cigar to the floor. A Negro boy dashed to pick it up. "I could use a drink," was all Donovan could say. He didn't trust himself to say more.

Tick, tick, tick. Why did clocks sound so loud in the darkness? Why couldn't she sleep? Why couldn't she forget Melinda Drake's performance at dinner—if the girl had fluttered her lashes any harder, she'd have flown right out of her chair—and why did the thought of Brice's leaving after the meal to see Annee rip her heart out? His leaving in the evenings was nothing new, after all. Oh, he was gracious enough during the day to afford her his company, but he was all too anxious to make his getaway when the lights went down.

Autumn rolled over, buried her face in the pillow and wished she could die. She'd married Roy Donovan, neither loving nor even liking him, thinking to share nothing more than a life without commitment or children, yet when Brice Donovan walked into a room, her knees went all wobbly and her mouth went as dry as cotton. Her toes tingled! She cuddled Sara Nelson and fantasized that the child was his. And hers. And . . . oh, God, if he continued to see Annee when they returned to Cayemite, she didn't know what she'd do!

She rolled from the bed, paced the floor, then dropped

into a chair before her dressing table. She stared at her zemis. Yes, she could see the resemblance between herself and the willowy spirits. But they had a seductiveness that she didn't, especially the zemi of fertility. The statue's hair was wild and flowing. Her eyes were more slanted and heavily lidded.

Leaping to her feet, Autumn bent at the waist and tossed her head, spilling hair over her toes. She came upright so quickly the room spun. But the effort had had its desired effect, and as she stared into the mirror, she was stunned at her reflected image. Her mass of hair appeared tripled in volume. It coiled around her neck and shoulders and breasts. It clung to her moist skin like the chemise she had chosen to sleep in on this uncomfortably warm night. The end of one tendril curled around her nipple, as if purposefully drawing attention to the taut sphere. So she touched her nipple, gently with her fingertips, watching as it hardened and thrust up against the filmy, ivory-colored material in a way it never had before. Then she touched it with her eyes closed. And she thought about Donovan. And it grew harder. And it hurt. She wet her lips with her tongue and thought if Donovan would only kiss her again, she might kiss him back.

Donovan, Donovan, what have you done to me, my darling Donovan?

She stared at the zemi. The zemi stared back. Thunder rumbled outside her windows, and the rain began without warning. With it came the wind, through her windows, dancing with the candle flame reflected in the mirror. The wind smelled of dust and cane and flowers. It smelled strangely of tobacco, and she wondered if Donovan was out there somewhere in the shadows, watching as he had been her first night on Cayemite.

Donovan.

She stared at the zemi.

"Donovan." She said it aloud, and thunder shook the house.

She smiled at the zemi. The zemi smiled back. Or perhaps it was just the interplay of light and shadow from the candle. Autumn imagined that if she wished very, very hard, she could bring Donovan home. The thought of pulling him from Annee's arms made her smile again. It made her heart pound as fiercely as the tides that crashed against the cliffs of Bachus Bay. She grew giddy with believing it. She squeezed her eyes closed and softly chanted, "Donovan, Donovan," and though she couldn't be certain, she thought the zemi chanted, too.

A great crash shook the house.

As from a great distance she heard the excited babble of voices, rising to a greater pitch as the house continued to shake. She was vaguely aware of the jalousie tumbling from its frame and clattering to the floor. The force of the wind smashed against her so brutally she stumbled, and in that same instant, the door flew open.

Donovan was there. His dripping black hair was plastered to his brow. His soaking white shirt clung to his skin, revealing the swirling black hair across his chest.

"D-Donovan?" She backed toward the window, heedless of the wind and rain that pommeled her back. Her eyes darted to the zemi, then back to the man at the door. "Donovan?"

His left shoulder leaning heavily against the doorjamb, Brice steadied himself ineffectually before lurching into the room. He smelled of liquor and roses. "Get dressed," she thought he said.

"Dressed?"

"We're leaving. Get . . . dressed."

"Donovan, are you inebriated?"

He roared a terrifying laugh in the direction of the ceiling before staggering toward the armoire where her clothes were stored. He threw open the wardrobe doors, snatched up her few belongings and flung them at her feet. "Get dressed!" he snapped at her again.

"I will not."

"Get . . . dressed."

He was facing her fully, legs apart and hands clenched at his side. But she wouldn't be cowed. "Not until you tell me what this is all about."

Slowly he began to stalk her; she backed away. "Always the stubborn one," he sneered.

"Stay away from me."

He slapped away her upthrust palm. "I said get dressed."

"I said no."

His eyes raked her so fiercely Autumn cringed. To think she had been fantasizing over such an insolent goat made her flush with anger as much as embarrassment as she futilely attempted to cover her abdomen and breasts with her hands.

Brice only laughed. "Don't bother, they're nothing I haven't seen before."

"Bas—"

"Careful," he interrupted, "your debts are mounting up, you know." Her chin jutted up sharply, and he laughed again. He took another step toward her, thinking that if her eyes grew any larger, they'd fall right out of her head. "Get dressed," he repeated, then said, "We're leaving."

"I'm going nowhere with a drunk, Mr. Donovan."

So they were back to *Mr.* Donovan. He snatched up her blouse and breeches and threw them into her arms. "If you don't put those on by the time I count to five, I'm going to carry you butt-up-to-the-rain over my shoulder, *Missus* Donovan." He had the decency to turn his back before drawling, "One."

"Oh!" She stamped her foot.

"Two."

She stuck one leg into her breeches. "Where are we going? I have a right to know that much."

"Home. Three."

She put the other leg into her breeches. "But it's midnight!"

"I've arranged for the *Venerable* to sail at one. Four."

"In this storm?"

"John Dearborne is a friend of mine and has sailed rougher seas than this. Four and a half."

She couldn't think of anything else to say, so just out of spite, she observed, "You stink of rum, Donovan." When that didn't seem to faze him, she added, "And Annee Rose."

He crossed his arms over his chest and grinned. "Careful, Missus Donovan. I might start believing you're jealous."

It was her turn to laugh. Her response was so abrupt that he jumped. Clothed now, she marched by him and snatched up her zemis. "Jealous over a brute like you? You flatter yourself, sir."

"Then why did you turn the color of pea soup when I sat by Melinda Drake at dinner?"

"Did you sit by Melinda Drake at dinner?" She batted her long lashes, imitating Melinda, and responded, "Why, Mr. Donovan, I didn't realize you were even *at* dinner."

He was getting really angry now, angrier than he had been at Annee earlier in the evening when she threatened to tell the entire island that she and he were to be married. Normally he wouldn't have cared, but he didn't want such a lie to get back to Autumn, and that made him mad, too. He shouldn't give one little damn what Autumn Donovan felt or thought—if she had any thoughts besides that frigging cane—but he did care, by God, and if it meant dragging *Missus* Donovan away from Jamaica in the middle of the night, he'd do just that.

"Get dressed," he hissed.

She stuck her face up to his and replied, "I am dressed."

"Oh?" One black brow shot up. He gave her a slow half smile. "I hadn't noticed."

Loz Nelson appeared at the door, silencing the retort burning the tip of Autumn's tongue. He looked uncertainly back and forth between his friends. "Ah. Your driver is ready."

"Good!" Brice barked, looking at the freckles across Autumn's nose.

"Wonderful!" Autumn responded toward his beard-stubbled chin. Tucking a zemis under each arm, she whirled on her heel, bent and snared her boots from the floor and stormed toward the door. "I cannot wait to get to Cayemite. I hope I never have to lay eyes on you again, Brice Donovan."

"That's going to be hard, considering we're living in the same house, Missus Donovan."

"Oh, please, don't remind me!"

"Yeah, well . . ." He thought a minute, then continued, "Well, there's more than one house to live in on that island, don't forget. If you don't like my company, I can always move out."

"Wonderful!"

But she didn't mean it, and by the time she reached the staircase, she regretted having said it.

"Fine!" he yelled at her retreating back. "I'll move out!" He kicked the damaged jalousie, hurting his foot. His head hurt, too. But not nearly so much as his heart.

After one look at the old brigantine Autumn knew they were in trouble. Half the size of the *America*, it hardly looked as if it could manage the ripples on a millpond, much less a gale-tossed sea. The *Venerable* rode high in the water, light of cargo, which explained why, unlike the *America*, she could maneuver through the treacherous reefs at the mouth of the bay and moor at the dock. The captain gave her no peace of mind, either. With a patch over one eye and a face sporting several days' growth of beard, Dearborne looked as if he might be running up a skull and crossbones before their journey was out.

There was a crew, sparse as it was. And all looked equally as unkempt as their captain. They stared at Autumn as if she had three heads when she came aboard. Then she realized they weren't accustomed to seeing women in breeches. As rank as they smelled, she realized they weren't accustomed to seeing women at all. A woman with any delicacy would not allow them within a mainmast's length of her.

Brice saw her below, his grip on her arm warning that he would brook no argument in front of the men. They moved down a dimly lit, narrow passageway that smelled of sweaty bodies and salt and rot, both of them stumbling as the keel swayed underfoot. Autumn passed easily beneath a cross timber hidden in the shadows. Brice wasn't so fortunate. His mind too occupied on seeing Autumn safely to their cabin, he ran into the timber, knocking his head with a resounding thunk that brought Autumn to a stop.

"Are you all right?" She looked back over her shoulder.

He groaned and ducked and shoved her on, beyond the door marked Captain to the last cabin on their right. She opened the door and entered a . . . closet.

"What, pray tell, is this?" she asked in disbelief.

"Home, for the moment." Brice rubbed his head and checked for blood on his fingers.

Autumn stared at the bunk, or what there was of it. "Oh, no. No, I won't sleep on that."

"Then don't sleep."

"But there are bugs on it!"

"Are there? Well, perhaps if you ask nicely, they'll move over. On second thought, considering how you hog the bed—"

"Don-o-vannn!" She turned and glared in the pitiful light inside the enclosure.

He pointed to the filthy chamber pot in the corner. "Your throne, m'lady."

"You're disgusting."

"Thank you." He backed out the door. "Keep this locked at all times, Missus Donovan."

"Don't!" She made a lunge for the door.

"Tut-tut, sweetheart. One foot out this door, and I'll see you keelhauled all the way to Cayemite. Do we understand each other?"

"Animal!"

"Ah, sticks and stones." He gave her a wink and blew her a kiss. "Good night, love."

Chapter 13

"Ain't you evah gonna get married, Miss Autumn?"

"No, Millie. Never."

"Dat's a shame. Nothing like snugglin' up to y'man in de evenin', when all the lights be out and you and him is d'only two people on dis earth."

"Are you afraid, Millie?"

"Afraid? Afraid of what?"

"Of having that baby."

"Lawd, it's gonna be grand. 'Magine lookin' in a chile's face and seein' y'man's eyes and y'own nose. I reckon I can stand a little pain if it means a part of me is gonna live forever."

Autumn remembered her friend Shelley's words: "The ache starts in your heart and melts into your stomach. It's in every breath you cannot find when he enters the room, in every jolt you get when he touches you with his eyes."

"Someday some man gonna sashay into yore life and set you right back on that breeches-clad behind of yores. I only hope I'm alive to see it."

Autumn stirred in her sleep and damned the day she'd ever set eyes on Brice Donovan.

Brice stood in the doorway, watching a hair-thin sliver of sunlight filter through the warped decking overhead and settle on Autumn's face. It was odd how the sunlight seemed to find her no matter where she was, odd how she could walk out into an otherwise dreary day and in five minutes the sun would be shining and the day would be cloudless. Watching her now, he felt like a youth again, one who had never had a woman but wanted one so badly that just dreaming about it made him wet his sheets. Three weeks ago his only worry in life had been to get Hunnington's affairs in order and ship out to Richmond. Now he had to concentrate just to remind himself that there was a Richmond, Virginia, and a tobacco estate that he had worked ten hard years to build with his own sweat and blood. Ten years to build a legacy for his children—and the only woman he had ever considered sharing it with didn't want children, or him either, for that matter.

Brice slammed the door behind him.

Autumn sat upright.

"You're home," he announced. He watched as she uncoiled her arms from around her zemis. "Sleep well?"

"Very funny."

He extended a hand as Autumn attempted to pick herself up off the floor. She ignored it.

Tyler was waiting at the dock. He doffed his hat as Autumn hurried to the carriage. Brice, hot on Autumn's heels, sensed that all was not well with his—their—overseer.

"Well, now." Hugh attempted to smile as Maîtresse Donovan climbed aboard the buggy. "What have y' got there?" he asked, pointing to the statues jutting from under Autumn's arms.

"Zemis."

"Zemis. Just what we need around here. More of them godalmighty spirits."

"I beg your pardon?" She arched one brow and stared down at the agitated Irishman.

Tyler leveled a look on Brice before responding. "We've had trouble."

"What kind of trouble?" Autumn asked.

"Spirit trouble," he responded to Brice. "The Indians are convinced the day of doom is just around the corner. They've taken to the hills like a drove of bleedin' ants."

"Well, we'll simply go and get them," Autumn answered confidently.

Both men stared at her in disbelief. "Beggin' yer pardon, Maîtresse Donovan, but it ain't that simple."

"No? Why not, Mr. Tyler?"

"It just ain't." He glared at Donovan.

"You may direct your explanations to me, Mr. Tyler. As you may or may not recall, thanks partly to you, I am equal owner of this estate. And please be assured that I understand English just as well as Mr. Donovan.''

Brice smiled. Tyler didn't. With a harrumph, he climbed into the buggy, along with Brice, then took up the lines. He headed toward Hunnington Hall.

The endless hours of tossing on rough seas hadn't dampened Autumn's spirits in the least. She had counted the days until her return to Cayemite, and now that she was back, she could hardly contain her excitement.

As on her first day on the island, the entire countryside was so rich in hue the sheer intensity of color almost hurt her eyes. It was all so breathtaking; even more so since this was all hers. Hers! Every tree and flowering shrub. Every fish in the blue lagoon and squawking parrot in the trees. Why, she could walk out her door any time of the year and pick bananas or coconuts or mangos from the trees and eat them to her heart's content—Eve in her paradise, and the only serpent was . . .

From beneath lowered lashes she slanted Donovan a peek. Serpent or Adam? she pondered. She had thought of him as Adonis once, beautiful and perfect in form. She'd also thought of him as a cheat and the womanizer Roy proclaimed him to be.

Who *was* the real Donovan? Green eyes—gray eyes, as changeable as his moods. Black hair badly needing a cut, but she liked it that way, she decided. It framed his face, highlighted his cheekbones and accentuated the hollows beneath them. And his mouth—even when he wasn't smiling, his lips seemed always to curl up at one side. Those lips were quick to smile, just as quick to cut her to the bone. And . . . those lips could kiss.

They had traveled only a short distance, approaching a sort of crossroads, when the stench, carried by the breeze, assaulted their noses. Gone suddenly was the delicious fragrance of blooming hibiscus, and with a gasp, Autumn buried her face in her sleeve and tried not to breathe.

"What is it?" she asked chokingly.

"See for yerself, Maîtresse Donovan." It was Tyler who responded. Lifting one enormous hand, he pointed to the clearing just beyond the crossroads.

She peeked through her fingers, and what she saw there made her stomach turn over. Within a circle formed by seven Indians and suspended from a rope stretched between two poles, hung the rotting carcass of a boar.

"A *baka*," Donovan explained. "Do you recall the morning of our meeting, when I was called away over boar trouble?" He pulled a handkerchief from his breeches pocket and handed it to her, lifting one brow as she pressed it against her nose and mouth. "Since the boar attacked a human, it is believed to harbor the soul of evil; a *baka* can take any form, human or animal or both. These men, considered to be the bravest on the island, have killed what they believe is a *baka* and are now waiting for the evil spirit to lift from the carcass. When it does, they will slay it as well." He pointed to the circle of dust surrounding them. "Sacred ashes. Pulverized bones of the dead. The evil ones cannot escape through blessed farine."

"But how can they stand the stench?"

"Chances are they don't even smell it."

Autumn groaned and jumped out of her seat. "I'm going to be ill."

"Again?"

Swallowing her revulsion, Autumn looked sideways at Brice, aware now that he must have known that the *Venerable*'s pitching throughout the night had caused her considerable discomfort and more time hunched over that filthy chamberpot than she was willing to admit. Narrowing her eyes—she wasn't about to give him another reason to gloat—Autumn sat slowly down into the seat next to Brice and said, "Never mind."

The grounds around the Greathouse seemed different. The house looked different, too. Many of the windows' jalousies had fallen to the ground, and the cobblestones on steps and walk had been displaced. The ground was buckled in places, as if pushed up by force from beneath. Autumn stared a long moment at the line of disturbed earth that sliced directly down the middle of the front garden. It stretched as far as she could see, disappearing into the line of trees on the farthest end of the estate's lawns.

"What on earth could have caused such a thing?" Autumn

wondered aloud. She toed the dirt with her boot before looking back toward the house.

"Gophers," she heard Brice say to Tyler.

"Biggest damn ground hog you ever seen," the Irishman responded.

And both men laughed, sounding so ridiculously like little boys, Autumn couldn't help smiling, too. To herself, of course.

She was about to question them further when Celie met her at the door, somber-faced and obviously eager to get on with her chores. Behind her, the servants were lined up, stiff and uncomfortable in uniforms that had obviously been in storage for some time. It occurred to Autumn that this was an acknowledgment, of sorts. She was being greeted as Maîtresse Donovan, instead of a stranger. It was an exhilarating realization that made her smile.

"My, but you all look so wonderful!" she exclaimed. They stood a little straighter. "And how wonderful the house looks." Lifting her nose a little, Autumn sniffed and said, "Why, Celie, is that fricassee I smell cooking?"

"Um-hm."

"How ever did you know fricassee is my favorite?"

"Didn't." She pointed toward Brice. "It's his."

"Oh." A little crestfallen, Autumn looked toward the arrangement of flowers placed near the foot of the stairs, thinking that all this sudden solicitousness was no doubt for Donovan as well. Any lingering excitement was dampened completely then, as the child's squeal of delight pierced the quiet.

"Donovan! Donovan!" Pierre flew into the foyer, his face radiantly happy as he threw open his arms and was taken aloft by Brice's hands.

Then Jeanette appeared, and Autumn felt her knees turn to water.

Jeanette, also in a uniform, dipped slightly for Autumn and smiled. "Welcome home, Maîtresse Donovan. I trust you had a pleasant sojourn in Jamaica?"

Autumn stared at Brice and Pierre, who, nose to nose, were beaming into each other's face. She didn't hear the question.

"Have you missed me?" the child asked Brice.

"Of course," he answered. "And have you been a good boy for your mother?"

His small, pink mouth twisting like Donovan's, Pierre nodded. "You missed all the excitement last night. The gods were angry and shook the island like this." He wagged his pudgy little hand in the air for all to see.

"But you weren't frightened," Brice said with all seriousness.

"Non!" Pierre shook his head, and his hair bounced like shiny black springs around his glowing cherub's cheeks. Then, throwing his arms around Brice's neck, he giggled and admitted, "But I'm so glad you're back."

Autumn turned without a word and started up the stairs, noting that she was halfway up before Donovan seemed to notice she was leaving.

"Autumn?"

She didn't turn.

"I'll see you in a moment," came his voice, so filled with affection for the child Autumn wanted to choke.

She was feeling ill again. The constant pitching of the ship had left her limp as a rag; the scene with the boar had about finished her off. Or so she'd thought. That was before the child had reminded her, like a slap in the face, that Annee Rose was not the only "other woman" in Brice's life. There was Jeanette. And to make matters worse, they had a child. Naturally he would be very reluctant to dismiss the mother of his son.

It doesn't matter, she told herself. Why should it matter? You married Roy Donovan to escape motherhood. You should be thankful that the arrogant goat has someone other than you to keep him happy.

She slammed the door behind her, feeling foolish as she did so. Forget him! she silently scolded. Brice Donovan is everything you have tried so hard to avoid. He would have her curled before a fire reading him poetry. She would be darning his socks and knitting him wool sweaters on winter evenings. He would have her pregnant every year until her body collapsed from the strain.

Falling back against the door, she pressed her palm across her mouth, and to her horror, the tears came from nowhere to scald her cheeks. They trickled down over her fingers and ran down the back of her hand into the cuff of her sleeve. Her head pounded, and she wanted to scream because, for the first time since her mother died, she thought she might actually enjoy reading a man poetry and darning socks and . . . oh, if she could only have a baby without having to give birth, she would have one, two, three, because no matter what anyone else thought, she *did* love children.

She heard Brice's voice, and then Jeanette's. They were at the top of the stairs a little way down the hall. Autumn left the door and walked to the window, hoping that the fresh air would miraculously alter her mood before Donovan entered the room. But from the window his and Jeanette's voices sounded as indistinct as a couple of bumble bees, and because misery feeds on misery, she tiptoed back to the door and pressed her ear against the wood.

"What the devil are you doing in that damned uniform?" Brice's voice crackled with irritation.

"I know my place here," Jeanette responded.

"You're not a servant, Jeanie. Let me talk to Autumn and explain—"

"No! I won't have her look at me that way, to know Pierre that way. You must promise me, Brice. For Pierre's sake, please!"

She'd heard enough. Autumn backed from the door, thinking if she didn't do something quickly, she was going to cry again. She swung toward the wardrobe, had thrown open its door and filled her arms with her belongings when Brice entered the room behind her.

Their eyes met over a stack of frilly petticoats.

"What are you doing?" he asked.

"What does it look as though I'm doing?"

"You're not supposed to answer a question with a question."

"You're not supposed to enter a room without knocking."

Brice stepped back and rapped on the open door. "May I come in?"

"Of course. It's your room."

"Aha. That's why you're moving out."

"I told you I would."

"I told you not to bother."

She marched past him without a glance. He followed her into the hall. "This is not necessary, Autumn. I'll move out."

"I wouldn't dream of inconveniencing you further, Mr. Donovan."

He caught her arm. The touch jolted them both. They stood glaring at each other in the center of the hall, each waiting for the other to speak.

Very slowly he reached out for her clothes. "Let's put these back," he said quietly.

Autumn flinched and clutched her garments more closely to her bosom. "No," was all she said.

"My room is more comfortable. It's bigger."

She shook her head.

His frustration growing, Brice kneaded the back of his neck. "I'm trying to be nice about this, Autumn."

"Don't exert yourself. I know what an effort it must be for you."

She watched his mouth flatten.

"Put the damn clothes . . . back."

"Don't raise your voice to me, Mr. Donovan."

Brice closed his eyes before, spinning on his heel, he reentered the bedroom from which they had come. Autumn followed, cautiously peeking around the door frame and watching as he jerked open the doors of the wardrobe and began collecting his coats. Without a word, he stomped past her and entered the adjacent room, kicking the door closed behind him.

How very silly, Autumn suddenly realized. She buried her face in her clothes. They were soft and cool to her cheeks. They smelled like lavender. Brice's door opened again, and this time, when she looked at him, he was grinning.

"Settled?" he asked.

She nodded and turned toward her room.

"Missus Donovan."

Autumn looked back over her shoulder, a little reluctantly. He was too tall and handsome; his shoulders were too broad and his eyes too intense and green for a woman who didn't want to have babies. She hid behind her pantaloons and said, "What is it, Mr. Donovan?"

I wish you would call me Brice again, he thought, but he didn't say it.

Saying nothing, he stepped back into the room and closed the door. God, but she missed him already.

Autumn lunched alone on the east terrace. This was a peaceful place, sealed off from the inhabited part of the Greathouse because of the recent fire. She'd busied herself for the past hour assessing the damage caused by Roy's drunken carelessness. Fortunately, most of the damage throughout the house was from the great amount of smoke that had boiled up from the old drapes and carpets and flooring throughout the east wing. The rooms that had sustained the most damage by fire were locked. Since Roy had died there, she was in no great hurry to view them.

But because the east wing had been shut off these months, little care had been taken with the gardens here. Bougainvillea and hibiscus were growing in a towering, drooping tangle around the courtyard, their vibrant blossoms masking all odor of smoke from the house. Hidden behind their thorny lair, she could gaze unobserved across the landscape, watching the distant caravan of ox-driven wagons and the men who were so tenaciously laboring to fill them. She wondered if anyone had bothered to inform them that the fruits of their labor was being wasted, that the few measly acres they managed to harvest per week lay rotting within storehouses in Bovier.

Autumn speared a chunk of banana and took it between her teeth, savoring its sweet, slick texture. It was warm from the sun, strangely arousing, conjuring images of Donovan's last kiss, the sensual thrust of his tongue into her mouth that had also been warm and slick and breathtakingly sweet. She curled her tongue around the banana, and closing her eyes, pretended it was Donovan. The sensation was so startling that her face turned as red as the hibiscus bloom bobbing over her head. She chewed it up and swallowed it as fast as she could.

She forced herself to think only of the estate. Where to start first? There was so much to do. Renovations on the house would have to wait. More important were the rebuilding of work quarters and the restructuring of the mill: the boiling house, where the sugar was made, and the still house, where the fermenting spirits were stored in puncheons, would have to be rebuilt from the ground up. Maureen Bovier had loathed the smell of the fermenting rum and had insisted that the mill be built as far away from the Greathouse as possible. Charles had obliged by erecting it out by the mountain, too great a distance to be seen to adequately.

Autumn studied the mountain. It jutted up from the center of Cayemite, all green at the base, purple in the center and slightly obscured at the crest by clouds. Shadows of those clouds moved in great dark splotches across the treetops until, finally, the mountaintop was revealed, looking barren and brown against the blue sky. From atop that mountain one could see the entire island: every cove, beach, developed or undeveloped section of land . . . and Hunnington.

Suddenly she knew *exactly* what her first effort as Maîtresse Donovan was going to be. She would scale Trempe Mountain!

Unfortunately, the Indians on Trempe Mountain weren't inclined to agree.

The stone-faced natives shook their heads in refusal a third time as Autumn attempted to explain her reasons for entering their village. "I wish to hire a guide," she told them.

Their heads moved in unison back and forth.

Autumn stared across their shoulders at the old man who perched on a tree stump, and she wondered if he was their chief. He looked as old as the island, his leathery brown face puckered and seamed around ageless eyes and a mouth hinting of humor. He smoked a pipe. His clothes were in rags and a crutch lay beside him on the ground.

She heard a horse approaching, and turning, her frustration mounted as Donovan slid from the animal and approached, his face dark and his eyes snapping like green flames. Her first instinct was to back away, but she didn't.

"Missus Donovan, what the hell are you playing at now?" he asked her.

"I've come to hire a guide."

"So I've been told. Why?"

She pointed up the mountain.

"I beg your pardon?"

"I wish to spend my first dawn back on Cayemite up there."

Brice's head fell back as he looked toward the towering crest. Trempe wasn't an overly tall mountain, average for so small an island. But scaling such a peak would take all of the remaining daylight hours and then some. Time and distance, he reasoned, weren't the least of the problems.

"You won't find a guide among these people. Not for such a frivolous cause."

"I'm willing to pay them."

"Are ya now?" He looked down again at Autumn. "With what? Money to these people means nothing. They have no use for it."

"Surely there must be something. Please, Brice . . ."

Brice. The word hit him like two tons of rock. And she knew it, by God. She stood there, with her freckles and with her hair swirling all around her shoulders, and her mouth parted just enough so he could see the pink tip of her tongue behind her teeth. Autumn Donovan could deny her womanhood until her dying breath, but she sure as hell had no qualms about dragging out the reinforcements when she wanted something badly enough. There was a name for women like her.

"Please," she repeated softly, then watched the irritation crumble from his features. He stared down at his boots and mumbled something to himself. Then he stared at her, really stared. He stared at her a whole minute without even blinking. And though she tried to stare back with equal intensity, she could only think of how ruggedly handsome he looked. He hadn't yet shaved, and the inky-black shadow across his face exaggerated his masculinity. The black leather vest he wore over his coarse gray osnaburg shirt added width to shoulders that were outrageously broad already.

Brice took a deep breath and asked, "What am I going to do with you?"

Autumn shrugged. Donovan watched the freckle at the corner of her mouth slide upward as she smiled and responded. "Humor me?"

''That's not exactly what I had in mind,'' he said more
to himself than to her. But she heard it, nevertheless, and
frowned. Brice gave her one last sideways glance and a
quarter smile before ordering, ''Get to your knees.''

''I beg your pardon?''

Brice went down on one knee. ''Get down,'' he told her.

Even on their knees he was half a head taller than she.
She stared up at the shock of black hair over his right ear
before he started rambling off words to the ground that
caused her brows to raise.

''*Atibo-Legba, l'uvri baye pu mwe, agoe! Papa-Legba,
l'uvri baye pu mwe. Pu mwe pase. Lo m'a tune, m salie
loa-yo.*''

''What does all that mean?'' she whispered.

''Knock, knock.'' His head tilted slightly toward her,
and he grinned.

It was the old man who responded. ''The barrier is
open. You are welcome!''

Brice helped Autumn from her knees, dusting off her
breeches so gently her heart skipped. Then, to add to her
confusion, he caught her hand in his and led her up to the
ancient one. And he didn't release it.

''Henri Touisannt.'' Donovan smiled at his friend. ''This
is Maîtresse Donovan.''

''*A nu bel fam!*'' Henri clapped his clawlike hands
together, his bones and purple-veined skin almost quivering under the gentle impact.

''Yes, she is.'' Brice looked down at Autumn. ''Very
lovely.''

Henri reached for his crutch. ''Will you honor us with
sharing our mélange?''

''Would we think to dishonor Legba?''

Henri's old voice was like gravel. ''Only if we are
ignorant.''

The straw-thatched village was perched on stilts. Children ran naked between, around and under the huts. Autumn
was keenly aware of the men's interest. They crowded
around her, babbling quietly among themselves and pointing to her hair. Once, when the wind blew it, they jumped
back so suddenly that several tumbled together to the
ground.

"It's the color," Brice explained. "They've never seen a redhead before. They believe you must have a passion for fire. Such passion holds great magic for these people, and they will probably come to revere you."

His eyes said something then, in their hesitation over her face. He looked away.

The women appeared. It was Autumn's turn to stare. They were nude from the waist up. She gripped her lower lip between her teeth and tried not to look or even react as they surrounded Brice with food and drink. They sponged his face with a cool, damp cloth, then tipped a hollowed coconut shell of water to his mouth. When they tried to feed him, however, he thanked them respectfully but assured them that he would prefer to do it himself. Disappointed, they sat back on their haunches, short skirts doing nothing to hide their femininity as they watched him sample their pepper pot stew.

Finally, he turned to Autumn and said, "Feed me." When she hesitated, he added, "It's the only way you'll be rid of them."

She took the bowl. Holding it just below his chin, she dipped two fingers into the greasy concoction and lifted a chunk of meat to his mouth, as she had seen the others do. She watched his mouth open, and her heart turned over. As his lips slid over her fingertips, her heart leapt right into her throat. Her mouth opened in anticipation, and when he took her fingers in his mouth with a slight sucking motion, his tongue wrapping around her fingertips, the shock caused her to gasp aloud.

"Oh!" her lips formed. "Oh, my."

His tongue pulled again.

She tried to swallow but couldn't. The pull on her fingers, all warm and slick seemed to reach all the way to her toes. "Mr. Donovan!" came the reluctant plea, and Autumn thought to herself that "Mr. Donovan" sounded ridiculously formal, considering what he was doing to her fingers. Finally, she managed to pull them from his mouth. Autumn stared into his eyes and wondered why that funny feeling in her nether regions didn't go away. If anything, it was worse. It centered between her legs and was as painful as it was discomforting.

"You're mine now," he said in so smooth and satisfied a voice that the tone rippled throughout her body. His next words, however, jarred her so abruptly from her thoughts that she forgot about tongues and bananas and naked women, forgot everything but the implication of his words.

They were: "You've just married me in the eyes of these people."

She tried to laugh. But she knew Brice Donovan well enough by now to recognize that look of certainty on his features. He wasn't teasing.

The women sighed, shrugged their brown shoulders and went back to their huts. The men smiled, laughed among themselves and had the audacity to slap each other on the back.

Autumn carefully placed the bowl on the ground and got to her feet. "I came here for a guide," she told them. "To take me up this mountain."

"Forget it," came Brice's voice from behind her.

"I will happily pay you."

"They do not understand you," Henri explained. He leaned a little harder on his crutch and shrugged his bony shoulders. "It would not matter if they did. No mortal would see you up the hillside. It is sacred land, forbidden to all but those destined to die. No mortal has ever returned after venturing there."

"Then see me halfway up, to just beyond the trees where the brown earth begins. I'll find my way from there."

Henri opened his skinny hands in a gesture of reasoning. "These are troubled times, maîtresse. The zemis who thrive on the mountains are disturbed. Just last night the islands shook, and this very mountain rumbled with anger. Even now the women of our people are preparing offerings to the great one who resides there so that no more trouble will besiege us."

"Then I'll simply go alone," she said stubbornly.

Henri puffed a little harder on his pipe.

Brice placed his bowl by Autumn's and got to his feet. He supposed there was no avoiding the inevitable.

Chapter 14

Brice cursed Autumn Sinclair Donovan for the third time in as many minutes and wondered what Henri had slipped into his pepper pot that had addled his mind enough to volunteer for such a venture. Had he allowed Autumn to start her trek alone, she might have turned back hours ago. Instead, she plodded along behind him, her hair wet with sweat and hugging her head, her shirt so damp it clung to her skin, revealing everything to his eyes.

Trying to stand straighter, he looked down on the top of Autumn's head, just as she looked up. Damn, if that wasn't excitement reflecting in those wide, whiskey-colored eyes. And though her face was red with heat and exertion, she smiled so breathtakingly that she put the setting sun to shame.

"I—is something wr-wrong, Mr. Donovan?"

"Don't you ever give up?" he asked her, after catching his breath.

"No. Never."

He watched her a moment longer, hoping she wouldn't realize that her shirt was plastered to her chest, revealing nipples the color of faded roses. "How did you get to be so stubborn?" He dragged his eyes back to her face.

"Practice, I guess." She sat down on the path and looked out across the water.

Brice swung the pouch from his shoulder and offered Autumn a drink, watching as water dribbled slightly from one corner of her mouth. She offered him a drink then. He pressed the opening to his mouth, enjoying it even more because her lips had been there a second before.

Shading her eyes with one hand, she squinted up the side of the mountain. "It certainly seems higher from this angle, doesn't it, Mr. Donovan?"

He flashed her a smile. "Don't you think you should start calling me Brice, seeing how we're married and all?"

Her hand came down sharply. "That's not funny. Marriage isn't a joke, Mr. Donovan."

"No?" Squinting, Brice looked back up the path. "Your marriage to Roy seemed pretty laughable." He hadn't meant to make the remark. But it galled Brice to think she'd jump into marriage and bed with a no-account like his brother yet could hardly walk into the same room with him without getting her back up.

He looked back down at Autumn, noting she hadn't responded, just sat on that rock and stared out over the water and forest and cane fields as if she hadn't heard a word he'd uttered. But her shoulders gave her away. She was spitting mad at the remark.

Let her simmer, he thought. He'd been simmering ever since she'd practically invited him to go live with Annee. He'd virtually mortgaged Willow Bend so she'd have enough money to see out her fantasy, and she couldn't care less if he dropped off the side of this mountain.

"You coming or not?" he snapped, angry as she turned confused eyes up to his.

She didn't say a word, just lifted that stubborn little chin up toward the mountain and said, "Yes, Mr. Donovan."

"Mr. Donovan" said it all.

The arching branches of the giant cieba trees allowed only occasional shafts of light to pierce the shadows. Autumn strained to make out the footpath appearing and disappearing through the undergrowth, her senses strung as tight as a fiddle as the two of them cautiously trudged through this last stretch of rain forest. It had been a suffocating tomb of never-ending green for the last hour, the vegetation so tangled and dense that not even the slightest breeze could reach them.

To her right the incline sharpened. To her left the tops of trees stopped where the base of others started, their gnarled, twisted roots grasping nothing but air, as well as the toe of her boot on occasion. Tripping again, she went down on one knee. Instinctively she reached out and grabbed Donovan by the ankle. He went down as well.

"Damn!" she heard him hiss.

Autumn buried her face in the crook of her elbow. "I'm sorry," she said looking toward the ground. She wanted to cry and didn't know why. She was tired, yes. She was hot, and she wished she had never suggested such an asinine scheme as climbing this mountain. But it hadn't looked so tall from the Greathouse. Then she heard Brice curse again, and she realized the mountain didn't have anything to do with her reasons for crying. She was upset over Donovan's earlier remark about her marriage to Roy. His opinion of her must be horrible. And forcing him into ridiculous efforts like climbing mountains that were bigger than they looked only worsened his opinion of her.

Lifting her head, she looked down her dirt-smudged nose and asked, "Do you want to go back?"

Brice glared at the sweaty, gritty fingers wrapped around his ankle. "Back? Hell, yes, I want to go back. I never wanted to climb this damned mountain in the first place."

"I know." She wiped her nose on her shirtsleeve.

Sitting up, Brice went on, "It's too late to go back. We have one hour of daylight left at the most, and I don't know about you, but there's no way this side of Hades that I'm sleeping in this damned forest after dark."

Her head fell to her forearm. "I hope it's easier going down."

She could hear Donovan breathing. She could hear the sigh of wind through the trees overhead and knew that if they could only make it out of this cloying tunnel of vegetation, relief would be forthcoming. She realized, then, that the wind in the trees and Donovan's breathing were the only sounds she heard. There was an eerie silence in the forest that throughout their journey had been a cacophony of squawking birds and humming insects. Then Donovan's breathing stopped. And the wind stopped. And it seemed the entire universe was holding its breath.

Slowly lifting her head, Autumn stared at Brice, and he at her. So it wasn't her imagination. He had sensed the sudden change as well. They listened to the silence, staring at each other and waiting as one waits for the crash of thunder after a brilliant streak of lightning has split the sky.

Nothing.

Donovan jumped to his feet. He grabbed her hand and began moving up the path, faster and faster, pulling her along behind him until the strain caused her legs to burn and quiver with fatigue. Her lungs ached. The skin on her wrist where his fingers clutched so tightly became chafed from the heat and pressure and grit that rubbed like salt into the irritation.

Then she smelled a sulfurous stench, like rotting eggs.

Onward they ran—up and up and up until each breath was a battle she was certain to lose if she didn't stop soon. She stumbled again, and he turned and yelled something so uncivilized in her face she could only gape and clamber to her feet to be dragged again, up and up and up, until her ears were ringing and her head was pounding.

The tunnel was darker, yet the sky, now a dull pewter-gray, could be seen more frequently through the sparser treetops, through the yellowing treetops, through the skeletal remains of dead tree trunks and limbs. Autumn covered her mouth and nose with her hand and wondered if another boar had been killed close by. Then she remembered that the Indians refused to ascend Trempe Mountain unless they were going to . . . die!

Oh, dear God, surely the smell wasn't—

The cloud rose up before them, around them, appearing from nowhere and settling among the dead and dying trees like a misty shroud. Like steam, it clung to their skin, hot at first then cooler, dripping from the bare branches overhead and plopping like raindrops on their faces and shoulders.

The air was noxious, burning her lungs, making her dizzy and sick in her stomach. She was going to die, Autumn thought, here among the rotting, stinking vegetation, among the spirits of dead Indians. Henri had warned them. Not just anyone was allowed by the gods to reach that peak. This was their punishment for trespassing on sacred ground.

She went down again, wondering why Donovan didn't curse her as he had before, why he didn't remind her of her foolishness and stubbornness, and ridicule her for marrying Roy. And though she tried to say, "Donovan, I'm sorry for all those things, all except for marrying Roy, because had I not married Roy I would never have met you," she couldn't. The words all buzzed around in her head in a confused jumble.

On her hands and knees, she stared at the ground and thought she only imagined its moving. "Don-o-van," she finally managed. With great effort she lifted her head.

"Don-o-van!" She wept it.

His vision, face down on the ground, swayed before her eyes. Then the roaring that filled her head began to vibrate the ground and the trees so violently that the tree limbs rattled; their leaves fluttered, damp and limp to the earth, landing lightly on Brice's back.

Autumn eased to the ground, stretched one hand out, and touched him. "So sorry," she said before closing her eyes. "So sorry."

The air smelled fresh, without the gaseous fumes that had sickened her earlier. Autumn lay for a long while with her eyes closed, her head nestled on her pillow. The illusions of climbing mountains and succumbing to the vengeance of angry gods had all been a very bad dream. Brice wasn't dead, and when she shared with him her nightmare, he would slant her that tolerant smile and say something like, "What am I going to do with you?"

She shivered and pulled her knees up to her chin. She hadn't been this cold since last winter, when a freak blizzard had rushed down through the northwestern range of mountains and blanketed Charleston with ice and snow. Teeth chattering, she reached for her covers. Her hand groped ineffectually over her knees before she realized there were no covers to be had. She must have kicked them away.

She sat upright.

A star winked above her, a beacon in the black velvet sky. Autumn stared at it several minutes, watching the overhead limbs sway with the frigid wind. She thought that were there enough light, she might see her breath. Her nose was so cold!

Then the memories flooded her, and the realization that the nightmare had been real brought a cry to her lips that echoed back through the endless pit of blackness below her.

Rolling over, she crawled forward mindlessly, searching, searching. "Donovan!" Her fingers found his boots and clutched his legs like a lifeline as she pulled herself up and over the backs of his thighs. "Donovan!"

Her hands twisting into his shirt, Autumn buried her face in his back between his shoulder blades. "Donovan, Donovan; my darling Donovan!"

He responded by groaning.

Had she imagined it?

He groaned again.

Sliding to one side, she turned him over onto his back. It wasn't easy. Her hands fluttered over his shoulders, his chest, up his throat and across his face, touching tenderly, like a blind man, searching for any telltale sign that he might have been injured. There was dirt on his cheek; she brushed it away. There was a leaf on his brow. She plucked it off.

Ah, blessed relief—his breath on her hand, warm and welcome. The whisker stubble on his jaw was slightly abrasive. She found his ears, covered with damp hair, and hesitantly she lowered her face, nestled her mouth into that hair and whispered, "Donovan?"

His arm came up around her.

"I thought you were dead." She laughed, then, and cried a little too.

"Are you all right?" He sounded drugged. The low, melodious cadence was a sweet rhapsody, however, to her muddled senses. And she clung to him harder.

"Oh, yes!" She wept, and laughed again. "I—I'm fine. I was so worried, Brice. Worried about you when I realized . . ." She cradled his head in her palms and stared down into his face, and though she could see nothing but its dark form, she knew every curve, hollow and angle of it.

His other arm hooked around her back. His fingers buried in her hair. "Worried," he repeated. His voice was raspy.

"This is all my fault. I'm so sorry, Brice. All I wanted was to see Cayemite. All of it. And I didn't realize . . . if anything had happened—"

"Sh."

"But—"

"It didn't." He pulled her closer.

She squirmed against him, not because her position astride him was disagreeable. Quite the contrary. But what was happening inside her was confusing, frightening; it made her feel dizzy again and breathless.

"Autumn."

The sound was ragged in the darkness, painful.

She stared down at his dark face and imagined she saw him smile.

"Autumn," he repeated, and before she could respond, his hand came up to the back of her head and pulled her face down to his. Their noses bumped, then his mouth found hers. The contact was shocking and she jerked away.

He pulled her down again, gently, merely touching his lips to hers, then applying more pressure until her mouth parted. His tongue skimmed through her silky lips, traced the even edge of her teeth, and more timidly than ever before, touched her tongue, retreated, then more boldly plunged until she was full of him.

He had never kissed her before like this. There was an urgency in the way his mouth slanted across hers, the way his tongue touched the roof of her mouth and the insides of her cheeks, the way he applied just the right suction so that she found herself kissing him back with as much eagerness, until her mouth was wet and slick, and he was wrapping his legs around the backs of her thighs and making groaning sounds someplace deep in his throat. Then his hips started rotating against hers, as they had that first night they'd slept together, arching, retreating, and the heat and hardness of him against her belly became painful and frightening.

His hands were on her back, her hair, her buttocks, squeezing, releasing. But when they slid in between their bodies and grasped her breasts, the realization of what was happening hit her bewitched reason. "Oh, no!" she gasped into his mouth. Then his hands had somehow found their way under her shirt, were running up and down her back, gently, not so gently, around her ribs where her heart was thumping so erratically she thought she might pass out again.

His body like stone, Brice lifted his face and buried it against the smooth arch of her throat, where her pulse hammered as wildly as his own. "You feel so good, Autumn."

She caught his wrist, allowing his fingertips to brush the side of her breast, but no further. "Oh, please," she begged him.

"Please what, Autumn? Has it been as long for you as it has for me?"

"Don't touch me that way, Brice Donovan!" His thumb had stroked her nipple.

"Say it again," he whispered. "Brice. That's my name, Autumn. Say it."

She wagged her head back and forth and wished he didn't feel so right and wonderful moving against her in such a sinful, animal way.

He felt her nipple rise and harden beneath his thumb, felt it all the way down to his aching manhood. "Oh, God," he groaned. She felt so good, so very good. He kissed the base of her throat, the skin where her shirt opened at the neck. Then he slid his hand down the back of her breeches, heard her gasp and felt her quake. Onward and around, insinuating his hand between their stomachs and down the hollow between her hips, inside her clothes, until his fingers found her mound of baby-fine curls that were already hot and moist with wanting him. And he slipped his finger inside her.

Her head fell to his shoulder. She was all liquid inside, like quicksilver, hot satin and glove-tight. He wished he could see her face. He could hear her breathing in painful little gasps, detected the shivers that passed through her body the moment he touched her. He grinned and said, "You like that."

She did. Heaven help her, she did.

"What else do you like, Autumn? Hmm?" He nibbled her ear. His finger moved in and out, in and out. His breathing became ragged. "What else?"

Autumn shook her head. She couldn't think. The forbidden rhythm of his hand moving against her had wiped all comprehension from her mind. Every nerve in her body was somehow centered between her thighs, and she could neither move nor speak, just ride the gentle wave of motion as he rocked her slightly back and forth. He was speaking quietly, whispering words in her ear that she couldn't understand. Island words, so soft and seductive they had a rhythm of their own.

"*C'est bien bon, ma chérie*. My love. Ah, Autumn it is so good. It *will* be good, if you will only let me . . ."

"No. No." It was a struggle to deny him, but deny him she must. With her last thread of reason she had to resist.

Was he moving too fast? He'd been so patient, waiting, wanting, since the moment he stood in the dark and watched her beautiful sleeping form in his bed those weeks ago, wanting to bury himself inside her, to know the sweet fulfillment that Roy must have known.

Roy. The name hammered in his head.

Roy.

The nagging vision of Roy and Autumn together welled up behind his lids, and his frustration grew as she denied him once again. He came slowly off the ground, his shoulders rolling and tilting as he rolled her over onto her back, his chest flattening her breasts and his knee wedging her thighs apart. The juncture beneath his hand opened like a tender, fragrant blossom, dewy and swollen with desire. He felt his own body throb in response.

Autumn closed her eyes. Nothing had ever felt so good, she thought. Nothing. Not skinny-dipping, running barefoot on the beach or sunning naked out by Brosnan's Creek. But how could she think of giving herself to a man who loved another? She wouldn't be used like Jeanette, then cast aside each time Annee Rose crooked her finger Donovan's way. And she knew in the deepest recesses of her heart that she couldn't bear to share him with either of those women.

She bit her lip and tried to remember those first tempestuous days with Donovan. She'd tried so hard to dislike him, to ignore those stirrings of attraction that surfaced each time he entered a room. But with one glance of those smoldering eyes he could make her forget all her resolutions; with one intimate touch of his hand he had her

stretching and purring and inviting him to know her as no
other man before him had.

Autumn threw her wrist over her eyes and sobbed, "Oh,
God!"

Brice stared down at her shadowed form, then slid his
hand from her clothes. "If you're worried about getting
with child—"

"I'm not. Really!" Acknowledging the truth was all the
more painful. It shattered her to her very core.

"I see." His voice came stiffly from the darkness.
"Had you denied Roy so vehemently, you might not be in
this situation now."

"Situation?" She stared at the star twinkling overhead.

"Being stuck on this island with a man you simply
cannot abide." Brice leapt gracefully to his feet. He walked
several paces up the path before her voice called softly
from the darkness:

"Brice?"

Donovan closed his eyes. Never in his thirty years had
he felt rejection so acutely and for an instant he wished he
had been more like his brother. Roy Donovan would have
had no qualms in taking what he wanted from Autumn.
None whatsoever.

Autumn, huddled against a rock, elbow propped on one
knee, thought that Brice Donovan could certainly brood.
He'd been doing it for the better part of an hour now. "It's
certainly cold, isn't it, Mr. Donovan?" She was tired of
the silence.

"Yep."

"It never occurred to me that the temperature would be
so much cooler after dark. I guess we're pretty high up,
though. What do you think? Ten thousand feet?"

She heard him chuckle. "More like one."

Autumn sniffed at his sarcasm. "Oh. Well, it certainly
seems high."

Several minutes passed and still Donovan said nothing.
Autumn rearranged her legs, once, then again, and stared
at the sky and stars and the ocean of blackness that stretched
forever around them. She heard Donovan shift, too, some-

where in the darkness. "So . . . what do you think made us pass out?" she asked him.

"Swamp gas."

"Swamp . . . on a mountain?"

"If you have a better explanation, Missus Donovan, I'm willing to hear it."

Autumn thought for a moment. "The gods might have caused it. You know what the Indians believe."

"The Indians also believe we are now married."

Her head swung toward Brice's voice. "What an absurd belief." She peeked over her rock and stared at his dark form, perched on a boulder, his shoulders hunched over his thighs and elbows on his knees. "Absurd," she emphasized more loudly.

"Hypocrite," he drawled. "You either regard their beliefs or you don't. You know, they say this mountain is haunted," he went on out of pure spite.

Autumn frowned.

"They say the souls of the dead wait here until allowed to join the afterlife."

"Absurd," she mumbled to herself, then crouched more closely to her rock.

"Good night," he said in a smug voice.

Autumn closed her eyes, but it was a long while before she slept.

Autumn wasn't sure what awoke her. She rubbed her eyes and stared out into the dense gray void and wondered if she were still dreaming. She was floating: there was neither sky above nor earth below her. Lights appeared and disappeared around her, pale, shimmering visions of no definite form, but oddly alluring.

"Donovan?" Her voice sounded muffled to her own ear.

A stirring of wind brushed her cheeks. Fingers of air lifted her hair from her shoulders and coiled it around her face. The song began, a sighing, haunting melody of awakening life, and as she stared, unblinking, into the eternal gray heaven, a sword of blinding white light streaked toward her so suddenly that she fell back against the rock and prepared herself for the thrust of its honed edge into her breast. It never came, but the white flash was followed by streaks of gold and red and green, like fingers of fire flickering in the mouth of a great, yawning hearth.

"Autumn!"

"Here!" she cried out in relief. Donovan materialized through the mist. They reached and touched, hands clasping, palm to palm, each finding strength in the other's presence. Autumn fell against him, wrapping her arms around his back, and wept. "Oh, God, we must be dead!"

He said nothing, just stared at the dawn, thinking she might be right.

They clung to one another and shivered.

They closed their eyes and thought heaven was here, in each other's arms. And if this was death, why hadn't they died long ago?

The sky began boiling then, whirling and tumbling around them, swirling in misty shapes of gray and white. Surely this was how God had seen it in the beginning, an earth without form, a void, a darkness upon the face of the deep. And with one swipe of His hand the firmament in the midst of nothingness took shape. The air was cold, then warm, then cold again. As they watched, clouds peeled away from the mountaintop, slowly, revealing a rock-covered precipice of sienna and black.

Onward the mist plunged, until the vague shapes of trees became visible but colorless still, their leafy fronds drooping toward the ground, heavy with dew. Where were the vibrant greens and golds of the coconut fronds, the metallic glint of banana leaves and the lightly bronzed tips of the star apples? There was only gray, interminable gray.

A ghostly white plume of smoke appeared, coiling up from the trees at the base of the mountain, then another and another, blending with the eddying currents of cascading clouds, and Autumn could almost imagine the Indians crouched around their fires, staring up the mountain and thinking her spirit was soaring with the zemises. Well, her spirit was soaring; her heart was hammering with excitement, and she was glad Donovan was behind her, holding her tightly around her waist, his lips in her hair, as he watched the spectacle with her.

She watched and waited, thrilled as she recognized

Hunnington's outbuildings, its orchards of oranges, lemons and limes. "Donovan, there. Do you see it? It's the kitchen gardens. Why I'm certain that's Celie's sweet potatoes and cassava I see!"

Donovan laughed and held her tighter. "If you can see that from here, sweetheart, you've got the eyes of a hawk."

"There!" She jumped up and down and pointed to undulating fields of cane. "We'll begin planting there, along that stretch of forest at the base of the mountain! And, oh!" She jumped again so suddenly she rapped him in the chin. "Oh, Brice, it's the house. Do you see it? There!"

"Aye, I see it."

The Greathouse shimmered ghostly white behind the tendrils of mist, its slate roof and black windows appealingly somber. Beyond the house the road appeared, twisting and turning like an ivory ribbon up and down the waking countryside, stretching from the sleepy village of Bovier, along the island's sandy coastline, occasionally through the forest, to the far side of Cayemite and Barrett Hall.

Yes, she could see Barrett Hall as well. It was a disturbing reminder that Donovan wasn't the only thing she shared with Annee Rose.

The fog seemed to stall over the water, and with growing anticipation Autumn and Brice waited for their first glimpse of the sea. Like a curtain of heavy gray velvet, the clouds parted, gradually revealing a colorless ocean. They stared at the horizon and waited again.

The shroud battled the sun for supremacy, and the sun won. It cast aside the dawn so abruptly that Autumn and Brice staggered from the impact of the brilliant light that spilled from the heavens, white and yellow and blinding. Brice threw his hand up over his eyes. Autumn buried her face in his chest. The sun crept over the watery horizon, obliterating the sky and washing the earth in heat.

And the sea turned blood-red.

Chapter 15

Dear Brice,

I will waste little time in pleasantries and get to the
point. I need your help. The situation here on Cayemite
is dire. Money is a problem. The people on the island
refuse to work, thanks to Annee Rose. She has convinced them that if they do so, they will risk the vengeance of Guede. She wants Hunnington, Brice, and I
suspect she will stop at nothing to get it. In short, I fear
my life is in danger.

I admit to having made a total wreck of my situation.
But you must understand what my life has been like
since Father's death. The responsibilities are enormous.
The isolation, day in, day out, has proven more than I
can tolerate. The damned place is impossibly lonely. I
have made efforts, however, to rectify the situation. I've
taken a wife, an enchanting child with brandy-brown
eyes. Autumn Sinclair hails from Charleston. The first
time I saw her she was riding astride along the beach,
wearing breeches, a man's shirt and no shoes, her curling copper hair swirling wildly about her shoulders. She
knows as much about planting as her well-to-do brother.
Unfortunately, I was forced to leave her in Charleston
until I could rectify the situation at Hunnington, but I
suspect she'll prove to be a very companionable partner,
out of bed as well as in, when I bring her to Cayemite.

Brother, I realize we have never been close, but I
beseech you; help me. For our father's sake and all he
worked for. You owe us that. Hunnington wouldn't be

in this trouble had you remained on the island and accepted your responsibilities as Patrick Donovan's eldest son, after all.

Roy

5 June 1831

Roy,

After four years and no word from Cayemite, your letter came as a surprise. You asked for my help, so I will give it. But I have responsibilities to Willow Bend that will occupy my time for the next few weeks. I should see you mid-July, at the latest.

By the way, congratulations on your marriage. Autumn Sinclair certainly sounds like the perfect young woman for the Donovan who has dedicated himself to be a successful planter . . . I think I'm in love with her myself.

Brice

Brice carefully refolded the letters and laid them side by side on the desk top. "I think I'm in love with her myself." He saw the words over and over in his mind. The feelings had started even then. He'd fallen in love with a fantasy that had embodied everything he'd ever wanted in a woman. And she didn't want anything to do with him.

Slouching in his chair, Brice closed his eyes. The urge to march up those stairs and beat on Autumn's door was frightening, but he'd made the decision while descending Trempe Mountain that the wisest move he could make at this time was to make no move at all. Too many complications could arise by becoming involved with Autumn now. He must keep his mind clear to sort out the problems on this island. Something was happening to Cayemite that had nothing to do with Annee Rose. Yes, she had terrified the workers into remaining in their straw-thatched hovels, but Annee had no control over nature, unless, of course, as the natives did, he was to believe that she embodied the soul of evil.

Well, she was evil, all right—and mad. And that was even worse.

Again, he opened his letter to Roy. I'm in love with her myself . . . I'm in love with her myself. Damn.

The memory came from nowhere, words spoken in jest. They wheeled into her foggy state of unconsciousness and sent her sluggish blood racing hotly through her veins. "Should there be a man who would marry me only for love and not strictly to beget him a long line of namesakes, I might consider the holy state of matrimony. Of course he would simply have to be the handsomest man in the entire world."

Those words haunted her now. How could she desire marriage to a man who didn't even love her? Who thought her a pain in the neck—that's how he had referred to her on their trip down the mountain—who only tolerated her presence because he had little choice? How could she envy Jeanette and Annee Rose because he used them in a way she had always scorned? Brice Donovan was right. She *was* a hypocrite!

Autumn squeezed her eyes more tightly shut and buried her face deeper into the satin folds of her pillow. She would stay here forever if she must, in this room with the door barred. She'd used the excuse, after returning to the house, that she was fatigued from that grueling journey up and down the mountain. No one had questioned it. Donovan had lifted one brow and, with apparent disinterest, left her to rest. She'd been miserable the entire time. She'd lain across the bed, hoping with every movement in the hall, with every creak of the floor, that Donovan would rap on her door and ask to see her. He hadn't.

Once she'd watched him from her window. He'd walked alone across the gardens to the beach below the house. He'd stood at the edge of the water, his hands in his pockets, and stared out to sea. Just looking at him had done queer things to her body. Her breathing quickened. Her heart raced. The sensation of butterflies in her stomach had turned into a heavy ache at the juncture between her thighs. The memory of his touching her there had made her uncomfortably hot and malcontent. Just thinking of it now accomplished a similar effect.

Rolling to her back, she kicked away her covers and opened her eyes. The flash of lights outside her bed caused Autumn to bolt upright. They arced overhead like meteors in the night sky. They danced in circles, in time with the drums, then exploded like sparks to drift toward the floor, then back up again. Blink . . . blink . . . blink—the yellow and white lights twinkled like the stars in heaven, a hundred lights so mesmerizing and enchanting that Autumn cried aloud.

Shoving aside her mosquito netting, she jumped from the bed. The lights flashed by her, around her, leaving phosphorescent little trails behind them. They swirled around her knees, and though she attempted to grab them, they eluded her hand, appearing and disappearing in the blink of an eye.

They circled the zemi across the room. As the statue's wide-eyed face appeared to blink at her in the darkness, Autumn ran for the door.

Throughout the house the tiny stars darted in the darkness, some in groups, others pulsing singly in time with the drums. Standing at the top of the stairs, Autumn called, "Donovan!" The lights zipped more hurriedly up and down the stairs and over her head. "Donovan!" she repeated.

Somewhere a door opened.

"Donovan, come quickly!"

He appeared at the bottom of the stairs. A light shone above his head, illuminating his features as he looked up at Autumn.

"Oh, Donovan, isn't it the most beautiful thing you've ever seen!"

Brice stared at her vision, swathed in white, a halo of light dancing around her shoulders. "Yes," he murmured thickly.

"It's like a thousand falling stars. Look at them dance!"

Slowly he started up the stairs.

Lifting the hem of her nightdress in one hand and grabbing the banister with the other, Autumn carefully tiptoed down the stairs. They met halfway. As on the morning they met on the Nelsons' staircase, Brice and Autumn eyed one another levelly.

"What are they?" she asked his eyes; for an instant they were all she could see.

"Fairies."

"Fairies?"

He nodded. "Fairies of Minetta."

A burst of light between their faces revealed his smile. Startled at the sudden tiny explosion, Autumn stammered, "Wh-who is Minetta?"

"The daughter of the last reigning chief on this island. She was evil and killed her father, wanting to rule over the people herself. She murdered them all because they would not acknowledge her as chief. The zemis of light sent their children to drive Minetta from Cayemite. Legend is that because they would not allow her to rest, she went mad."

"Mad."

Brice stepped closer. "Mad. There's a legend concerning this island and those . . . fairies. Stare at them long enough and you, too, will go insane."

"Do you believe that?"

"Every man or woman who's ruled this island, according to legend, has gone insane."

Autumn laughed. "Even the Donovans?"

"Some believe my father killed himself."

The words came like a blow from the darkness. Her reaction was instinctive. Cupping her hands gently along his cheeks she waited until the next pulse of light brightened his features before saying, "Oh, Brice, I had no idea. I'm so sorry."

"And Roy . . ." He turned his head slightly and said into her palm, "And me."

"You aren't insane."

"No?" He gently caught her wrist as she attempted to pull away. "I must be," he said in a husky whisper.

The fairies flickered around their shoulders, whirling in circles so quickly that they formed a close-knit chain of unending star shapes in the darkness.

Donovan pressed his mouth against the blue-veined skin of Autumn's wrist, touched it with his tongue, then ran his lips lightly to the edge of the lace-trimmed cuff of her three-quarter length sleeve. She closed her eyes, and behind her lids she visualized Donovan's face, highlighted with the soft pulse of the lights. When she looked again, the tiny torches seemed to have settled in his eyes, flashing with such feral heat her heart stopped beating for an infinitesimal moment. "Oh, Donovan," she moaned. "Donovan."

He was too weak to resist.

Sliding his arm around her waist, Brice moved up and against her, crushing the soft mounds of her breasts against his chest. Her nipples felt like hard buttons as they pressed through the light material of her wrapper and into his shirt. Her head fell back, exposing the pale arch of her throat and sending the riotous waves of her burnished-copper hair tumbling beyond her hips.

His hands moved over her, the flat of his palms brushing the sensitive tips of her breasts through her gown, down her stomach to the warm place between her thighs. The cotton became damp where his finger dipped tenderly into the soft recess, and though she pressed her legs together, he wedged his knee between them, pulling the gown taut beneath his hand.

She thought of a hundred reasons why she should run from Brice Donovan's embrace, then cast them aside in deference to the exhilarating rush of desire that caused her head to swim and her heart to thrash in her breast like a drowning person's. She was doomed. She knew that. She had fallen under his spell, that magical lilting cadence of his voice and the drowsy, hypnotic enchantment of his eyes. He made her feel alive. He made the blood sing in her veins just by entering a room. He made the nerve endings throughout her body vibrate with musical tension that filled her being with unbearable anticipation.

And when he touched her, as he did now, with his breath smelling lightly of brandy and his lips slightly sticky with the liquor, her world tumbled end over end, and she was helpless to stop the fall. And she didn't want to resist. She wanted to stay here forever. Yet, as his hands burned their mercurial path up the curve of her hip to her slender ribs and cupped her breasts in his palms, she sensed there could be more. So much more. Those forbidden images of men and women together flashed through her mind as startlingly as the sudden bursts of light swimming in the darkness of that stairwell, images that spoke of pain and death . . . and she didn't care. She didn't! She knew only that she wanted Brice Donovan so badly, in a way she couldn't even understand, that she would willingly sacrifice her body and soul for one promise of forever from those searching, demanding lips. For although she had everything she had ever dreamed of—independence and her own plantation—she couldn't shake free of the realization that without Brice it would all mean nothing.

His dark head came up. She glimpsed his closed eyes, their long, straight lashes and the tiny lines along their outer corners that looked deeper in the flickering light than they really were. He kissed her—a touch at first—then his mouth opened and his tongue swept her lips with its velvet tip before plunging inside her mouth, then withdrawing and plunging again in a way that matched the thrust of his hips against hers. But when she might have fled, afraid of the confusing responses in her body, he caught her buttocks in his hands and held her closer, so close that the length of his long, hard manhood jutted against her stomach and throbbed with a life of its own. A warm flood oozed through her lower body, and he sensed it.

His body like stone, Brice backed away. He stared at Autumn's swollen mouth, at the nipples high and hard and protruding through the gown like little rosebuds. "Will you come with me?" The query raked the inside of his throat. "Will you?"

"Where?"

He laughed, an abrupt, tight sound that vibrated Autumn from the tips of her tingling toes to the ends of her auburn curls.

Tracing her jawline with the tip of one tapered finger, he said softly, "Naïveté becomes you, love. Very well, if you're more comfortable with games, I don't mind. You know I want you, and I ask you to come with me to bed."

Autumn closed her eyes. He was too near, too damnably near for her to think rationally. But then, all rational thought had fled her the first moment she'd put eyes on Brice Donovan weeks ago.

The pounding started. Autumn thought, for a moment, that the expectation she was feeling throughout her body had somehow settled in her ears. But as Brice turned away and moved down the stairs, she realized that someone was beating frantically on the front door.

"Donovan! Damn you, Donovan, open this door!"

Annee Rose.

Donovan froze on the bottom step.

Like cold water in her face, the shock of hearing Annee's voice left Autumn winded. Clutching the banister, she began backing up the stairs.

Brice slowly turned to face her. "Autumn, stay where you are." The lion's head knocker again reverberated through the darkness. The tiny blinking lights began a frenzied assemblage against the ceiling that cast an eerie glow on Donovan's shoulders. "Stay," he told her again.

Autumn turned and, with gown lifted to her knees, fled up the stairs.

"Autumn!" Brice started up the stairs but the frenetic pounding on the door stopped him in his tracks. "Autumn, please! Dammit, Autumn . . . Autumn! Ah, damn!"

Anger mounting in her breast, Autumn slammed her bedroom door behind her. How could she have forgotten? How could he make her forget that Annee Rose existed? And Jeanette? And Pierre? He couldn't be satisfied with them—oh, no, he had to add her to his little harem, and she had almost allowed it. She, who had sworn never to be used by a man, had pressed her body against his and practically invited him to defile her. Why, for a moment she had actually fantasized love in his eyes and in the way her name had shuddered almost reverently against her ear.

Stupid girl! She wouldn't believe that any more than she would believe the lights wreathing her head were . . . were . . . fairies!

She swung at the light nearest her face. Her palm connected sharply with the tiny body, sending it spinning to the floor. "Oh, my!" Her offending hand clutched against her breast, Autumn stared, horrified, as the light shimmered weakly at her feet. Oh, dear God, she hadn't expected . . . oh, what had she expected? She dropped to her knees.

The pale light pulsed against her fingertips, and she jerked her hands away. "I'm sorry, so sorry," she cried to the fairy. "But, you see, now that Annee is back, he doesn't want me. She's just so beautiful. And I'm so frightened of having babies. A man like Brice Donovan deserves to have children. He's so handsome. And kind. He really is. He's been so patient." She covered her face with her hands and cried, "I didn't mean to hurt you!"

Stumbling to her feet, Autumn ran for her candle and lit it, babbling promises to the tiny injured creature that she would do everything humanly possible to save her. That she hadn't meant to be cruel; she was just so upset . . .

Autumn screamed as she turned. Where once the enchanting beauty of fairies had darted in the darkness, the tallow light revealed huge, ugly beetles swarming about the room and crawling over the furniture.

Falling back against the wall, Autumn slid to the floor, buried her face in the crook of her arm and wept. Her fantasies were crumbling one by one.

Annee Rose stumbled backward as Brice came at her through the door. Catching herself, she snarled, "How dare you do that to me!" then jumped at his face, fingers crooked, and buried her nails into the flesh of his neck. "How dare you humiliate me in that way!" she went on. "How dare you walk out on me in Jamaica without a word!" She beat his shoulders, chest and arms with her knotted hands, then his back as he doubled over in an attempt to shield himself from the blows. On and on she battered him until he could take no more.

He lunged at her like a cat in the darkness, catching her off guard. She tripped and fell to the ground, throwing her arm over her face as he lifted a menacing hand. But he didn't thrash her. He stood over her, arm raised as he threatened, "Come at me like that again, you little bitch, and I'll make you sorry you were ever born."

"Don't you dare threaten me!" she flared.

"I'll kill you, Annee, I swear to God!"

"What's wrong, lover boy, did I interrupt your little

tête-à-tête with your brother's wife?'' Annee threw her head back and barked an obscene laugh to the black sky. Then she asked, ''Does she have you mewling over her already, my darling Donovan? Has she convinced you that she finds you the most appealing man on the face of this earth? As she did Roy? She wanted nothing from Roy but this estate, and she used her body to get it. Now she wants it all, doesn't she? And the only way to get it is through you.''

''Shut up!''

''According to Roy, he wasn't her first, you know. She had such a widespread reputation, no man in Charleston would have her.''

''Roy—''

''Had an equally tawdry reputation and didn't care. Besides, she was the first woman he'd met who actually enjoyed his perverse ways of lovemaking. Oh, she would never do for you, Brice. Can you imagine taking her back to Virginia and introducing her to society? What will you do when you accidentally meet up with one of her former lovers? You'll be a laughingstock.''

Brice didn't move.

Shifting to her knees, Annee smiled her little-girl smile and continued, ''Why, she doesn't even want to have babies. She loathes children, according to Roy, just as much as he did. What of all your dreams, Donovan? What of the home you've built in Virginia? Who will it go to, if not your son?''

He brought his hands up slowly and pressed them against his ears. ''Shut up,'' he repeated in a craggy voice.

She ran her hand up his thigh. ''I can give you a son. Many sons. We're good together, Brice. You remember. Forget Autumn Donovan. Your brother's wife. Imagine how he must have used her. He told me how he used her. Would you like to hear how he used her?''

Ah, God! She's lying, she's lying, he repeated to himself. Yet there was no denying that the same thoughts had forced him from his bed many nights since Autumn's arrival.

Realizing her words were having their desired effect, Annee went on, ''You called me whore before leaving Jamaica, said the idea of your marrying a tramp was ludicrous. Well, at least I'm honest about what I want from you, Donovan.'' Her fingers plucked at the buttons on his breeches before she purred, ''Is she?''

Blink, blink, blink—the lights in the trees condensed in a cloud and moved silently across the gardens.

Brice stared unseeing at the ground. He didn't want to believe Annee. Receiving Roy's letter in Virginia, he had allowed Autumn Sinclair Donovan's image to obsess his mind, to fill the long hours of drudgery and the sleepless nights with the hope that somewhere there was another woman like her. And, when he reached the island and learned of Roy's death . . . ah, how he had dreamed. Her arriving then on Cayemite had been too good to be true. *She* was too good to be true, too beautiful, with her tumbling auburn hair and flashing eyes the color of sparkling brandy. Dammit, why couldn't Willow Bend be enough? Why?

''She doesn't want you, Brice.'' Annee smiled as Donovan's eyes shifted to hers. ''Haven't you more pride than to be used by that woman?''

He pushed her hand from his thigh. ''Go home, Annee.''

''Only if you come with me.''

The lights pulsed and hovered.

Brice thrust one hand through his black hair, kneaded the back of his neck. ''Not now,'' was his weary response. ''I—I have to think.''

''Why? I love you, Donovan. I have since we were children. Every man who came after you meant nothing.''

''You love the chase,'' he said. ''Once we were married, you'd grow bored, just like you did with your last three husbands. Besides, I have no intention of rotting on this damnable rock any longer than necessary.''

Her head came up. Pushing herself to her feet, Annee stared at Brice a long moment before speaking. ''But you said—''

''That I'd remain on Cayemite long enough to get Hunnington's affairs in order.''

Blink, blink, blink . . .

''I won't let you leave me again.'' Her voice was low and guttural. It was enough to send shivers up Brice's spine.

They stared at each other in the darkness, her threat hovering in the air as audibly as the sigh of wings that beat more frantically in the stillness.

"I'll do everything in my power to keep you on this island," she continued. "Everything."

The first light dodged past her nose. Annee gasped and stumbled backward. Another followed, then another and yet another, darting so thickly about her face that her terror-stricken features were cast as brightly as day. She swiped at them frantically and, backing away, hissed and growled so vilely the hair on the back of Brice's neck prickled. "Make them stop!" she screeched. "Stop!" Annee turned and ran for her horse.

Blink, blink, blink. The fairies followed.

Chapter 16

Autumn and Hugh Tyler stared curiously at the dark, expectant faces. "What do they want?" she asked him.

"T'pay tribute, I'm figurin'."

"For what?"

Tyler gave her a sideward glance. "They're thinkin' yer blessed." He pointed to the bowls of ground corn, dried fruits and what appeared to be plant roots that had been placed in a semicircle at her feet. "Since these are all offerin's to the spirits I'm reckonin' that's what they're believin' y'are, lass. Y've traveled t' the mountain and come back again, so y'must be."

"But that was days ago." She rubbed her temples, the throbbing within a reminder of how many sleepless nights had passed since her venture up and down Trempe.

"Y've been hearin' the drums at night?" As she nodded, he went on, "Their council's been mullin' over the idea. No doubt Henri smoked some of his farine whatever and decided anyone who goes t' the mountain and returns is the next best thing to an angel."

Autumn stared at the *gammelle* of water at her feet. "What about Donovan?" she asked Hugh softly. "He went with me."

"Their spirits are female."

"So, what am I suppose to do now?" She shoved her hands into her pockets.

"Whatever yer wantin' t'do."

Autumn looked up. Their eyes met. "Very well," she said. "Do they speak English?"

"Some."

"Do you speak their language?"

He nodded.

"Then tell them this: I wish for them to work for me, in

222

the building of the sugar mill and the planting and harvesting of sugarcane. By doing so they will be rewarded."

Hugh stared down on the top of Autumn's head. He missed that spark of enthusiasm that had reflected in her voice and manner upon her arrival on Cayemite. Her slender shoulders were drooped slightly and her eyes were shadowed. The reality of Hunnington's situation was bearing heavily on her mind. The fact that Donovan had moved out of the house hadn't helped matters.

He turned to the Indians and spoke to them. They responded with silence. "I reckon they're gonna have t' think on that one," he said then to Autumn.

Leaving the natives muttering among themselves, Autumn and Tyler moved down the path toward the few blacks who were struggling so diligently to build the new mill. Thank heaven there were those on the island whose lives weren't controlled by the whims of spirits.

The child's laughter caused her stride to falter, and though she tried desperately to keep from glancing toward the clapboard house beyond the stables, she couldn't help herself. Brice was there, with Pierre and Jeanette. He had been living with them for the past week.

Slowly Donovan walked their way, his hands in his pockets and eyes on the ground. Judging by the fatigue in his face, he had slept little the past few nights. He hadn't shaved that morning, and he wore the same clothes he'd worn the day before.

"Tyler," was all he said at first. He glanced toward the laboring blacks, looked at the ground and added, "Missus Donovan."

They all stood in silence, watching the grass grow and hating every moment of it.

Finally Tyler cleared his throat. "I imagine the cylinders'll be arrivin' in the next day or two."

Brice pursed his mouth slightly and looked at Autumn. She looked at Tyler.

Tyler looked at them both, one to the other. "Don't y' imagine?"

Brice and Autumn nodded in agreement.

Hugh went on, "I've been riggin' up a wagon large

enough t' carry 'em from Bovier to the house. We'll have t' bring 'em in one at a time."

They all looked toward the men laboring on the boiling house, Tyler thinking he had never met two more stubborn people, Autumn wishing Brice would move back into the house and Brice wishing he could.

But Brice, with Annee's help, had convinced himself that Autumn was a user of men, had been used by men and suffered no remorse over either. Even if Brice could forgive her her past, which he could easily do if he allowed himself, she would want no part of Willow Bend or of him because she had everything she'd ever wanted here on Cayemite . . . except his half of the plantation. And he wasn't about to let that go . . . yet. Letting that go meant letting her go, and he couldn't. In spite of everything, he couldn't.

Autumn had convinced herself that the misery she was feeling was entirely due to loneliness. These past days had been hectic with making plans for planting and discussing with Tyler her ideas on the building of storage barns and barracks for the workers. But the nights, ah, those nights, those long hours from sundown to dawn, had been monopolized by tedium. There were books in the library, but the words had continually blurred into a vision of green eyes and a taunting smile.

She spent hours in the tub, up to her neck in jasmine scent and bubbles. Afterwards she would slip on the gown Mary had given her, feeling foolish as she did so because there really was no reason to wear it. But she had come to enjoy the sleek coolness of the gossamer material; she liked the way she looked in it, and for the next few hours she would fantasize Donovan's walking through her door and finding her in it. Autumn practiced her surprise:

"Why, Mr. Donovan, whenever will you learn how to knock?"

"For shame, Mr. Donovan . . . walking in on a young lady during her toilette."

"Oh, do you like it, Mr. Donovan? It was just something I threw on in passing."

"I've missed you so, Brice. Please come home. Please."

Turning her back to Donovan, she said to Hugh, "I'll

be riding out to the east fields to see how the clearing is
coming. Will you have Tullius saddle me a horse?''

"Aye, maîtresse, I'll have 'em saddle the roan y' rode
yesterday.''

She thanked him and returned to the house.

The babbling of excited voices reached Autumn before
she stepped into the kitchen. She stared in disbelief at the
spitting cauldron of stew as it bubbled over into the fire. A
bowl lay shattered and dumplings were strewn across the
floor; a decapitated chicken was running across the floor
and bumping into the walls, splattering blood all over the
room.

"For heaven's sake, what is happening here?'' she
demanded.

The women's jaws snapped closed. No one moved.
Autumn watched as the beheaded fowl flopped onto its
back, pointed its feet toward the ceiling and died. Taking a
deep breath she asked, "Where is Celie?''

The Negress closest to the door pointed to her dark-
faced companion and suddenly wailed, "She done it! She
done kill dat *koklo* in dis room an' I tol' 'er not to. Go t'
de *Maître Source*, I tol' her, to kill dat *koklo*, but she
would not do it!''

Louder now, Autumn asked, "Where is Celie?''

"Lorgina no go to the *Maître Source!*'' the accused
woman railed. "Bahd lady cahm ahnd nail Lorgina's ear
to a tree. Wants no *koklo* blood in Source, no way, de
bahd lady say!''

"Where . . . is . . . Celie?''

"Tonnerre! Majeur, you be, and nothing more!''

Patience at an end, Autumn stamped her foot against the
floor so hard that pain shot up her leg. *"Assé-a!''* she
screamed. Pointing then to the dead *koklo* she ordered,
"En e, si'l vous plaît!''

They all gaped at Autumn as if she'd sprouted horns.

"Is there a problem here?'' came the deep voice behind
her, and it was all Autumn could do not to whirl, bury her
face in Brice's vest and weep. Instead, she turned very
slowly, and with slender shoulders squared, said, "No,
thank you.''

Donovan's hooded eyes took in the mess at Autumn's

feet. "I heard you screaming all the way to the boiling house."

"Did you?"

Brice smiled and nodded. He slid his hands into his pockets.

"Well." She motioned toward the floor. "They've killed a chicken in the kitchen."

He regarded the blood-spattered walls. "Seems our little feathered friend had a hard time giving up the ghost."

"Yes." A bubble of laughter swelled up inside her throat. She was so glad Brice was there she could almost pop! Subduing her excitement, however, she went on, "We seem to have misplaced Celie."

"Aha."

"Have you seen her?"

He stared at her boots, her knees, her waist, breasts and mouth. "No," he finally said looking into her eyes. "I would imagine she's off somewhere pouting. She wasn't pleased that you rotated all her workers."

"I only thought that the women working in the kitchen would be more suited to planting." She pointed to the workers. "These women are so much smaller than those Celie was using."

"There's a reason for that." He leaned his shoulder against the door frame and asked, "Would you like to know why?"

Up went her eyebrow. "I'm certain you are going to tell me, regardless."

"No."

"Oh. Well, I'm always open to suggestions, Mr. Donovan. Go on. Tell me why these women were used in the fields."

"They're Arda women."

Autumn frowned. "And that means?"

"You don't put two Arda women within speaking distance of each other, and certainly not together in a house. They make pitiful domestics and will quarrel among themselves just for the sake of hearing themselves talk."

Her face burning Autumn said, "Celie should have said something."

"It is not Celie's place to inform the maîtresse of the

house rules. *You* make the rules.'' Looking down at the watchful women, he ordered, ''Get this mess cleaned up, then *poussé allé.*'' To Autumn he added, ''Your horse is saddled.''

She waited, thinking he would leave the doorway. He didn't. Edging around him was difficult enough without his green eyes pinning her to the tiny space between him and the doorjamb. Autumn tried sucking in her breath, believing if she could avoid touching him in any way, she would be safe from the disquieting emotions that continually assaulted her senses when he was near. His presence brought sunshine to a day that was abnormally cloudy.

What, she wondered, could he do to her nights?

She dashed from the house to the saddled horse attended by Tullius. ''Would you care to join me?'' she called to Brice, but she didn't look back.

''Would you like me to?''

Tullius helped her to mount. Autumn looked down as Donovan looked up. Their eyes locked. ''You're welcome,'' she answered softly.

He waited a lifetime before saying, ''I'll be along directly.''

Directly. Just how long, exactly, *was* directly? Autumn thought that if she made her horse walk any slower he would doze. Attempting to turn her mind to something besides Brice Donovan, Autumn regarded the panorama around her. Dead or dying cane stretched as far as she could see, its stunted growth proof of soil depletion. Even if they cut it to the ground, it wouldn't continue to grow, so she had decided to section the fields and burn them. The ash would, in turn, be turned over and would eventually fertilize new crops.

The day was overcast, with dingy clouds that obliterated the blue of the sky. Autumn stared a moment at the mountain, or what she could see of it. For the past three days its blunt peak had been hidden by a depressing fog.

Since there had been no rain for the past week, Autumn surmised she should be thankful for the clouds. The unrelenting sun could be devastating to both man and beast, sapping their strength and consuming the streams with its hellish heat. Already her skin was browning, even through her clothes. The hat she had begun to wear had helped little, as the sun reflected off the parched earth and tinted her cheeks a honey-gold.

Reining her horse, she listened to the steady tempo of the *simidor* drums. Florilius, Tullius's youngest son, had taken to blowing the conch as well; the music blended so beautifully she was sometimes tempted to dismount and dance.

The workers were lined up and down the stream that ran crookedly through the center of the field they had begun to clear. Dismounting and tying her horse just inside a row of trees, Autumn approached them cautiously, curious over the ritual they must go through before any land was worked. Because their god resided in water, and because a stream ran through this particular field, sacrifice must be made to the *Maître Source:* Master of the Stream.

Along the stream were placed bowls of oil, peas and coconut milk. Henri, pipe jutting from his mouth, held a dead chicken in the air and prayed, *"Maître Source, moin mande pou ou gade jardin moin vini fait ici."*

"Enjoying yourself?"

"Brice!" Whirling, Autumn beamed a smile up at Donovan that sat him back on his heels. "I thought you weren't coming."

"And miss one of Henri's performances?" He laughed quietly. "Not on your life, sweetheart."

Autumn forced herself to look back at the ceremony. "What is he saying?" she asked him.

"Master of the Stream, I pray you to protect the garden I have just made here."

"Fascinating."

"Yes." The word brushed her ear.

Tipping her chin up at Brice she inquired, "How is Jeanette?" Good God, she thought, just go ahead and stick the knife in a little deeper, Autumn.

He looked surprised. "Fine."

"And Pierre?"

"Fine."

They stared at the ceremony a while longer.

"Pierre is certainly a beautiful child," Autumn suddenly blurted. "You must be very proud."

His brows knitting together, Brice looked down into Autumn's freckled little face. "He means a great deal to me."

She swallowed. "That's understandable."

Brice frowned a little harder.

The drums beat a little louder.

Autumn wanted to die, and she knew that if she stood there beside Donovan any longer, she was going to cry all over his shirtfront. Turning abruptly, she started back for her horse.

"Where are you going?" he called.

"I've just recalled an appointment."

"With *whom?*"

"I've some letters to write!"

"Are you sending them out by pigeon?" Her shoulders snapped back at that one, and Brice laughed to himself.

The horse shied at her approach. It tossed its head nervously and skittered sideways as she attempted to mount. "Whoa," she soothed him, and patted his neck. The animal quieted, and again she attempted to mount. Brice came up behind her, cupped his palms around her buttocks and hoisted her up and into the saddle. Her cheeks like hibiscus blooms, she blinked down at Donovan and offered, "Thank you."

"My pleasure." They both looked toward the hand he had rested on her thigh. He slowly removed it.

Gathering her courage she ventured, "Will I see you back at the house?"

"Is that an invitation?"

"It is your house, too. I hardly think you need an invitation to come and go inside its walls."

A half dozen John Crows burst from the treetops, their giant wings beating the air like muffled gunshot. The horse whinnied. The foliage on the trees rattled strangely, and for a moment the pounding of the *simidor* drums ceased. There was silence again, like those few moments of silence on the mountain when it seemed the entire earth had stopped moving. They were waiting. For what?

Florilius was the first to look toward the hill. His eyes

wide in terror, he pointed to the robe-clad figure riding the startlingly white horse and cried, "Ahhh-eee, Minetta!"

Donovan's horse screamed and bolted, tearing its reins from the bushes on which it had been tethered, and fled across the shallow stream. More John Crows lifted from the treetops and a roaring like distant thunder began to vibrate the very earth where they stood.

Autumn felt the mare tense beneath her. Like a possessed thing, it threw up its head and reared, its front hooves pawing the air so recklessly that Donovan was forced to dive to one side to avoid being struck. Autumn clutched at its mane and dug her knees into the animal's side to avoid tumbling backward. Her efforts did little good, however, as the mare began to buck and kick, and though she clutched desperately to stay astride the beast, her fall was inevitable.

The world was a mad cacophony of sounds in that moment. She heard Donovan cursing, heard him call out her name even as she rolled backward over the horse's rump. She heard the terrorized screams of the workers as they ran into the stream and prayed to the *Maître Source* to save them from Minetta. And the roaring was louder, and she wasn't certain, but she thought she saw Donovan falling, too, as if the earth had somehow slid out from beneath his feet. He was going down, down . . . just as she had, and she wondered, before she hit the ground, if the fall would kill her.

She dreamed she was back in Charleston. There were Mary and Mitchell. Lollie was saying something like "I tol' you some man was gonna sit you right back on that breeches-clad behind o' yores!"

Oh, Lollie, Lollie, how could you know?

Mary and Mitchell were arguing again. "But she's in love with him," came Mary's strident cry. "It is written all over her face!"

How could you know?

Mitchell stared down at her with tears in his eyes. "He'll be good to you, for you. Just give him a chance, Autumn."

How did you know?

Her eyelids fluttered open. Autumn stared at the canopy over her bed and wondered how she came to be here.

"Hello," the child's voice whispered close to her ear.

Turning her head, she blinked into Pierre's black-lashed green eyes. "Hello," she said.

"I've been watching you sleep."

"Have you?"

He nodded and a curl of ebon hair tumbled over his brow. *"Oui.* Do you know there are more than five freckles across your nose?"

"Are there?"

"Oui. Do you know how I know?"

"How do you know?"

"Because I can only count to five and there are more than five that I cannot count."

"I see."

He studied her for a moment. "I'm glad you did not die," he stated then.

"Are you?"

"Oui. Do you know why?"

Her head hurt, but she shook it, nevertheless.

"Because I like your hair. I have never seen hair the color of fire."

"Do you still think I'm a witch?" Autumn asked him softly.

His little face screwed up in a frown. After considering the question, he stated, "Yes. We all believe you have brought good magic to the island. I like you very much. So does my *maman.*"

Her eyes throbbed. So did her head and shoulders and back.

"I have something for you." Pierre's voice held a child's breathless expectation. He dived toward the floor, then was back again, holding the overturned glass up with a great sense of pride and accomplishment. "Do you like it?" he asked, and Autumn wanted to cry.

The mammoth butterfly, swirled with red and yellow and black, pumped its tissue-thin wings in time with her heartbeat.

"Oh!" she exclaimed. "A butterfly!" And carefully, she touched the glass.

His eyes widened as a tear ran over the bridge of Autumn's nose and dripped onto the satin-lined pillow. "Don't you like butterflies?"

"Yes. Yes, I do. Do you know that when I was a child, I used to chase them?"

"Did you catch them?"

"Oh, no," she responded in all seriousness, "I was never fast enough to catch them."

Out went his little chest, and he looked so much like Donovan that Autumn had to bite her lip to keep from crying that much harder. "I caught this one myself," he boasted.

"Did you!"

"*Oui!* Would you like to come with me to the valley and catch one yourself?"

Autumn smiled. "I would like that very much."

"When your head is better, I will take you there." He shimmied off the side of the bed. "I have to go now. Donovan told me to tell him when you woke up." Pierre looked back over his shoulder, that familiar grin curling up one side of his lips. "I believe Donovan likes you very much."

"Oh?" Her heart stopped beating.

"He was very upset when he carried you in. You had blood all over your face."

Her fingertips tenderly explored the swelling at her hairline.

Holding the glass-caged butterfly against his chest, Pierre went on, "He slept beside you all night."

"Upset," she repeated, in disbelief.

"Yes." He walked to the door, hesitated and looked back. "I never saw Donovan cry before."

Autumn was still staring at the door five minutes later when Donovan came in. He was carrying a tray of food.

Brice stopped inside the door. "Hello," he said, much like Pierre had earlier.

Autumn smiled in response.

"I thought you might be hungry."

"Yes," she lied.

He slid the tray onto the bedside table, then helped

Autumn to sit upright by piling pillows behind her back. Then he gently tucked a napkin into her collar and placed the tray across her lap. Sitting down beside her, he waited for her to eat.

Autumn stared down at the chicken and wrinkled her nose.

"You don't have to eat it if you don't want to," he assured her.

"After yesterday, I'm not certain I will ever eat chicken again."

He took the tray from her lap and set it aside.

Tick . . . tick . . . tick. The timepiece on her dresser sounded like the monstrous clock on the courthouse that fronted on Charleston's town square.

They waited in silence.

Autumn's head was pounding, but the discomfort was nothing compared to the ache that was battering her heart in that moment. Donovan looked so . . . solemn. And tired—defeated, even. His eyes were red-rimmed. His clothes were rumpled. He still hadn't shaved. The burden of his thoughts weighed so heavily on his mind that his dark head drooped slightly between his shoulders, so he buried it in his hands.

"What's wrong?" she asked him, dreading the answer.

He stared at the floor.

Her world swimming, Autumn sat upright, her fingers lightly touching the bunched muscles of his upper arm through the coarse material of his osnaburg shirt. He leapt from the bed so suddenly she sat back in surprise. "What's wrong?" she repeated.

Rocking back on his heels, Brice glared down into Autumn's face. It was white but for the sprinkling of freckles and the tiny spots of color on her cheeks. "Stop looking at me that way!" he bellowed so loudly the plate of chicken rattled on the tray.

The words crashed against her ears. "How was I looking?"

"All sloe-eyed and innocent, that's how!" Brice paced the room. "Dammit, I've been half out of my mind with worry."

"Oh?"

"Oh?" he mocked her. "You damn well know it, Missus Donovan."

"Please," she said softly. "Call me Autumn."

Donovan stopped dead still. "Oh, no. You'd like nothing more at this point than to twist me around your little finger, as you must have done to my brother. Well, I won't get caught in that trap."

"Trap!"

Squaring his shoulders and thinking they had never felt so heavy, Brice steeled himself one last time. "I want you off this island."

Her eyes burned. So did her throat. She stared at the sheets that covered her feet and swallowed hard. "I know that," she forced herself to reply. Finally lifting her tear-spiked lashes she looked at Donovan and said, "I know you don't like me much, Mr. Donovan."

He glowered.

Autumn went on. "Oh, you were kind enough while my brother was here, though I've often wondered why you chose to participate in my little ruse. I would suppose it was because you had little choice. Hunnington *is* partly mine, after all. And since I have no intention of selling it . . . perhaps you thought you could change my mind?"

A heavy lock of hair slipped over his brow and tickled the bridge of Brice's nose. He brushed it back with a flick of his hand.

"Or perhaps you thought you might marry me in hopes of gaining control over it all?"

He laughed.

"Well, it won't work." Her voice was hard now. "I won't be used for any reason. You have Annee and Jeanette to engage freely in your deviate pleasures—"

"Deviate!"

"You don't need me for that. Neither will I be tricked into handing you my half of Hunnington. It is mine!" She thumped the bed with her fist. "I won't leave this island!"

Brice wanted nothing more than to leave the discussion at that. But he knew, for her own safety, that Autumn should leave the island. It was a dilemma he had struggled with since the very moment Tullius had found him in the fields and announced that Maîtresse Donovan had arrived on Cayemite. "But it isn't safe for you here," he tried to reason.

"Really, Mr. Donovan, I fear you overreact. I suffered only a small bump on the head, and you act as if the entire island is about to crumble on top of us all."

Brice turned toward the window. "The natives killed your horse."

"What?"

"They believe the miserable, frightened beast was a *baka*, and hung the animal at the crossroads."

Autumn slumped into her pillows. Imagining the beautiful mare dead and hoisted between two poles was enough to make her dizzy again.

Propping his hands against the window frame, Brice listened intently to the water's distant hissing across the sand. It was hard to believe that the day before that blue-green serenity had been disturbed enough to slosh waves up over the road and halfway to the house. In all the years Brice had spent on Cayemite, even through some of the most treacherous storms, never had he seen the water behave in such way without a strong wind disturbing it. But there had been no wind, no movement at all—except the occasional trembling of the earth. That alone should be enough to convince Autumn to leave the island. And yet he stood there irresolute, with his jaw locked and reason out of his reach. He couldn't let her go. But with that decision came the sobering realization that he would somehow have to deal with Annee.

It could no longer be delayed.

Chapter 17

The cylinders arrived the next day. Autumn was kneeling
among the thigh-deep purple foliage of potato plants when
Pierre came dashing around the front of the house, his eyes
sparkling and his hair flying in the wind.

"They are here!" he called to her. "Come quickly,
maîtresse; the cane squashers have arrived!"

Brice called them cane squashers, so Pierre did, too.

The ensuing excitement was tangible, vibrating in the
air. The mill workers dropped what they were doing and
rushed toward the road. The domestics ran out from the
house, a splendid array of brightly colored flowing skirts
swirling around bare feet and ankles. Autumn joined them,
caught up in the anticipation that crackled the air.

Around the bend the horseman appeared, riding low in
his saddle, his white shirt billowing around his forearms as
he rode into the wind. And as the men and women making
their way down the road separated to let him pass, Donovan reined his frothing animal up beside Autumn and
offered his hand.

"Your cane squashers are here," he said, gazing down
into her watchful eyes. His mouth twitched into that
bewitching smile, making her forget that only yesterday he
had stated that he wanted her to leave the island. She took
his hand, and with a simple flex of his arm, he hoisted her
onto the rump of his horse.

The schooner, all sails lowered except the mainsail,
rode the swells of the deep, clear bay, then headed up into
the wind to come alongside the dock. From the deck the
shiny steel cylinders reflected the sun, and Autumn hugged
herself in excitement.

"Ho, there!" the captain called. "Are ye Donovan and Donovan Company?"

"Aye!" Donovan called back.

"And have ye hailed me to deliver these machineries from Montego Bay?"

"Aye!" Brice smiled askance at Autumn and yelled, "We've ordered two cane squashers from Jamaica!"

"And would this be them?"

"It would!" Autumn joined in. "Indeed it would!"

Donovan and Donovan looked at each other and laughed.

The smell of weathered wood mingled with the tang of sea air. A sudden gust of wind whipped at the taut standing rigging. Autumn blinked the tears from her eyes, and when Brice asked her softly what was wrong, she lied and said the wind had tossed sand in her face. She felt foolish. While other women throughout the world were fawning over voluminous skirts and whalebone corsets, she was becoming emotional over mill machinery. Then, thinking again, she realized it wasn't only the equipment; it was Donovan, too. She could easily believe that he was enjoying himself, that he looked at her with pride on his face and that he understood her need for accomplishment.

Within an hour the entire island knew that Maîtresse Donovan's cane squashers had arrived; the *ahhh-oooo . . . ahhh-ooo* of Florilius's conch song had told them. The natives came from the hills and forests and their village, women bare-breasted and children riding goats. They all stared in awe at the glittering round contraption that was strapped to the back of Tyler's wagon. Behind him came a smaller wagon loaded with *taches* and iron gutters. Inquisitive children clambered aboard, despite their parents' warnings to stand back.

It was a day Autumn would never forget. The Indians, apparently having discussed her proposition at some length, joined in the festive occasion. Donovan, however, kept his distance. Several times throughout the day Autumn saw him speaking quietly with Tyler. Then there was Jeanette. The young woman was distressed, weeping upon occasion and arguing with Brice so heatedly that he had mounted his horse and ridden away, only to return after several minutes to continue their discussion in a quieter tone.

Autumn was overseeing the placement of one of the cylinders when Jeanette approached her. "Maîtresse?" came her softly accented voice.

Autumn watched the workings a little longer before turning to face her.

"I must speak with you on a matter of extreme importance. It is concerning Donovan." They walked silently across the grounds before Jeanette found the courage to speak further. "He is going to Annee tonight."

At a loss as to what to do with her hands, Autumn crossed her arms over her breasts and fixed her eyes on some distant object. "I see," was her only response.

"This does not distress you?"

"It's really none of my business."

Her head tilting slightly, Jeanette stared unblinkingly into Autumn's face. "Then it's true? You do not care for Brice?"

"How I feel toward Mr. Donovan would have little effect on his behavior, I fear." Unfolding her arms, she slid her hands into her pockets. "He's proven that by moving in with you."

Jeanette frowned.

Autumn went on after a slight hesitation, "I'm certain if anyone could convince Donovan to stay home, it would be you and Pierre. He is, after all, devoted to the boy."

"But I cannot convince him. He believes if he goes to her, you and the island will be safe from harm. She is an evil person, maîtresse. She has killed her last three husbands!"

Autumn froze. The hammering and singing and the barked orders of the *busha* became as muted as the hazy sun that penetrated through the leaves of the breadfruit and banana trees overhead. "Killed them," Autumn repeated.

"Yes! We all fear her, maîtresse, because she thinks nothing of killing or torturing the people on this island. Donovan is inviting his own death if he goes to her."

Autumn thought of Patrick Donovan.

Stepping closer, Jeanette beseeched her, "Convince him to leave the island, maîtresse, and go with him yourself. Yes! You must go with him. And take my Pierre, too!"

"Pierre!"

"Yes! This island holds no future for my son. It will destroy him as it has all the others." She fell to her knees and, gripping Autumn's hand in both of hers, wept. "I cannot die knowing my son has been sentenced to the same fate as I!"

Oh, my! Autumn dropped to her knees before the trembling woman, looked into Jeanette's moist brown eyes and said, "You should speak of these matters to Donovan. He is the child's parent. As his father—"

"Father!" Jeanette's dark face turned scarlet. Wiping her tears, she repeated. "Father! Oh, no . . . No! Maîtresse, you believe . . . Brice is not my Pierre's father. Roy was Pierre's father!"

The confession sat Autumn back on her heels. Breathless, her face bloodless, Autumn stammered, "B-but, I—I thought since you and Donovan are lovers—"

"Lovers!"

"Well, aren't you lovers?"

"Maîtresse, Brice is my brother!"

Autumn jumped to her feet.

"Patrick Donovan was my father." Jeanette stood, too, and faced Autumn squarely. With as much courage as she could muster, she explained, "My mother was from the village. He took her into his house as a servant even before his wife died. I was raised as Pierre is being raised now, given the freedom of coming and going as I pleased, but I could never be allowed acknowledgment as his daughter. It is not done."

"But Roy—"

Jeanette interrupted, "I do not like to speak ill of the dead, and I know he was your husband, but Roy was a bad man. He was cruel to all these people and misused us when he could. He hated the idea of having a Creole for a sister and had no second thoughts about using me."

Her face burning, Autumn grabbed the girl's shoulders and demanded, "Did he rape you, Jeanette?"

"Yes, maîtresse. Many times."

"But how could Brice allow it? Why did he do nothing to stop him?"

Jeanette laughed, a sad little laugh, and shook her head. "Has the stubborn man told you nothing of himself? No?

Brice left this island twelve years ago. As a young man of eighteen he traveled to Jamaica and lived for two years in Montego Bay. He then traveled to Virginia, where he built a respectable home for himself and his future family. He returned to Cayemite only because Roy pleaded for his help. Roy had lost everything. Everything! All the banks between here and Charleston had cut off his money and were threatening to foreclose on Hunnington!''

Autumn turned away. She felt cold, then hot. And as she looked out on the nearly completed mill, the waving fields of sun-splashed cane in the distance, the horrible realization hit her that *none* of this was hers. It belonged to Brice. He had paid off the loans with his money. He had purchased the cylinders and *taches* and gutters; they were his alone.

Feeling awkward in the silence, Jeanette lightly touched Autumn's arm. ''I beg you, consider what I have told you. Donovan is filled with guilt over leaving his father those many years ago, because Roy convinced him that Hunnington's failure was due to his shirking his responsibility as Patrick's oldest son. Give him a reason to believe in himself once more. If you care for him at all, do this, please!''

Autumn blinked. The cylinders didn't seem quite so shiny or magnificent now. ''I have to think,'' she said more to herself than to Jeanette.

Autumn walked down the path, beyond the stable yards filled with cattle and oxen. She thought of Donovan on the evening Mitchell had perused Hunnington's accounts. Lies, all lies. He'd watched from the shadows and said nothing. She recalled the morning in the Bank of Jamaica, Brice sauntering in with his cocky smile and his assurances that her dreams were just around the corner, were there for the asking. She had grabbed them and run, convincing herself that, thanks to Roy, the world had been laid at her feet. Roy had bequeathed her nothing, really. Brice had given her everything.

She had a horse saddled. Leaving the stables, she rode past a silk-cotton tree; under its great shading limbs were babies sleeping on bright scraps of multicolored cloths. Their mothers were stooped in the nearby kitchen gardens,

tending sweet potatoes and peas. Giving the animal its
head, she rode long and hard through the cane fields, the
towering stalks a yellow-green blur out of the corner of her
burning eyes. She raced along the pearly line of coastal
beach, eternal-blue to her right and forever-green to her
left, each vista ready to swallow her with its fathomless
beauty.

The brilliant splash of red from the giant poinsettia tree
ahead caught her attention, and Autumn headed toward it,
her horse diving into the dense shadow of the forest and
out again. Bursting into the harsh yellow sunlight, she
blinked, reined her animal and blinked again.

In the center of the mostly barren field stood the poinsettia tree. A woman was hugging its massive trunk.

"Help me!" The vague voice drifted on the sea wind to
Autumn's ear. "Help me!"

Donovan slouched in the damask-covered chair and listened to the light tinkling of crystal behind him. In a
moment a glass was suspended over his shoulder; he took
it and stared down into the swirling brandy without a
glance at the woman beside him.

"I'm glad you're here," she said softly, against his ear.

He took a drink.

Annee walked slowly to the settee across the room. Her
red silk wrapper belled around her knees slightly and
flapped open as she turned to face Brice. She wore nothing
underneath. "Will you come sit beside me?" she asked.
Sitting, she patted the overstuffed cushion beside her.

Very slowly he left his chair and joined her.

"Remember when you courted me?" Annee slid one
flattened palm across his chest, up his throat, and cupping
his jaw in her hand, forced his face around to hers. She
swept his lower lip with the pad of her thumb. "I would
make you wait here in the parlor and speak with my father
while I dressed."

He had never courted her. Never. Brice stared into her
eyes and waited.

"Do you know how long I've waited for this, my
darling Donovan? Since the day you left Cayemite, I've
fantasized your returning to me. Now you have, and I

wonder why." She kissed him lightly, just a small, dry peck. Then she smiled knowingly. "She's turned you away, hasn't she?"

He shook his head.

"Come now, Donovan. I know you wanted her. Now you know how I've felt all these many years, remembering the times we had together and aching for them so badly I would have done anything to get them back."

"Just what might you have done, Annee?" The deep timbre of his voice in the quiet room was like a sudden crack of thunder. The shorthaired dog beside the door lifted its head, blinked its yellow eyes at Brice, and growled.

"Waited," she said simply. Throwing her arm along the settee behind Brice's shoulders, she leaned against him and smiled again. "I knew you would eventually have no choice but to return to Hunnington."

"Once my father and brother were dead."

Annee feigned a little pout. "Such an unfortunate set of circumstances."

"Annee, I don't believe my father killed himself. I think someone pushed him from that cliff. He didn't jump." She smiled and ran one long, tapered fingernail along his jawline to his chin and finally to his mouth. He swallowed and went on, "I don't believe Roy accidentally caught his bed on fire. I think he was drugged and the bed set afire."

"Roy was a drunk, my darling, and Patrick was a depressed old man who finally realized he was a failure as a planter." Further dismissing his remark, she said, "You have an overimaginative mind, Donovan, and are far too suspicious for your own good. Besides, who would do such a thing?"

She was daring him to say it, so he did. "You."

The wrapper slid off her thigh as Annee sat back. One white breast swung free of the silk bindings. "I?" she asked. Rising from the settee Annee paced back and forth across the room. "Whoever gave you such an asinine idea, Donovan? It was that old man, wasn't it? Henri Touisannt?"

"No."

"That old bastard hates me," she spat out so vehemently the dog curled its tail closer to its body. Her robe open, legs spread and hands on her hips, Annee demanded, "Was it he?"

"No," he repeated.

"He's a liar if he said it!"

His head came up. "He's your grandfather."

Her eyes like violet fire, Annee swept her hand over the nearest table, sending its procelain contents shattering against the floor. "I deny it!" she snarled, baring her teeth.

Slowly Brice got to his feet. "Keep your voice down, Annee. I'm in no mood to deliberate with a banshee."

Moving against him, Annee pressed her body against his and whined, "They all hate me, you know. My mother hated me so much she killed herself. My father wanted nothing more than to turn me over to those godforsaken savages and their heathenish ways, but even they turned me away. Well, I showed him. I showed them all that Annee Rose is more powerful than their weakling spirits. Now I control them all!"

And as if to prove her point, she coiled her arms around Brice's neck and forced his mouth down to hers. He kissed her back, not because he wanted to, but because he must. He'd grown tired of the game. It was time to end it—one way or another.

When Annee pulled away, her mouth was wet and cherry-red. "You'll make her go?" she asked, meaning Autumn.

Brice nodded.

"Swear it."

Closing his fingers around her white throat, he smiled coldly, wanting nothing more than to squeeze the soul, should she harbor one, from her beautiful body. "I told you long ago that Autumn's stay was only temporary. I gave her two months to play planter. At the end of those two months, I intend to pack her away on the next ship to Charleston."

Pleased, Annee smiled. "Come with me up the stairs," she begged him.

He closed his lids and pretended her eyes were as golden-brown as fine Irish whiskey and her hair was a jasmine-scented cloud of tumbling auburn curls. It would be easier that way.

The dog growled and Brice looked around.

Autumn stood in the doorway.

Their eyes clashed and Autumn looked away, around the room, and finally at the floor. Brice shoved Annee away. "What the hell are you doing here!"

Annee whirled toward the door, doing nothing to cover her nudity. She only laughed.

Every drop of blood seemed to have puddled in Autumn's face. She stared at Brice with such wide and innocent eyes that he felt like cutting out his own heart and throwing it at her feet. "Well?" He yelled it.

She flinched, stepped back, and for the first time since the moment they'd met, she appeared to be at a loss. "Oh, I—I—I didn't know . . ." Finally her chin came up and her eyes flashed. She looked beyond Brice to Annee Rose. "I am here to speak with Maîtresse Rose."

"Indeed?" Annee purred.

"Yes. Yes, I am. Myah!" she barked. He heard a shuffling of feet. Suddenly next to Autumn there was a young Indian girl, her shoulders stooped, her face and left shoulder covered in blood. She was cupping her ear in her hands and trembling. "Madame Rose," Autumn continued, "I have just learned that you have misused one of my employees in the most despicable way. I found Myah with her ear nailed to a poinsettia tree."

"And what does that have to do with me?" Annee asked.

"She tells me it was done by your decree."

Autumn glanced at Brice. He stared at Annee.

"I found her stealing from my property," Annee finally responded.

"What," Autumn demanded, "did she steal, exactly?"

"A banana."

"Banana? Only a banana! You have disfigured this child for the sake of a banana, when there are thousands to be had on this island?"

"It was *my* banana." Hooking her arm through Brice's, Annee taunted, "I assure you, Maîtresse Donovan, the man or woman who takes anything of mine will sorely regret it."

Autumn stepped closer. "Never, under any circumstances,

will you mistreat my people again. Should they break any civil law, you will bring it to my attention, and I will deal with it. If you ever harm one of them again, I will contact the authorities in Jamaica and press charges against you. Am I understood?''

Brice felt the shiver that passed through Annee's rigid body. She didn't respond to Autumn's ultimatum, and he surmised it was only because she had been stricken speechless. Annee Rose was not accustomed to taking orders, and though he could have grabbed Autumn Donovan up in his arms and kissed her for her heroism, he knew there would be hell to pay.

As Autumn turned from the door, cradling Myah's shoulders in her arm, Brice disengaged Annee's hand and stepped after her. ''Donovan!'' Annee cried. ''You aren't leaving!''

Autumn looked around, then away, concentrating her efforts on helping the injured girl. Brice stared at the blood dripping onto the white marble floor and said simply, ''Yes.''

''But our plans! You promised me, Brice—''

''I'll be back.'' The words caused Autumn to hesitate. He noticed, then repeated. ''I'll be back.''

By midafternoon word of Annee's misdeed had reached the natives. They disappeared into the forest as quickly as they had appeared that morning. Sitting upon an overturned *tache*, Autumn watched the few lingering blacks struggle with their chores while she thought about Brice.

Brice with Pierre balanced upon his broad shoulders.

Brice with Sara Nelson cuddled in his arms.

Brice as he looked with fairies dancing in the dark about his head.

And Brice with Annee—kissing her, holding her, breaking Autumn's heart, and he didn't even know it, or care. But why should he care? She'd accused him of being a cheat, a gambler and a womanizer. Well, she could discount his being a cheat and a gambler, and though she had been mistaken about Jeanette, she couldn't dismiss Annee. Closing her eyes, she tried to wipe the image of his holding Annee from her mind. It wasn't possible, and as the picture bore painfully into her memory, she dropped her forehead onto her upraised knee, and sighed.

"Hello." The little voice was a melody.

She tilted her head and peered out of the corner of her eye. A butterfly at the tip of her nose beat its butter-colored wings next to her cheek. "Hello," Autumn said.

Pierre sidled up to her. They each studied the insect on his finger, watching as it lifted, as softly as a breath, into the air and fluttered away.

"Good-bye," he sang to the butterfly.

"Good-bye," Autumn echoed.

Pierre turned his wide gray-green eyes up to Autumn's and asked, "Would you like to come to the valley with me now?"

"The valley?"

"My secret place. Where I go to chase butterflies."

"Is it far?"

His curls bounced with the shake of his head. "Oh, no. It is never far to any place on Cayemite. But we must be careful. My *maman* warned me the bad lady might get us. Are you afraid of the bad lady?"

Autumn thought a moment. "No," she replied.

"I told them all you would not be afraid. I told them all your magic is stronger than the bad lady's."

The tears came. She couldn't help it. Lightly touching his flushed, damp cheek with her fingers, Autumn said, "I've no magic, Pierre."

Pierre's face took on a solemnness that was startling for one so young. "But you do, maîtresse! You made Dono-van happy, and that is good magic."

"Did I, Pierre? Tell me how I made Donovan happy."

"By coming here."

"Was he unhappy before I came?"

"Oh, yes. Very unhappy. He would sit in that dark little room with the angels near the ceiling and drink *clarin* all the night."

"You are certain?"

The boy nodded. "I sneaked from my bed sometimes and watched him. I prayed to my loa that he would not turn into a bad man like his brother." He wiggled in the manner of all little boys, then scratched his nose. "He sat on the settee with a bottle in one hand and a letter in the other.''

"Letter?" Autumn lifted one brow, curiously.

"I saw it in the desk once, but could not read it. I don't know how to read.''

Autumn smiled. "Perhaps we should teach you. Would you like that?''

His eyes, wide, suddenly sparkled with excitement. "Could you teach me to read, 'I think I'm in love with her myself'?''

She caught his smooth cheeks in her palms and stared down into Pierre's eyes, so much like Brice's. "Why?" she asked him. "Why would you want to read something like that?''

"So I can read the letter, too.''

"The letter.''

"Yes. Donovan's letter. I sat in the shadows and heard him read it: 'I think I'm in love with her myself', it read.''

Jumping from his perch, Pierre caught Autumn's hand and coaxed her, "Come along, maîtresse, and we will go to the valley. I will catch you the grandest butterfly on Cayemite.''

"Promise?''

"Yes!" He bounded down the path, a miniature of Brice Donovan, making Autumn smile despite the mounting pressure in her head and heart. And she followed him, remembering all those butterflies she had chased as a child, and all those brightly colored dreams that had slipped through her fingers and fluttered away. Well, she could run a little faster now and fight a little harder. Her dreams, she realized, were there for the taking.

Chapter 18

She had believed, standing atop that grassy knoll, that she was looking on a valley of flowers; they were butterflies, all of them, with tiny transparent wings pulsing in the crystalline afternoon air. Closing her eyes now, she could see again Pierre's dashing into the living rainbow; the yellow and blue and red cloud rose into the nearly colorless sky and drifted on the breeze before settling again onto the waving, knee-high grass. She and Pierre had chased butterflies until they both fell exhausted to the ground. She'd caught a thousand of them, it seemed—a thousand dreams, a thousand fantasies, and all of them with Brice Donovan's face.

Jeanette knocked softly on Autumn's bedroom door, then entered quietly, a silver service balanced upon her upturned palms. "I have brought your tea, maîtresse." Autumn looked at her thoughtfully from behind her jasmine-scented bubbles. Jeanette moved gracefully to the bedside table, and there placed the beverage and bowl of fruit. Facing Autumn again, she said, "I would like to thank you for your kindness to Pierre."

Smiling, Autumn sank a little farther into the tub.

Jeanette went on, "He has grown very fond of you."

"And I of him."

"Pierre is an easy child to love. He has a good heart, like his uncle." Her hands nervously plucking at the folds of her skirt, Jeanette mustered her courage and said, "Donovan has packed."

Autumn quickly looked away, down into the frothy, glittering bubbles, and remembered Donovan in a tub, with bubbles. "What would you have me do?" she finally asked.

"Stop him."

"How?"

"Beg him, if you must. You have seen Annee's cruelty for yourself. She will destroy Donovan. This entire island is not worth his life or happiness."

Autumn shifted. The water had grown cold. "You love him very much, Jeanette."

"He was always good to me. Since his return he has been like a father to Pierre." Lowering her dark lashes, Jeanette confessed softly, "Yes, I love him. His is my brother."

"I don't know what I can do," she lied, while her heart pumped double-time in her breast.

Jeanette moved to the window with the long, easy stride of an island woman and opened the jalousie. The drums were there, filling the night air with a somehow disturbing rhythm. "It is warm," she said quietly, looking toward the darkness outside the house.

Minutes ticked by before Jeanette went on, "My people are celebrating the coming of life, as there are children about to be born in the village. They are praying to the zemi of life to grant the infants safe passage into the mortal world. They will pray to the zemi of fertility to bless them soon with more children." Staring out the window, Jeanette added, "You can hear it in the drums, can't you?"

One, two, pulsed the drums. "Yes."

"It is warm tonight," Jeanette repeated. She moved toward the armoire.

Autumn stared into the tepid water as Jeanette laid the filmy gold negligee out across the bed. Jeanette padded silently on bare feet to the door, closing it behind her as she left the room.

Brice tried to focus on the letter in his hand. His inebriated mind would not allow him to concentrate, so he dropped it again into the desk drawer and reached for his bottle. Who was he kidding? All the *clarin* between here and Jamaica couldn't change the fact that Annee Rose was waiting at Barrett Hall. He'd made his decision; there would be no turning back. He would do what he'd come to Cayemite to do: end Annee's madness, end her obsession with a man who no longer existed, who had never existed, really. He'd never loved Annee, had never vowed a love for Annee, but in her own twisted mind she'd convinced herself, those long years ago, that he did love her.

He took a long drink of the clear liquor. No, he didn't love Annee. But he would enjoy what she could do for him, if he allowed her. His memory wasn't so foggy that he couldn't recall their times together, the passionate, stolen moments of two young people enjoying the first delicious taste of manhood and womanhood. The things they'd done had been animal—things he'd never done before or since, and probably never would repeat.

Brice slammed his glass onto the desk. The image of those brandy-brown eyes turned up to his that afternoon in Annee's house kept cropping up to haunt him. Damn Autumn Donovan for turning his wretched existence inside out with one glance of those eyes—bewitching, seductive, childlike—flashing innocence, then temptation, with a single blink. He wasn't surprised that Roy had been suckered into marrying her. He'd marry her, too—if she'd have him.

But she wouldn't have him. She had what she wanted. And if he went to live with Annee, perhaps she would continue to have it for a while—at least until he forced Autumn to leave the island. And she would leave. She would have little choice.

With great effort Brice rose from his chair. He stood at the window, watching the shadows change with the shifting night clouds. The mountain was there beyond the fields and forests, waiting in the darkness. As a child he had thought of Trempe only as the Indians' sacred grounds, where their dead went to die, where their spirits resided and controlled their lives at a whim. Even now, he might never have realized the truth had the quakes not started, had the gas and steam not condensed against the peak and gradually begun to cover the island.

"There y' are!"

Tyler's unexpected greeting caused Brice to jump. Closing his eyes, he took a deep breath before turning.

Tyler was staring at the valise near the desk as Brice faced him. "Well, now." One heavy brow lifted in consideration as Hugh said, "Seems to me someone plans on goin' somewheres."

Donovan slumped back against the windowsill. "So it seems."

"Yer a fool, Donovan."

"Maybe. But if Annee is happy . . ."

"Lord, deliver us from martyrs, especially ones who are feelin' sorry for themselves."

Brice's head snapped up.

"Don't like the truth much, do y', lad?" he thundered. And when Brice stood a little straighter he went on, "Found yer pa standin' at that window many a time, starin' out over the garden and thinkin' t' himself. 'Irish,' he'd say, 'I'd give my last share of cane t' see Brice again. Don't figure he'd care t' see me, though.' Then he'd slump into one of his moods again and reach for his *clarin*. Then Roy'd slither in and both of 'em would hurl insults at one another for the rest of the evenin'."

His blue eyes softening, Tyler said, "Yer just like 'im, y' know. You and yer pa are like two peas in a pod. Y' look just like 'im. Talk just like 'im. Hell, y' even walk just like 'im. I think that's what hurt him the most. When y' left the island a big piece of 'im went with y'."

Brice groaned quietly.

Looking beyond Brice's shoulder and out the window, Hugh, his voice thoughtful, asked, "Have y' heard the talk? The damned savages are sayin' the end is near, that the dark ones have returned and are waitin' out in the forests to make their move. The men are killin' ever' bleedin' animal that looks at 'em cross-eyed."

Crossing to the desk, Brice poured himself another drink. "I've heard," he responded.

Tyler watched as Donovan quaffed the liquor as he would water. Then he said, "They're believin' Annee Rose is behind all this upheaval. She's convinced 'em of it."

"Well, that's what makes *us* civilized, isn't it, Tyler? Because we *don't* believe it."

"Maybe. But y' can't deny somethin' is happenin', Brice."

"I never denied it."

Hugh wiped a rough hand across his mouth. "It's been comin' for a long time, I reckon. Even before yer father died, the tremors had started. But it's been a while since the last ones. A year maybe."

Brice continued to stare into his empty glass. "Maybe it'll be a year before the next one," he commented absently. He was thinking of Autumn.

"Aye. Maybe." The Irishman glanced again at the valise, then looked at Brice. "Think about it for a while," he said. "Yer father and brother are dead and buried down at the crossroads, son, and no amount of revenge is gonna bring 'em back."

"But if I hadn't left—"

"This habitation would still be in a mess. Cayemite is gonna produce exactly what she wants to and nothin' more, regardless of who's maît of Hunnington Hall. I'll tell you what I told yer father, and yer brother, pitiful excuse for a human bein' that Roy was; sell Hunnington to Annee Rose and get out. Hell, *give* it to her. Y' don't need the money, Brice, not like yer father did."

For the first time since Tyler had entered the room, Brice met his eyes and didn't look away. "But we both know it's not just Hunnington she wants."

"That's no reason t' wrap yerself up in a nice bright ribbon and plunk yerself on 'er doorstep! Even Roy had the God-given sense to fight her!"

Those words struck a chord of surprise in Donovan. Had he sunk lower than his brother?

Hugh turned and walked to the door. "Think about it," he repeated before leaving the room.

Brice continued to stare at the door long after Tyler had departed, and for the first time he asked himself why he had chosen to go to Annee. The excuse he'd made to himself yesterday wouldn't hold up in light of what Hugh had said. Giving in to Annee's demands wouldn't solve Cayemite's problems, wouldn't make the cane grow or the Indians less superstitious. And it wouldn't bring back his father or brother. They had each known Annee and what she was capable of doing. But they'd remained on Cayemite, had cleaved to Hunnington like lovers because—like himself—they had nothing else. Perhaps, just perhaps, it was Hunnington that had killed them. She had sapped their very life, and when they could fight no more, they just gave in, as he was doing now.

Brice sank again into his chair. A breeze, heavy with impending rain, gusted through the window, causing the hot puddles of wax over the cherubs' heads to drip like tears over their little faces. Laying his head on the desk, Donovan closed his eyes.

Autumn moved silently down the stairs, pausing frequently in the darkness, listening to the creaks and groans of the old house as the rising night wind shook the shutters and rattled the jalousies in their frames. For the hundredth time in the last hour she visualized the rambling home without Brice's presence. The emptiness during the past week had been hell, with his living with Jeanette; her believing they were lovers had only intensified the ache. She now knew that barren space called loneliness, and she didn't like it.

She had convinced herself, even as she slid into the diaphanous wrap, that her reasons for doing this were nothing short of noble. She would save Brice from Annee and thereby save Hunnington, too. But she knew, even as she descended those last few steps, with her heart pounding so wildly in her chest she could scarcely breathe, that her reasons weren't noble at all. She wanted Brice Donovan for reasons that had nothing to do with Hunnington Hall: He made her heart sing with every intense glance of those green eyes; he made her toes tingle with every twitch of those lips. And ah, their touch; even now the very thought brought goose bumps to her arms, and she shivered. Just the thought of his being in the next room flooded her senses with presence, *his* presence, and as always, her body responded, surged with exhilaration, vibrated with expectation until her knees were like water and her stomach was fluttering.

"Donovan," she whispered, too winded really to speak. In the back of her mind her reason struggled with her heart. Yet even as she tiptoed across the marbled foyer to the open library door, she knew the battle was lost.

He was seated at the massive desk, his head resting on

one forearm, and he appeared to be asleep. She entered the room quietly, crossing the carpeted floor to the puddle of pale yellow light that spilled from the single burning candle over her head. That last thread of reluctance tugged through her body as her eyes drifted over the broad expanse of his shoulders to the thick black hair that lifted and fell with the wind that raced up his back, fluttering his shirtsleeve.

He groaned. The sound went through her like lightning, fusing her feet to the floor and jarring every nerve ending throughout her body. It was frightening, this desire—overwhelming. Dizzying. She thought she might faint. She swallowed and listened to the faraway drums pound strangely in time to her heart and watched the heavy rise and fall of Brice's back as he breathed.

One, two . . . one, two.

"Donovan."

He stirred.

"Donovan?"

Oh, Donovan, wake up quickly before all my resolutions desert me!

"Donovan!"

His head popped up, bobbed groggily between his shoulders, and he blinked at the desk. Then slowly, slowly, he lifted his face. He blinked again, first sleepily, then disbelievingly.

He stared.

She stared back.

Finally, "Au-Autumn?"

The rich timbre of his voice went through her senses like ripples on a pond, touching each hidden recess in her body. She swayed under the impact of the sound.

Brice tried to swallow. He was afraid to blink, afraid that if he shut his eyes for even a second, she would be gone when he looked again. Enchanting, bewitching, beguiling—Autumn was all of those things. His eyes were riveted on the apricot skin that showed from her shoulders to the plunging lace décolletage barely shielding her breasts. Swallowing again, he whispered:

"God."

A timid smile touched the corners of her mouth. "I—I

couldn't sleep, so I thought"—she saw his eyes narrow—
"perhaps I would get a book."

"Wrong room."

Her glance swept the parlor. "Oh, well, yes. I guess it
is. Well . . ."

Her bravado floundered. Then her eyes fell to the valise
at the foot of his desk. She rallied her courage.

"I . . . I understand you're leaving?"

Brice sat back in his chair, his brows beetling over the
bridge of his nose as he frowned. The cherub above
Autumn's head drenched her in halos of shimmering light.
It reflected from her shoulders and her tumbling hair and
glowed softly from the gossamer ivory lace over her breasts.
The effect was far more powerful than any quake that had
previously shaken the island. He couldn't speak.

Say something, she thought.

He tried.

"Well?" If he didn't say something soon she was going
to bolt. "Are you going to see Annee?"

His eyes fell to the tiny fisted hands that clutched frantically at the front of her gown, pulling it taut over the swell
of her hips. He was beginning to understand. "And if I
was?" He eyed her breasts.

"I . . . I would ask you not to."

"Why?"

The abruptness of the response was frightening. "Because."

Up went one eyebrow, and his gaze shifted to her face.
"Because *why?*"

"I don't want you to."

"Why not?"

His directness was infuriating. Battling for further courage she blurted, "Because I'm asking you not to!"

"Aha." Brice drummed his fingers on the chair arm.
"It wouldn't be because of a conversation you overheard
between myself and Madame Rose, would it?"

"Conversation?"

"Our discussing the fact that I intend to make you leave
the island?"

The distant chimes of the tall case clock rang through the
quiet. Autumn closed her eyes and tottered slightly from

the shock of the disclosure. "Leave," she said in a strained whisper, "leave Cayemite?"

Brice left his chair very slowly, wondering if the weakness in his knees was due to the *clarin* he'd been drinking or the sight of Autumn so damnably near and so beautiful he could hardly breathe. "Is this how you convinced Roy not to leave you?" He circled her, staring at her shoulder blades beneath the satin ribbons that held up her gown. "Did you?"

Autumn shut her eyes and clapped her hands over her mouth. One thought drummed over and over, He's making me leave Cayemite!

He touched her hair with trembling fingers. "I might be convinced to let you stay. Convince me, Missus Donovan, as you convinced my brother to have you come."

The realization of what he'd said hit with blinding force. She whipped about so suddenly that the flowing skirt of her gown twisted around her ankles. He was tall, nearly blotting out the cherub's light above and behind his head. Autumn's head fell back as she looked up into his dark face. "My reasons for coming here had nothing to do with your sending me from Cayemite."

A cynical smile curled his mouth. "Why don't I believe you?"

"But you must!" She placed a hand on his chest. His heartbeat accelerated so suddenly his entire body was jolted. Before she could speak again, he grabbed her wrist and drew her quaking frame against his.

"What words did you use on him?" he growled. "Perhaps, 'I love you'?"

"No!" Autumn shook her head, sending her coppery hair shimmying to the backs of her thighs.

"Say it. Say, 'I love you', Missus Donovan, and make me believe it. Maybe then I'll let you stay."

"I love you."

It came without a moment's hesitation. So easily, so prettily and oh, so believably that Brice was left winded and pale.

"I . . . love you," Autumn repeated and realized in that instant that she did indeed love Brice Donovan. She closed her eyes and raggedly admitted one last time, "I love you."

His arms came around her then, one curling around her waist and the other up between her shoulders where his hand buried into her hair. His fingers twisted into the coiling copper-colored mass so suddenly she cried aloud in surprise. "Pretty little liar," Donovan hissed. "You'll regret having lied to me."

"I'm not!" she wanted to say, but the words wouldn't come. She could only stand mute in his iron grip and tremble like a little sparrow as he devoured her with his eyes. He kissed her then with raw abandon, covered her mouth bruisingly with his until the pressure forced hers open so that his tongue could boldly plunge between her teeth.

In response her arms flew up around his neck; her body arched against his, satin against steel, and his arm tightened with bone-crushing pressure around her ribs. He possessed her tongue with his, then he was pressing his entire mouth across hers, until finally he broke away to gulp a long, excruciating breath.

She hung there, arms around his neck, with her head thrown back and the butterfly pulse of her pale arched throat turned up to his lips. His breath was moist against her skin, hot, then hotter as he stared down into her flushed face, her vibrant lips and sooty lashes reflecting like gold in the cherub's light. And as he watched, a tear, glistening in the candle's glow, welled through those lashes and trickled into the hair at her temple.

He was besieged with frustration, searing pain that shattered his heart and mind. Autumn loathed him so strongly she could not even tolerate his touch, it seemed. He kissed her again, telling himself it would be the last time. He'd rather whore himself to Annee Rose, because she at least, in her demented little way, loved him. He kissed Autumn forcefully, wanting to imprint his taste, his feel, his memory on her mind for a lifetime, as she was imprinted on his. For in that instant he knew her desperation; it wasn't easy to let go of a dream; Cayemite was as much a part of her fantasy as she was of his. The difference was, she was still fighting for hers. Perhaps he should do a little fighting himself . . .

Autumn felt the shift in his emotions. It surged through Brice's rigid body and flamed in his eyes. His finely carved mouth turned up in devastating coldness that caused her heart to plunge to her stomach. There was something in the green depths of his eyes that reminded her of others—of Roy—a madness fueled by hopelessness and rashness that she had been too naive those many months ago to notice. She recognized it now only because it was foreign to Brice's eyes. And because of that she was frightened even more.

She touched his face. "Brice, I—"

"Shut up!" He knocked her hand away. "Not now," he whispered through his teeth. "Don't 'Brice' me now, Missus Donovan, or do you need to remind yourself whom it is you're trying to seduce?"

Stunned by his insinuation, Autumn stumbled backward, suddenly feeling conspicuously naked before his condemnatory, defiling glower. She covered her breasts with her arms. "I—I only wanted—"

"I know what you want," he informed her in a low, savage tone. Slowly he circled her, so close that the sleeve of his shirt brushed her arm. "You want Hunnington. Well, love, you'll have to work a little harder this time to get it."

Voiceless, Autumn could only shake her head. As he moved up behind her and the hard musculature of his thighs pressed against her buttocks, she dug her tiny doubled fists into her mouth and bit her knuckles to control the cry of confusion and pain that welled up in her throat. After years of denying herself love, after succumbing to it, it was being twisted into something shameful!

"Why don't you pant a little harder!" came the taunting voice at her ear. He flicked the slender strap of her gown off her shoulder so that it dangled on her arm. His hard brown hands covered her shoulders then; his thumbs massaged the nape of her neck, beneath her hair. "Hurry," he jeered, "Annee's waiting."

Oh, dear God! she inwardly wept. Dear God! She wanted to flee but couldn't move. And as his hand slid down over

her shoulder into the lace supported only by her upraised
arms and cupped her breast, her knees turned to jelly and
her senses tumbled in turmoil.

She moaned.

"That's better," Donovan said softly. "You like that,
don't you, pet?" He felt the nipple pucker in his palm and
grow hard. "As I recall, you like this as well." He slid his
hand down, down over her flat stomach, feeling her flinch
and shiver, and he knew even before he buried his fingers
into the satin folds of the gown between her thighs that she
would be warm and damp and inviting to his touch.

His breath escaped him in a long, painful rush as she
whimpered, "Oh, Donovan . . . Donovan . . ."

He jerked her around.

Their bodies collided. So did their eyes, their mouths.
She left the floor in his arms, dancing on tiptoe as he
smothered her again with his plundering, searching mouth,
as his tongue dipped and raked the sweet, wet cavern that
was at once intoxicating and maddening. He went down on
his knees, first his right, then his left, clutching her to his
chest even as he laid her out on the rug, even as he pressed
his hips against hers and ground them to the floor with the
primitive rhythm that pulsed with the wind, inside his
heart and loins. One, two . . . one, two.

He fumbled with his trousers.

She closed her eyes. This was certain madness, this
desire to give herself to a man who did not love her, and
for one overwhelming instant she knew the bliss of self-
sacrifice that love can bring, the insane need to give her all
for the man who fired that emotion, regardless of *what* he
believed. So when his hand ran up the inside of her thigh,
she opened her legs freely and gasped as he slid his fingers
inside her.

Like the petal of a flower she closed around him, sleek
and damp and warm, so fragrant he had to struggle or he
might have lost all control. He kissed her breasts, pulled
the rosy hard peak gently, insistently, between his teeth
until she was thrashing back and forth on the floor and
whimpering. He forgot his anger, forgot there was any
other woman on the face of the earth, or any other man
who might have had her. He didn't care. In that moment

he would have given her anything if she would let him love her: Hunnington, Willow Bend . . . his heart, but then, again, she already had that—completely.

She yielded to the white-hot need that teased her every nerve. She stretched and purred beneath his experienced hands, arched and opened until a warmth rushed deep inside her and gathered between her legs.

He sensed it. He shifted his weight above her, looked down into her passion-drowsy eyes, briefly kissed her mouth as he wedged her legs open further with his knees. He felt the cool satin of her gown against his flesh, where his trousers were open and pulled down around his hips. As his tumescence nestled into the baby fine hair there, between her legs, he was overcome with such need that his entire body throbbed with pain. He lifted and poised.

Her eyes flew open and locked on his as the first probe of his body against hers lurched her love-drunk senses back to normality. The realization of what was happening was as sharp as the sudden splintering pain that tore throughout her lower body as he drove inside her. "Oh, no," she gasped, "Ple-e-ase, no!"

He didn't understand. Lost in that first, hot plunge he knew only the rapture of consummation. The barrier was baffling, frustrating. He thrust again, deaf to the cry of pain that tore from her throat. But this time, as her fragile body arched from the floor and her lips pulled back in pain and denial, as the satin sheath surrounding him gave with the insistent pressure, he realized—and froze.

Autumn turned her face away, gritting her teeth and praying the humiliating, excruciating pain would subside before she screamed, "Oh, God," she cried over and over. "Please, please, please."

With a growl of self-contempt Brice melted onto Autumn, pinning her body on the floor beneath his. He was afraid to withdraw, afraid of hurting her further.

"Please!" The cry shuddered against his ear. "Please, don't!"

Burying his face in her hair, he murmured. "I didn't know. I swear, I didn't know."

"I—I hate you!" she cried.

"No! Ah, Autumn, you should've told me. Why didn't you tell me?"

She dug her elbow into his rib so forcefully Donovan groaned. When she did it again he caught her wrists and pinned them down to her sides. "I'm sorry," he whispered. "I'm so sorry."

The cherub over his shoulder seemed to peer quizzically at Autumn, its halo of yellow-gold light reflecting from its wax-streaked face as the fixture swayed to and fro in the breeze. She wanted to cry, not because of the pain, but because she'd asked for it, because she'd known all along that the act would be horrible, and she was disappointed when it was.

Brice gently slid from her body, feeling her tremble as her thighs battled to shield herself from further abuse. As he rolled to his side, she rolled away, drawing her knees up to her stomach. His eyes fell on the crumpled pool of satin that had lain beneath her hips. It was stained with blood. With a particularly vile curse, Brice rolled to his back, adjusted his breeches, and glared at the ceiling, thoroughly disgusted with himself.

He listened to the drums. He listened to the soft, plaintive sobbing of the wounded girl beside him. He listened to the wind and the first gentle patter of rain that thudded on the sun-baked earth outside the window. Turning his head, Brice watched Autumn's shoulders shake, feeling at a total loss over what he should do, though he knew what he wanted to do. He wanted to take her in his arms, to hold her, soothe her, and take away the pain and humiliation. But he was afraid. He was so afraid.

"Autumn."

Autumn flinched. Burying her nose further into the rug, she snapped, "Don't touch me!"

"I won't." He moved up against her back so his lips were but a breath from her ear. "Look at me," he beseeched her.

"No."

"I didn't mean to hurt you."

"Liar."

"I didn't know you were a virgin, for God's sake."

Autumn sniffed and opened her eyes.

"You should've told me, Autumn."

"You—you might have asked."

Brice smoothed her damp hair back over her shoulder. "You were a married woman, *Missus* Donovan, or have you forgotten? I thought you and my brother—"

Coming up on one elbow, Autumn interrupted, "Considering he left me at the altar, we had little time to say more than good-bye, which was just as well, because had I had to endure that disgusting act with Roy, I certainly wouldn't have followed him to Cayemite looking for more!"

"He never told me," came the quiet reply. "I'm sorry."

She forced herself to cry a little more, even though the discomfort had subsided somewhat. She liked the effect it was having on Donovan.

"Autumn . . . look at me?"

Autumn shook her head and lifted her chin stubbornly toward the window. She heard him take a long, weary breath, then release it. Her heart leaped in her throat as he shifted; a thousand flimsy excuses she might use to detain him ran through her mind. But as she sat upright with a thought to stop him, he dropped down before her, and smiled. He looked pale and haggard. It was all she could do not to touch him.

"I suspect you're going to make this as uncomfortable for me as possible," he said.

Coyly lowering her lashes, Autumn stared at the floor beneath his knee.

The etched lines about Brice's mouth deepened as he laughed softly. "My God, you're beautiful when you do that."

She peeked at him just a little.

"I love your freckles," he teased. " 'Specially that one." With one bent finger Brice brushed the freckle at the corner of her mouth. The fact that she didn't move away was encouraging. Catching her chin with the tip of his finger, he tipped her face toward his and waited for that first flash of amber behind her lashes before he implored, "Forgive me."

She watched the convulsive tightening of his throat. His face was red. There was a sheen of moisture across his brow. Autumn took perverse pleasure in adding to his discomfort by not responding to his entreaty. And when he tried to kiss her again, she turned her face away, so his lips only brushed the corner of her mouth. It was odd that even after the horrible experience, she longed to turn her mouth up to his again.

Donovan backed away. He took a deep, unsteady breath, then released it. "Don't do this," he said. "Say something."

"You're making me leave Cayemite."

"Forget the goddamned island."

"It is all I have."

"There are other plantations."

"But they're not mine."

The cherub overhead rocked back and forth. The candle flame flickered and sputtered in the quiet.

"I'm going to make you forget the island," Brice stated softly.

The distant case clock sounded the hour. The jalousie rattled in the window. Autumn's heart jumped as Brice rose from his knees to stand above her, so tall her head fell back completely as she gazed up the length of his tall lean body to his eyes. He reached for her then, through his own shadow, and though she cowered slightly, the first touch of his fingers on her skin left her weak and eager for more, in spite of everything that had happened earlier.

Donovan lifted her in his arms, one hand riding gently beneath her buttocks, the other curled possessively over her breast as she rode in his arms up the stairs. Though her body cringed with the memory of pain he had inflicted earlier, the desire was there, as heady and mystifying as it always was when he was near, and though her heart raced madly, she melted against his chest and closed her eyes.

Chapter 19

The door clicked softly closed behind them. The room was in deep shadow; all but one of the candles had been doused. Donovan walked purposefully across the floor to the bed, and as the first blue-white flash of lightning burst outside the open window, he laid her gently onto the turned down sheets.

The storm rolled over the thrashing waters of Ravel Bay and shook the house. Autumn, unable to speak, even to blink, was curled inside the sheltering *baire* with her fingers knotted into her palms and her knees close to her chest. She trembled with fear, with expectation and reverence as Donovan began to undress.

Slowly he tugged the tail of his shirt from his loosened waistband. Her eyes dropped to the vee of skin that was exposed below his stomach. He peeled the shirt from his shoulders and she shifted her glance over the broad, bronze expanse of his chest, feeling the rush of a strange anticipation overcome her fear of lying with Donovan again. Strange that even after the crucifying pain, she shook with the need for him to touch her again.

This was longing, she realized. This was the need to belong, to sacrifice, to share. To love and be loved. Oh, if he only loved her!

From behind her closed eyes she heard the thump of one boot upon the carpeted floor, followed by the other. She looked again, shy and quaking and unsure, unprepared for the sight of his trousers sliding down over his hips, to his knees and finally to his ankles. Her heart thrummed a frantic rhapsody in her bosom as he stood tall and naked, and looked at her through the narrow opening of the mosquito *baire*.

Adonis, bold and beautiful and perfect. Donovan.

The bed shifted. His shoulders filled the gauzy opening, the covers of the bed sliding toward the place where his knee buried into the feather mattress. He searched her face with his eyes. Smiling, slightly, he said: "Hello."

Her lower lip trembled.

"Come here." He lifted his hand. She shook her head. "I won't hurt you again," he told her.

"Please, I cannot bear it."

"I'll make it good for you, *chérie.*"

"That can never be good!"

"But it can." He breathed it. "It can."

"I—I think I would rather die," she lied, and Brice laughed softly.

"Yes, my love, you will die just a little. As I will."

Uncomprehending, she shook her head again.

Brice dropped his hand. "All right. Then I'll hold you. Nothing more."

"Put on your clothes," she ordered, struggling to keep her eyes on his face.

He shook his head. "No."

"You . . . you won't touch me like that again?"

"No."

"Promise."

"I promise."

Autumn frowned and Brice smiled. "I don't believe you," she said.

Donovan stretched out on the bed, laying his head on the pillow beside her knee. He stared at the canopy overhead and listened to the rain and wind and waited for Autumn to relax.

Silly girl, she scolded herself. One part of her yearned to run from the room, the other wanted nothing more than to rest beside him, to know the warmth of his hand on her skin, and the delicious caress of his mouth on hers. It was a struggle not to allow her eyes to roam his entire body. More than once they slid to the shadowed indentation of his navel, where the hair on his chest had narrowed into a thin dark line; she'd drag them back up to his chest, to the smooth skin that looked gold in the mellow candlelight, then to the muscled arms that were corded from years of hard labor, and finally his hands, hard, brown . . . gentle.

Her nipples hardened. Her breath failed her. Slowly she slid down onto the bed and lay stiffly beside him, waiting . . . waiting . . . waiting. Rolling her head, she looked up over his shoulder. His eyes were closed. "Are you sleeping?" She saw his eyelids tremble.

Donovan smiled. "I promised you."

Autumn stared at the canopy.

The minutes ticked by. Then Donovan rolled to the edge of the bed and sat up. Autumn came up on one elbow, and as he began to move from the bed, she stopped him by calling, "Brice!" He froze. "Don't go," she pleaded, remembering the times he'd left this bed in the middle of the night, and how lonely she'd been after his leaving. Recalling, too, that Annee was waiting at Barrett Hall, she beseeched him, "I beg you: stay." Reaching, she touched her fingertips to the broad, flexed muscles of his back. "Stay."

He laughed. His dark head turning, he looked down into her upturned face and said, "I was only going to blow out the candle."

Oh. Her fine brows knitting over her eyes, she repeated aloud, "Oh!" As he laughed again, she closed her hands onto his pillow and swung it against his shoulder. He laughed that much harder.

Brice fell atop her, knocking the pillow from her hands so it tumbled to the floor along with the counterpane. They twisted and tangled in sheets, legs and arms, until finally she lay beneath him with her gown hiked to her waist and one breast mostly exposed for his eyes. He was still laughing.

"You arrogant swine," Autumn joked half seriously. "You can leave this room this very minute. See if I care in the least."

"You care."

"I don't! You're a brute, Brice Donovan. A defiler of innocent women!"

"Innocent my foot, Missus Donovan. You came to that room with the intent to seduce me."

He stared down into her eyes.

"Kiss me," she whispered against his mouth.

"No. I made you a promise—"

"Kiss me," she repeated, the urgency in her voice as audible as the escalating storm outside the house.

The touching of their mouths was brief, too brief. Closing her eyes, she groaned and pleaded, "Again."

"Ah, God," he moaned, and the sound vibrated his chest, and hers. He did kiss her, hungrily, possessively, branding the taste of his mouth and tongue on her and in her, filling her mind and body with such explosive expectation that she shook to her very toes. Wrapping her arms around his neck, she kissed him back, matching the thrust of his tongue with her own, delving, retreating, plunging, until he was moaning and twisting his fingers in her hair so he could grind his mouth more forcefully against hers.

"Autumn." It was a prayer, a reverent, worshipful whisper that was desirous and warm and beckoning. Burying his face against her throat he rained kisses from the tender underside of her chin to her ear, then down to the fragile sweep of her shoulder, nibbling, scattering the moist touches of his lips along her pulse points until she was whimpering and pleading for more.

"Donovan, Donovan. My darling Donovan." She almost wept it, a sweet hosanna to the night and to the man, to the blissful beatitude of awakening desire . . . and love. She was aflame inside, burning with a need that surpassed even the pain of their earlier coming together. She wanted him—oh, God, yes! She wanted him, all of him. Inside her, where the growing ache was pulsing, throbbing for his touch.

Her body, with a will all its own, twisted against him as he bent down to her breasts, arching so the straining, swollen tips jutted rosy-pink and proud to his searching mouth. He took one, all of it, wrapping his tongue around the nubby peak and sucking it hard, almost painfully, so she cried softly aloud:

"Oh, Brice! Please!"

Her fingers slid through his hair, tightened over his nape and pressed him more closely to her breasts, first one then the other. His breathing grew ragged, and the muscles in his arms quivered under the agony of restraint. When his head came up, his eyes were fathomless seas of green that reflected the fire of the bedside candle.

"Before God," he rasped in a pain-induced voice, "I beg you, Autumn, don't send me away again."

Her heart pounding against her ribs, Autumn touched his face, so warm and large and near her own. "Send you away? I would rather die, Mr. Donovan."

He knew her meaning.

Brice caught her hand with his own. Palm to palm and fingers laced, he pressed it into the pillow, over her head. He rolled to his side. With his free hand he began to explore her. He eased the pad of his thumb over her nipples, and felt them respond. His fingers ran lightly down the trough of her waist, hesitated over the downy softness between her legs, then slid down the length of her inner thigh, nearly to her knee, then up again, oh, so slowly until the mounting pressure inside her blossomed so forcefully she opened herself to him without shame, without a thought of what might come after, without caring.

He touched her there; gently placing his hand upon the damp cleavage. His eyes touched hers before he parted the silken flesh. She tensed, and he withdrew.

"Easy," he told her. "We'll wait, Autumn. We'll wait until you're ready."

"I'm ready." Surprised at her own admission, Autumn bit her lip, wondering what insanity had pervaded her mind as well as her body.

"Not yet. You're not ready yet. I want it to be good for you next time. I'll make it good for you, I promise."

His words hummed in her veins. "Donovan." She sighed.

He caught her hand, and as he shifted, Autumn became aware of his intent. Eyes wide, her head rolled slightly from the pillow as she attempted to jerk her hand away. "No! Oh, Brice, I can't—"

"Please."

She shut her eyes and held her breath as he closed her hand gently around the smooth hot skin of his burgeoning desire. Her breath left her in an unsteady exhalation of surprise, and when she might have tugged her hand away, he wrapped his fingers more forcefully around her wrist and, much to her consternation, began moving her hand slowly up and down. He trembled and groaned. His dark head dropped so that his hair tickled her chin and nose.

And as his hand left her wrist, his hips pumped in that rhythm with which she had grown so familiar.

She almost withdrew her hand, but instead she let it slide, gently, over the sleek skin, amazed at how incredibly hot he was in her fingers, how magnificent he felt to her touch. "Don't stop," he whispered in her ear. Then his exploration began again, slowly, touching lightly with his fingertips behind her knee, below her buttocks, then tracing the underside of her arm from her wrist to her elbow.

Autumn closed her eyes as he again found her breasts, cupping each one and teasing each tip until it grew so incredibly hard it hurt. And she found that the rhythm he'd set with her hand had suffused her own body. It was natural to move against him with the easy tempo, yet she found that, strangely, it wasn't enough. A hunger was building, coiling in her nether regions that was, at once, painful and wanting.

"Donovan," she murmured to the darkness over his shoulder. "Donovan."

His head came up. Eyes meeting hers, Brice smiled, and as thunder rolled somewhere over the bay, he kissed her while he slipped his hand between her legs. This time, she didn't flinch.

They rolled together, he catching her hand now and pulling it up around his neck. He felt her heart race against his, and through the shadows inside the bed he saw her eyes widen and her lips part in silent question. "Hush," he soothed her. "If it's bad, I'll stop." He went up on his outstretched arms, and poised.

She opened.

He entered, slowly, as he should have the first time, guarding her tender threshold with patience and care. The sheath yielded slowly, so agonizingly tight and wonderful he thought he would explode in spite of his battle for control over his own body.

A flicker of pain crossed her features, and he froze. Closing her eyes, Autumn prayed for the courage to continue, because she wanted this, regardless of the burning discomfort inside her. She ached to be near him, to hold him close in every imaginable way. Drawing her legs around his buttocks she pulled him inside her, lifted her hips to impale herself on him as he groaned and sank against her, driving deeply, so their bodies joined completely together.

She went all liquid inside, pliant and hot and desirous. He filled her to the point of bursting, it seemed, and she wanted to laugh with joy, with the inexplicable exhilaration of the union that sang wondrously in her heart. "This is wonderful!" she cried in his ear.

He laughed, husky and deep in his throat. "This is nothing, my love. It gets better, believe me."

She looked up at him with those innocent eyes, and it was enough to bring a growl so feral from his chest she shrank slightly beneath him. He began moving then, slowly, in and out, rocking her with easy motion until her head and heart and body were drowning in a tide race of pleasure. She began moving with him, allowing her body to respond to his every whisper, every thrust and roll of his hips against hers. The sharp pain of their earlier joining was gone, but a new pain was growing, baffling in its pure, sensual pleasure. Odd that she could beckon it, wanting more of it, and not understand why. But it was building, surmounting the roar of wind outside the house until she was whimpering and calling his name, clutching at his shoulders and pleading for . . . what? There was something, she sensed, just out of her reach, so sublime she would die if she could not touch it soon.

The green-gold sheen of his eyes reflected her face before he sank against her, burying his face into her hair and the pillow at her throat. As his hips twisted against hers, her hands ran over the taut, bunching planes of his back, spreading over the moist, working blades of his shoulders and down, down to the small of his spine, and the feel of his buttocks working so furiously was enough to bring an animallike whimper from her lips. The mounting pleasure spread outward, singing through her veins to every inch of her body until her limbs were thrashing, until the frenzy of their meeting was overwhelming her with the drowning ecstasy.

It came suddenly, so violent, so heart-stoppingly wondrous that she wept his name aloud to the fluttering canopy above his shoulder, until he turned his damp face to hers and muffled the outcry with his mouth. She clutched at his arms, his back, his hips as she spiraled backward, falling over the precipice of pleasure that rent her world in its glorious upheaval.

Breathtaking, this carnal magic, depleting, searing, beautiful. She drifted back to reality, rocking in his arms, basking in the deep caress of his drawl as he soothed her in French and creole, his voice tight and painful as it brushed her ear. In her sensitive state she could feel him still, bold and erect inside her. Innocent yet of nature and the ways of a man's body, she didn't realize his sacrifice as he slowly withdrew and lay down beside her. On his back, he stared at the canopy, drawing several long, uneven breaths.

Autumn rolled to her side, resting, partially, against his ribs, her fingers absently trailing through the soft hair on his chest and stomach as she peered down into his face. "Is anything wrong?" she asked him.

He looked into her eyes and smiled. "No. Not if you enjoyed it."

Autumn smiled back. "I had no idea . . ." Blushing, she admitted, "It's wonderful, isn't it?" Almost timidly, she kissed his cheek, feeling the stubble of his beard against her tender lips. "Thank you," she whispered, feeling seductive and beautiful and womanly.

Donovan groaned and closed his eyes. Wrapping his arms around her, he pulled Autumn against his chest, so her head nestled beneath his chin and her knee wrapped leisurely over his thigh. They listened to the rain until its steady patter put Autumn to sleep. For several hours Donovan lay with his eyes open, until the candle burned to nothingness and buried them in darkness.

And the ache inside him grew.

Chapter 20

The first thing she noted on awakening was the zemi staring at her from across the room. Blurry-eyed and blinking, Autumn stared back. She could tell without looking that Brice was still beside her. The warmth of his body was evident and welcome.

Autumn stirred, but when she closed her eyes and started to drift back to sleep, the sudden crowing of a rooster near her ear made her sit up in bed. The red-and-green-and-white cock was perched on the canopy top, and it ruffled its feathers before crowing again.

A goat bleated, and Brice sat up.

The Donovans stared in disbelief at the menagerie in the room.

His voice husky with sleep, Brice thundered, "What the hell is going on here!"

Suddenly the door was flung open. Celie, her hands on her hips, stormed into the room, her dark face as righteous as any preacher's they'd ever known.

"*Plaçage!*" she bellowed loud enough to scatter the goats toward the door.

"The hell you say." Brice jerked the sheet across his hips. "*Plaçage*, my ass."

"You got *koklo*." Celie pointed to the rooster. "You got goat and pig and horse. You got house and you got woman. You got *plaçage* union."

Sheet clutched to her breasts and her face aflame, Autumn looked into Brice's tired eyes and asked, "What is *plaçage* union?"

He spoke so matter-of-factly that the sheet slipped from her fingers. "We've just been betrothed, my love. Congratulations."

Her head throbbed. So did her eyes, and other places. . . .

Propped up on one elbow Brice continued, "If a man owns a house, a field, ten to twelve goats, a few pigs and a horse, he is marriage material. If he lives with a woman and has relations with her, it's as good as marriage." Autumn's face went white. Her eyes glittered like dark topaz and her mouth dropped open. "What's wrong?" he asked her

She didn't know, but suddenly everything beautiful that had taken place between them the night before seemed different in the light of day. She was tired. Her limbs were leaden, and she thought she must look a fright. "Nothing," she finally responded.

Celie left the room. Donovan, stretching and lying back on the bed, yawned then teased, "Ah, the ole morning-after blues. This is where I'm expected to pour out my heart to you, convince you that last night meant something, that you're special and we'll live happily ever after."

Pulling her legs up to her chest, Autumn rested her forehead on one knee and closed her eyes.

"Autumn?" Sliding his hand up her back, Donovan laughed a little and said, "I was only teasing, love. Come here." He tugged on her arm.

She pulled back. Her head tilting slightly, she peered at Brice from behind her curtain of hair and asked, "Are you going to make me leave the island?"

"Yes."

"When?"

"On the next ship."

She couldn't look at him, and when he rolled toward her and pressed his mouth against her back she jumped from the bed in a fury.

"Did you think that if you seduced me, I'd change my mind?" came his deep voice behind her.

She shoved aside a goat that was standing on her breeches. "Perhaps I didn't think at all," she snapped, knowing even as she said it that it was a lie. She'd done nothing but think about Donovan since the moment she'd met him.

"Don't you even want to know why I'm sending you away from the island, Autumn?"

Pulling her shirt down over her head, she whirled to face him. "Oh, I know, all right. So you can continue your relationship with Annee Rose and so you can have Hunnington all to yourself!''

He came off the bed, wrapping the sheet around his lean hips so it draped down his leg and onto the floor. His black hair hanging nearly to his eyes, he pointed one long straight finger in her face and said, ''That is the stupidest thing I've ever heard you say, Missus Donovan. I don't give a damn about Annee or this godforsaken plantation!''

''And you expect me to believe that?'' She grabbed up her boots. ''After all the money you've spent on renovations to Hunnington? A man who doesn't give a damn about something doesn't spend a fortune on it. She must be very important to you, Donovan, if you were willing to put that much money into her.''

Autumn stalked out and slammed the door behind her. Then sinking against the wall she wondered what had happened to her senses. Pressing the heel of her hand to her throbbing temple, she continued unsteadily, down the hall.

The sun hurt her eyes. It made her feel hot and sticky, and she wished she could bathe. She wanted to scrub Brice Donovan's scent from her flesh, for occasionally it would drift to her nostrils and fill her body with all those sensations that made her dizzy and weak. She felt suddenly, horribly ashamed of herself; ashamed of snapping at Brice, and ashamed of her behavior the night before. What must he think of her now? She was no better than Annee Rose, throwing herself at him that way. Then, recalling the intimate, tender assaults he'd made on her body, she blushed even hotter.

Then she remembered that he was going to make her leave the island. Despondency swallowed her.

To her own amazement she realized she wasn't nearly as upset over leaving the island as she was over leaving Brice. The vows she'd made last night had not been lies. She was in love with Donovan, which was dispiriting in light of the fact that he cared not a whit for her. Lollie had explained men's ''needs'' to her more than once. But she'd forgotten to relate how a woman's ''needs'' could drive her to behave irresponsibly. Well . . . she'd acted irresponsibly with Donovan. And the fact that she'd do it again given the opportunity, was enough to make her ill.

Jeanette was sweeping the front porch of her quarters when Autumn walked up. Autumn watched silently for a moment. Yes, she could see it now, the resemblance between her and Brice. The noble line of the brow and the fullness of the lower lip were the same in both of them.

"Good morning," she greeted softly. Jeanette stopped sweeping and looked up.

Their eyes touched. The bond between them was instant; their shared love for Brice Donovan was achingly apparent as each blinked away their tears.

"Good morning," Jeanette responded.

"Might I come in?"

Jeanette propped the broom against the house before nodding, somewhat nervously. Autumn walked by her into the tiny house. A wooden bed with a plumped mattress was against one wall, a smaller one—Pierre's—was beside it. A tattered settee decorated another wall, while a spindle-legged table had been placed before the window.

"Would you like tea?" Jeanette asked.

Nodding, Autumn waited in silence as the woman hurried to the chore. When they were both stirring sugar into the hot brew, Autumn said quietly, "Donovan is home."

"I know." Jeanette added without taking her eyes from her cup, "Thank you."

They sipped the hot tea. Then, taking a deep breath, Autumn announced, "I would like you to get your things together, Jeanette. You and Pierre are to move into the main house."

Jeanette nearly dropped her cup. "I don't understand."

"You're moving into the house; it's as simple as that. You're Brice's sister, and your place is there. You're a Donovan." The word brought a lump to Autumn's throat. "A Donovan," she repeated more urgently, doing her best to block out the connotations the name brought to her mind and heart. She herself was a Donovan, but it mattered little. She wasn't wanted here.

"But I told Brice—"

"This was my idea. I have not discussed it with Donovan."

"You're very kind, maîtresse."

"The name is Autumn." She put her cup down and stood up. "You'll join us for dinner, of course. As you will from now on."

"But I've nothing but this to wear!" Her hand fluttered over the thin cotton blouse and skirt, then over her hair, slightly damp around her temples.

"That will be remedied soon enough." Autumn paused at the door. "I'll have Tyler move your things into the house."

She left the house and didn't look back.

Autumn moved through the next hour in a state of numbness. Her headache was back. She felt feverish, and more than once she rested in the shade to escape the heat. She hated those moments of inactivity, for then she could do nothing but think about Brice, and that made her head—and her heart—hurt more. She was in love with Brice, and he was sending her away, away from him and away from Cayemite. The two most important things in the world to her. Why? What had she done wrong? The staff, though wary at first, was beginning to accept her. Yes, she'd made mistakes where they were concerned—Celie was still disgruntled over the kitchen affair—but she'd made up for it by turning control over all domestic matters to her. She'd placed the Arda women back out in the fields and had almost convinced the Indians to work. They would be here at this moment had Annee Rose not nailed Myah's ear to a tree.

Damn Annee Rose. This was all her fault!

She was besieged with anger and . . . jealousy. Yes, she was jealous, green-eyed with it. She'd never been jealous over anything, except maybe Anita Cunningham because she'd stolen her dearest friend in the entire world right out from under her nose. But Annee's stealing Brice and Hunnington was far different. She was destroying Autumn's future, and Autumn was simply allowing it.

It was happening already! Autumn suddenly realized. Like every other woman, she was allowing her love for a man to override her better judgment, to weaken her, to transform her into a simpleton who could hardly think on her own, much less react in a crisis.

With a flash of her old defiance, Autumn jumped to her feet. The horizon pitched, and even as she struggled to regain her balance, she tumbled to the ground. The cieba leaves overhead spun dizzyingly for a moment before the world slowly righted and stilled.

"Maîtresse!" A dark face hovered above her—then another. Each looked concernedly down on Autumn as she covered her face with her forearm, feeling foolish. Gently, the blacks helped her sit up. "Go get Donovan," one man said to the other.

"No!" She caught his arm. "I'm fine. Really. It's just so hot . . ."

The men exchanged glances.

Blotting her face with the sleeve of her shirt, Autumn got to her feet. "I was just going to the village. It's not fair, you know . . . you're working on the mill with no help. Not in this heat."

She thanked them again for their concern, then slowly made her way to the stables.

Cutting across the west section and over the creek bed was the quickest route to the village. Still, it seemed to take interminably long. She stopped once, not far from the coastline, and watched the reddish-black crabs scuttle on their pointed little legs across the sand to the water, claws held high. So numerous were they that they made a distinct clicking noise as they bumped and clattered over rocks and shells and each other. She saw a crocodile once, lying hidden partially in swamp mud. Nearby, John Crows feasted on the remains of a school of goddammies that had washed ashore, lying dead and rotting in the sun.

She was allowed entrance to the village without Henri's approval. The Indians were all huddled outside a hut, chanting. At the far end of the village, beneath breadfruit trees, several somber-faced natives were beating their drums. The spellbound groups hardly noticed as she entered the leaf-thatched hovel.

The woman was on her back, knees up and legs open. Whimpering in pain, her tiny fists pounding the floor, she labored in childbirth. Henri was at her side, smoking his pipe and tamping gray dust inside a bowl. Taking in the shabby, dirty surroundings, Autumn frowned. She frowned even harder as Henri added water to the farine and started to pour it down the expectant woman's throat.

"Stop."

Henri looked up.

"How long has this woman been laboring?" Autumn went down on her knees beside him.

He held up two fingers.

"What is this?" She pointed to the concoction in his hand.

"For the pain."

"Don't give her any more. It's slowing her labor."

He lifted the woman's head anyway.

Autumn grabbed the bowl from his hand. "The pain will not kill her, but if you continue to numb her *you* will."

"It is the way of our gods."

"It is not my way, and I am maîtresse of Hunnington Hall. I know what is best for this woman." She watched his eyes narrow in suspicion. "Remember," she added, "I have gone to the mountain, and know . . ." Shoving the bowl to one side, she ordered, "Bring me hot water and clean blankets and—"

Outside the door, someone screamed. Autumn leapt toward the opening, just as a woman threw herself to the ground and began writhing in apparent agony. Before Autumn could react, Henri explained, "She is the girl's mother. She is relieving her daughter's pain by taking it into her own body."

Autumn looked down into the laboring girl's glassy eyes. "That's ridiculous," Autumn muttered. On her knees again, Autumn looked intensely into her face and said, "Scream, if you must." When the girl looked confusedly back at her she demanded Henri, "Tell her what I said."

"It is not our way."

"Tell her what I said."

"It is—"

"*Asse-a!*" Her eyes flashing in anger, Autumn glared at the old man and threatened, "If you defy me, you defy every god on the mountain."

That sat him back. Henri puffed on his pipe a little

harder as he sized Autumn up. When he made no move to speak to the woman, Autumn turned for the door.

"Wait."

Autumn listened as he spoke softly to the girl. The young woman's eyes widened, and she shook her head. Beside her in an instant, Autumn smoothed the hair from the woman's forehead and nodded, smiled, and in a soothing voice assured her that she must no longer contain the pain. It would help the babe to be born if she would stop fighting it.

But she did try to fight it, with every last vestige of strength she had in her contorting body. Soon, however, without the numbing effect of Henri's potion, the discomfort became so unbearable that she had little choice but to cry out.

The men and women outside the hut scrambled into the trees.

The woman laughed, then, in relief, and with the next contraction she screamed a little louder. The child was born moments later.

Autumn didn't realize until later, while sitting back on her heels and watching Henri gently handle the infant, that during the ordeal she had not experienced one moment of fear. It was an odd time to think of Brice. But his image came unbidden, hovering in the air so clearly he might have been standing there beside her, smiling that cocky little smile that said, I knew you could do it. Strange that her accomplishments now were never complete without him, never quite so satisfactory without him telling her that he approved.

And he did approve. Sitting there with her legs crossed while Henri cut the umbilical cord, Autumn thought that, despite Donovan's usual annoyance over her stubbornness, he had always looked at her with respect. He had never belittled her for her motives or actions. Not as Mitchell had.

The knife sliced cleanly through the membrane, cutting that natural bond between mother and child. Autumn looked on the mother's face and smiled—until Henri opened his *paquett* and withdrew a length of candlewick. He tied off the cord with the wick, then dug again into his pouch.

"What are you doing?" She wrinkled her nose at the gray material clinging to the end of his finger.

"This will heal the navel." He began dabbing the filmy substance around onto the babe's distended little belly.

"But what is it?"

"Web of the spider."

"A spider's web!"

His knobby head bobbed up and down.

"That's disgusting," she declared.

He squinted at her from the corner of his eye.

"Take it off," Autumn told him.

"We have used web for generations."

"And no doubt many have died from the fever. Take it off!"

He did.

The day seemed darker when she left the hut. Though it was only a little past noon, the sky was dull with clouds and the heat was oppressive. Her shirt and hair clung to her back. Her head throbbed. As Henri offered her water, she drank deeply, then asked for more. She drank, then poured the remaining water into her hand, and bathed her face.

The woman who had birthed the child only moments before appeared at the hut door, the baby wrapped in dirty clothes in her arms. The others crowded around her, took the child and proceeded to place the baby within a circle of bowls. Autumn cautiously approached, eyeing the water they used to bathe the blood and mucus from the child. It smelled foul and looked little better. Murky brown and thick, it clung to the child's flushed skin like molasses.

"What are they doing?" she asked Henri. He had ambled up beside her, leaned on his crutch, and was smoking his pipe.

"Warding off the evil ones."

"With?"

He puffed and she repeated, "With?"

"Spices, *bois-caca* leaves, manioc mush, coffee and *clairin*."

"Well . . . it smells awful."

She watched in silence as they placed the child in a tiny basket. To her surprise, an agile young man, after tucking the basket beneath his arm, scurried up the side of a tree and wedged it between the fork of two limbs. The infant's wail of disapproval drifted up through the towering limbs and into the pewter-gray sky as Autumn blinked in amazement.

"The babe will remain there for nine days," Henri explained as she looked disbelievingly into his rheumy eyes. "He is not considered born until that time. If he survives, then I will name him."

"But what will he eat?"

"*Eau-sirop.* A mixture of cane juice and water."

"But what of animals?"

"If he survives, it is the will of the gods. If he dies, it is the will of the gods."

"Bring the child down."

His old mouth puckered like a dried persimmon.

"Down," she repeated.

Henri thought for a moment, then called to the boy in the tree, "*Á té! Á té!*"

The crowd stirred and the people mumbled among themselves. They looked at Autumn suspiciously, and as she returned their stare, they backed away.

"They are afraid of you," Henri said softly.

"Are you?"

She heard him wheeze slightly as he inhaled. "I had a dream of fire," came the response at last. "Ogu was among us, burning."

Autumn watched as his eyes flickered over her hair. She remembered Brice's mentioning they believed she had a passion for fire. "And is Ogu bad?"

"She is strong. She will protect us against the evil one."

"Who is . . ."

"Minetta."

The boy placed the basket and the squalling child at Autumn's feet. She took it and offered it to the baby's mother. Ignoring Autumn and child, the woman turned her back and reentered the hut.

"The child does not exist," Henri explained. "If he is worthy of life, he will survive."

"The baby needs nourishment, clothing." Looking into Henri's watchful eyes, she added, "Love! The child exists as surely as yourself. I cannot abide this neglect. You must convince them—''

"You convince them."

Instead, Autumn looked down at the infant. "What are you doing?" he asked as she took it in her arms.

"I'll return the child in nine days. Until that time, he is mine."

There were bullfrogs calling from the swamps before Autumn was halfway back to the house. It was getting that dark. The air felt damp on her face and smelled foul enough to turn her stomach.

Celie stared at Autumn and the infant in astonishment as Autumn announced, after arriving back at Hunnington, "We'll care for the child for the next nine days. I'll need a wet nurse, of course. I shan't allow the baby to starve." Laughing as the infant rotated his head and nuzzled her breast, Autumn added, "I think you'd better hurry, Celie! Oh, and see that the room nearest mine is made ready. We'll room the baby there so I can see to him during the night."

She lost her voice, then, as Donovan walked through the door.

A head taller than she, he looked down at the squirming bundle in her arms, his face full of amazement and curiosity. His presence permeated the air and her body and made the room seem so warm that she thought she'd faint if he stared any harder.

"It's a baby," she said.

He made a funny clicking sound with one corner of his mouth. "Is that what it is?"

"Those silly Indians were going to plant him in a tree for the next nine days."

"The very idea."

"The poor thing might have starved."

"Undoubtedly."

"I thought we could just put him into the room next to mine—"

"We?"

"I, rather."

"Rather." Tucking the tips of his fingers into his breeches

pockets, Brice leaned against the doorjamb and looked so unabashedly sensual that Autumn's face colored.

"Will you excuse us?" she asked him.

"No. There's something we have to discuss."

"Oh. Well, I—"

"I missed you."

Her eyes searched the deepening shadows about them.

"We have to talk," Brice told her—he was closer now—and this time he spoke more urgently.

Voices drifted through the house, one a good-humored baritone and the other horrifyingly recognizable. "John Dearborne!" she exclaimed. Clutching the mewling infant to her breast Autumn looked up into Brice's troubled face, and all the fears and dreads she had managed to shelve throughout the morning surfaced in the cry, "He's brought the *Venerable* to take me back!"

"He's brought Clarence Dillman."

Dillman . . . Dillman . . . Where had she heard the name? There was a flash of Annee's angry face before Brice shocked her further by announcing: "He wants to buy Hunnington, Autumn. I'm considering his offer."

"Mrs. Donovan!"

She was still staring into Brice's eyes when the portly man stepped around Donovan and extended his hand.

"My, my, my, my, my!" he clucked good-naturedly at the squirming baby. "Now isn't he a robust little bairn."

They all stared down at the baby's shock of black hair.

"Yes," Autumn replied as steadily as possible. The tears were choking off her voice and threatening to spill. It didn't help when Brice gently caught her wrist and gave it a reassuring squeeze.

Autumn quickly excused herself as politely as possible.

Brice watched her go, noting the little shoulders that weren't so erect now, and he sensed that something inside Autumn had died a little as he made that announcement. He shouldn't have blurted it out like that, he realized, not until he could sit her down and explain why he was considering Dillman's offer.

"Is something wrong?" Dillman asked, and Brice, watching Autumn disappear up the stairs nodded, thinking that a little of him was dying too.

Chapter 21

Autumn was sitting on the edge of her chair, hands clasped and pressed between her knees, when Pierre came bounding into the room. His cheeks were apple-red. The air whirled about him, smelling like the sea and sand and the banana frond that dangled from his hip pocket. His eyes wide with excitement, he flew to the reed basket on the table and looked down at the child.

"Tonnerre! Un bébé, oui?"

"Yes."

"Celie said you found him growing in a bunch of bananas. Said you just peeled off the skin of a banana and there he was."

"Is that what she said?"

"Yes. But I don't believe her. I know where babies come from."

"Do you?"

"Oh, yes. Everyone knows the zemi leaves them." He threw a glance toward the zemi on Autumn's dresser, and with a half grin, added, "I figure you'll be getting one soon."

Autumn stared at the zemi for a full minute.

The zemi stared back.

"Will you teach me to read now?"

Pierre's voice shattered the spell. With a yearning in her heart that left her shaken and weak, she looked wistfully down at the sleeping baby and nodded.

Within minutes an ink well, quill and paper were provided; so quickly, in fact, Autumn suspected the tyke had hidden them outside the door. They sat a long while before the secretary. Autumn would carefully print out a letter and Pierre would parrot it over and over until he could close his eyes and write it with a flourishing finger in the air.

"You're a very bright young man," she told him.

"I know," he responded. He then wiggled with such pleasure she couldn't help but laugh.

She then printed out his name. "Pi-erre. Pierre. P-i-e-r-r-e."

He ran his little finger over it almost reverently, disappointed when he smeared the P. "Write your name." He pointed his blue-smudged finger at the paper.

She did so.

"Autumn." Pierre stared at it a long while, repeating it, rolling the sound on his tongue, closing his eyes and memorizing the look of the word. And soon, as if the image had suddenly planted itself on his mind, he tilted sideward, looked back over his shoulder and said, *"Tonnerre!"*

"Is something wrong?"

"No, something is right! It is very right!"

"Well tell me what it is, because I need something that is very right, right now."

"Oh, I cannot do it. It's a secret, I think."

"I thought I was your friend."

"You are!" he stressed in all seriousness. "I would never take someone who was not my friend to see my butterflies." Lifting one eyebrow he asked, "Will you come to the valley with me again to chase butterflies? I saw a blue one this morning as big as my hand."

It could very well be her last opportunity to chase butterflies, she reasoned. Autumn then thought of Donovan's words, "I'm considering it," thought again that at this very moment he was down those stairs manipulating her future, and the longer she thought about it, the madder she got.

Pierre's eyes widened. "You have that look again on your face."

"What look?"

"Donovan calls it your spitfire look. He said to keep clear of Maîtresse Donovan when she gets that spitfire look on her face. He said someday your freckles will catch fire and pop right off your nose."

"He did, did he?"

"Oh, yes. But he was laughing when he said it."

"Does he laugh at me often?"

"Yes. I think so." Autumn's mouth twisted sideways, making Pierre giggle.

Then he did something that brought tears to her eyes. Wrapping his little arms around her neck, he said, "I love you, maîtresse."

Touching her forehead to his, she looked him in the eye. "Do you?"

"Yes."

"And I . . . I love you, too, Pierre."

"That is good. If you will wait until I grow up we can be married."

"But I'll be an old woman by then."

"No one grows old on Cayemite. Except, of course, Henri."

The thought occurred to her that he was right. Most people on the island were barely older than Brice.

"I think I would marry you even if you were old," he went on.

"Well." Releasing a long sigh, Autumn smiled. "You are a very special young man, Pierre."

"I know. Would you like to know how special I am?"

"Of course."

"It is a secret, and you must not tell a living soul; promise."

She crossed her heart.

He wiggled from her lap. "Promise!" he reiterated, and his eyes blazed so intensely into hers that Autumn sat back in her chair. Speechless, she nodded.

Pierre walked to the window. Staring out over the gardens, he said, "Close your eyes, maîtresse." She stared a moment longer, and he repeated, without again turning to face her, "Close them."

She closed them.

"Make a wish," he said. "Any wish."

Autumn smiled at the game. "Very well."

The wind blew in, smelling of salt and flowers.

A Negro man, standing in the distant cane field, stopped his chore and looked back toward the house. That's the

image she saw in her mind before shifting her thoughts to
other things; to Donovan and Hunnington and . . . butterflies.

Pierre's head fell back, his child's laughter filling the
room as lightly as the wind that ruffled the *baire* on
Autumn's bed. She opened her eyes. When at last he
turned to face her, his green-gray eyes dancing with
humor, he said in so knowing a voice that she shivered:

"But he will never leave you, maîtresse. Never."

She stood at the window, looking out at the Negro man
in the center of the distant cane field. He paused periodi-
cally, and looked back toward the house.

"Autumn."

The sound was as melodious and heartrending as ever.
Autumn clutched at the windowsill, forcing her anger under
control, convincing herself that nothing had changed since
her arrival on Cayemite—not herself or her circumstances.

But they *had* changed. Just as she had always feared,
her love for a man had sapped her strength, had diverted
her from her goals and left her with little more than
tingling toes and a heart that was doing somersaults in her
constricted chest.

"Go away," she finally managed.

"Not until we talk."

"We can't talk, Mr. Donovan. We never could."

His silence was a taunt in itself. With as much courage
as she could muster, Autumn turned slowly from the
window.

He was bent slightly over the basket, his left hand in
his breeches pocket, his right lightly fanning the spray of
hair on the baby's head. His own hair had tumbled over
his forehead, and it was through that black fringe that
Brice peered at her when he finally drew his eyes from the
child.

Damn you, Donovan, for making my heart melt to my
stomach!

"Never thought I'd see this," he said with a sly grin.

"What."

"You with a baby."

"It's not as though he were my own, of course."

"You have a real way with children, you know. Pierre's in love with you."

"I know. He's asked me to marry him."

"Did you accept?"

"I'm considering the offer."

He straightened to his full height. She always forgot how tall he was, how broad his shoulders were, or how intense his eyes. He could fill up a room just by entering it. She found herself backing away until the small of her back was pressed against the windowsill. "You—you forgot to knock," she announced, sounding ridiculously nervous.

"It is my room."

"Not anymore." Her voice was higher. "It is *my* room and I have no intention of leaving it. Ever!"

"Autumn."

Her arm came up. Palm out, she demanded, "Stay away from me, Brice Donovan. You got what you wanted from me. Our contract was fulfilled—"

"Contract!"

"Yes, contract, and keep your voice down; you'll wake the baby."

"Contract!" he repeated, irritation so thick in his voice it almost choked him.

"The fine print, I think you called it."

"Is that what you think took place in that bed last night?" He jammed one straight, shaking finger toward the bed and demanded, "Is it?"

Up went her chin, and squaring her shoulders, she snapped, "It was disgusting!"

"That's a lie, Missus Donovan." He was pointing at her now. "You know what I think?" he went on, "I think it meant just as much to you as it did to me. More, maybe, because for the first time in your life you felt like a woman. Did that upset you, Autumn? Didn't you enjoy being a woman for the first time in your life?"

"Why, you bastard!"

"Tut-tut, Missus Donovan, is that any kind of language to be using in front of a child?"

She flew at him in a rage and out of the need to touch him and be touched by him. She hit him with such force he groaned and stumbled backward. She beat his chest with her fists, each blow striking her heart as it did his chest. "I hate you for doing this to me!" she railed, then cried a little louder, "How dare you do this to me when I neither needed you nor wanted you nor loved you! You're inhuman, Brice Donovan, with the feelings of a jellyfish!"

When he could take the punishment no longer, he caught her flailing wrists, and, jerking her squirming little form off her feet and against his rigid body, he declared, "I should whip you, Missus Donovan."

"You don't have the backbone," she jeered.

"You know what I'm tired of?" he jeered back.

"I'm certain I don't care."

"It's bossy women."

She thumped him again, this time with her knee.

"You and Annee have been pulling me back and forth like a goddamned rope in a tug of war game."

"I've done no such thing!" she argued.

"Yes you have, Autumn. You have."

His voice had dropped so disquietingly low that Autumn couldn't help but raise her face from his chest and look up into his eyes. A mistake, she realized immediately as those swimming green pools drowned her in desire. "Put me down," she whispered.

Brice moved toward the bed.

"Not there!" Panic surging in her voice, Autumn kicked ineffectually at his legs as he shouldered aside the mosquito *baire* and dropped her into the sheets. She rolled away and he sprang at her. He tugged at her clothes as assuredly as he whispered playful words to shatter her resistance.

"I thought you came here to talk!" she muttered into the mattress.

"We'll talk later," he said with a mouthful of her hair.

"But people don't do this kind of thing in the daylight!"

Donovan chuckled so lasciviously her ears turned red.

"Hush," he told her, "you'll wake the baby."

"Brice Donovan, take your hands out of there this minute! Oh! How dare you! Ouch! That tickles! Stop . . . stop . . . oh, Brice. Brice . . ."

The bed creaked beneath their weight.

"Still want me to stop, Autumn?"

She closed her eyes, sinking beneath his shoulders and chest and the pressure of his hips against hers. Her breeches were around her ankles. He caught them with the sole of his boot and shoved them over her feet, to the edge of the bed, where they slipped to the floor.

His hand came up slowly, beneath the tail of her shirt, skirting, lingering over her hip, to her ribs to the place where her heart drummed frantically inside her chest. "It's racing," he said softly. "Here." The shirt came up around her armpits. He pressed his mouth against the underside of her left breast. "And here." His fingers closed around her arm, biting into the blue-veined skin of her wrist. "And here, too." His face came up then and nuzzled against her throat. Autumn thought that those weren't the only places where her pulse was throbbing.

Her lashes fluttering closed, Autumn shivered as his mouth dropped again to the pink, pointed tip of her breast. He molded it with his lips, exploring it with his tongue until it jutted against his teeth. "You're beautiful," she heard him say. He moved back and forth from one breast to the other as if undecided as to which brought him more pleasure. And all the while, his hands were moving, stroking, burning her with such intense pleasure she thought at any moment she would cry aloud. His tongue dipped into the well of her navel. Autumn gasped. His hand ran up the inside of her leg, and Autumn trembled.

Then Brice showed her exactly what he could do with his tongue.

When she thought she would surely unravel at any moment, Donovan moved back on his knees. His fingers plucked at the catches on his pants, and almost with a life of their own they peeled down around his hips, to the tops of his thighs. She reached for him without hesitation, without embarrassment, thinking nothing had ever seemed so beautiful as Brice's body in her hands.

She opened and he poised.

He plunged and she guided.

He braced his weight above her, his palms sinking into the mattress beside her head and his elbows bracketing her shoulders. "Ah, damn," he groaned. "Damn." And their world trembled in that blissful moment of joining.

He took her quickly beyond consciousness, beyond awareness of filtered sunlight and *baires* that fluttered with every little breeze. There were glimpses of reflected bodies in the dresser mirror that made her heartbeat triple. And all the while, there were his words, those lilting island words that she wished she understood, for they moved her as forcefully toward that scaling of pleasure as his long, slow strokes inside her.

She trembled with sensation. She ached, full of herself and him, until she wept his name and cried for release. And still he took her, up, up, his own body straining and his fingers digging into the mattress by her shoulders until, on outstretched arms he rode above her, their sexes touching, but nothing else except their eyes—until even that became too painful, the touch too intense.

His name came, without sound, formed on lips that were open and wet and yearning. So he kissed them again, more intensely than ever before, his tongue driving and drawing while his hips went driving and drawing until she was mindless. His head went back then. His entire body went hard. He prayed softly at the canopy overhead, and she watched from her tunnel of dim awareness as he said her name to God and the *baire* with such desperation she thought he'd wept it.

The pressure mounted, coiled and tautened to the point of bursting. And still he stretched and filled and pounded inside her until the flood came, a glorious miracle that rushed beyond mortal limits to the divine, to the sublimity that was shining, boundless.

She cried his name, and she cried. The tears in her eyes blotted on the sheet beneath her cheek as she rolled her face toward the bed, unable to bear seeing him above her, so splendid that even the joining of their bodies wasn't enough. She wept because he couldn't know what loving him had done to her.

With a soft curse he rolled away, so quickly her body was left shivering and empty for lack of his warmth. He moved to the far edge of the bed, his back to her, his knees curled slightly toward his stomach. He gulped several long, uneven breaths before the broad, tense planes of his back and shoulders relaxed even a little.

"Donovan," she said. She touched his back and he stiffened again.

"Don't," he implored her.

Autumn ignored him. Rolling up against him, she slid her arm over his waist and asked, "Have I displeased you?"

Brice said nothing, just rolled a little more into the bed.

"I'm sorry if I cried. It's just so—"

"Wonderful." His voice was tight.

Autumn smiled. "Yes."

She thought she heard Donovan groan.

Autumn pressed her cheek against his back, ran her hand leisurely across his chest, to his stomach, until he caught her hand and hugged it tightly against his body.

The baby whimpered.

Autumn sat up, pulling the tangled sheet across her legs and hips. The child was a reminder of the purpose of the act in which she and Brice had just participated. It was the consequence that struck her. She waited for its impact. It didn't come, but a slow warmth that germinated in her heart ebbed through her body and pulsed so serenely she almost smiled.

And for the first time since her mother died, the thought of having a man's child—this man's child—filled her with wonder. She knew in that moment what her argument against leaving Cayemite would be.

Leaning slightly over Donovan's shoulder, she peered down on his tense profile and said, "Would you make me leave Cayemite, Donovan, when there is a chance I could be with child?"

His head came around as he rolled into her arms. "You're not," he said simply, causing the confident little smile on her mouth to diminish.

"But three times we've—"

"My God, are you that ignorant, Autumn?"

Sitting back, she blinked in disbelief.

He came at her then, his green eyes stormy and his body rigid with tension. Catching her hand he took it down his belly, to the silky hardness that earlier had driven her mad with desire.

"See for yourself," he said through his teeth. "I've put no baby in you now, or the time before."

"But—"

Brice groaned, not knowing whether to laugh or curse at such innocence. Rolling her to her back he interrupted, "It has to happen for me, too, Autumn. The magic. It hasn't happened for me. I wouldn't let it, knowing how you feel."

No màgic. How could that be when she had exalted in the glorious, the wondrous magic, and died the most beautifully blissful death she could ever hope to imagine? Her hand moved slightly; Donovan closed his eyes and whispered:

"Don't stop."

She didn't.

And it happened for him, too, though not so gloriously or wondrously because he experienced it alone. But it was a release, and Autumn understood now why he'd put no baby inside her, and wouldn't, knowing how she felt. And as he found that release without her, as she had found hers without him . . . the ache inside her grew.

Autumn knew the moment she awakened that something was different. Brice was gone. Afternoon had settled into the room, deepening the corners with shadow and relieving the hot air with the scent of flowers.

The armoire door swung open, the one emblazoned with *D,* creaking slightly as it did so. Autumn sat upright in bed, staring through the *baire* toward the wardrobe, then toward the dresser. The zemi of fertility was gone. So were the combs and brushes she had always spread out upon the dresser. The baby was gone as well.

She dressed quickly and left the room. Her ear strained for any familiar sound. By now Celie should have begun their evening meal. The clanging and ringing of pots and the smell of fricassee or akee should now be making her stomach growl. But there was nothing, not even the *simidor*'s serenade as the workers made their way back to the house.

From the top of the stairs, she saw John Dearborne and

his first mate leave the house. She heard Clarence Dillman call Brice's name, then Brice's response.

"I thank you for this, Dillman. Signing those papers has brought a great relief to my mind."

The men stood facing each other outside the library door. They shook hands, then Dillman went the way of Dearborne, pausing only as he looked up the flight of stairs toward Autumn. Tipping his hat, he said, "Madam Donovan, I'll see you at the ship." Then Autumn saw her trunks standing just outside the door.

She was leaving Cayemite.

Donovan waited until Dillman had boarded the buggy for Bovier before coming to the stairs. He seemed to take an abnormally long time before meeting her eyes.

"How dare you?" she asked him softly.

He appeared to flinch.

"How quickly you tire of the hunt when the fox has been treed, isn't that right, Mr. Donovan?"

He shook his head.

She came down the stairs slowly, chin up and fingers clutching the banister for support. When they were at eye level, she slapped his face. "I won't leave, Donovan. You cannot force me to leave. Half of this estate is mine and—"

"She'll kill you if you stay." He said it softly, his cheek aflame and his intense eyes on hers. "Annee will kill you the same as she killed my father and brother. And if she doesn't kill you, the island will, as it did my mother and father and brother. As it did Bovier and Barrett. It will suffocate you with loneliness. It will work you until you're broken and bleeding in here." He pressed one finger against her heart, and as her mouth went soft and opened in surprise, he twisted her shirt front into his fingers and, stepping up beside her, lifted her from her toes. "By God, I will not allow it. I love you too much."

She felt suspended, unbelieving, joyous. Her arms came around him, and his around her. She pressed her lips against his cheek for a brief moment, feeling the heat of her earlier slap and the coarseness of his unshaven skin. She smelled his scent of salt and musk, a little brandy.

"I won't leave! How can I leave?" She wept into his shirt collar.

"I'll meet you in Montego Bay." He kissed her temple.

"Come with me now, Donovan. Now!"

"I can't. Ah, God, Autumn, I'll do what I came here to do or I'll never live in peace."

"Then let me stay. I'm not afraid of Annee Rose or—"

"It's not safe!" Brice shook her. "Even if I deal with Annee, there's the island—"

"I don't believe in legends or zemis who control people's lives at a whim. It's a fairy-tale, Brice; like the fairies and the boars and the people who are supposedly possessed with good or evil."

Grabbing her wrist, he pulled Autumn down the final few stairs and out the front door. He dragged her down the stone steps and on reaching the road whirled her around toward the island's horizon. "Look at her," he demanded. "Look at her, then convince me that what's happening to this rock is fairy-tale!"

A stream of black smoke billowed from Trempe's crown into the sky, and hung over the west island.

"A fire?"

"Yes. But inside her, Autumn. Trempe is a volcano, which explains the gases that nearly killed us and the tremors that spooked your horse. The goddamned island is crumbling beneath our feet."

"But it—it can't be!"

It started then, as if to belie her denial, beginning beneath their feet and rippling outward, toward the water, back toward the house, then streaking more quickly toward the mountain. Sounding like thunder, it rolled from the ground in undulating waves until they were pitched like a boat in a storm. Brice grabbed Autumn before going down, then they toppled together, feeling the ground tremble and pulse under them as they clung to each other. Yes, they thought, the island was crumbling beneath them!

But unlike the times before, the tremor didn't stop, but rolled into the center of the island and, with one great heave, went driving up Trempe and escaped in an explosion of fire and rock and gas. The servants ran from the house. They ran from the fields, wide eyes looking back

over their shoulders in terror as the sky rained glowing ash
over land and churning water. When they could run no
farther, they fell to their knees on the sand. With white-
capped waves fretting their ankles, they chanted in homage
and fear to the angry gods on the mountain.

And the trembling and thunder ceased.

If Brice had held on to any selfish doubts concerning
Autumn's leaving the island, they now vanished. Helping
Autumn to her feet, he hurried her to the awaiting buggy
and ordered the trunks to be loaded.

When she opened her mouth to protest, he pointed his
finger in her face and snapped, "Don't!"

They were halfway to Bovier before she could control
her shaking enough to speak. "Come with me," she said.
Looking out the opposite side of the buggy from Brice, she
added, "Please."

"I've instructed Dillman to send help just as soon as he
returns to Jamaica. I can leave then."

"But why must you remain?"

"I have a certain responsibility to these people."

"And I don't?" Her face turned sharply to his.

"No," he replied, "you don't."

Steam and dust hung over the trees, kept aloft only by
the south wind that stirred the crystalline sea waters. The
sun setting on the west horizon glowed like a great ball of
fire behind the curtain of lingering smoke.

A flurry of activity greeted Autumn and Brice as they
entered Bovier. Upon seeing Donovan, the natives rushed
to the buggy, their cries of "Maît Donovan, Maît Donovan, grace, *diabs!*" climbing to a fever pitch as they
pointed to the mountain. Shoving them aside, he escorted
Autumn to the dock, both stumbling over the people reaching and plucking hands and fingers as they cried out for his
protection.

Seamen hurried to load Autumn's trunks. John Dearborne
was planted at the ship end of the gangplank, forbidding
any of the frightened natives to force themselves aboard.
"I've taken me load, ya cowardly savages now, *poussé
allé!*" came his resounding threat.

Beside him, Clarence Dillman was fit to be tied. "Mr.

Donovan!'' he called, ''I beseech you, man; leave this cursed place now, before it is too late!''

''I'll leave with the others,'' he said to Autumn.

Jeanette and Pierre appeared in the crowd. The little boy dodged through the frantic people, and as he approached Autumn and Brice, she went down on one knee and opened her arms.

''You are leaving!'' Pierre said to her. ''But maîtresse, you must not leave!''

''She's leaving,'' came Brice's voice above them, absolute and deep. He turned then to Jeanette and added, ''I'd like you and Pierre to go as well.''

''Not I. But Pierre . . .'' Looking down at her son and Autumn, she added bravely, ''Take my Pierre from this island, maîtresse.''

''Noooo!'' The boy stumbled from Autumn's arms. His eyes wide with fear, he grabbed his mother's skirts and wept against her leg. ''We must not leave Donovan alone. I cannot leave him! Help will come, *maman,* I promise you.'' Whirling back to Autumn, he pleaded, ''You must stay, maîtresse! I cannot help you if you leave on that ship. I cannot help you!'' He then threw himself into Autumn's arms again, and kept repeating, ''I cannot help you if you leave the island.''

Autumn looked up into Brice's eyes. ''Please. It isn't fair,'' she told him.

''Get on the ship.''

''Please!''

Pierre moved away as Brice reached for Autumn's hand. Pulling her up into his arms, he said in a voice raw with emotion, ''I'll not lose you to this goddamned island. This island has taken everything I have ever loved. It will not take you, too.''

''You love me.''

''I love you.''

''Yet you can turn me away.''

''Because I love you.'' Cupping her face in his hands, he said, ''I love your freckles. 'Specially that one.'' His thumb brushed the spot at the corner of her mouth.

''Blimey, Donovan,'' came Dearborne's harangue, ''Are ya gonna stand there for the duration, or what? This ole crate ain't gonna stand up to those bits of ash again, I'll guarantee ya. Ain't nobody gonna leave this hellhole if she catches fire!''

Brice grinned at Autumn. ''I'll see you in Montego Bay.''

Her heart was breaking. ''Swear it,'' she demanded. Her voice was breaking and the tears were beginning to fall.

''I swear it.''

He kissed her with all the passion he felt in his heart. Then he pushed her away. ''Good-bye.''

She turned stiffly toward the gangplank, her shoulders aching from the strain of holding back the sobs in her chest. And when Pierre's little hand caught hers, it was all she could do not to cry aloud.

Tucking something into her hand, he whispered again, ''I cannot help you once you've left the island.''

She walked on.

''Missus Donovan!''

Heart pounding, Autumn paused and slowly, slowly, looked back over her shoulder.

His hands were in his pockets. ''What do you think of Virginia?'' Donovan asked her.

''I have never seen Virginia,'' she admitted.

Brice grinned. ''What do you know about raising tobacco?''

''Nothing.''

''Didn't know much about growing cane either, did ya?''

''But I learned.''

''Aye,'' he said softly. ''You learned a lot.''

Her feet were like lead, her heart barely lighter. The scraping of the plank behind her as she stepped aboard ship was as wrenching as the sight of Donovan standing there, his legs spread slightly and his shirtsleeves fluttering in the wind.

Dearborne barked his orders and the mangy crew of seamen hustled to the rigging.

The wind was with them. As it billowed the mainsail, the *Venerable* moved smoothly into the tranquil sea. Clutching the rail so tightly that her knuckles popped, Autumn called to the diminishing figures on the dock, "I'll see you in Montego, Donovan!"

He said something, but the wind caught the words and threw them back on the island.

"I think I might enjoy growing tobacco!" she added, and she thought she saw him smile.

"I don't like it," Dillman said, now standing beside her. "No man makes out his last will and testament as suddenly as he did unless he expects something is about to happen. That man will never leave that island, Mrs. Donovan, you mark my words." Then looking into Autumn's white face he added, "I certainly hope you know something about tobacco, my dear."

"Why?" Her voice was dry.

"Because Donovan has left you everything he owns."

She watched numbly as Dillman, agitated and sweating, hurried toward Dearborne.

The paper Pierre had thrust into her hand fluttered from her fingers where it caught in a crosswind on the deck and danced around her feet. Only then did she realize she'd dropped it. As the wind shifted again, the paper lifted to her fingers, and she grasped it.

"Roy," it began, and it ended, "I think I'm in love with her myself."

Autumn closed her eyes.

Oh, Donovan. My darling, darling Donovan.

Chapter 22

He knew the madness now for what it was—blackness and despair. It was pain so intense that the mind burned. It was holding something you love and having it slip through your fingers, no matter had hard you tried to hold onto it.

It was losing Autumn.

He was staring out to sea when Annee Rose found him. He sat alone on a rock, the wind whipping his face and the turquoise water reflecting in his eyes.

"She's gone," Annee said.

Donovan's head lowered slightly. He stared at his hands.

"Poor Donovan. It is horrible, isn't it? The pain. Yes, yes it is. I cried every night for twelve years after you left Cayemite." She stood before him, the silk of her dress flapping and billowing in the wind. Her hair drifted like a black cloud around her shoulders. "I'll make you forget her," she added softly.

She gently caught his face in her hands, pressed his head against her bosom, and stroked his dark hair. "Poor Donovan," she soothed him.

They stayed there for several minutes before she continued. "It was inevitable, you know. You were destined to return to me. You're mine, and you always have been . . . just like Hunnington. Both of you are mine now that *she* is gone." Turning toward the water, she smiled. "See for yourself. She's gone. Forever and ever."

His head dropped to his hands.

Smiling brightly, Annee walked toward the water before facing Brice again. "We'll celebrate. Tonight! Oh, darling, it'll be just as it used to be, the two of us together. It'll be wonderful!"

Her smile fled as Pierre topped the rise. "Damn!" she hissed so vehemently that Brice looked up in surprise.

Pierre, his child's face serene, smiled at Donovan. "I have come to see you back to the house," he told his uncle.

Annee backed away as he approached Brice.

Offering his little hand to Donovan, Pierre said, "Don't worry. Maîtresse will be back. I promise you."

"She won't!" Annee snapped.

Resting his hand consolingly on Donovan's shoulder, Pierre looked directly at Annee Rose and ordered, "Go away."

Her eyes narrowed.

"Away," he repeated.

She backed toward the water. "I'll see you tonight, darling?"

Brice looked again to the horizon. The ship was gone.

The house was empty. Brice stood in the center of the room, staring around at the furniture, seeing Autumn as she rearranged this or that piece, as she sat in the high-backed chair and threw one leg over the arm as they discussed the building of the mill. And there she stood, beneath the little cherub, an angel herself dressed in gold silk and ivory lace.

He was torturing himself, yet the visions came: Autumn striding through hip-high weeds, standing coolly while a headless chicken hopped around her feet . . . struggling in his arms and finally surrendering. He remembered the way her body molded against his, the taste of her mouth. And he felt like dying.

He fell into a chair, a bottle of *clairin* in one hand, a glass in the other. He drank until he was bleary-eyed, until his head was so heavy he could hardly lift it. He tried to drink himself into oblivion, but unconsciousness was always out of reach, taunting him with the relief that would ease his heartache and his dread of facing the night. He drank until he should have been too numb to feel anything any longer, but he still felt the black despair, the madness. He knew now what had driven Bovier and Barrett and, yes, Patrick Donovan, too, to the brink of insanity. Love, sublime and suffocating; they had loved Cayemite—beautiful, bewitching Cayemite—and Brice had loved, still loved, a woman.

Stumbling from his chair, he stood in the middle of the room, beneath the bronze cherub, as the walls spun around him. "Stop!" he yelled at no one, at everyone, at all the faces that stared back at him from the mirrors hanging on each of the four walls of the room. He saw Patrick Donovan's face, and Roy's face, too.

"Damn you, papa!" he roared. "You're the one who told me never to come back. If you'd've written, ah, God, just one letter I might've come back!"

He threw the bottle into the mirror and heard it shatter as he staggered around to look at the other face. "You son of a bitch!" he jeered at Roy. "If you were alive, I'd kill you myself. Come on out here so I can kill you myself!" He aimed the crystal tumbler at the glass and hurled it. He missed. Taking a paper weight from the desk top, he threw it, too, against the wall, followed by a book and a candlestick. Finding no satisfaction in that, he swiped his arm over the desk, sending paper and pens and a conch shell to the floor. He kicked a chair, toppling it backward.

Jeanette appeared at the door, as did several open-mouthed, wide-eyed servants. Pierre hung on her skirts. His face turned up to hers, he wept. "He is like the bad man, *maman!* Make him stop!"

Picking up a blue-and-white china vase, Brice flung it against the wall.

"Quickly!" Jeanette told her son, "Fetch the Irishman, Pierre. Run!"

Closing his hands around a tissue-thin glass, Donovan felt it crumble in his fingers.

The servants scattered, leaving the house as they had during Patrick's and Roy's tirades, babbling about *bakas* and madness, and wasn't it a shame that the maît had followed in his father's and brother's footsteps. They decided to go to the *Maître Source* and pray for his soul.

Donovan watched them out the window. "Look at 'em run," he said loud enough for them to hear and peer back over their shoulders. "Run, you bunch of bleedin' savages, and see if I care! If you want to pray for something, pray I don't shoot your butts when you come back!"

Tyler, with Pierre fast on his heels, barreled into the room. "Mother of God, the man's in his cups. Bring me some coffee, Jeanette, and make it black."

His hair in his eyes, Brice clumsily turned to face his overseer. "Get out," he snapped.

"I don't like seein' y' like this, son."

"Who as'ed ya!"

"I know yer upset about Autumn—"

"Don't!" The sound of her name drove him back against the wall.

"All right, I won't say no more."

"I'm drunk."

"Aye, and y' hurt."

Staring at the ceiling, Brice laughed and shook his head. "God, how I hate this place."

"Then leave it. Y' should've left with Autumn."

"Don't . . . say . . . it!"

"Why did y' stay?" Hugh asked. "Just t' get even with Annee? Did y' ever think that just leavin' the island would destroy her faster than a bullet between the eyes? Look at yerself, Brice. Yer killin' yerself, man. Open yer eyes and see it."

"But if I hadn't left in the first place, they might still be alive." His eyes burning with memories and anger, Brice looked directly at Hugh and said, "I as good as killed them myself."

"Nobody forced either one of 'em t' stay. They could've picked up and moved on any time."

Brice waved the argument away. Turning his back to Tyler, he tried to focus his sights out the window. The world rocked and swayed like a pendulum before he managed to right himself with both hands. He blinked, then cursed himself for getting so damned drunk he'd begun to hallucinate.

Autumn Sinclair Donovan was walking up the road.

She was standing on the last tier of stone steps when Donovan left the house. His face was white. His hair was a mess and he smelled like a still when at last he stopped before her.

Autumn, her eyes swollen from salt water, lifted her

chin and returned Brice's disbelieving stare. Her hair lay plastered to her head and clung to her still-damp clothes. She was without her boots.

"You—"

"Jumped ship," she replied in a husky voice.

"Little fool. You might have been eaten by something."

"Or drowned."

"You're too stubborn to drown."

She looked into Brice's face and thought he'd never looked so handsome.

He looked into Autumn's face and thought she'd never looked so beautiful.

"So." He swallowed. "You're back. Remind me to keelhaul Dearborne the next time I see him."

"It's not his fault. I told everyone I was going to my cabin and I wasn't to be disturbed until we docked in Jamaica. I simply slipped over the side when no one was looking."

Brice closed his eyes briefly. "You might have drowned," he repeated.

"But I didn't. Donovan, are you inebriated?"

"No. No, I'm not 'nebre-bre-ited." They both laughed. Then he admitted, "God, I missed you."

She stepped closer. Her lips were swollen and crusted slightly with salt. There was seaweed in her hair. "Will you help me to the house?" she asked Brice. "I'm so tired."

He turned his face away, back toward the west horizon that was blotted by dust and steam and ash. The setting sun shimmered like fire beyond the clouds, causing him to blink. He reached for her; with an effort he pulled her up against him as he sank his face into her hair and cradled her shoulders in his arms. But though he tried, he could not lift her.

They tumbled to the ground in each other's arms as they rolled in the cool grass, their mouths searching for and finding one another and their hands clutching at each other's backs.

"I love you," he told her.

"I love you."

"Marry me," he pleaded.

"Yes." She wept. "I will. I will. I'll be Autumn Sinclair Donovan Donovan, if you'll have me."

"If I'll have you." He laughed and rocked her a little more. "Silly girl." Then he added, "You might have drowned."

"But I didn't."

Brice lay on his back, the evening dew seeping through his shirt as he pressed Autumn's head against his heart. "Thank God," he whispered. "Thank God."

The house was dark when Hugh Tyler finally came down the stairs. He almost stumbled over the tiny shadowed form at the bottom.

" 'ey, lad, but I almost conked y'. Will y' be sittin' there the entire evenin' or will y' be off t' bed?"

A single moonbeam found Pierre's face as he turned it up to Tyler's. "I'll stay awhile," he responded.

"Right, then." Fluffing the boy's hair with his fingertips, Tyler bid him good-night.

"Tyler?" Pierre called quietly.

Hugh stopped and turned.

"Is Donovan all right? And Autumn?"

"Aye. They're both a little worse f' wear, but they'll be fine in the mornin'. Sleep's the best thing for 'em both." Hugh disappeared through the shadows.

The wind moaned in relief.

Pierre sat on the step, arms clasped around his legs and his chin resting on his knee. He counted the chimes of the tall case clock—ten, eleven, twelve—watching the door and waiting. He stood as it opened.

"She's back," he whispered.

"No."

"She's back."

Annee Rose stood in the doorway, her eyes locked on the boy's. "Liar! I saw her board the ship—"

"She's back and with Donovan now."

When she started to enter the house, Pierre lifted his hand and said, "Go away."

"He's mine!" She wept it.

"Go and if you come again, you'll regret it."

"Don't threaten me, child. You are only a child."

"Am I, Minetta?" Pierre smiled. "Am I?"

She backed away.

"Don't ever come here again," he repeated.

"You'll pay," Annee growled. "You'll all pay. Donovan especially."

"Go." As he stepped from the stair, she turned and fled. After closing the door behind her, he locked it.

Autumn, her eyes burning, stared out the *baire* opening, trying to remember just how she came to be in bed with her clothes on, beside Brice. She hurt horribly in her head and her bones; when she moved, her muscles rebelled by contracting so violently her entire body bowed. Her throat was so raw she could hardly swallow and her tongue was swollen. Her skin was on fire. The discomfort was so intense that she was tempted to remove her clothes. Instead, she kicked her sheet away and rolled from the bed.

There was a reddish pall about the room. A glance at the clock told her the hour was early. So where was the soft, pale light of dawn? The fragrant scent of flowers and dew and saline water that had always refreshed her upon awakening? She struggled to the window and looked out.

She tried to call Donovan's name. The sound lodged at the base of her throat and would go no further. When she tried again it came out as a rasp. Brice stirred.

He raised up on one elbow as Autumn pointed out the window, to the night fire that torched the sky. "Hell," was all she managed to croak before the trembling started.

The glass prisms on the lamp globes began to tinkle like chimes. The door on the armoire swung open. Brice and Autumn locked eyes as the big house trembled. It creaked and groaned and rained plaster onto their shoulders. The floor heaved and the bed and dresser slid across the floor.

Brice staggered toward Autumn, stumbling as the floor shifted beneath him. Then he went down, as did Autumn, the mirrors and pictures on the walls and the jalousie in the window. The roaring intensified until they covered their ears in anticipation of the explosion that would surely follow.

But no explosion followed. Only silence.

Autumn was afraid to move or even to breathe. She and
Brice looked at each other as they waited. One minute
passed, then two, then three. Blood trickled from a laceration over Brice's eye and ran down his temple. Autumn
touched the wound gently before pulling herself into his
arms. They waited a moment longer.

Jeanette's voice came through the wall. "Brice!" she
called. She forced open the door, and finding Donovan
and Autumn just climbing to their feet, threw herself on
her brother and wept. "It is Pierre! My Pierre is missing. I
cannot find him!"

"When did you see him last?" When Jeanette didn't
answer, Brice shook her and repeated the question.

"He has not slept in his bed," she finally answered.

His face pale with fear, Donovan pushed Jeanette aside
and started for the door. He met Hugh in the hall. "Get
the hell to Bovier and raise the distress flag."

"It's been done."

"Get as many men as you can find for a search party—"

"They're all off chantin' t' that godforsaken mountain," Hugh cut in.

With a low curse Brice turned down the corridor, jumping over heaps of wood and plaster as he made his way to
the staircase.

Autumn remained where he'd left her until her trembling
ceased. Slowly she climbed to her feet and made her way
outside.

The mill was gone. Only scraps of lumber and rock
remained. The cylinders, gray with ash, lay dull and dented
beneath a toppled ceiba tree. It wasn't the melee of scattered barns and outbuildings, or the terrorized bawling of
cattle or the squealing of pigs, however, that rooted her
attention. It was Trempe. Beautiful, beckoning Trempe
was boiling with fire.

Autumn made her way through the rubble to the barn. A
wide-eyed Negro man stood soothing the frightened horses,
his face melting in relief as Autumn entered. "Where has
Donovan gone?" she asked him.

"To de village, ma'am."

"Saddle me a horse."

"But ma'am—"

"Do as I say. When Donovan returns, tell him I have gone to the valley. Perhaps Pierre has gone there."

It took two tries before the skittish mare allowed the saddle to be strapped on her back. When the man finally led the horse from the barn, Autumn was pacing impatiently up and down the patch of potato plants Celie had planted outside the kitchen door.

"Do you know the valley?" Autumn asked. Swinging her leg over the horse's back, she look down on the man's face.

"Yes, ma'am, I know it."

Without another word, Autumn pulled her horse about and started on her course.

The air was foul and difficult to breathe. The gas and smoke and dust clouded the sky as suffocatingly as a shroud. The closer to the mountain she rode, the denser it became until it seemed that deepest twilight had overtaken the island. But the fire was there, at Trempe's crest, glowing red into the sky.

She reached the valley in minutes.

There were no butterflies and no Pierre. The land was scorched and smoking.

Sliding to the ground, Autumn dropped to her knees. The dizziness had gripped her again, this time much worse than before. She'd thought when she awakened that her weakness and lightheadedness was due only to the ordeal of swimming the bay yesterday. But even that should not have weakened her so.

Coming up on one leg, she reached for her horse.

The spear came from nowhere, whistling by her ear and thudding dully into the animal's breast. The horse stumbled, tossed its head one last time before rolling to its side. Autumn blinked, uncomprehending in that first few seconds, until the thunder of encroaching hoofbeats warned her of approaching danger.

She was hit by a massive blur of white that knocked her winded to the ground. Her reaction was instinctive. She rolled, scrambled, dodging the razor-sharp hooves by inches as they came at her again. On her feet, Autumn began running across the flat bed of smoldering grass where once she'd chased butterflies. The terror deafened her, blinded her to all but the forest up ahead, yet dimly she wondered why the beast had not struck again. For that's all it was—a great white beast with flaring nostrils and hooves that was trying to kill her. She fell into a clump of mangrove at the edge of the forest and tried to hide.

Many of the straw- and frond-thatched huts in the village were smoldering. Some had toppled during the force of the quake or had been crushed beneath falling rock. Brice had heard the drums long before breaching the people's imaginary barriers. Where was Legba, guardian of gates and protector of homes when he was needed?

They were on their knees, surrounding Henri, in the center of the village. His arms outstretched and pointed up the mountain, the old man rocked and moaned and prayed for the gods to spare their souls.

Stepping over bowls of *afibas* and *rapadous,* Brice caught Henri's shoulder and spun him around. "I'm looking for Pierre," Donovan said loud enough to be heard over the chantings. "Have you seen Pierre?"

Henri's head fell back. His corded old neck flexed convulsively as he hummed.

"Damn you, old man, I asked a question. Have you seen the boy?"

Henri opened glazed eyes before singing out, *"Maît-bitasyon!"*

His frustration mounting, Brice turned to the others. "I need help in finding the boy!"

They ignored him. But why should he be surprised? These were the same people who ignored their newborn children for nine days and didn't dare cross a threshold without praying to Legba first, who slaughtered animals believing they might actually be some demon spirit intent on killing them.

He ran to mount his horse and headed back toward the coastline, skirting the frothing waves, their turquoise color cloudy now with mud. The shoreline was strewn with fish, their white bellies bloated and opened by the John Crows hopping from one carcass to another. Driftwood bobbed just off the cay, burned flotsam that briefly caught his eye before sinking in an undertow.

He rode on.

He thought of Autumn as he rode by a smoking cane field. This had been the best of the crop. Now its smell was rank with ash. He thought of his father and his brother as he passed the crossroads; both were buried there with his mother. He wondered if, when this was all over, there would be anyone left alive on Cayemite to bury him.

Where once the road had jutted nearly to the sea, now there was a flooded pool, and Brice was forced to change his course. He headed west, back toward the mountain, feeling its heat even from this distance, watching it spew its fire and gas high into the dark sky, where the sun should have shone.

Hunnington's front portico was partially gone, toppled onto the flagstone piazza where he'd played as a child. Tullius was standing among the stones, rolling his sweat-stained hat in his hands.

"Have you found Pierre?" Brice asked when approaching.

"No, maît, sir, no find de boy."

Onward. To Annee Rose.

His horse was in a lather when he finally arrived at Barrett Hall. The Greathouse appeared untouched by all the pandemonium. Even the servant who met him at the door seemed unconcerned about the danger.

Shoving him aside, Donovan stormed across the marbled foyer and into the drawing room. Spinning around on his heel, he demanded of the domestic who followed him, "Where the hell is Annee?"

The black shook his head.

"I'm looking for a boy. Pierre. Have you seen him?"

"No, Maît Donovan. No boy come here."

Lifting one brow, Donovan glared so fiercely at the Negro that the man backed from the door. "If you're lying to me—"

"No! No child be here. Ever!"

"Perhaps I should see for myself."

The black clasped his white-gloved hands together.

Brice left the room and took the broad, polished mahogany stairway to the second level, and there threw open every door he came to. Those he could not open with his hand, he kicked open, heedlessly splintering the fine wood.

He found the rooms barren of furniture, empty of everything but the mountain's firelight that spilled through the cracks of boarded windows and puddled on the deep embrasures of the mahogany sills.

Satisfied that his upstairs search was complete, he descended the stairs again.

The lower level of Barrett Hall *was* Annee Rose. Elegant and splendid with black lacquer woodwork, the furnishings hinted of Annee's love for Oriental design. Brice worked his way from room to room, sensing that his time would better be used searching elsewhere. Knowing Annee as he did, however, he was taking nothing for granted. She would be furious that he had again turned to Autumn, and she was cruel enough to use a child in her revenge.

He almost missed the narrow door in his hurry to finish his search. It was obscured in shadows at the end of a long, dark hallway.

The space was small, without windows, a room within a room. He stood inside the door and stared at the life-size portrait on the wall. Gowned in white silk robes and a jeweled headdress, the woman had lifeless eyes that seemed to stare through Brice. Her face was painted white. Her lips were red. The plaque beneath read Minetta.

Staggered tiers of candelabras were arranged in each corner of the room. Smoke streamed from each steady flame, smudging the low ceiling. Tables were draped in black cloths; black pillows lay strewn on the floor at the base of the portrait. The room reeked of female scent and of roses.

The door creaked behind him. Brice spun. The Negro who had earlier greeted him looked through the portal and whispered, "Come out of dere, mahn. Dat bahd place. Much trouble you find if Maîtresse Rose see you dere. Come out now."

"What the hell is this?" He peered about the dimly lit quarters, noticing manacles dangling like glistening black snakes from the wall.

"Come out," the black repeated with such urgency Brice stepped toward the door. When he hesitated once more, the man reached one big hand for his arm and pulled him from the room. "You a fool fo' a white mahn," the

Negro said. "A fool to be here in dis house, on dis island. Leave dis place afore de maîtresse come back and find you."

"Where is the maîtresse?" Brice continued to stare inside the room, a sense of understanding beginning to claw like cold fingers up his spine.

"Don't matter," he responded. "She be back soon. She always come back." Pulling the door shut, the man pointed Brice up the hall and warned, "She catch you here, and dere be nothin' I can do. Go now. Go!"

Brice left the house and rode back to Hunnington.

The sky was churning, boiling clouds of steam and dust and gas that obliterated all but the spray of fire from Trempe's crest. A huddle of people stood outside Hunnington's doors when Donovan arrived. Jeanette detached herself from the crowd and greeted her brother with a relieved smile.

"My Pierre is safe!" she told him. "He crawled into Celie's potato bin and fell asleep. With all the noise, no one heard him calling for help until moments ago."

Brice laughed in relief.

Peering up at Brice, Jeanette noted the worry on his face as he looked back toward the mountain. "Will it stop?" she asked him, meaning Trempe's eruption.

"I don't know."

"It is the quakes I'm most frightened of," she admitted. "I fear the earth with open up and swallow us all."

"Help will come. The *Venerable* should be docking in Montego soon, if she hasn't already. Dearborne will be returning with other ships and we'll *all* be able to say good-bye to this godforsaken place."

They reentered the house. Celie was busy overseeing the domestics, the stronger ones shoving the massive furniture back into place. Already the carpets were being rolled and removed for cleaning, and the thump, thump, thump of reed beaters sent puffs of gray dust into the air, making breathing nearly impossible.

"Where is Autumn?" Brice asked. He stepped over broken dishes, pausing in the foyer as he looked across Jeanette's shoulder and into the drawing room. The damage he saw there made his face burn. The shattered mirrors and splintered crystal had been rent by a very different sort of upheaval.

"I have not seen her."

Jeanette's response forced his mind back to the present. Brice glanced up the stairs. He swung toward the door, and as Tullius ambled in among the rubble, Brice called, "Where has Maîtresse Donovan gone?" to anyone who listened.

Tullius smiled a great, toothless smile, and answered, "De stables, monsieur."

"When?"

"Umm." Staring at his bare feet, Tullius pondered the question for a ridiculously long time. Finally he said, "She follow you, Maît."

"Followed?"

He left Jeanette, working his way out the back of the house where the workers were still pounding the carpets and, children were shooing chickens and goats back to their quarters. His eyes scanned the ground, halting over the ruined cylinders. He moved swiftly down the path, looking, searching, until finally he broke out in a run, frightening the horses as he entered the sagging stables.

The stable boy jumped up. "Where the hell is Missus Donovan?" Brice thundered.

"The valley," the boy responded. He pointed one trembling finger out the door and repeated. "The valley."

Chapter 23

Autumn crouched for what seemed like hours within the undergrowth, biting her lip as she was repeatedly stung by insects. She didn't dare move or make a sound. Once a great black spider had crawled onto her leg. She'd closed her eyes and prayed harder than she'd ever prayed in her life, and when she looked again, it was gone. Perhaps if she prayed hard enough, the demon that was trying to kill her would go away, too.

The sky was brighter now, not from daylight, but from fire. A red-and-gold haze shimmered over the entire island; the mountain was like one great ember in the midst of smoldering ash. Several times the trembling had started; nothing more than a slight vibration of the ground and the leaves overhead. But it was enough to make her heart pound and bring tears to her eyes.

She actually dozed several times. Having grown so weary of the worry and fright she'd slipped into unconsciousness, imagining briefly each time she awakened that it was all a bad dream. It was a nightmare, but it was all too horribly real. Someone had tried to kill her, was perhaps out there now, waiting for her to move so he could try again. Still, she could not stay here forever. And Autumn realized now that she was ill, burning with fever.

She crawled through the fallen and rotting vegetation, deeper into the jungle, hoping to put enough distance between her and the area of the attack, so that when she did make her run back across the valley, she wouldn't be noticed. Still, she hadn't traveled far before she was forced to rest. Each movement was like a knife through her muscles; each burst of pain shot directly to her head until she was all but blinded by the excruciating discomfort.

She rested, then continued, weeping quietly because she

ached so badly. The pain was so intense she almost wished
the white demon would find her and kill her, just so her
suffering would end. But when she thought of dying, she
remembered Brice, and the thought of him kept her going.
He wanted to marry her because he loved her—truly loved
her—for herself, and not because he wanted only the
children that would come from the union. He'd told her
that having children didn't matter. He'd proven to her that
it didn't matter. But it did matter. It mattered to her
because she loved him, too. And she couldn't think of
anything more wonderful than to have his baby.

Oh, if she could only live long enough to give him a
child.

Up on her hands and knees, she moved more quickly in
and out of the bushes. Finally, after carefully assessing her
surroundings, she moved unsteadily to her feet, crying
aloud as the pain pricked like needles to every point
throughout her body. She ran, in and out of the deepest
shadows, her will to survive driving her onward when her
strength would no longer sustain her. Each time she fell it
was a struggle to climb to her knees and even harder to
force herself to her feet.

She saw him then, the horse, white mane flowing and
front legs hoofing the air. She knew he'd been following
her all along, and on his back was . . . death? Beautiful
and ghostly, her face a mask of white, she was smiling.

Autumn ran.

The mangrove tree reached up to grab her, its fleshy,
sickly looking leaves rank with rot and its gnarled, twisted
black roots tripping her. She went down again, sinking up
to her wrists in the oozy soil of the swamp. The mangrove
roots jutted from the slime like thousands of snakes contorting together in the darkness. They looked like snakes,
writhing around her arms and striking her face. She flailed
at them with her muddied hands, clawing at her face until
the realization that it was her own nails inflicting the pain
brought her back from her feverish illusions.

The foul-smelling muck sucked at her feet and knees,
pulling her down, weighting her exhausted limbs as she
tried to stand. And the horse was there, over her shoulder,
moving soundlessly through the trees, the specter on its

back now laughing with garish red lips, taunting, beckoning. It would be so easy, Autumn thought, to lie down and die.

She stumbled from the mud, grasping the same roots that had frightened her so before, pulling herself out of the slime onto firmer ground. She ran again, plunging deeper into the trees until, in the shadows, every form grew grotesquely twisted and menacing. She ran into a spider's web, so finely spun it was like silk against her face. She slapped it away, screaming as she saw the tiny black bodies, hundreds of them, scurrying to every point around her head. Autumn fell backward, the ghostly web trailing from her fingers and hair like slivers of filmy ribbons.

And the horse came closer.

The drums. She could hear them now. On her hands and knees again, she crawled toward the source of the beat. But the distant rhythm surrounded her, giving no direction. She looked to the sky and saw no light, only the tangled limbs of vegetation where the sun should have been. Then she remembered there was no sun. In hell there was no daylight or dark.

But she wasn't dead, she reminded herself. Death was there, over her shoulder, waiting in long white robes and so beautiful she might have been tempted to join her. But always, when she thought of that surrender, she remembered Brice. He'd loved her long before she came to Cayemite. He needed her, of that she was certain. She would be his friend, his companion, his partner and his wife. She would live long enough to give him a child.

She raised her head from the ground, the world above her spinning slowly in a blur of dark green. Her eyelids were so heavy she could hardly open them.

The child stood within a clearing, a child with Brice's smile. He lifted his hand and waved her on. "This way!" he called.

Her head fell back on the ground, and Autumn groaned. She was falling, falling down a tunnel in her mind, and always the voice was calling, "Quickly, maîtresse, I am here to help you!"

She reached for his hand.

He waved her on.

"Pierre. Pierre."

"I have come to help you!"

The pain. Oh, the pain.

"I have come to help you!"

She struggled to her knees. Her hair, entwined with vines and dusted with the spider's web, dragged over the ground around her hands as she crawled toward the child. He was always out of reach, beckoning her onward, dodging in and out of the tree, frightening her with his sudden appearances and disappearances.

Once she thought she heard the ocean rolling, thought the pounding in her head was actually the billowing breakers crashing upon the coast. She heard, too, the squawking of birds, their *ooo-ahh, ooo-ooo-ahh* chorus in the shifting tree limbs sounding dimly through her burning mind. But when she thought she would stop and rest, the child was back again, calling, "Come quickly, maîtresse!"

The horse was closer, the rider's face a white mask of anger.

Heaving herself to her feet, Autumn began running again.

The brush whipped against her face. Thorns tore at her skin until she was burning as hotly on the outside as she was on the inside. She stumbled over a sleeping crocodile once, thinking it only a dead, fallen log. Its bellow and hiss vibrated the leaves over her head, and its tail cracked the ground like thunder. She could hear the horse behind her, its hooves pounding the earth as forcefully as her heart pounded against her ribs. Closer, closer—the animal's pungent odor of sweat overpowered even the fetid stench of decay around her. The beast's breath wheezed through its flaring nostrils until she was certain that the apparition at her heels was a great winged dragon, snorting fire and reaching for her with hooked claws and razor teeth.

When she could run no farther, when her lungs burned with exhaustion, she fell again for the last time. She rocked on her knees, too weak to raise her head. With desperation she saw the clearing ahead, the magical valley, and there stood the child, hip-deep in swaying green grass and sunshine, butterflies hovering about his shoulders like a butter-yellow cloud.

The horse appeared behind her, prancing and rearing in time with the drumbeats. Then the roaring started. The ground pitched. Autumn clung to the earth, her fingers digging into dirt and grass as the flash of fire lit up the sky. "Oh, Donovan," she cried. "Donovan."

"Hush and let me help you," Brice said softly.

"Pierre! I must get Pierre!"

"Pierre is fine, love. Autumn, open your eyes and look at me."

Her lips were cracked and bleeding. Her head, damp with sweat, rolled back and forth on her pillow. "He's there. I saw him." She wept.

"You're dreaming. Pierre is here. Open your eyes and see him."

Pierre touched her face. "It is all right now," he soothed her. Moving closer, he whispered, "You're safe now, maîtresse."

Donovan looked toward Jeanette. "We'll get her out of these clothes." He reached for the muddied breeches, but his hands dropped to the coverlet he had thrown over her legs. "My God, what was she doing on the edge of that forest? She might have died. . . ." His words trailed off; again he reached for her breeches.

"Don't touch me!" Autumn's eyes, wide and frightened, were an odd red-brown, as if lit by a fire from within.

"You're shivering, pet."

"Then let me shiver."

"I only want to help."

Sitting straight up in bed, she screamed so savagely that Brice leapt to his feet. Celie, standing at the door with a tray of weak tea, dropped the service and backed away. Her jowls quivering, she howled, *"Diab! Monter diab!"* Turning away, she ran from the room.

Donovan kept his distance, though it wasn't easy, and did not approach her again until she had wilted back onto her pillows. Jeanette hurried in, her arms burdened with moist towels and a basin of fresh water. Without looking toward her brother, she said, "The servants have left us. Celie has told them that Autumn is possessed with a devil."

"It's only a fever."

"They believe—"

"I heard what the hell they believe!" Brice looked out the window. The sea was gray and hazy through the fog. And beyond the crook in the road where the buggy tracks approached the water was the crossroads. Brice groaned. The cruel implications of Jeanette's announcement now struck him. "You don't think . . ." he began. "No. No, they wouldn't, they couldn't. . . ." Looking at Jeanette, he asked, "Could they?"

His eyes drifted again over to the jalousie, then to the door, where they lingered for several moments. Brice took a deep, unsteady breath and wondered aloud, "Where is Tyler?"

"In the library."

"With the weapons?"

"Yes."

Dragging his gaze back to Autumn, he stated in a low voice, "I'll kill every one of those goddamned savages before I let them take her."

Autumn moaned. Her lashes fluttered. Brice slid onto the bed, his fingers nudging aside a strand of rust-brown hair that had adhered to her cheek with mud. "Hello," he said when she opened her eyes.

"Hello."

"Are you feeling better?"

She looked at him blankly, then asked, "May I have some water?"

He lifted her gently in the crook of his arm so he could press the cup against her mouth. She didn't drink. The water dribbled from the side of her lips and off her chin. Brice dropped his mouth to the top of her head and kissed her.

"This is my fault," Pierre murmured in so soft a voice only his mother heard him. "She was looking for me."

"The fever has been coming on for days." Jeanette hugged her son. "It was bound to happen. Autumn will be fine, and she'll never have to worry over getting the fever again.''

"Promise?'' He looked at Jeanette through large, pleading eyes.

"We will pray she recovers.'' She was making no promises.

Jeanette lit the candles as Brice remained on the bed, holding Autumn in his arms, his hands gently smoothing the hair from her damp brow. He felt the tremors pass through her, over and over, until it was impossible to detect when one left off and another began. Eventually, with Jeanette's help, they peeled the sodden clothes from her body, bathed her flushed skin in cool water and wrapped her in blankets. And when the blankets clung damply to her, they repeated the efforts, so she stayed dry and warm at all times.

Autumn's fevered brain saw lights of red and yellow, warm colors that collided behind her lids and spiraled outward like the fireworks she'd once watched in Charleston. At other times a coldness pervaded her, a brittle blue stretching eternally around her. She shivered violently, as much from the emptiness as from the aching chill.

She cried Mitchell's name, as she had that time during her childhood when he'd taken her to see the fireworks. "The lights!'' she'd called out, all full of breathless excitement. He looked down at her and said, "I love you, little girl. I'm so proud of you; I always have been.'' She danced around his feet and said, "I love you, too.''

To open her eyes was a struggle, but she did so on occasion. Always there was a tall, dark man with intense green eyes looking down at her. "Who are you?'' she asked him once. She thought he'd been struck, so wounded did he look over her query. "I have a right to know,'' she added.

He smiled rather wearily and responded, "Yes, you do.''

"Well then . . . who are you?''

"A friend.''

"A friend?''

"A very *good* friend.''

"Oh, well . . . in that case.'' She drifted again. Looking up from her pillow, she stared, unblinking, into her father's stern face. "How is mama?" she asked him.

"I'm sorry to say she is dead, child."

"Dead."

"The babe as well. A damned shame it is, too. A son; another son. Well . . . life must go on."

And on and on and on. She thought that right now she'd really rather die, but the man with the green eyes would not allow it.

"Leave me alone," she told him once, "and let me die."

"I can't do that."

As he reached again to bathe her with that annoying cold cloth, she snatched it from his hand and flung it on his face. "I will hit you if you touch me with that again!"

"And I just might hit you back."

"Well, I can see you're no gentleman."

"Madam, I never professed to be." He smiled at her so warmly she forgot her anger.

Then the pain would seep back into her bones, and she would sink into darkness, a deep, spiraling fall that roared in her ears with such fury she was driven to weep and plead, "Help me. Oh, help me."

"I'm here," the voice would soothe her.

The fiend on horseback appeared, hovering outside the window, the beast's hooves slashing the air as the gowned rider laughed with horrible red lips. "She's coming!" Autumn wept. "She's going to kill me!"

"A dream. It's only a dream."

"No! She was there. In the valley and the trees. Pierre was there. Ask him!"

"Drink this."

"I won't."

"Please, Autumn—"

"No. You can't make me. Oh, the pain. Make it stop. Make it stop." She thrashed with her hands and feet, making horrible noises in her throat as she tried to swallow.

"She's strangling!" came a woman's voice in the darkness. Then someone was grabbing her up, making her roll to her stomach and forcing his fingers down her throat. She bit them savagely until pressure at the sides of her

jaws forced her to release the grip. Autumn slumped in a
heap off the side of the bed.

Jeanette grasped Brice's hand, but he pushed her away,
his fingers dripping blood over the breadfruit floor as he
lunged for Autumn. They both hit the floor in the same
moment, her head knocking against the wood as he thudded onto his shoulder.

Donovan groaned, then muttered, "Damn."

Jeanette rushed to help him. Calling over her shoulder,
she ordered Pierre, "Fetch us tatters, *mon petit,* quickly!"
Doing her best to lift Autumn from Brice, she asked her
brother, "Will you do what I ask now? I beg you, for her
sake as well as your own—"

"I can't."

"Look at your hand."

"I can't tie her."

Rolling Autumn onto her back, Jeanette shook her head.
"Her fever is high, Brice, and will get higher before this is
over."

Donovan clutched his wrist, attempting to stem the flow
of blood from his hand. Pushing to his knees, he leaned
against the bed, shoulders tight and face white. He heard
Pierre return moments later, as well as Tyler. He remained
on the floor, his bleeding hand resting on one thigh and his
head back against the bed. With his eyes squeezed tightly
closed, he listened as they bound Autumn's hands and feet
to the bedposts.

"Not too tightly," he finally said.

Jeanette came to him, took his hand in her own and
wrapped it gently with cotton. "You need rest," she told
him.

"No."

"You'll do Autumn little good if you're too exhausted
to see to her needs."

Brice curled his fingers over the makeshift bandage,
released a long sigh and said, "Leave me alone."

The hours dragged. Darkness filled the room with heavy
silence. Brice sat in his chair beside the bed, watching the
rise and fall of Autumn's chest, leaning with elbows on his
knees toward her each time her breathing appeared to
falter. With a rush of his heartbeat he would nudge her,

first gently, then not so gently, if the prod brought no response.

Once she rolled her head his way and opened her eyes.

"Mr. Donovan." Her lips barely moved.

"Missus Donovan," was the reply.

"What if I fail?"

"You won't."

"But what if?"

He touched her face. "I won't let you."

"Promise."

"Before God."

Her eyes fluttered closed again, and she slept a little more soundly.

Autumn's fever grew worse through the morning hours. Brice was constantly bathing her, her face and arms, and when he tenderly sponged her breasts and stomach, she sucked in her breath and mumbled something that soundly strangely like, "It's wonderful, isn't it?"

He laughed softly, thinking it was only the fever talking. But when her eyes, like warm golden brandy, looked into his, he allowed himself to believe that she knew exactly what she was saying. "Yes, you little nymphet."

Her face screwed up in a frown. "You're always laughing at me, Donovan."

"Am I? Sorry, love." Leaning closer, he brushed her lower lip with the pad of his thumb and said, "God, you're sweet."

"Sweet?"

"Like marzipan."

"Oh, I love marzipan. . . ."

"So do I," he whispered. "So do I."

Dawn brought the promise of a clearer day. There was a brisk west wind that stirred the ash clouds over the open sea, allowing dappled sunlight to infiltrate the drab countryside. Trempe was quiet and, after stumbling almost drunkenly from his chair, Brice was relieved to find the mountain's crest no longer so menacing. He scanned what he could see of the horizon, hoping to detect a sail, but there was nothing.

"I've brought you breakfast," came Jeanette's voice behind him. "I've brought Autumn some broth."

He ignored his own and reached for Autumn's, setting it aside as he unbound her hands and rubbed her slightly swollen and bruised wrists with his fingers. Sliding his arm beneath her shoulders, he raised her slightly and said, "Be a good girl and cooperate."

She lay limply, without response.

"Ah, me," he sighed. "Always the stubborn one." After a moment he went on, "If you don't eat, you will die. If you die, well . . . so shall I. Do you want that on your conscience, marzipan?"

"She cannot hear you," Jeanette said.

He kissed Autumn's brow. "Who's to say whether she hears me or not?" Then he tipped her flushed face up to his and kissed her mouth.

Jeanette watched him solemnly as he turned his face toward the window. A ray of sunlight lit up his mouth. "You need rest," she told him. "I'll call you if there's any change."

"Do you remember where our father was when my mother died?" he asked her, hugging Autumn closer. "No? No, I suppose you wouldn't. You were too young. He was out there." He nodded toward the window. "There was some problem with the cane—a blight or something. Whatever, it was more important than my mother. She died when he was talking cane talk with Tyler." Easing Autumn back onto the bed, he said, "I won't leave her."

The first quake came an hour later.

Brice lay on the bed next to Autumn. Forcing open his heavy lids, and staring at the ceiling, he heard a rumbling like distant thunder. He rolled and grabbed her, holding her feverish little body against his as the house shivered around them.

"The fire is back!" Jeanette stared toward the mountain, her face reflecting the reds and golds of the flames. "Where is Dearborne?" she wondered aloud.

"I suspect he'll have trouble locating us in this stew pot."

Jeanette looked at the sea, barely visible beyond the coast. She saw Tullius's lanky frame running barefoot up the beach. "Maît Donovan!" he called as he neared the house. "Come quickly, Maît Donovan. Donovan!"

Brice rolled from the bed.

He met Tyler in the hallway. They hurried downstairs to the front door, its great timber barricading them in, as well as locking the frantic servant out. As the door swung open, flakes of white plaster drifted like snow to their shoulders. Tullius, his hat in his hands, hopped from one foot to the other and babbled so incoherently neither man could understand him. He pointed down the beach.

"Ship," was all Donovan needed to hear.

He ran through the garden, hurdling the boxwood, forgetting his earlier lethargy as he made his way to the shore, no longer a tropical white. His eyes strained for the sight of flapping sails, the hulky shape of Dearborne's old brigantine as it cruised toward Bovier. But he could see nothing through the dense cloud of ash. Visibility was at a minimum.

The flotsam caught his eye, as it had the day before, bobbing in the shallow waves, catching on the reef banks. His pace slowed, then stopped. The ground around him was strewn with wood. At the edge of the water was a body lapped by the waves—John Dearborne.

"Mother of God," Tyler said behind him. "They never made it."

Brice fought back his nausea before turning to look at Hugh.

Tyler bent low and, partially lifting a black-edged plank of wood from the sand, said quietly, "She burned."

The chanting came then, beyond the raw-edged bank of upthrusting rock. Donovan and Tyler hurried up the embankment, and, under cover of fog, watched the primitive ritual in shock. At the crossroads, where once hung the carcass of a boar and a mare, now hung the effigy of a woman.

Donovan hit the road running, with Tyler on his heels as they entered the house and replaced the timber barricade. Jeanette came halfway down the stairs before asking, "Has help arrived?"

"Help is not coming," Brice responded grimly. "But the savages are. For Autumn." Looking up at his sister, he asked, "Can you shoot a gun?"

"I—I don't know."

"Will you try?"

"If I must."

With weapons in hands, they waited, realizing that should the natives storm the house, the three of them had very little chance of holding them back. As afternoon crawled toward dusk, Brice looked out the window, at the silent, watchful faces of the men who surrounded the house. "What are they waiting for?" he wondered aloud.

"It's Autumn," Tyler ventured. "If they're believin' she's possessed by some sort of *diab*, they'll think twice before doin' anything that might upset the applecart. 'Specially if they're thinkin' she might have anything t' do with that mountain."

"We'll have to convince them that it's a fever."

Hugh turned resigned blue eyes on his employer and said, "If she dies, it might be best just to give 'er to 'em."

Brice moved like a striking rattlesnake. Though Tyler outweighed Brice by three stone, Brice gripped Hugh's shirtfront and, before the Irishman could twist free, had thrown him up against the wall with enough force to knock the wind from his lungs. "Don't even think it," Donovan hissed in his face.

"All right, lad. I was only thinkin' aloud. I'm just meanin', if she's already dead—"

"Well, she won't be. She's not going to die. I won't let her!"

"All right, then. All right."

His torrent of blind anger subsiding, Brice backed away.

Hugh shook his head. "Get some rest. Yer gonna need it before this is all over."

Rest. Yes, he needed it. Attempting to think back, he couldn't remember when he'd last slept—a night, a week, a fortnight . . . a bloody year? A lifetime, or so it seemed. His entire body ached.

He took the stairs slowly, half listening as Jeanette prepared him for Autumn. "She's worse . . . hallucinating . . . strapped again . . . convulsions." Still, he wasn't prepared. Nothing could have prepared him for what he found.

Autumn was conscious. She looked at him through dull,

slitted eyes and smiled. He felt his heart break, but he smiled back.

"I thought you'd gone," she rasped.

"Where would I go?"

"With Dearborne."

Brice shook his head.

"Is he coming?"

She's dying, he thought. What harm could come of lying? "He'll be here." He took the chair beside her. She was too weak to roll her head, so Brice did it for her, allowing his palm to cup her bloated cheek.

"I was dreaming," she said. "About marzipan."

"Sweet dreams."

Autumn laughed weakly. The action caused her lips to crack and bleed. "Will you stay awhile?" she asked him. "I'd like to sleep again, but I'm afraid."

"Don't be. I'll be beside you all the time."

Her eyes closed. "I feel like a trussed-up guinea hen, Donovan."

"You'll be better soon."

"I suppose it'd do little good to discuss my plans for harvesting that west section of cane," she teased in a slight voice.

Brice grinned. Autumn peeked at him from beneath her lashes and grinned back.

"Don't worry," she told him then. "If I'm too stubborn to drown, I'm too stubborn to die of fever."

"I'm counting on that."

"Do you know what I wish?"

"Tell me."

"I wish . . . I wish we could have been married. I wish . . ."

"Tell me . . . tell me quickly, marzipan, before you slip off to sleep again."

But she slipped away, nevertheless.

The chanting began just before midnight. Brice stood by the window, staring out at the torch fires dotting the darkness. Jeanette entered the room and stood for a long moment, hesitant to disturb him. But as her eyes traveled down his arm, her heart stopped.

He heard her soft inhalation. Without leaving the window, Brice looked back over his shoulder and, lifting the flintlock casually, pointed to another at Autumn's bedside and asked, "Do you think I'll have the guts to do it? To nuzzle it against her temple and pull the trigger?" With his shoulder against the wall, Brice frowned and studied the weapon in his hand. "I should have little trouble with my own. I fantasized it enough times these past years."

Autumn groaned. Brice dropped onto the bed beside her. "She's a fighter," he said without turning.

"Yes, she is," Jeanette responded.

"Is she over the worst yet?"

"I don't think so."

Autumn thrashed in delirium. In a dry voice she cried out his name. He went down beside her, afraid to hold her too tightly, afraid the slightest touch would torment her more. His own body was burning, not with fever but from fatigue, despair and heartache. He should have turned her away that first morning she'd barreled into the library. He should have told Mitchell Sinclair the truth. Autumn would have been safe in Charleston now.

A soft hand touched his shoulder. "Have you considered having Henri treat her?" Jeanette asked him.

The light shock of his breath against Autumn's temple disturbed the coiling tendrils of fine hair beneath his lips. He struggled to swallow before saying, "I've considered it. But I'm not certain I've grown that desperate yet."

"She is going to die if something is not done."

"You're certain?"

"Yes. We may be too late already."

Brice lay for a long moment, his head on the pillow beside Autumn's, his arm looped over her breasts. "What d'ya say, marzipan? Shall we give him a try? Think you're up to a little mumbo jumbo and farine Guinée?"

"Marzipan," she repeated weakly.

Brice rolled from the bed and took up his gun.

Chapter 24

Brice walked straight out of the house toward the solemn-faced natives. The silence vibrated as he stood before them, the night wind whipping his shirtsleeves and the top-heavy hibiscus nodding around his thighs.

"What do you want?" he asked them.

The torch flames fluttered in the breeze.

More loudly, then, he asked, "Why are you here?"

"You know why they are here, little boy."

"Ah, Henri. I'm glad you're here." Brice searched the shadows. Henri's gnarled old frame was silhouetted beneath a coconut tree, his pipe casting a red-orange glow across his face. "You may tell them all to go back to their village," Donovan said.

Henri puffed a little harder on his pipe.

"Maîtresse Donovan is ill," Brice announced loudly. "She has a fever. Nothing more."

"They do not understand you."

"Then tell them."

Henri didn't respond.

Frustration crept over Brice, but he didn't show it. Calmly he took the final few steps to the road, noting with satisfaction that the natives shied nervously at his approach. He walked without hesitation over to Henri.

"You have forgotten yourself," the old man stated. One eye, glittering with torch fire, turned up at Brice.

"Legba," Brice drawled, "is no longer welcome at Hunnington."

Henri humphed and turned his wrinkled face toward the sea.

Stepping closer, Brice said, "Don't you think you've manipulated these people long enough, old man? Between

329

you and Annee, you have them afraid of their own shadows.''

"It is custom. As old as time."

"Whose custom? The blacks? The Indians? No, it's yours. You've taken a dash of African and a plug of Indian and concocted your own religion. There's no foundation for any of your beliefs."

"Do you deny the legend?"

Stepping closer to Henri, Brice thrust one finger toward Trempe and said in a lower voice, "There is your legend. A volcano, and nothing more. It wasn't gods, good or evil, who blanketed the island in darkness for years. It was only Trempe doing exactly what she's doing now. She's the reason the earth trembles and the animals react. There are no *bakas* or *diabs* except in here." He tapped Henri's skull with the same finger he'd jutted at Trempe.

"Careful . . . little boy."

"You don't scare me, Henri. Not anymore."

"Foolish, foolish boy."

Reaching over Henri's shoulder and gripping the smooth bark of the coconut tree with one hand, Brice said, "You will come with me now into the house, and though it galls me to do so, I will ask—no, demand—that you do what you can to help Autumn."

"But I thought you didn't believe—"

"In spirits with sharp, pointed fangs and bat wings."

The pipe wheezed in Henri's lips. Then he replied, "I'll think on it."

Brice withdrew the flintlock from the waistband of his breeches and, pressing it into the crepey underside of Henri's chin, stated coldly, "I should think on it quickly, my good man, because if you don't, the top of your prickly old head is going to be residing up this tree with those coconuts."

Henri reached for his crutch.

Donovan's determination withered with the sight of Autumn, damp with sweat and so pale that even her freckles had disappeared. Her hair, matted from hours of tossing upon her pillow, streamed off the side of the bed, nearly to the floor. The shallow rise and fall of her breasts was further evidence of her declining state.

Pulling Henri to the bed, Brice said, "As you can see, she is in no state of possession. She is ill, desperately ill, and I fully expect you to heal her."

"And if I can't?"

"You can. I've seen you at work, don't forget."

"That was many years ago."

Brice laughed softly, tiredly, but not without threat. "Don't tell me, old man, that you doubt the power you carry in that *paquett* on your belt."

"It would depend on what illness grips her, of course, whether natural, or—"

"Or what?" Grabbing one skinny arm in his fingers, Brice gave Henri a shake before repeating, "Or what?"

"Who would benefit most from her death?"

"Are you saying Annee Rose has somehow done this to Autumn?"

Turning a toothless smile up to Brice, Henry hunched one shoulder and replied, "Who is to say? Perhaps we will never know. If she lives, no. If she dies . . . My remedies cannot help the *ouanga*." Looking down at Autumn, he said, "There will be a cost."

"Absolutely. Your life, if she dies."

"I'll need my privacy."

"No."

"Then you will sit yonder and be quiet."

But Brice paced. "What are you doing?" he asked the old man.

"Removing the blankets."

Then he questioned, "What are you doing now?"

"She has rested too long on her back. Her lungs are full."

Frowning, Brice said, "I don't like you pawing her like that."

"Her muscles are too tight."

"What are you giving her?"

"Cabbage water."

"Why?"

"It is healthful."

Brice leaned against the bedpost. "What are you doing now?"

"Lighting my pipe."

"Is her fever down?"

"No."

"Is she any better at all?"

"No."

"Is she going to die?"

"Yes, I suspect so."

Brice closed his eyes. Between clenched teeth he groaned aloud, "It's Annee, isn't it? Of course—the woman in the woods. I thought she'd dreamed it, but it was she. Annee, goddamn her, I'll kill her! I'm going to kill her."

Donovan left the house before dawn. The sky was an eerie sight, glowing red on the west horizon. The moon hung between the two ragged clouds of steam on the east that topped each wave on Ravel Bay in a snowy cap. He stood with his face in the wind, allowing his last thread of reluctance to be swept away in its soothing current. He knew now that Autumn was lost to him and, coward that he was, he could not stay and watch her slip away. She was beyond pain, beyond dreams, and Autumn without dreams . . . ah, that was no Autumn at all. Better to remember her with flashing brandy-colored eyes and a freckle that wouldn't be still.

He climbed onto his horse's bare back and rode toward Barrett Hall.

Annee Rose was standing on the bottom stair when Brice entered the house. She wasn't surprised to see him.

"Hello, darling. You look like hell," she told him.

"I've been through hell, Annee. But I don't suppose that comes as any news to you."

She feigned a pretty little pout before sighing. "Yes, this dreadful volcano has the entire island in an uproar. The ash should do wonders for future cane crops, however."

"I didn't come here to discuss cane."

"Oh?"

"I came here to discuss us." Her eyes widened, causing Brice to smirk. "Come now, Annee, did you think I would let you get away with it again?"

"Away with what?"

"Murder."

"I haven't murdered anyone."

"You pushed my father off that bluff, burned Roy in bed and now . . . how *did* you manage Autumn?"

Surprise flushing her fair complexion, Annee leapt from the stair and skirted toward Brice. "Autumn is dead?"

"No. Not yet. But she will be, I've been told. Does that please you, pet?" Before she could respond, Brice caught her chin, his fingers digging so cruelly into the flesh of her jaw that Annee whimpered. "Is there an antidote?" he hissed in her face.

"I don't know what you're talking about."

He shook her. "You fed her poison. That's how your father killed Bovier, isn't it? Poisoned him little by little?"

She clawed at his hands. "You're insane, Donovan."

"If that's so, Madame Rose, I would not push me too far, if I were you. You are in a very vulnerable position at this moment. It would behoove you to cooperate."

Annee laughed. Pressing herself up against Brice, she said, "If I *had* somehow managed such a feat, why would I want to cooperate now?"

"Then you're admtting it." His fingers bit deeper into her skin.

"I'm admitting nothing. But are you willing to risk her life on the off chance that I didn't do it?"

"What the hell do you want from me?"

The question exploded through the house, bursting with as much frustration as anger. Annee only laughed. "Your soul," came her response.

"That I cannot give. It is lying half-dead with Autumn."

"Then your body will do."

"And if I give it?"

"And if you don't? All I ever wanted, Donovan, was you." Catching his hand, Annee pulled him toward the stairs. "Caleb!" she called to the Negro in the shadows. "You'll bring us drinks in an hour. We don't wish to be disturbed until then."

The child stood at the window, his smooth face, glowing in the moonlight, turned up to the sky as tears ran down his cheeks. Autumn heard him sniff, then watched as he wiped his nose with the back of his hand.

"Pierre." She only mouthed it, but he turned, nevertheless. "Help me?" she whispered.

He tiptoed to the bed.

"I'm glad the old man is gone," she told him. "He frightened me."

Pierre took her hand in both of his. "He thinks you are dying. He said there was nothing more that he could do for you."

"But you can, Pierre. You can help me. I know you can."

His small shoulders lifted as he took a breath.

"Pierre? Where is Donovan?"

"Resting." He stared at his feet. A tear dripped off the end of his nose. Looking at Autumn again, he asked softly, "You must believe very hard that I can help you, or it won't work. It only works with Annee because she believes it. She believes in herself so very much she cannot help but believe in me. Do you understand me?"

"No. I don't think I do."

"My *maman* calls it faith."

"I understand faith."

"Good." Climbing onto the bed, he wrapped her in his arms and legs, then closed his eyes. "Let's think of butter-flies," he whispered. "Shall we?"

Tyler was beaming as he entered the room. Autumn, propped up on pillows, weakly returned his smile. His hands on his hips, he declared, "Yer a sight for sore eyes, lass, and that's a fact. Welcome back t' the livin'."

"You're too kind, Tyler."

"Is there anything yer needin'?"

"A bath."

"Yer wantin' *me* t' give y' a bath?"

Laughing shakily, she replied, "Perhaps if you just supply the water."

Jeanette entered the room, her arms full of soft, frilly undergarments that Autumn hadn't worn since leaving Charleston. As she spread them on the bed, Autumn couldn't help but smile. It was odd to think that at one time she'd cringed at the very idea of dressing in those feminine little fripperies. Now she looked forward to it. It must be the illness, she mused. The fever had left her feeling as fragile as a porcelain sparrow.

As Tyler turned toward the door, she asked, "Has Donovan returned from the village?"

"No, lass."

"He's spending a lot of time away from the house, isn't he?"

"There was a lot of damage in the last quake," Jeanette joined in.

"But I haven't seen him since my fever broke." Frowning, she added, "Is Mr. Donovan purposefully avoiding me?"

"No!" they chorused.

Jeanette added, "You've been asleep the last couple of times he's come in. He's very hesitant to disturb you."

"Tell him to disturb me. I'd like to see him, please."

Tyler walked out the door. "I'll get your water."

"Tyler!"

"Aye, maîtresse, I'll tell 'im when I see 'im."

Jeanette followed him into the hall. "Will you see him now?" she asked quietly. "Will you go to Barrett Hall and speak with Brice? I cannot lie to Autumn forever."

Hugh kept walking, down the stairs and out of the house.

Annee answered the door when Tyler knocked. Dressed in a flowing silk gown of royal blue, she smiled stunningly into his eyes.

"Good morning," she greeted him.

"I didn't come here to exchange pleasantries, Annee, I've come here to see Donovan."

"Really, Tyler, why can't you accept Brice's decision? He has chosen me over Roy's urchin widow, and that is that."

She tried shutting the door. Tyler stopped her with his foot. "He's been here three days without a word from 'im. Have y' killed 'im, Annee, like y' did the others?"

"How dare you! Remember, sir, who you are. You'll

be answering to me soon, and you'd do well to remember it."

"I'll swim all the way t' Kingston before I answer t' you!" he bellowed. "Fact is, I'd rather take my chances with every shark between here and Jamaica. Now let me see the boss."

"He doesn't wish to be disturbed."

"Let me—"

"No!"

She slammed the door in Tyler's face.

Caleb stood in the shadows of the staircase, wringing his hands and watching Annee as she lay her head back against the door. "Fools," she said aloud. "Fools, if they think he'll ever return to them. He's mine, Caleb. Mine! He came to me on his own accord. No one forced him. Did I force him to come here?"

"No, ma'am," came his uncertain response.

"No. He came because he loves me. He's always loved me. It was just a matter of time before he realized it." Smiling more pleasantly, she directed the servant, "It's time for his tea, Caleb. You know Brice enjoys his tea promptly at noon."

"Yes, ma'am. I'll bring it directly."

"And make certain it is hot. It won't dissolve the sugar properly unless it's hot."

Bobbing his head, Caleb hurried from the room.

She swept down the hall, blue silk billowing like a bell around her knees, her fingers jabbing hairpins into the neat chignon on the nape of her neck. Entering the drawing room, she took a deep breath, smiled and said brightly, "Good morning, darling." Crossing the room, Annee went down on her knees. "I've some sad news, I'm sorry to say. They buried Autumn." She sighed. "Oh, dear, I've distressed you. Please don't be angry. I swear to you that I had nothing to do with her death. It was only a fever, after all. It really didn't occur to me to use poison on her. Besides, I couldn't do anything that might endanger you."

Burying her cheek against the inside of his knee she squeezed his leg tightly and giggled like a girl. "Oh, isn't this wonderful? It's just as it used to be, the two of us, sitting in Papa's drawing room and discussing our plans to marry. Here's Caleb with your tea. Put it here," she directed the servant. He placed the service on the table, but as he reached to help her stir milk and sugar in Donovan's cup, she stopped him and said, "I'll do it myself." When he hesitated, she snapped, "That will be all!"

He paused at the door and, looking back over his shoulder, watched as Annee heaped two spoonfuls of sugar into Brice's cup. Turning, Caleb hurried down the hall.

The sound of a cantering horse brought Autumn off her pillows. "Jeanette, is it he? Is it Brice?" She watched hopefully as Brice's sister ran to the window.

"It's only Tyler."

Autumn's heart sank in disappointment. "I don't understand. Why is Brice avoiding me, Jeanette? I know I must look dreadfully bad, but—"

"He's terribly busy."

"Oh, for God's sake, will you stop making excuses! The man has avoided me for three days, and I demand to know why."

Smiling slightly, Jeanette turned from the window. "You're better, for certain."

"Don't try to change the subject."

"Very well." Taking a deep breath, Jeanette blurted, "I'll let Tyler explain it!" Then she dashed out of the room.

Tyler was just coming up the stairs when Jeanette accosted him. "Have you seen him? Is he returning? Is he alive?"

He shook his woolly head before replying. "I would not have believed it, lass. But with my own eyes I saw him."

"Believed what?"

"Mistress Rose met me, by God, at the door. She said Donovan had made his choice, then slammed the door on me so hard my ears rang."

"That's no proof!"

"Aye, so I told m'self. Then I hotfooted around the house and gandered through the windows. I saw him, finally. Both of 'em, havin' themselves a tea party right there in Barrett's own morning room!"

"Tea! Brice hates tea." Whirling from the Irishman, Jeanette shook her fist and repeated, "I won't believe it. He loved Autumn more than his own life. He'd give his soul to spare her one moment of pain. He's proven it time and again. Why would he, how could he walk away from her with hardly a second thought?" Her black eyes flashing, Jeanette stared at Tyler and asked, "You're certain it was Brice you saw?"

"Sittin' there wearing one of Annee's dead husband's dressing robes, I suspect. Some black thing with gaudy red dragons and tassels on the belt. She was fawnin' over him like he was some babe still wet behind the ears, stirrin' his tea, wallerin' all over his feet. It was enough t' make me upset m' breakfast, I don't mind tellin' y'."

Her spirits lagging, Jeanette dropped onto the stair. "She'll have to be told."

"It won't be easy."

"She's so weak."

"Aye . . . but she'll have to be told."

The sponge bath refreshed her. In clean attire and with her hair braided, Autumn rested against her pillow, fighting the exhaustion that kept her dozing fitfully throughout the day. She was determined to stay awake long enough to see Brice.

Celie entered the room, hesitating at the door, her eyes studiously watching Autumn for any sign of devils. "Come in," Autumn told her. Smiling weakly, she teased, "I promise you, Celie, I shan't grow horns and a spiked tail. What have you there?" She pointed to the tray the big woman balanced on her palm.

"Sugar cakes."

Before Celie could cross the room, the shaking started, rattling the glass prisms on the lamp beside the bed. The tremors had grown so commonplace the women hardly gave them a second's notice.

"Sugar cakes." Autumn sighed. "How wonderful, Celie. I've had the most unusual craving for sweets since I've been better."

The trembling continued, rolling through the house and

the countryside. A spray of fire and ash shot into the sky from Trempe's crest.

"Oh, my," Autumn said in a strained voice. Looking worriedly up at Celie, she suggested, "Put the tray down quickly, Celie, before you drop it."

"That be a bad one, maîtresse."

"We're going to be fine. Help should be arriving just any day from Jamaica and—"

"Ain't no help comin' from nowheres," the big woman countered. Wringing her hands, Celie whispered, "That bad woman, she fixed us all. She say Minetta send the fire and smoke to banish the irreverent ones from the island."

"But Minetta is dead. She died over two hundred years ago."

"She back. Henri say she be back to do battle with the blessed one."

"And who is the blessed one?"

"Don't know. Don't nobody know."

"But John Dearborne—"

"That was a shame. A real shame. You was lucky for sure, yes'm, for coming back to this island like you did." Celie turned and walked back to the door.

"Lucky. Why?"

Her button-black eyes round, Celie frowned and said, "Why, don't you know? That big boat of his burned up. John Dearborne, be buried down by the crossroads, what was left of him after the fish and the John Crows got him."

Fear shook her, more powerful than any quake that had yet rent the island, more bone chilling than any fever that had gripped her. With her head spinning, Autumn sat up from her pillows, forgetting the sheet that fell to her waist, revealing the gossamer cotton of her chemise. Rolling to one hip and almost to her knee, she reached to stop Celie before the woman left the room.

"Wait. Wait." As the dark face turned back toward hers, Autumn forced the question out through her dry throat, terrified of the answer. "Donovan . . . where is Donovan? He hasn't, he isn't . . . dead, too?"

"Ain't they told you nothing?" she responded.

"Oh, God." Oh, God.

"He done gone yonder three days ago, and he ain't come back."

"Yonder? Where is yonder? Celie, where has Donovan gone?"

"To Barrett Hall."

"To Annee."

"Ain't surprised. It was a matter of time, was all. She done had every man she ever wanted and then some: Patrick Donovan, Roy. She would have had Maît Brice long ago if you had not come here. She got a way with her men. Magic, I want to say. Makes 'em lose their heads. Makes their loins so hard they is driven to ruttin' animals. After they done had her, they don't want nobody else. Drives 'em mad, it does. Mad.'' Celie left the room.

I won't believe it. Autumn repeated the words over and over in her mind, and yet, how else could Donovan's sudden disappearance be explained? Falling back on the bed gripping the pillow, she closed her eyes, feeling her body shake, and knowing that this time it wasn't caused by fever.

Donovan was with Annee.

She saw again Annee pressing her scantily clad body against him that morning in Barrett Hall's drawing room, saw him kiss Annee. Autumn felt her own lips part for want of that touch. Donovan with Annee. How could he? How could he?

When Jeanette and Tyler entered the room, the fire in her eyes would have put Trempe to shame. Hesitating just inside the door, Jeanette asked her, "You wanted to see us?"

"Sit down." Autumn pointed to two chairs next to the bed. When they were settled, she said, a little less determinedly, "I want to thank you both for seeing me through my ordeal. It was a decidedly debilitating illness, I'm certain; now that I'm better, however, I wonder why you've not given me a reason for Donovan's absence."

Jeanette and Tyler exchanged glances.

"Where is he?" Autumn demanded.

"The village," Tyler responded, wincing as he did so.

Jeanette lowered her eyes. "You know, don't you?" she asked Autumn.

"Celie informed me. I've learned, too, that the *Venerable* never reached Jamaica."

"We only wanted to spare you," Jeanette said. "You were so very ill."

"Then it's true. Donovan has finally given in to Annee." Her mouth twisting bitterly, Autumn slumped onto her pillows. "Why?" she said toward the *baire* overhead. "Did he have so little faith?"

"Henri told him you were dying. He told him that Annee had caused your illness."

"So what did he hope to accomplish by going to her now?"

"Revenge," was Tyler's simple response.

"Then why didn't he simply kill her and come home? Why has he chosen to stay with her?"

They all sat in stilted silence, listening to the surf pound between the intermittent rumbles of the mountain. Autumn finally looked back at Jeanette and Tyler in total dejection.

"Is it true what they say?" she asked them. "About her power over men? Brice is so strong—his willpower, I cannot believe he . . . perhaps he's dead?"

Hugh ducked his head. "I saw him this very morning. You can rest relieved that Donovan is still alive."

Drained of what little strength hope had lent her, Autumn closed her eyes and repeated, "Yes. Relieved."

When sleep came again, it brought no rest. Autumn wept in her dreams. Her strength waned under the despair of losing Brice.

Chapter 25

Pierre skipped down the beach, his cheeks kissed with color and his green eyes flashing with excitement. He turned and ran back toward Autumn, skirting the foamed-topped water as it lunged and hissed across the sand. His head thrown back and his black hair whipped with the misty wind, he was a fantasy that had kept her alive these past few days. With Pierre, she could always dream of what might have been.

Jeanette had scolded her for leaving the house on such a dreary day. The fog was heavy and smelled of rain. Thunder rumbled as threateningly as Trempe trembled the earth. Somehow she sensed the end was near. The mountain, quiet for days, had resumed belching and spewing its fiery ash over the island, scorching woodland and cane field, destroying most of the village with crashing rock and the first hint of lava flow. Oddly, through it all, there was little panic among the people. Their faith that somehow their supreme god would save them from Minetta's power had carried them through the tribulation of burying those killed in the last rock slide. Still, standing now upon the rock where she'd perched that first morning after her arrival on Cayemite and staring out to sea, Autumn wondered if there was anyone, *anyone,* there to help them.

She followed Pierre's footsteps up the beach, continuing where his ended, her shoulders hunched against the wind and her eyes watching the sand shift in tiny dunes against driftwood and boulders. A great white bird drifted overhead, its black-tipped wings arching heavenward before it screeched and dived toward the water; then, mere inches from the turquoise bed, it swooped back toward the beach at an angle.

She came upon Brice by sheer accident. She'd not started

on her journey with any intent of seeing him. But there he stood with fingers of water surging around his bare feet and wind dusting his trouser legs with sand. His head was down. One hand was inside his breeches pocket; in the other he held a conch shell to his ear.

Had he sensed her there? His head turned and their eyes touched.

Why? hers asked. Seized with the need to fly down that flat stretch of sand and touch him, she trembled in her place, frozen at the sight of his eyes—unseeing, cold and as gray as the clouds around them. They weren't Donovan's eyes.

He continued to stare, unmoving, unblinking, until slowly his grin appeared, tugging at one corner of his lips, relieving the pale gauntness of his face. The trade wind came in a blast, rocking him backward; the shell dropped from his hand and began floating back out to sea. The wind whipped sea spray and sand into blinding whirlwinds along the beach, forcing Autumn to cover her face for several instants. When she looked again, Annee was with him.

Wretched woman.

"What are you doing here?" Annee asked him. "I told you to never . . . you! What are *you* doing here?" she spat at Autumn. "Leave this beach this instant. You're trespassing! Caleb! Caleb, call the dogs this moment! Get off! Get off this beach!" She picked up a stone and flung it at Autumn.

A howling cacophony came at her from over the rise. Autumn backed away, her eyes on Brice and the woman who was pulling angrily on his arm, who was shoving him back up the beach. Still backing, Autumn called, "Donovan!"

He didn't turn. His head down and his feet dragging noticeably, Brice continued up the beach.

"Brice!"

He hesitated. Her heart quickened. And when he looked back over his shoulder, there was such confusion in his eyes that she knew in that moment that Donovan wasn't himself.

The dogs came around the bend, ears flat and teeth bared. Autumn froze as Annee shrieked, "Kill! Kill!"

But they didn't kill. As Autumn closed her eyes, preparing herself for the assault, the animals stopped, went to their bellies and whimpered.

"Really, maîtresse, you must take more caution when walking on these beaches." Pierre skipped up to Autumn and took her trembling hand in his own. "You'll catch a fever again if you don't bundle up."

Her throat tight with terror, Autumn managed only, "The dogs."

Pierre smiled. "Oh, they know me. Disregard the dogs."

"But—"

"They won't hurt you," he assured her. Then, laughing, he added, "I won't let them."

The incident on the beach had weakened her considerably. Nevertheless, Autumn stood in the center of the drawing room and faced Jeanette and Tyler squarely.

"I have seen Donovan this morning. Something is terribly wrong with him." She wavered in her efforts, the trembling that had assailed her at seeing Donovan now creeping like a fever chill throughout her body. Leaning back against the desk she announced, "He needs our help."

"But he made his choice—"

"Did he?" Staring down at her sandy boots, Autumn shook her head. "He looked at me as if he didn't know me at first. And when I called his name, he appeared startled. He looked almost as if he were sleepwalking." Her head coming up again, she asked them, "Has it ever occurred to you that perhaps Donovan has been kept at Barrett Hall against his will?"

"There's no keepin' Donovan somewheres if his mind is set t' leave it," Tyler responded. "Just as there was no keepin' him here when he decided t' go see Annee. We both did our best t' stop him." He nodded at Jeanette.

"Very well. But what if his mind is not his own?"

Celie entered the room in that moment. All watched silently as the Negress poured them each coffee. Handing Autumn a cup, she said, "*Mapou*."

Autumn peered at Celie over the edge of her uplifted cup. "*Mapou?*"

"The sacred tree. It is believed to house the spirits of everlasting peace. The Indians make a drink from its roots that make them happy like when Donovan drink his *clairin*. The Ardas use it, too, but they call it happy root." With that the big woman sauntered out of the room.

Trempe's explosion came moments later.

"Idiot! Idiot man! I told you! I told you never to leave this house without me!" Caleb watched, horrified as Annee brought the switch down onto Donovan's back. "How dare you defy me? Caleb, bring Mr. Donovan's tea. Quickly. I said bring it to me now! Now! I said *now!*"

Caleb ran from the room, stumbling as the house pitched beneath his feet. Looking back at Annee, he begged her, "Maîtresse, we got to leave this place. That mountain gonna come down on us all soon!"

"That mountain cannot hurt us." She laughed. "I control that mountain. Now do as I say unless you wish to join Donovan in a lashing!"

She turned back to Brice. "Get on your knees," she told him.

He groaned and rolled away.

Bringing one foot sharply into his ribs, she sneered, "Do you love her so much, Donovan? Do you? Well, I'll see the little witch dead if it's the last thing I do. And the others; their disobedience can no longer be tolerated. It is time I show them who is in control of their lives. This island is mine. Mine, I tell you. My father wouldn't believe it. He thought it was his. But I showed him. Fool. Just like the others: Patrick, Roy. They used me, just like my husbands, and they all paid with their lives. I said get on your knees!"

She kicked at him again. This time he was ready.

Catching her ankle, Brice gave a yank that sent her flying. Annee hit the floor, and the entire house seemed to shake under the impact. Candelabras rocked. Plaster rained from the ceiling, dusting them with fine powder. Brice lunged for her throat, but the manacles around his wrists held him back, tearing into the raw flesh of his arms.

Annee rolled away as Caleb entered the room. "Bastard," she hissed over and over. Crawling to the silver service, she began heaping spoon after spoon of sugar into the cup until the hot tea was thick as molasses.

"This will show you. How dare you defy me? I see we've been too long since our last dosage, darling. Hold him, Caleb. Open your mouth. I said, 'Open your mouth.' Darling. My darling Donovan, please open your mouth. I said, 'Open your mouth!' "

Holding Brice's head gently in his hands, Caleb looked pleadingly into his eyes and whispered, "Please do as the mistress say, Mr. Brice. Won't do you no harm." He added more quietly, "Trust Caleb, Mr. Brice. Won't do you no harm."

Brice drank, his eyes questioning Caleb as the Negro backed to the door.

Annee smiled. "Now, isn't that better? It will all be better soon. This will all be ours. Our Eden. Just the two of us." Jumping to her feet, Annee said, "I've an appointment now. I shouldn't be long, and then you'll truly be mine, darling—all mine, forever and ever and . . . ever." The door closed with a bang behind her.

Brice sat against the wall, waiting for that first rush of lethargy that would leave his mind too muddled to think. There had been enough laced sugar in that cup to kill him, he thought. He closed his eyes. The realization had been the first rational thought he'd had in days.

But with reason's return came the excruciating pain of remembrance. Autumn. The thought of her had driven him these past days to lose himself all too willingly in Annee's drug-induced slumber. Since word had arrived of Autumn's death, he'd cared little about life. He still was indifferent about his own, but he knew that with the walls about him now shaking almost continually, he must somehow get back to Hunnington. Jeanette was there, and Pierre. Tyler would need help in getting the people off the island—if he hadn't already. Brice realized in that moment that he had no idea just how long he'd been trapped here. Hours? Days? Weeks? Perhaps help had arrived from Jamaica long ago. Perhaps Pierre, Jeanette and Tyler were safely away from the island.

He hoped to God that they were.

* * *

The natives appeared to have given up any hopes of praying the angry gods into submission. Men, women and children hurried toward the sea, their long canoes stretched between them as the sky showered them with molten rock and fiery ash.

The east wing of Hunnington Hall had crumbled with the last quake. In horror, Autumn and Jeanette stood in the rubble and watched the ground heave, yawn and devour the barn and what was left of the mill. Scrambling over a timber that had once supported one of the house's massive stone walls, Autumn ran toward Tyler as he mounted his horse.

"I'm going with you!" she shouted over Trempe's roar.

"Ye'll get yerself, Jeanette and Pierre down t' that water and get in a boat. I'll see t' Donovan m'self!"

"But Annee—"

"I'll see t' the lady!" He patted the gun in his waist-band, then digging his heels into the horse's sides, tore off toward Barrett Hall.

They met Henri on the road. Sitting on a crumbled stone wall, crutch at his side and pipe jutting from his mouth, he appeared completely at ease.

"Get in a boat," Autumn told him.

"Seems I was wrong," he responded.

"About what?"

"You. You didn't die after all."

"No I didn't. Now get in a boat."

He cackled so pleasantly that Autumn stared at him in disbelief.

The following jolt from Trempe sent both Henri and Autumn to their backs. Screams of terror welled up from the natives as first one canoe, then another, was shoved into the choppy, muddy water and paddled out to sea.

"Maîtresse!" Pierre's urgent cry brought Autumn to her feet. She ran as fast as her trembling knees would allow toward the boy and his mother. Jeanette was on the ground, her bloodied head resting against a rock.

"Get in a boat," she told him.

"But maîtresse—"

Plucking Pierre off the ground, she shoved him into the arms of a passing woman. "I'll see to your mother, Pierre."

He set up a howl of refusal, kicking and screaming as the woman battled him all the way to the boat. Seeing Tullius, Autumn called him over, and together they lifted Jeanette into a boat and set it adrift.

Autumn was headed back up toward Henri when a Negro on horseback approached her. "You are Donovan?" he asked her in a heavily accented voice.

"I am."

"You must come. Donovan and Maîtresse Rose have been injured. They ask for your help."

The ground pitched. Autumn grabbed the man's leg for balance. "Where is he?"

He pointed back toward the mountain.

"There?" She eyed him suspiciously. "I don't believe you." As he turned his horse to leave, however, she stopped him. "I'll come."

"Maîtresse, no!" Pierre jumped out of the canoe, avoiding the woman's attempt to grab him.

The black offered his arm, hoisting Autumn onto the rear of his horse.

"Maîtresse, you mustn't go!" Pierre called, running as fast as his little legs would carry him up the beach. "It's a trick! Tyler will be back. Maîtresse!"

Autumn looked back over her shoulder, unable to hear Pierre over the crash and rumble of the mountain, over the frightened babbling of the natives. "Get back to the boat!" she ordered him, then wrapping her arm around the man, headed away toward the mountain.

Caleb stood in the foyer, wringing his white-gloved hands and cringing beneath Tyler's torrent of obscenities. "Damn you, man, I won't ask you again. Where the hell is Donovan?"

He finally broke. Falling to his knees he beseeched the Irishman, "Grace, I did not do it! It was her, the evil one, she make us do it. She slay my brother in the cane field 'cause he disobey her. With her own hands—"

"I said, where the hell is Donovan!"

He pointed one trembling finger toward the back of the house.

Lifting the man by his lapel, Hugh growled, "Show me."

They ducked as the great chandelier above their heads came crashing to the floor. The house tilted, timbers and stone creaking and grinding as the walls leaned to one side, yet, remarkably, refused to fall. The mahogany spiral staircase sagged, cracked, and as Tyler and Caleb dodged beyond its curve, it crumbled like matchsticks to the floor.

Digging into his pocket, Caleb withdrew his key. He fumbled for what seemed like minutes at the lock until finally the door flew open.

"Son of a bitch," Tyler shouted. He blinked in disbelief at the chained, sweating man huddled in the corner of the smoking room.

Donovan looked up, a relieved grin tugging one corner of his lips. "It's about time," he said.

"Mother of God, I can't believe what I'm seein'."

"Believe it—then release me. Please."

Tyler yanked a cowering Caleb inside the room with one jerk of his beefy arm. "She was right, after all," he went on.

Blinking the sweat from his eyes, Brice watched Caleb jab at the steel cuffs around his wrists, hearing Tyler ramble on, but not fully comprehending everything the Irishman was saying, until he heard the word, "Autumn." The chains tumbled to the floor with a clank as Brice looked up and questioned, "What?"

"I'm sayin', Autumn knew somethin' was wrong the minute she saw y' this mornin'. She was tellin' us—"

"Autumn." He'd begun to shake.

"Aye. Y' remember the little red-haired girl with the chin?"

"She's alive?"

His bushy brows curling over his nose, Tyler looked into Brice's white face, and grabbed his shoulders. "God, man, y' look like y've just seen a ghost."

"She told me Autumn was dead."

"Well I won't deny she came close t' dyin', all right. Fact is, it was a damned miracle that she didn't. But the

lass is alive, maybe not as sassy as before, but I'm figurin'
once y've explained to 'er why y've been spendin' yer
time up here, she'll be more inclined to perk up a mite.''
Hitching Brice's arm around his shoulder, he added under
his breath, ''That is, if we get off this damned powder keg
in time.''

As they stepped from the crumbling house, the island
shook again, and Trempe finally erupted, filling the sky
with fire and boiling smoke. They were hit with a gust of
hot wind and fell to their knees, huddling against the blast
that blistered their faces and singed their hair. Yet through
it all Brice could think of only one thing. Autumn was
alive. Alive!

They had just managed to calm Tyler's terrified horse
enough to mount when Brice glanced down the road. He
blinked, wondering if Annee's *mapou* juice was still
affecting him.

''Donovan!'' Pierre wiggled from Henri's hands, then
jumped from the plodding ox's back. He threw himself
into Brice's arms.

Down on one knee, Brice hugged the boy tightly. ''What
the devil are you doing here? Why aren't you with your
mother and Autumn?''

''My mother is safe, but Autumn has gone to *her*.''
Pulling back, he looked into Donovan's eyes and finished,
''To Annee.''

Clamping one hand on Brice's shoulder, Tyler asked in
as calm a voice as possible, ''Where have they gone?''

''I know,'' Henri said. Sitting on the animal's back, he
puffed on his pipe and grinned serenely at Brice.

They all stared at the old man and waited. Finally he
pointed toward the mountain.

Brice handed Pierre up onto the back of Tyler's horse.
''Get him off the island,'' was all he said.

The figure stood before her, white face and red lips a
mask of calm in the hellish storm that shook the very
ground beneath their feet. Autumn knew for certain now
that she hadn't dreamed her.

''Annee, what have you done to Brice?'' she asked.

"Minetta."

"Very well. Minetta, what have you done to Brice?"

With a flick of her white silk robes, Annee paced. "I really didn't want to kill you, you know. The two of us have a great deal in common: we both love Hunnington and Brice. Had you simply left the island with your brother, this might all have been avoided."

"Brice," Autumn urged her. The heat was becoming unbearable.

"You really don't believe I would hurt Brice, do you? We're going to be married. He's promised me. We're going to spend the rest of our lives making Cayemite the most productive cane plantation in the world."

Autumn looked nervously up the side of the mountain, knowing she must stay calm, she must not anger Annee Rose in any way. "Annee, the island is crumbling beneath us. If you love Brice, you'll want to get him off the island as soon as possible."

"Minetta!" she shrieked, causing Autumn to stumble away, into the arms of the Negro who'd brought her to this crude temple of sorts. "I tried to warn you as I warned all the others. I won't tolerate this disobedience any longer. They must all be taught a lesson." Pointing one finger up the mountain, she said, "I can stop this eruption any time I want."

Raising her voice, Autumn screamed over the escalating thunder, "Are you certain, Minetta? Perhaps it's the zemis who are controlling the mountain. That's what Henri says. Henri says the zemis reside on the mountain and are prepared to stop you in any way they can."

"He's a liar!"

"The Indians believe their redeemer has come—"

"Fools! I'll show them, I'll show them all! I know who I'm dealing with. Imagine their believing I wouldn't know. Imagine a god pretending to be a child."

"The Indians believe this zemi is more powerful than all others who have come before him—"

"Shut up! Shut up!" Sweeping aside her robe, Annee withdrew a gleaming machete. Its steel blade reflected the fire from the encroaching lava flow into Autumn's eyes.

Struggling now in the man's arms, her terror of Annee

surpassing even her fear of the mountain, Autumn cried, "What about Brice, Annee? He'll be upset if you kill me."

"He thinks you're dead already." Annee smiled and fingered the machete almost reverently. "It worked out marvelously, you know. His coming to me thinking I had caused your illness was all I needed. He actually believed that if he came to me, I might be convinced to help you." Her fingers tightening on the knife, Annee turned her violet eyes on Autumn and hissed, "I know why he did it. He wept your name when he . . . well, I laughed in his face when he pleaded for my mercy. I made him promise me he'd never leave if I supplied Henri with an antidote. I took such pleasure in informing him of your death. But then he, he . . ." Her voice trailed off. Her eyes became distant.

"Poor Brice. Poor darling. My darling Donovan, did you love her so much? I know the feeling. I loved you and you left me. It *is* horrible, isn't it? The emptiness. Oh, don't weep, my darling, I'll make you happy." Annee looked again at Autumn. "I tried. I tried so hard. But he, he just didn't care. Do you know how that made me feel? Watching him die every day because he just didn't care. I tried to make him forget. The *mapou* made him forget, until *you* showed up."

A violent explosion rent the air and Autumn and her captor were pitched to the ground. She scrambled from his hands as fire and ash and rock fell from the sky. Before she could regain her feet, however, Annee was over her, her robe smoldering in spots and her thick white face powder streaked with sweat and tears. The rouge on her mouth had smeared from the corners of her lips. She held the machete high above her head.

"You won't get away from me again!" Annee shrieked.

The machete fell, slicing the air in front of Autumn's throat with a muffled whoosh. Throwing her head back, Annee laughed as Autumn screamed and covered her face with her arms.

"You should have stayed on board Dearborne's ship," she cried. "You might have stood a better chance of surviving. And I had planned it out so carefully, too. I set that fire in the hold knowing it wouldn't be discovered until you were too far out to sea to do anything about it. And when I chased you down in the forest. I'd have killed you then had Brice not happened along."

God help her! Whoosh. Whoosh. The skin on Autumn's arms burned and bled as Annee lifted the weapon one last time for the kill.

Donovan appeared suddenly from the forest, a shadow in the ash fog, the fire reflecting on his sweat-dampened face as he threw himself onto Annee. They hit the ground in a heap of white silk and long raven hair. Autumn rolled to her unsteady legs, watching as man and woman grappled for the weapon in Annee's hands, crying out as Annee struck a blow against Brice's shoulder, cutting deeply, almost to bone. Jumping to her feet, Annee lifted the knife over her head and stared down at Brice.

"Go away." The small voice came from the melee like a song on a breeze. "Go away."

The fire glow of approaching lava reflected from the upraised steel into Pierre's eyes. Standing on the edge of the rock plateau, the boy gazed steadily at Annee.

"You!" she railed. "You can't harm me. I'll bring this mountain down on your head, little boy. You are only a child!"

"Is that what you believe, Minetta?"

Brice rolled toward Autumn, clutching his arm. He grabbed her to his chest, twisting his bloodied fingers into her hair with painful ferocity.

Her eyes wild, Annee stared at them both. "You!" she shrieked at Autumn, "What are you doing here? Caleb! Caleb, call the dogs!" The ground trembled. Rocks crashed within inches of Annee, but she didn't move. Spinning, she stared up the side of the mountain, straight at the rolling fire bed and screamed, "Kill them! Kill them all! I demand that you kill them now!" With that, she whirled back toward Autumn and Brice and lifted the machete.

The blast of wind came from nowhere, roaring like a windstorm before the rolling rock bed, sounding like a thousand voices so crystal sharp that the force was staggering. It froze Annee where she stood, her terror-filled eyes on the child, his hand upraised and his head thrown

back in what might have been a desperate cry for mercy
from the gods.

"Avatar. Avatar," it sounded like.

Staggering to his feet, Brice pulled Autumn up against
him. He plucked Pierre from the ground, his good arm
wrapped about the child's waist, and the three stumbled
from the clearing, hesitating only long enough to look
back once. Annee, her back to them, faced the mountain
of molten rock, her arms upraised, white robe whipping
around her. The searing wind torched her hair and appeared
to evaporate the very skin from her bones. Then she was
gone.

They met Henri on their path down. He was perched on
a tree stump, his pipe jutting from his mouth and his
grizzled old face wearing an amused smile. "There is a
boat," he said, "down by Barrett Cay. It is hidden within
the reeds. My granddaughter was not so devout in believing that her powers could withstand the gods." His eyes
shifted to the child, his head resting limply on Brice's
shoulder.

"It was only the wind," Brice told him. "No gods."

Henri chuckled, then said, "Foolish boy."

Brice left him, knowing the old man would refuse his
help, knowing his beliefs would carry him peacefully from
this world to the other.

They met Tyler on the way, with Caleb at his heels. The
Irishman took the boy from Brice's arm and handed him
off to Annee's house servant. Brice went to his knees, loss
of blood and exhaustion draining all strength from his
limbs. Autumn fell beside him, kissing his face and pleading:

"Please. Please, Brice, we've not much farther."

With Tyler's help, Donovan struggled to his feet.

The boat was hidden in the reeds just as Henri had said.
Tyler helped Autumn in, then Brice and Pierre. Grabbing a
trembling Caleb, he shoved him toward the boat and said,
"That'll 'bout do it."

Autumn came off her seat, rocking the canoe perilously
in the water. "Tyler, get into this boat."

"There's no room, lass. I'll be makin' m' way back
around to Hunnington, just t' be certain how everyone is

farin'." He met Brice's eyes. "I've been responsible for these people too long, maît. I can't turn m' back on 'em now."

"There's a boat for you?"

"Aye." He shoved their boat further into the choppy water. Directing Caleb, he shouted, "Get them paddles up, man, and paddle like hell!"

Caleb took up one paddle. Brice and Autumn each took up another.

Donovan didn't last long, the injury to his arm forbidding more than a half dozen weak strokes. Still, the long, narrow boat had been built with speed and maneuverability in mind, and it wasn't long before Autumn and Caleb put distance between themselves and the disintegrating island.

Unable to see through the dense curtain of smoke and ash, they stroked the water, watching the display of red-and-yellow fire in the distance, hearing the roar and hiss of steam as the land yawned and the sea rushed into the boiling guts of the mountain.

Autumn felt as if that distant fire had found its way into her own body. Her muscles burned with fatigue; each laborious stroke wrenched her arms at the sockets. Her shoulders felt as if they were being torn apart, and a sharp pain in her side sliced through her ribs. But she closed her eyes and counted each stroke, damning Caleb silently for keeping such a fast pace, but knowing they had little choice if they wanted to put any distance between themselves and the building explosion.

They heard the end coming before they felt it. The rolling thunder, not unlike the vibrations that had rent the air over the past few days, filled the sea and sky, eddying the waves around the little boat until it was lifted back toward the island and the exhausted occupants began to fear that all their efforts had been for nothing. Paddles were torn from their raw hands and tossed into the swirling currents. Then the sea floor heaved.

The blast was ear splitting. Caleb ducked his head to his knees. Brice clutched a whimpering Pierre to his chest and fell back into Autumn's lap. She wrapped herself around them both and dropped to the boat bottom, her face buried in Donovan's hair, her fingers twisting into his shirt as the first rush of gaseous steam swept over them.

She thought of Tyler, knowing he hadn't escaped. She thought of Henri, who was no doubt still sitting upon that tree stump, talking to Legba and truly believing the guardian of gates and homes would protect him. She thought of Hunnington and wept for them all.

There was sun on her face. It was a gentler heat than Cayemite's fire. Autumn squinted slightly as the golden light wedged through her swollen lids. She blinked, then looked blearily into the sapphire sky. How long had it been since she'd last seen a blue sky?

Gradually, she became aware of where she was. The boat rode the gentle waves smoothly, the light slapping against the sides almost hypnotic enough to send her back to sleep. Brice's head was on her stomach. Smiling, she touched his face, rough with stubble, then remembering his arm, she sat up and reached to touch his shoulder. The bleeding had stopped, and though he clutched his arm to his chest, he appeared to be resting comfortably.

Pierre was sitting upright. He was looking out to sea with his back to Autumn. "It is gone," he said. His head turning, he looked at her and smiled. "Cayemite is gone."

Autumn looked back, over a sleeping Caleb. The turquoise water stretched eternally before her. "How do you know?" she asked him. "We might have drifted miles."

He pointed to the sky. "The birds. Do you see them?"

Shading her eyes with both hands, she watched the gulls swirling in a cloud out over the water.

"They're searching for land, for Cayemite." Looking again at Autumn, he finished, "For home."

The occupants of the low-riding boat wondered, over the next two grueling days, if they would ever see home again.

The first hint that they were no longer alone came with a resounding, "Ahoy, there! Castaways, be you Donovan and Donovan Company?"

Autumn and Brice blinked skeptically into each other's

eyes, each wondering if the long hours of food and water deprivation had finally robbed them of their senses. As they struggled to sit up, however, the chorus of shouts and cheers brought their heads around with a snap.

The ship was nearly on them, bright and spanking new, under full sail. The vessel was the same one that had delivered the cylinders to Cayemite.

Loz Nelson, with a weeping Shelley at his side, looked down from the schooner and hailed back to the captain, "By God, it's them! We've found them!"

Had there been one ounce of strength left in her body, Autumn might have wept as Brice swept her up against his chest and held her. Caleb, his dark skin pitifully gray, hugged Pierre in his bare arms. The next pair of heads that they saw, however, did bring a cry from Autumn's parched throat. "Mitchell!"

"By God, Brice Donovan, you have some answering to do!"

Mary, tearfully fluttering her hankie in the air, added, "Oh, I am sorry, Mr. Donovan, but I let our little secret slip. Oh, my. Oh, dear, Autumn, are you all right?"

"Dammit, Captain, I want that man arrested for impersonating my brother-in-law!"

"Oh, do shut up, dear. Please."

Looking concernedly into Brice's puffy eyes, Autumn frowned. "Can he do that?" she asked him worriedly. "Have you arrested for impersonating Roy?"

"I think the crime he cited was impersonating his brother-in-law." A grin tugging at one corner of his dry lips, Donovan pulled her closer and said, "Given five minutes with a preacher, I think that problem might be rectified."

"Do you still want me?" She touched his cheek, thinking that even with his face red as a beet and overgrown with beard he was the handsomest man on the face of the earth. "After all," she went on, shooting him a glance from behind her salt-tipped lashes, "Hunnington is gone. And I know how desperately you wanted my half for your own."

He pondered her a long moment, thinking that with her hair hanging in strings to the bottom of the boat where it floated in sea water, she had never looked so beautiful. "I'd marry you just for that," he said as she smiled.

"For what?"

"That." Lifting one sunburned finger, he gently touched the freckle at the corner of Autumn's mouth. "Come 'ere," he said with a growl.

She did.

Chapter 26

They were married two weeks later at the very spot where they had picnicked once, a shelf of land overlooking the Bogue Islands. Shelley and Loz Nelson attended them, while Mary and Mitchell, Pierre and Jeanette looked on.

Autumn wore a gown of pale yellow, a gift from Shelley. Braided into her hair were pink blossoms to match the bouquet in her hand. She stood at Brice's side, clutching his arm, and he her hand as the clergyman spoke of loving and cherishing, for richer or poorer, and Autumn thought she'd love Brice Donovan no less if he were the ugliest man on the face of the earth and didn't have a cent to his name.

They returned to the Nelsons' and toasted their marriage, but before the first sweep of dusk blanketed Jamaica, Brice and Autumn Donovan returned to Montego Bay. Clarence Dillman had offered the use of his seaside town house as a wedding gift. The solicitor had assured them that after spending two-and-a-half days adrift, he had no inclination to partake of a scenic ocean panorama anytime soon.

It was a quaint abode, not overly large. Its creamwashed walls and gleaming breadnut floors and high ceilings gave it a cool, airy appeal that was refreshing. The bedroom overlooked the bay. With French doors open, the breeze, laden with hibiscus and sea tang, filled the quarters with heady sweetness.

Brice stood on the veranda, a glass of champagne in one hand, a bottle in the other. The door opened and closed behind him. He turned and stared.

"So," he said.

"So." Autumn echoed, leaning back against the door, smiling at her husband.

"Dillman has supplied us with enough champagne to last us a couple of weeks."

"Is that all?" Her voice was husky.

The bottle brushed against Brice's leg. "Nice dress, Missus Donovan."

"It's Shelley's."

"It's still nice."

"Thank you."

"You're welcome."

"Will you put the bottle down?"

"And the glass?"

"Oh, certainly, the glass, too."

The glass and bottle tinkled together as he placed them on a table.

Coming away from the door, Autumn walked slowly toward her husband. "I have something for you, darling."

Brice grinned. His eyes twinkled.

Pulling the gift from behind her back, Autumn placed it in his hands. "It's from Mattie. You do remember the store-keeper in town, don't you?"

Unwrapping the present, Brice stared at the flowing-haired zemi in his hand. His face dark with irritation, he looked back at Autumn. "I thought we'd done with this nonsense." He plunked it onto the table.

Sweeping his arm around Autumn's waist, Brice pulled her closer. "May I kiss my wife now?" he asked.

"I'd be hurt if you didn't."

Hesitating, he cocked one brow and threw a glance toward the door.

"Is something wrong?"

"I expect Mitchell to come barreling in and threaten me if I so much as glance your way."

"He's just outside the door," she teased. "Shall I fetch him?"

Lifting her from her feet, he whispered against her mouth, "Not on your life, Missus Donovan."

Closing her eyes, Autumn pleaded, "Again."

"Missus Donovan."

The embrace was rocking. Heart to heart they met, lips touching tenuously at first, then more demandingly, insatiably, their impatience to love as fervid as any fire that had threatened to burn them in the past. His kiss drove her head back; his hand was buried in her hair, and his tongue plunged to the delicious depths of Autumn's mouth until, drowning in wondrous currents of sensuality, they parted, weak from the storm tide of desire that had overcome them.

- He looked in her eyes and said, "I love you."

"Then do so."

She smelled of jasmine, as he knew she would, beneath those endless layers of frilly underthings that Shelley had lent her. "I like your breeches better," Brice teased her somewhere between her second and third petticoats. "They're easier to get off."

The petticoat sailed across the room and landed in a heap on the floor.

"Oh, Donovan." She sighed.

Kneeling before him, she gently slid her hands beneath his coat, easing the satin lapels over his shoulders and down his arms. Her fingers tenderly skimming the bandage above his elbow, she looked concernedly into his smiling face and asked, "Are you certain you're all right?"

His face was suddenly intense. Catching her chin in his fingers, Brice responded in a tight voice, "Do you know how long I have ached to have someone worry over me?"

"No." She shook her head.

"A lifetime. I waited for you a lifetime, Autumn Dae Sinclair Donovan Donovan." He smiled.

"Well, wait no more, Mr. Donovan. I'm yours forever."

Their clothing drifted to the floor.

He came to her gently, tenderly. Slowly, watchful for any sign of distress, he balanced one knee on the bed and outstretched his hand.

"Hello."

She smiled.

"Come here," he said.

Autumn took his hand and thought of butterflies, the kind she chased as a child, before her arrival at maturity had made it improper to engage in such childish pursuits. Donovan was one shining fantasy that would not elude her.

Brice rolled to his side, taking Autumn with him into

the plush comfort of the down bed, his fingers tenderly plucking the combs from her hair, so it tumbled in a mass across the white sheet beneath them. It filled his nostrils with the scent of flowers and sunlight that had drenched her during their wedding. But when he might have covered her tantalizing body with kisses, she stopped him.

"No, Donovan."

Autumn rolled on top of him, unprepared for what the sight of his dark head and broad shoulders pressed into the bed would do to her. The explosive warmth started in her heart and melted to her stomach. It tingled in every limb and in every crevice until she was breathless.

His fingers slid along her head and drew her mouth down to his. "I love you," they said together, before the blissful meeting.

His mouth opened under hers, allowing Autumn the freedom to lead. Clumsily at first, even timidly, Autumn touched her tongue to his. He groaned. She did it again, and he shivered. She ran her hands over his shoulders, her lips down the palpitating column of his throat to the diamond-shaped thatch of fine hair on his chest. Meanwhile his hands stroked her head, her face, the delicate curve of her ear, brushing the little freckle at the corner of her mouth and the proud chin that had given him such pleasure in past weeks.

Her hands explored him, bringing an intake of breath and a moan of pleasure. They swept his stomach, his thighs and in between. They inched slowly, slowly, up the length of his burgeoning desire. But it wasn't her fingers that brought his shoulders off the mattress, his teeth clenching and his stomach tautening as if someone had driven a fist into his lungs.

"Christ," he groaned. "Ah, Autumn, love. Love, what are y' doin'?"

Her face came up, smiling, and haloed by hair. "Showing you exactly what I can do with *my* tongue, Mr. Donovan."

His head fell back to the bed. His fingers twisted into the sheets and his body broke out in a thousand tiny pinpoints of such intense pleasure he wanted to cry aloud. "Ah, love," was all he could manage.

She moved back on top of him, her worshipful gaze holding his. If he had been a weaker man, he might have cried, so moved was he by her love. Her apricot shoulders blanketed with copper-colored hair, she smiled and said, "You made me feel like a woman for the first time in my life, Brice Donovan. I want to give you the same joy."

And she did. She lifted, impaled herself on him and sank to the wondrous oblivion that only his presence inside her could bring. She took him to that sharp-edge plane of sublime madness, where love and desire are one. And she knew, as she denied that supreme ending with all the control her starving body could muster, what Brice's sacrifice had cost him before.

His eyes closed, his head arched back onto the bed, the blood roared like a windstorm throughout his burning body as Brice lost himself in the velvet warmth encompassing him. The sensuous undulation of Autumn's hips against his, the arch of her spine that lifted the golden, rose-tipped breasts to his hands and lips nearly drove him over the brink. Rolling his shoulders from the bed, he buried his face against those breasts and cried her name aloud.

"Autumn. Autumn. Ah, love I can't hold out any longer." Sliding his arms around her back, he started to roll.

"No." She clamped his shoulders to the bed.

His breath escaping sharply through his teeth, he looked into her eyes and said, "You don't know what you're doing."

"I know exactly what I'm doing."

He groaned. His head thrashed from side to side and she knew he was as close as she. She took his hand and, palm to palm, she pressed it into the bed above his head and whispered, "Oh, Donovan. My darling Donovan, I am your wife, and I love you."

The flood came—an explosion, an earthquake—blinding, breathtaking, celestial. They twisted and lunged one last time, the tempo of nature binding them in ecstasy. He cried out her name, and she his, the culmination of love lost and found and forever spiraling in the whirlwind of emotions that shuddered within the four-poster bed. It was completeness at its most complete. It was sublime, joyous, infinite. And as the pulsing life of his loins bathed her womb, she knew more love, more fulfillment—and more hope—than she ever had in her life.

Autumn nestled against her husband. His arms came around her. His hands buried in her hair. "Are you certain it's what you want?" Donovan asked her.

Autumn listened to the frantic pounding of Brice's heart and knew, as he held her, that he was holding his breath. "More than anything," she said. He sighed in relief and love.

There was another sigh of sound, as the wind whipped through the open doors, fluttering the sheer curtains at the windows and the *baire* on the bed. A butterfly danced in the current and landed on the flowing-haired statue with the wide, watchful eyes.

Autumn smiled at the zemi.

And the zemi smiled back.